THROUGH THE FIRE

Mary Perrine

Water's Edge
Publishing, LLC

REVIEWS

A deeply emotional novel about reclaiming self-worth and navigating complicated familial legacies. -K.C. Finn

This masterfully written story is filled with suspense and memorable characters while exploring themes of identity, trauma, and family in a brilliant way. -Christian Sia

Author Mary Perrine delivers a beautifully written, emotional, yet powerful story of acceptance and identity. This is the perfect thriller filled with secrets and psychological suspense. -Rabia Tanveer

Perrine is an exceptional storyteller. Through the Fire *will keep readers on the edge of their seats. From the very first sentence, they will be drawn into this mesmerizing tale of lies and hidden truths.* -Rhea Karras

Fans of psychological thrillers and family sagas will be drawn into Perrine's endless twists and turns. The small-town imagery, intricate plot, and diverse cast of characters make this a must-read. -Damon Ellis

ALSO BY MARY PERRINE

Hidden
The Lies They Told (Cedar Point Novel #1)
The Road of Lies (Cedar Point Novel #2)
Life Without Air
Outside the Lines
The Storms of Eddie Greer

PART ONE

Chloe Chambers, Summer St. John,
& Ellery Gray

ONE

The *truth* was a lie—a web of deceit woven with flawless precision. Every. Single. Word.

For eighteen agonizing years, she had existed as *Summer*, a name that felt more like a burden than an identity. Her life had been shaped by her mother's fragmented reality, wedged into the spaces between neglect and hopelessness.

After sixteen years of hiding under a new name swiped from a phonebook, a staggering revelation knocked on her door, shattering everything she had always believed. *Summer St. John* had been a role cast on her by the woman who raised her, a villain who dreamt of living the life of a wealthy leading lady, like in the novels she plunged into. But that meant trapping the perfect man.

When the truth of her life finally broke, it unleashed a storm inside her. The revelation forced her deeper into the shadows, where she wrestled with the miracle she had prayed for her entire life. Rage and joy cycled through her as she played and replayed what could have been—all that the woman had taken from her.

She had been born Chloe Jade Chambers, the youngest daughter of an affluent Minnesota family. Yet, at just eight days old, she vanished without a trace. She was never destined to be the daughter of a cold-blooded predator, but somehow, she was caught in a sinister game orchestrated by a woman whose malice knew no bounds. The woman had turned her life into a narrative that felt plucked from the pages of a novel filled with deceit and manipulation. Chloe had been nothing more than a pawn in her evil game.

Once she learned about her birth family, the journey of acceptance had taken her two long years. Before she could move forward, she had to reconcile her past identities of Chloe Chambers and Summer St. John with the person she had become after the explosion that had obliterated the small cabin she once called home. The decision to torch her old life had been the only way to escape. And from those flames, nearly a thousand miles away, emerged eighteen-year-old *Ellery Gray*.

As Ellery neared Hunters Cove, Minnesota, uncertainty and excitement consumed her. Her stomach churned with nerves. She clutched the steering wheel to steady herself. The weariness from the long drive threatened to push the 1996 Camry off the road multiple times. It wasn't the twenty hours behind the wheel that drained her; it was the emotional fatigue from twenty-two months of anticipating the moment she would finally meet her *family*—people she knew only from online pictures and stories. They were virtual strangers who had no idea their lives were about to be capsized.

According to her contract, a new book was to land on her agent's desk in less than eight months. The story had a working title and a byline but nothing more. Instead of outlining the story or letting her imagination pull her into the world she had started creating for her readers, she had spent most of the past two years researching her family, the one Ellery had lost before she had barely opened her eyes. Each discovery intensified her desire to reclaim her rightful past, but as the miles faded into the rearview mirror, regrets swelled.

Ellery had packed and repacked boxes and bags a dozen times. It was not until 9:00 p.m., eight hours before she was to venture out on the trip that would change her life, that she finally settled on two suitcases, a small plastic bag of toiletries, and a tote filled with information about the family who had no idea she was returning home. If things did not go well, she would retreat to Schenectady before the public learned her identity. If they went better than she expected... *They wouldn't.* Almost nothing in her life ever had.

Ellery Gray was a household name. Her fame echoed across the world. Money, she had. Friends, she did not. In Schenectady, New York, she was known as the shy and somewhat reclusive Elle Gray. Residents never linked the woman with the downcast face, hiding behind the oversized sunglasses and worn Schenectady Blue Jays baseball cap to Ellery Gray, the famous author behind the narratives that delivered a whiplash of emotions for her readers. They were fiction to everyone else. But to Ellery, they were sharp, broken pieces of truth that cut so deeply, she bled.

As she passed a weathered sign declaring she was within half an hour of Hunters Cove, Ellery felt her stomach lurch into her throat as waves of emotions surged. Fear swirled within her. She squeezed the leather steering wheel of the old car, a relic from a life intertwined with Gus and Millie Walker, the elderly couple she had cared for in the quiet town of Schenectady. When they passed away, she had inherited everything, right down to the kitchen sink.

A *New York Times* bestselling author with a handful of novels should be sitting behind the wheel of a BMW or something equally flashy, but that was not Ellery's style, despite what her bank account suggested. Hiding from her past, she was anything but showy. Her threadbare purse, plucked from a free box at the edge of her neighbor's lawn, screamed modesty. The black army boots were hand-me-downs from Amelia Lopez, her agent. And the jeans with the holes in the knees were not a fashion statement—they were simply old—a testament to years of living in stolen garage sale clothes and, later, hiding in plain sight. No one suspected a best-selling author to dress as she did.

A quick Google search about her unveiled a carefully crafted narrative. Like the novels she penned, it was a *story*, one Ellery wanted the world to believe. It painted her as an only child growing up in the backcountry of northern California, where her father worked as a day laborer for a vineyard. The bio described a selfish mother who abandoned her family when Ellery was nine, leaving her to navigate her youth without a mother's love. Each detail had been carefully chosen to paint a subdued picture that would not draw attention. Not a single word held a whisper of truth. The storyteller within her had spun an elaborate facade woven from her imagination.

To the world, author Ellery Journey Gray was an enigma as elusive as the blue Himalayan poppy. When she ascended the ranks to hit the bestseller list, reporters swarmed like locusts, chasing leads, badgering Amelia, and pleading with her publisher for the inside scoop on the author. A morsel of information or a blurry photo was more than they had. Still, as hard as they tried, they always walked away with blank notebooks and a promise to themselves to break the story.

The people Ellery trusted—a handful at most—formed an impenetrable fortress around her, protecting her at all costs. She was their maestro of words, twisting sentences into epic plotlines that clung to the reader long after the final page. It didn't hurt that her novels fattened their bank accounts. And the mystique of Ellery Gray gave them prestige in the publishing community. They could not afford to out her.

Even in her isolation, Ellery felt an intoxicating sense of freedom she had never experienced. For those first eighteen years, she had been tethered to the woman she believed was her *mother*. However, that bond felt more like a chain than love. Ann St. John, or Karma, as she had rebranded herself after her husband's sudden death when her daughter was three, was a sinister force of nature. She was Satan on steroids. Everywhere Karma went, she left chaos in her wake. Her presence radiated a kind of malevolence that sought to unravel the decency within Summer—as she had been known during her childhood. Never again would Ellery claim that name.

Minutes from Hunters Cove, a chill ran up her spine, and an uneasiness clutched her stomach. Shadows fluttered at the edges of her mind. She could almost hear the whispers of the past—a painful reminder of what had been lost when Karma kidnapped her and raised her in what could only be described as hell.

As each mile passed, Ellery felt herself being pulled into the black hole of uncertainty. Resurfacing had the possibility of exposing two shocking revelations. The first: Summer St. John had not perished in that tragic fire eighteen years before. The second was a darker truth entangled with the first: Summer had not been just a victim of circumstances, a cruel twist of fate set in motion by an insane woman; Ellery had been the architect of her destruction—the one who burned down the cabin.

Worst of all—according to everything she found online— arson was a felony. She was a felon.

TWO

Ellery maneuvered her car onto the shoulder of the road. The gravel crunched beneath her tires, reminding her of the commotion she was about to launch. Across the road, Hunters Cove Lake glistened like diamonds under the sun, welcoming her home. She had never been this close to having a real family, but even with the possibility of reuniting, she focused on the potholes ahead rather than the joy. A U-turn was by far the safest choice.

Feeling her mission tighten across her chest, she drew a deep breath. Rocking her shoulders back and forth, she slowly exhaled and closed her eyes, allowing herself to imagine weaving back into the Chambers family, into the life that was meant to be hers—the one that had been wrenched away from her by her vile mother.

Her palms were slick with perspiration, something she had felt often on the long drive. Trembling, she ran them down her thighs. The knot in her stomach twisted as she rehearsed her plan again, the details flickering like a vintage movie reel as she envisioned what lay ahead. Her pulse quickened when she conjured up images of the faces she had never met in person yet knew intimately through nearly two dozen months of research. It pounded like a jackhammer, matching her frenzied thoughts. The air felt electric. The soon-to-be encounters felt dizzyingly distant yet impossibly close.

Until she had met every Chamber and carefully mapped out her approach for revealing her identity, she would introduce herself as Elle Gray, a newcomer looking for a fresh start—close enough to, yet far enough from, family living in the

Brainerd Lakes area.

Her story would include a modest inheritance from her grandfather, granting her the luxury of time without the immediate pressure to find a job. If pressed about her past, she would acknowledge she had worked as a barista in the South—an obscure yet believable role. The more closely her fabricated backstory resembled the truth, the easier it would be to persuade everyone. Besides, the faint hint of her southern accent was a dead giveaway to the past she desperately wanted to keep hidden.

Ellery caught a glimpse of her reflection in the rearview mirror. Fatigue from the long trip wrapped around her like a heavy cloak. The edges of her mouth tilted down in disgust. Dark shadows and puffiness had settled beneath her eyes, a testament to the hours spent in the car. A soft sigh escaped; a yawn followed. She reached into her felt tote and fished out a 1940s leather make-up bag decorated with delicate pink flowers. It was one of the countless remnants of Millie's life she could not part with. Skillfully, she began her transformation from exhausted to... Who was she kidding? A swipe of color on her lips, cheeks, and lashes would not change the fatigue that had settled into her bones. Still, she tried.

Her choices for lodging away from the tourist crowds were limited. To protect herself, she had carefully considered her options, finally settling on a room at the Harmony House Bed and Breakfast, a charming throwback from the 1880s that sat on the edge of town. Based on the website photos, Ellery knew tales were hiding in the walls. The arched doorways, the timeless elegance of a turret, and the welcoming front porch would surround her with positive memories she would carry with her. When—not if—things went south, they might be the only good ones she had of Hunters Cove.

A glance at her phone told her it was too early to check in. Her stomach grumbled. The fast-food burger from the previous night and the morning's gas station coffee and cinnamon roll had only angered the hungry beast. As much as she yearned to meet her family, the pull of food won out. A good night's sleep and a shower would be the perfect prelude to her family reunion.

She eased her car back onto the highway leading into town; the tires hummed against the asphalt. Butterflies danced inside her chest. Slowing, she scanned the historic, timeworn storefronts lining the main street. A car behind her beeped when she came to a sudden stop in front of the first restaurant she came to—Clara's—a charming brick-front Norwegian eatery. Sweeping an apologetic hand through the air, Ellery pulled forward until she found a parking spot.

. The twenty-hour drive, with only a few breaks, had left her muscles stiff. Limping to the sidewalk, she stealthily stretched while she walked the half-block to the restaurant. As she approached, a sign on the door caught her attention. *Uff da! You must be hungry! Get on in here, and we'll take care of that!* A smile lifted her cheeks. No one needed to tell her twice. "Clearly, we're not in New York *or* South Carolina," she whispered as she wrapped her fingers around the handle and stepped back in time.

A small bell hanging over the door tinkled, announcing her arrival. The noise was nearly swallowed by the clanking of dishes and laughter that seeped beneath the kitchen door. As she stepped deeper inside, she was instantly surrounded by a medley of delightful aromas—the warm, yeasty scent of freshly baked bread blended with the irresistible saltiness of broiled fish. The smell of sweet and tangy cider with its fruity essence drew a begging from her stomach. An unexpected smile spread across Ellery's face as she pressed a hand against it. She could not have chosen a more welcoming restaurant.

A stunning woman with blonde hair pulled back into a cascading ponytail greeted her. Her face shined with warmth. Embarrassed by what she had seen in the small rearview mirror, Ellery ran a hand through her dark locks, smoothing the tangles that had undoubtedly grown there.

"Hi. I'm Clara. Welcome."

"I'm Elle..." A soft flush crept up Ellery's cheeks as she nearly revealed her full name.

"Nice to meet you, Elle." Clara's smile broadened. "Will anyone be joining you?"

Ellery shook her head. "It's just me."

The woman picked up a menu and silverware wrapped in a cloth napkin. "In that case, I have the perfect table." Before leading her to the hub of the restaurant, Clara flashed a knowing smile at Ellery. She set the menu and silverware on the table and pulled a chair out for her guest. "This is the best spot to eavesdrop on every conversation." She winked at her. "That way, you won't feel so alone."

Ellery chuckled. "Thank you. I appreciate that."

"Sure thing. I'll be back to take your order." Clara disappeared into the kitchen.

Settling into her chair, Ellery pulled a book from her tote and randomly opened it. For the next thirty minutes, she immersed herself in the surrounding conversations without turning a page: fishing tales, adventures, and personal missteps. Ellery saw hugs, heard laughter, and caught wind of a sale at Serendipity Studios, the same gallery owned by her brother, Liam. If that wasn't serendipitous, she didn't know what was.

THREE

After ten minutes on the front porch, at precisely 3:00 p.m., Ellery pushed open the heavy door of the Harmony House Bed and Breakfast. It swung with a soft, nostalgic moan. Oh, the stories that door could tell—murmurings of long-ago secrets. In a few moments, it would hold another—the return of Chloe Chambers.

As Ellery stepped inside, overloaded with two ancient suitcases, a plastic bag, and a large tote, the floor creaked beneath her, announcing her arrival. While caring for Millie and Gus, an elderly couple in Schenectady, Ellery had become a pack mule, never allowing them to lift a finger.

Setting her luggage at the end of the green velvet couch, Ellery closed her eyes briefly. She pressed her hand to her spine and leaned backward, fighting the knots that had grown there on her long drive. Even without the weight of her bags, she felt the heaviness of her secret.

"Welcome to Harmony House." The voice of the woman behind the desk was as soft as butter. "Oh, my goodness!" she exclaimed, noting the lack of wheels on the vintage bags. "I haven't seen a suitcase like that since… Well, my parents might have had one years ago."

She extended her hand in welcome. "You must be Miss Gray."

"Please, call me Elle."

"I'm Susan. Paula's delivering fresh flowers to your room, but she should be back shortly."

"Flowers?" Ellery's face went white. Had they figured out she was Ellery Gray, the author?

Susan moved gracefully around the desk and opened a large wood-covered book. "Yes, our rooms always have flowers."

The soft scratch of a pen filled the air as Susan wrote in the register. "Mary Lou's Blooms is next door. She shares the flowers that are too old or..." She snickered. "I can't believe I'm telling you this...the ones she rescues after funerals."

Ellery's eyes narrowed in curiosity. "Rescues after funerals?"

Paula entered through the café doors behind the counter. "Sometimes Susan overshares." She smiled through tight lips. "But, since she started to tell you, Mary Lou doesn't believe in wasting anything, so after weddings and funerals, she sneaks back into the church and takes the ones families leave behind. Some she reuses, others she repurposes and drops off here."

"Wait. Are you saying the flowers in my room could be..." Ellery cleared her throat, "funeral flowers?"

"Well, not today." The corner of Paula's mouth curled upward into a crooked grin. "It was a good week for folks around here. Nobody died." Her eyes sparkled with a hint of mischief.

Glancing at Susan, her demeanor shifted to a more practical tone. "The ones I put in your room are fresh." She raised her hand slightly. "Well, *reasonably* fresh. I'll change them when they begin to wither. But since you're staying for two weeks, you *could* be subjected to some memorial flowers."

"Okay. I can *live* with that." Paula snickered while Ellery dug her wallet from her bag.

She handed Susan her credit card. The woman's eyes lingered on the card for a second too long. A rush of warmth bled up Ellery's neck and onto her cheeks.

"Isn't there a famous author named Ellery Gray? Paula mentioned it to me when she took the reservation. I told her it had to be a coincidence. I mean, seriously, why would any famous person stay here? Why would they even be in Hunters Cove?" Susan pressed the credit card to the reader and waited for approval before returning it.

"Well…" Paula's face twisted in a theatrical flair. "There was that circus clown who passed through on his way to *find himself.* And that guy who robbed… Well, let's forget about him." She flapped her hand through the air. "But there was that ventriloquist…"

"Who was so bad, they kicked him off of *America's Got Talent* after he drop-kicked his dummy across the stage for not moving his lips when he talked." Susan gave her *the look.* "Not famous—just stupid."

A nervous laugh escaped from Ellery, briefly breaking the tension in the room. "I get asked that a lot. That's why I go by Elle." She returned her card to her wallet and slid the key off the counter. "Thank you." Anxious to retreat behind closed doors, she turned away quickly.

Paula retrieved the crumpled plastic bag from the couch and hung it over her forearm. The bag swayed as she bent down, her fingers wrapping around the thick leather handle of one of Ellery's suitcases. She looked over her shoulder at Susan. "I highly doubt a woman as wealthy as *author* Ellery Gray would be packing her…" Paula straightened her back and humorously shifted into an Italian accent. "Armani and Versace clothes in an old, I mean, *vintage* suitcase."

A gentle wave of relief washed over Ellery. An unexpected laugh gurgled. "Or drive a 1996 Camry." She made a funny face as she hoisted her tote over her shoulder and adjusted it before grabbing the other suitcase and following Paula up the right side of the double staircase.

An hour later, Ellery sat in the clawfoot tub, enveloped in hot water that rose nearly to her chin. The iridescent bubbles glimmered like tiny pearls in the sunlight that streamed through the transom window near the ceiling. Her hands had turned a vivid shade of crimson; she could only imagine the rest of her body mirrored that fiery hue.

Moments before, her anxiety had spiraled into a storm.

Waves of emotion crashed through her, each thought dangerously close to spinning out of control, dangling precariously on the edge of chaos. The encounter in the lobby could have gone horribly wrong. To avoid more of the same, Ellery promised herself that until the Chambers family knew the truth, she would live as a ghost—entering and leaving the B&B with the stealth of a skilled thief. In many ways, it was no different than how she had navigated her first thirty-six years.

Wrapped in her pajamas and a thick white terry robe she found hanging in the bathroom, Ellery plopped into one of the chairs with her tote. She removed the thick stack of papers, information about her family she could have recited by heart.

As she shuffled through the pages, nostalgia washed over her. Standing before the full-length mirror, one by one, she brought the photos of her family close to her face, searching for similar traits. Her siblings were all varying shades of sun-kissed blonde. In stark contrast, she had dark brown hair, the color of dirt. The only commonalities she shared with them were the striking blue eyes and the distinctly pointed chin. She was an outlier, a daisy in a field of red roses. Karma's choice of which twin to kidnap had almost been predestined. As an infant, Ellery had not resembled the exhausted woman who had fallen asleep on the park bench nearly thirty-seven years before.

Even though the photos showed her as an outsider, DNA proved otherwise. Vanessa Chambers was indeed her biological mother. Ellery had kept her results private on the website; Vanessa had not. Obviously, her mother was hoping to find her daughter one day. But Ellery had discovered her first.

The air felt thick with hope. *Tomorrow.* Tomorrow, the tangled threads of her past would unravel. Everything she had kept hidden from the outside world would come to light. *Tomorrow*, seven lives would be profoundly changed—hers, most of all.

FOUR

Long before dawn, Ellery jolted awake, her body drenched in a cold sweat. She threw the covers off and sat up. Remnants of the scrambled nightmare slipped through her fingers like sand through an hourglass. To soothe her racing thoughts, she reached for her phone, a distraction to keep her from attempting to piece together the horrifying dream. She lost herself in rereading Karma's obituary, perusing old articles about the fire and explosion that had ended Summer St. John's life, and searching for new information about the Chamberses.

As the hands of the clock inched toward seven, Ellery peeled herself out of bed, pushed back the red curtains with the delicate gray and tan foliage pattern, and carefully pulled up the brittle roller shade. The early May sun shimmered on the lake's surface, sending shards of light across the back wall of her room.

She turned on the television to push away the silence. Knee bends, jumping jacks, and arm circles helped her release pent-up energy. Just as her heart returned to its normal rhythm, a sharp knock on the door sent it into a wild dance again, nearly buckling her knees. She grabbed the edge of the small table to steady herself as the hair on her arms stood at attention.

"Good morning, Elle," Paula called from the other side of the door. "I'm leaving a tray with a carafe of coffee and a couple of rolls on the table out here. Breakfast will be served around nine."

Panic surged inside her. The mere thought of joining Paula and Susan for breakfast felt like facing a firing squad. Her stomach churned just thinking about the tales she would need to tell. Lying had never been her forte. Hiding was where she excelled.

"I think I'll skip breakfast this morning. But thank you for the coffee and rolls. That's way more than I need."

There was a slight pause, and she could almost feel Paula's disappointment through the thick door.

"Are you sure? The B&B's empty. As you can tell, this isn't our busy season." The muffled sound of her voice didn't betray her dejection.

"I appreciate your kindness, but I'm not much of a breakfast eater." The lie felt heavy, reminiscent of every time Karma opened her mouth.

"Okay. But if you want more coffee or another roll, just let us know."

"Thank you." Ellery pressed her ear against the door, straining to hear the faint sound of footsteps retreating down the corridor. She dropped onto the bed, tugging the covers beneath her chin to seek solace from the reality outside her room.

A whirlwind of thoughts twisted through her, each pressing down on her more than the last. *What if her family didn't want her? What if the passage of time had eroded any possibility of a reunion? What if she was forced to return to Schenectady alone?* The possibility of rejection loomed over her like a dark cloud, nearly suffocating her.

Ellery was only three when the man who knew her as Summer, his daughter, was no more. From that moment, Karma tossed her aside like a china doll that had been glued together but would never be the same. Her life was broken. There was no doubt about it. She had been the deceptive lifeline that bound Brant St. John to Karma. As soon as he was gone, she had no need for a child. Nor did it seem she wanted one. Summer had become a burden, a constant reminder of all that had been lost. All she wanted, all Summer ever wanted, was love, but her mother was a narcissistic, hateful woman who was incapable of loving anyone but herself.

After Brant's death, Karma had spent weeks in bed in a fog

of despair, neglecting the child she had renamed Summer. On the day she picked her up from the hospital, after the accident, she shed her maternal title, no longer allowing her daughter to call her mom. Instead, she became *Karma*, a name she wore like a badge. She desired pity, yet she despised it.

Karma looked *through* her instead of at her. And because of the fictitious birth certificate, Summer was barred from experiencing the world beyond the walls of their apartment, not even to attend school. The illusion of *homeschooling* was nothing more than a joke. Her lessons came from the stacks of novels her mother lost herself in and from hiding in the shadows on the nights she snuck out, people-watching and digging through dumpsters and garbage cans, thrilled to find second-hand food larger than a bite or a broken toy that would entertain her.

Many nights, Karma left the apartment with a slam of the door, seemingly forgetting she had a daughter. She would often stumble in during the early morning hours. That time alone granted Summer a reprieve. By the time she was five, it was a toss-up for who hated whom worse.

Ellery crawled out of bed, tiptoeing to the door on the uncarpeted floor. With a quiet twist of the handle, she quickly opened the door and snatched the tray from the table, praying she could sneak in and out without being noticed. Guilt plucked at her for lying to Paula, but the rumbling in her stomach was more pressing than her conscience.

After setting the tray on the small, painted table, she dropped onto the matching chair, inhaling the first roll without tasting it. She poured coffee into the delicate white teacup adorned with tiny blue forget-me-nots and drank it while savoring the second sticky pastry.

Still too early to enter her brother's art gallery, Ellery decided to shower. Steam filled the air, blurring the reality of what would come. With a towel wrapped around her, Ellery opened the door and stepped out of the bathroom, waiting for the thick cloud to dissipate. She dried her hair in front of a full-length mirror before applying more makeup than she had ever worn in her entire life. Ellery stood back and studied her reflection. Never had she considered herself pretty, but then again, she had never tried to impress anyone before today.

As the clock ticked closer to 9:30, the hair on the back of her neck rose. A tidal wave of anticipation swelled in her stomach, and she began to pace. The possibility of having a family was like a new pair of shoes—you loved the idea of them, but they were uncomfortable until they were broken in. The seconds stretched like elastic, and the waiting was killing her.

9:55 glowed on her phone. Ellery slipped on her coat and inched the door open and closed without a sound. The click of the lock announced her departure. Without looking back, she descended the narrow back staircase on tiptoes, each step a countdown to what lay ahead. The door to the outside world creaked open, and she rushed across the porch and down the winding path that meandered along the lake.

The street was almost deserted except for the few people who drifted in and out of the Higher Grounds Coffee Shop and Nel's Cafe on the main drag. Sitting on the stone bench, Ellery could not peel her eyes from the gallery. Suddenly, the inside lights came on, and the *open* neon light flashed to life. *10:08.* Clearly, her brother was somewhat of a slacker.

She wanted to rise, to be the first one through the door, but she was frozen in place. One minute passed, and then another. Ten minutes slipped away while she decided whether to continue her mission or abandon ship. Standing, she turned toward the B&B, but a sudden surge of resolve changed her direction. She waited for the lone car on the street to pass before she continued. Determination to meet her brother was the only motivation she needed.

Like at Clara's, as Ellery stepped into the gallery, a delicate chime from a tiny bell announced her arrival. Yet, no one greeted her. The air felt thick, almost as if it were holding its breath.

"Hello?" Her voice faded into the long space. "Is anyone here?"

Silence.

Perhaps it was a sign she had made the wrong choice. As doubt crept in, Ellery's gaze landed on a painting on the far wall. The colors were a harmonious dance. A spectrum of blues and purples depicted the tranquil lake; the pinks of sunset kissed the lake's surface, reflecting into the water. She stepped closer, captivated. Turning toward the front window, she took in her brother's exact view when he painted it. The painting, ironically, was called *Home*.

In Schenectady, the same painting hung across from her bed. She had ordered it as soon as she learned Liam was a painter. Every night before she closed her eyes, she whispered, "There's no place like home. There's no place like home."

But now, standing in the unfamiliar gallery, staring at the very familiar painting, a question loomed heavily: Would this ever truly be home? Or was this another cruel twist of fate, a slap across the face from a universe that seemed to toy with her hopes and dreams?

FIVE

Footsteps thundered down the stairs behind her, each thump reverberating into her thoughts like a drum in an empty room. The conversation she had played out hundreds of times fought for her full attention. Ellery could feel the warmth creeping onto her cheeks, a rush of heat that betrayed the calmness she hoped to display. She kept her back to the sound, bracing herself for whatever would come next—acceptance or denial.

"I'm sorry. I didn't realize anyone was here. Hi, I'm Liam, the owner of the gallery."

Ellery turned. Surprise flickered on Liam's face.

The lines across his forehead deepened. A moment's hesitation hung in the air as his lips parted.

"H-have we met before? You look so familiar." The rhythm of his words was uneven. Ellery swallowed hard under the intensity of his gaze. His statement frightened her.

Ellery wondered if Liam could hear her out-of-control heartbeat. "No." Because of the chaos churning inside, she wasn't sure if she'd spoken the word aloud.

Liam shook his head. "Wow! That's weird. There's something about you that makes me think we've met."

As her brother stepped closer, Ellery's hands began to shake.

"What's your name?"

A jagged breath caught in Ellery's throat as a tumultuous wave of angst crashed over her. She had rehearsed this moment countless times in front of her mirror, but now, standing an arm's length of her brother, it felt surreal. With a determined inhale, she closed her eyes and slowly released it. "I'm…"

Just then, the bell on the door chimed. A woman with pink bangs stepped inside. "Hi, Monica." Liam eyed Ellery, silently pleading with her to stay. "I'll only be a moment. I want to figure out how I know you."

As Liam disappeared into the back room, fading from view of the door, Ellery felt a surge of panic. Quietly, she slipped through the door, the bell sirening her escape.

Stepping into the entryway of the photography shop next door, Ellery bent forward, her fingertips digging into her jeans as she fought to steady her racing thoughts. Colors and shapes melded together as tears threatened to spill. Moisture pooled on her lashes as she squeezed her eyes shut. Her breath came out in quick, shaky bursts.

Ellery had never been a crier. She was a survivor, a fighter who hid in the shadows and trained her heart not to care. But knowing she didn't belong to Karma and that she had a family, a real family, had changed all that. Now, emotions and doubts flooded through her like a river.

She argued with herself. *I can't do this. I have to do this. It's why I came. But what good will it do? You'll have a family.* What if Liam rejected her and sent her packing? But what if he didn't? With every question, a new wave of panic washed over her, pulling her deeper into the storm.

Opening her eyes, Ellery stared down at a pair of black boots that were not hers. Pushing herself upright, she looked into Liam's face.

"Am I glad to see you. It's cold out here." Liam rubbed his hands together. "Let's go into the gallery." He led Ellery back toward the shop, checking over his shoulder twice to ensure she had not disappeared again.

He pulled the door open, but Ellery froze, unable to cross the threshold.

"Are you okay? What's going on?" Liam's eyes held a deep concern.

Ellery opened her mouth, but her words were impossible to find.

"Come on. I promise I won't bite." Liam smirked. "The only person I've ever bitten was my brother, and believe me, he deserved it."

Finally, she stepped inside and followed Liam to the checkout counter. Liam pulled two padded stools with short backs from beneath the carpeted worktable and waited for her to sit before he did. The way he tracked her every move, Ellery knew he was afraid she would bolt.

"As I recall, you were just about to tell me your name."

Ellery drummed her fingers on the countertop. "I guess I was," she whispered. "It's ah, Elle Gray." She swallowed past the lump in her throat. "Ellery, actually." She studied his face, searching for a sign of recognition.

Liam's eyes clouded in thought. "That's not a name I recognize. Where're you from?" The sharp edges of his question hung in the air, ready to attack any answer she gave.

She debated lying. If things went south, she did not want him to find her. Finally, she settled on being *vague* rather than telling an out-and-out lie. "Here and there. Most recently, out east."

He pulled back in surprise. "Well, you're a long way from home, Elle Gray."

At that moment, the truth felt like a stone had lodged in her throat. She could feel the pressure. The struggle was a tug-of-war between honesty and self-preservation. Suddenly, her words found momentum. "I *am* home."

"Oh, you live here now?"

"I used to." She swallowed hard. "My real name…" Attempting to make peace with the news she was throwing at her brother, she squeezed her eyes shut. Her hands twisted anxiously, matching her inner turmoil.

The moment moved in slow motion; a cloud of uncertainty hung in the air. Finally, Ellery unveiled the truth, which had been hidden for almost thirty-seven years, the one she had cloistered for nearly two years. "My *given name* was…" Her face twisted as she looked Liam in the eyes. "Chloe Chambers."

The name landed with a thud.

Liam pulled away from her. "Is this some kind of a cruel joke?"

"No." The massive wall clock ticked ten times as she let him digest the news. "I have the DNA documents to prove it." She retrieved the folded papers from her tote, smoothing them on the table. "It says Vanessa Chambers and I share DNA. Look." She pointed to a statement that proved them to be *mother and daughter*.

Liam stood motionless, absorbing the shock. Unable to contain his whirlwind of emotions, he began pacing, periodically stopping to scan the results again. He dug his fingers restlessly through his thick hair. Finally, he distanced himself from Ellery by standing behind the counter.

"So, where in the hell have you been the last thirty-some years? Living under a rock?" The pitch of his voice rose, anger tugging at his features. "My family is very influential. The story of your kidnapping has made national news at least two dozen times since then." A fierce eruption of anger filled the room. "How could you not have known you were her—*Chloe*?"

Ellery's eyes shimmered. "It's a long story."

Liam moved to the entrance of the gallery. With a quick twist, he locked the door, cutting off interruptions. He switched off the *open* sign and cut the lights, giving the impression he was closed. In a burst of frustration, he slammed a hand against the wall, the sound echoing in the stillness. Ellery could see his jaw flex.

"Well, I've got nothing but time." Liam pressed his mouth into an angry line.

Two hours of explaining Karma, her escape from Beaufort—minus the fire, explosion, and the identity of the person who showed up on her doorstep two years before—left Ellery exhausted and starving. Still, she hung in there, answering every question Liam tossed at her. A hint of relief washed over her as she noticed the tension on his face had fallen away. It almost seemed like he believed her.

After a half dozen questions, he fished his phone from his pocket. His fingers moved quickly over the screen.

Before he finished, Ellery gently placed her hand on his arm. "Please don't tell anyone else yet." Her eyes searched for his understanding. "That news needs to come from me."

"It will. Believe me." Liam tipped his phone toward her, revealing the text he was ready to send.

Meeting at 6:00.

BIG news.

"Wait for it!" He opened his hand and began counting down, folding fingers with each number. "Five, four, three, two, one…"

His phone dinged numerous times as responses from his siblings flooded in. He positioned the phone between them. Ellery leaned in, her eyes sparkling with curiosity as she read the incoming messages.

*I call BS. The last time you
said that, you wanted us to
paint the gallery.*

*You better not be lying.
I'm gonna miss
Harlow's first softball game.*

*There better be chocolate
ice cream.*

*And remember the cherries
this time.*

*And mint chocolate chip
ice cream, or I'm leaving.*

What's wrong with you?

Nobody makes a sundae with that.

Says the dork who eats
his ice cream cone with a spoon.

Liam dropped the side of his fist lightly on the counter. "Are you sure you want to be part of this family?"

Ellery's shoulders sagged. "More than anything." Suddenly, a wave of panic coursed through her like a dark cloud shadowing a sunny day. "Will your parents be there?"

"You mean *our* parents?" A gentle smile spread across his face. "No. Dad's on a business trip, and Mom has a city council meeting tonight. It's just the four—well, *five* of us."

Their conversation was interrupted by the buzz of his phone. Moments later, the soft ping sounded twice more as additional messages arrived.

So help me, Liam,
if this is another one of your
"I want everyone to see my
new shoes" meetings,
we're going to drown you
in the lake—tonight!

And I've had a crappy day,
so I'm all for taking you out!

Oh, hell yes!

Liam typed a short message before turning his phone so Ellery could see it.

Same shoes.
This is BIG!

He punched the *send* button and tucked his phone back into

his pocket. "Now, let's go find something to eat. I'm starving."

"You can leave the gallery?"

"I own it. I can do anything I want."

He placed a hand on Ellery's back. She instantly recoiled.

Liam quickly withdrew his hands. "I'm so sorry. I didn't mean to scare you." His voice was ripe with regret.

Ellery's expression softened as she glanced downward. "You didn't. I just…" She hesitated. "I've dreamed of having a sibling for so long…" She met her brother's gaze. "And now I have four. To be honest, I haven't been touched by *family* since my da—I mean since Brant died."

A frown creased Liam's brow. "That's the saddest thing I've ever heard."

"Yes, but if all goes well, in a few hours, all that changes, right?"

Liam chuckled. "First, it already has." He poked a finger into his chest. "Me. I'm your brother. Second, you read the texts. You may not be so happy about having siblings once you meet that crew."

A smile spread across Ellery's face. "Oh, I don't think there's any chance of that happening."

Liam glanced toward the stairs. "If I go upstairs and get my coat, promise me you'll be here when I return."

Ellery raised her right hand. "Promise."

Liam ran up the stairs, returning in record time.

"Where are we going?" Ellery slipped her arms through the sleeves of her jacket and zipped it up.

"First, we're gonna go eat before I starve to death. Then, we need to pick up everything we need for sundaes. The meeting caller's responsible for ensuring we have *more than* enough fixings. And don't let me forget the cherries. *One time.* One time, I forgot them, and I've never heard the end of it."

"Cherries! Check!"

"Some families drink. Mine hits big news head-on with ice cream." Liam shot her an impish smirk.

"Interesting tradition."

"It started when we were kids." Liam held the door open for her, locking it behind them. "After Mom left, we had a lot of *meetings*—and ice cream." He placed a hand on her back and turned her toward Nel's Cafe. "After that, we'll head out to Dad's."

"Wait! I thought you said he was gone." Ellery's face furrowed in confusion.

"He is, but that's where all family meetings take place. They always have."

"Is there going to be anyone there besides the five of us?" The closer she got to meeting her siblings, the more her nerves felt like they were on fire.

"Just Edda. She's Dad's housekeeper." Liam rolled his eyes in a humorous gesture. "Like Dad needs a housekeeper—or a gardener—or a landscaper—or pool boy—or... It's just him here. He could handle everything himself."

A surge of surprise shot through Ellery, her neck instinctively pulling back. "How rich *is* your family?"

"Rich?" His head wobbled back and forth. "Hmm, not Bezos rich, but probably more than Clooney."

"Clooney?"

"He's an actor. You have been living under a rock, haven't you?"

Ellery nodded. She tried to imagine that lifestyle as they walked the few blocks. "I really don't want Edda to know who I am before I tell your...*our*...parents." Her mind drifted inward, and panic fluttered inside. "I don't know if I'm ever going to get used to saying that."

"You will." Liam opened the door to the café and ushered Ellery inside. "Edda leaves at four. With Dad not there, she may already be gone."

"Hi, Liam." A frazzled-looking woman grabbed two menus from behind the counter.

"Hey, Nel. This is Elle." He laughed. "You guys rhyme."

"Nice to meet you, Elle. Welcome to the diner."

"Thank you."

The woman led them to the only cleared booth near the back. She set the menus on the table and sighed heavily. "We're a little backed up. The breakfast crowd seems to have nowhere to go today. You'd think they didn't have jobs." She swung an arm across several empty tables, setting what appeared to be a new employee in motion. "Good help is hard to find. I've never had to invite a busser to do his job." Nel rolled her shoulders back and folded her hands. "Jen'll be with you in a few minutes."

"No problem."

After Nel left, lines deepened across Liam's forehead.

"What are you thinking?"

"Money." The word was a complete sentence that spoke volumes. "My family may think that's why you showed up."

"I don't want or need money. What I need is a family."

He held his palms outward. "We are a very protective bunch. Hopefully, they'll believe you."

Liam's concern played out in Ellery's head. How would she explain she did not need their money without telling them who she had become in the past ten years?

SIX

Liam eased his Jeep down the winding gravel road to what he referred to as the *main house*. Ellery's jaw dropped when the building came into view. The sheer size left her awestruck. It dwarfed the B&B in town. She had never seen anything so stunning.

Red bricks covered the lower level, emanating timelessness. Black shutters framed each window, adding a slice of charm. The upper level offered a striking contrast, covered in white shakes. Five dormer windows jutted out like curious eyes.

After cutting the engine, Liam pointed to the middle window. "That's my room." His words were matter of fact, as if everyone had bedroom windows the size of a bus.

Ellery's eyebrows shot up in surprise. "You *live* here?"

"Not on your life. But I grew up here. You'd know what a geek I was if you saw my room. It looks exactly the same as when I left home at eighteen. Same posters. Same CD player. Same bulletin board with girls' phone numbers pinned to it." His grin broadened. "Mom hasn't changed a thing."

"I thought your parents were divorced."

"Not divorced. Separated. There's a difference." He held up his index fingers and moved them far apart. "Divorced." Then he held two fingers on the same hand and spread them apart. "Separated."

Ellery tipped her head in question. "So, they remained married because of you kids?"

"Something like that. It's been over thirty years, but Mom still runs Dad's life like a CEO. And to be honest, he wouldn't survive without her."

"Don't you think it's odd they never got divorced?"

"It is what it is." He continued to stare at his bedroom window. "We don't touch their relationship with a ten-foot pole." Liam shifted in his seat. "Mom redecorates the main part of the house every five years or so—in case she decides to return."

"Is that a possibility?" Liam's shrug was barely perceptible, making her believe it was part of an off-limits topic, so she refocused. "She doesn't remodel bedrooms?"

"Are you kidding? Those rooms are a shrine to our teenage years—except…" He held a hand up. "Never mind."

Ellery pointed to a small, white cottage nestled to the right of the house. "Is that a neighbor or a guest house?"

"Wow. Look at you. Asking a million questions," Liam teased. He wagged his head back and forth like a metronome. "Guesthouse, more or less. Dad owns it, but Baily and Ben and their daughter, Piper, live there."

"She didn't move far from home, did she?"

"None of us did. We all stayed in Hunters Cove. But you're right; for some reason, Baily wanted to stay on the property. When she and Ben got married, she told Dad they'd fix the place up if they could live there." Liam opened his car door and grabbed the ice cream from the back seat. Ellery picked up the canvas sack they had filled at the grocery store.

As they walked up the steps of the main house, Ellery mentally calculated the distance to the cottage. It couldn't have been more than a hundred feet away. With windows open, she was sure the gentle breeze would carry their voices, quashing any privacy.

Edda's voice rang out as they crossed the threshold. "Shoes off! I don't mop this floor every day because I want to."

The hardwood floor gleamed in the sunlight that streamed through the wall of floor-to-ceiling windows facing the lake of the great room.

Liam cast a sideways glance toward Ellery, his face hilariously distorted. In a low whisper, he remarked, "She's a liar. Dad hasn't been here for four days, but she still mops every morning. You can't tell me she doesn't want to do it."

Edda stepped into the foyer, wiping her hands on a faded gingham-checked apron. "I heard that, smart-ass." She brushed a few strands of her shoulder-length gray hair back from her face as she sized up Ellery. "So, who are you who dare barge into this house when the master is not here to defend his castle?" Her eyes spread in question as she turned toward Liam.

"You've seen too many episodes of *Knightfall*." He gestured toward Ellery. "This is…" He walked over and pressed the off button on the television remote, throwing the room into a loud silence. "Geez, Edda. You must be going deaf in your old age."

Edda raised a fist in a warning. "Who you calling old, boy?"

"I'm Elle Gray." Ellery extended her hand.

Edda crossed her arms, ignoring the gesture. "That's not even a name. It's a letter." Her tone dripped with sarcasm. "L? Why in the hell would any sane person name their kid after the alphabet?" Suddenly, she slapped the heel of one hand against the other. "Ohhh, so you come from a long line of hippies."

Ellery shifted awkwardly, a nervous chuckle escaping as she fidgeted with the zipper of her jacket. "It's E-L-L-E."

With a dismissive eye roll, Edda's expression conveyed her skepticism. "Whatever. It's not a name fitting for a person or a dog." The housekeeper's voice was ripe with condescension. "So, what are ya doin' here?" Suddenly, she batted her eyes at Liam, snickering. "Or is she your flavor of the month?"

A grin tugged at the corners of Ellery's mouth. Her eyes held a glint of mischief as she glanced at her brother. "Flavor of the month, huh?"

His cheeks pinkened, annoyance creeping into his voice as he shot back, "She's just a friend, Edda. That's all."

The housekeeper scowled at Liam. "A friend, huh?" She gave Ellery the once over. "Boy, you could do a whole lot worse than this one here. I've seen some of those bimbos you've dragged home."

"Enough, already." The words echoed in the massive foyer.

Edda eyeballed Ellery again. "Well, Alphabet, if you've got a brain in your head, you're already battin' better than the others."

"My name's Elle." Frustration nibbled at her. "I really am just a friend."

Liam pushed past Edda, his broad shoulders brushing against her as he entered the prep kitchen. In each hand, he gripped a bucket of ice cream, frost forming on the outside of the plastic. Ellery trailed behind, lugging the heavy bag with an array of toppings, including not one but two jars of cherries.

Edda raised an eyebrow. "Must be a serious meeting." She traipsed behind them so closely, Ellery could feel the woman's hot breath on her neck. "It appears to be a two-bucket showdown." She chuckled, pointing her thumbs and fingers like guns.

"We're not meeting 'til six, so you're dismissed for the day." Liam gave her the evil eye.

Edda's head bobbed as she silently mimicked Liam's message. "Fine! But remember, this ain't a self-cleaning house. So, make sure you and Alphabet clean up after yourselves."

Liam set the buckets on the counter and closed his eyes briefly. "That line never gets old." He pulled the freezer door open, blocking Edda from his view, tipped his head back, and stared at the ceiling before shoving the ice cream inside. That told Ellery everything she needed to know about Edda's relationship with Liam, if not the whole family.

Edda disappeared into the back room, returned with her coat and purse, and shot daggers at Liam before turning to Ellery. "Bye, flavor of the month. Next month, maybe he'll bring home someone named M." She waddled out the front door, her high-pitched laughter piercing the air.

"Sorry about that. Edda's been here since before Chloe…" Liam scrunched his face. "I mean before *you* were taken. I have no idea why Dad keeps her. She's such a pain in the ass. There was a time when she honestly cared about us, but that was before Mom left. After that, it was like being raised by a grandmother who only tolerates you."

Ellery carefully unbagged the toppings. "How long ago was that?"

"I suppose it would have been around the time you and Baily would have been three." His voice was steeped with nostalgia. "One day, Mom woke up, packed her bags, and moved back to Minnetonka. I remember that day like it was yesterday. She lined us up on the couch and told us the house didn't feel like home anymore, and it wouldn't until you were back."

"That's awful. You must have been devastated." Ellery carefully folded the empty bag, avoiding Liam's eyes.

"Devastated? No. I was four. I was absolutely crushed. None of us could understand how she could leave us for someone we barely knew." Liam kept his back to her as he stared out the window. "No offense. I know that seems awful, but we only knew you for eight days."

"I get it."

"To help us understand, she reminded us about the time Jacqui lost her favorite doll. Mom made us spend the rest of the day looking for it. Mom said she knew the doll wasn't important to us, but Jacqui needed our support, so we had to help her."

When he turned around, he had a massive grin on his face. "Of course, Mom had no idea Preston had given the doll a haircut and then got scared and buried it in the backyard." He stretched his neck. "Years later, Dad's old hunting dog dug that dang doll up."

"Seriously?"

"Yeah. Dad made us give our allowance to Jacqui for an entire month. She was twelve by then and didn't care about dolls, but she loved watching us suffer." The look on his face shifted as his thoughts spun. Ellery could see the whiplash of emotions in his eyes. "I remember the day she left like it was yesterday. She said you were waiting for her somewhere, so she had to go."

"Mother's intuition. That would have been around the time

my dad, sorry—Brant died. She was right. I *did* need her. That's when Karma's fangs came out."

Liam leaned against the counter. "Brant sounds like he was a great guy. You never have to apologize for loving someone who loved you back."

Ellery joined him at the counter. "What's always bothered me is that he died without ever knowing he wasn't my biological dad." Her shoulders inched downward. "Of course, he didn't know Karma kidnapped me either. Had he known, he would have moved heaven and earth to make sure I made it home."

"Everybody keeps secrets for one reason or another. I'm sure you've done something you're not proud of."

That statement was heavier than Liam knew. Ellery's heart thudded as a truth, bigger than Chloe's return, threatened to burst out of her. Secrets swirled, each darker than the last, yet none compared to the fire and explosion that convinced Karma of Summer's demise.

Granted, the cabin she had rented was almost a hundred years old, was less than three hundred square feet, and had gaps between the logs so large that she could practically watch the stars lying in bed at night. At the top of the market, the cabin was worth maybe fifty thousand dollars. Insurance would have covered the loss. But even so, when Ellery received the advance for her first book, she knew what she had to do. She collected hundred-dollar bills from banks all over New York, put seventy-five thousand dollars in a sturdy cardboard box, and anonymously sent it to her former landlords. But even though she had paid her dues, the secret was almost more than she could bear. Only Millie and Gus knew the truth, and they had taken it to their graves.

"What's wrong?" Liam's voice was low with concern as he stepped closer to Ellery.

"Nothing," Ellery lied. "I was just trying to imagine what it must have been like growing up in this house."

Liam huffed. "You don't want to know. Thanks to Edda, it

was like growing up in the military. We had to keep our rooms spotless, had chore charts, and were given an allowance that was docked for any infraction. Most weeks, I owed more than I got. Preston and I often ended up borrowing from *Jacqui, the perfect*. When Mom left, Jacqui took on her role—mostly because Edda became a psycho monster. That's when life here turned into boot camp."

"Did you ever see your mom after she left?"

"We did, but it wasn't the same. *She* wasn't the same. When we were with her, she was more focused on finding you than doing anything special with us. She came back for birthdays and holidays, but she was always quick to leave again."

"But you knew she loved you, right?"

Liam paused. "I suppose, but she always seemed more like a distant aunt who appeases her guilt by giving you a gift and then disappears until she feels obligated to return."

"I'm sorry. I feel like that's my fault. If only…"

"It's not your fault."

"Maybe not, but I can't lose the feeling that I am somehow responsible for the pain this has caused everyone."

"No. Mom and Dad made choices. When you disappeared, we lived in Minnetonka." Ellery watched the sharp edges of Liam's memories slice into him. "We moved back here within the year. I was too young to remember life before you disappeared, but Jacqui did. Mom wanted to stay in the cities in case the person who took you had a change of heart, but Dad wanted us to put miles between us and that day. Pops, Mom's dad, was the police chief in Minnetonka when Karma took you. Dad was so angry with him. He blamed him for not doing a good job keeping the scum out." Each word was a brush stroke of a picture, telling the story of a life Ellery had not known.

Ellery followed Liam onto the front porch and sat in a swing. "I read about my kidnapping. I saw pictures of Chief Cole and watched an old interview with him."

"Pops is amazing. But after your kidnapping, he spent so much time searching for you that Nan, Mom's mom, couldn't stand who he'd become, so she left." Liam held up a hand with two fingers spread wide again. "They didn't divorce either. But her leaving was another of the reasons Mom moved back to Minnetonka to take care of Pops. She and her dad joined forces. All they did was search for you."

Liam's shoulders fell. "When I was eight, Dad took us up there to spend time with Mom while he spent a few days at a meeting in St. Paul. The walls were covered in photos, notes, and strings. Pops had recreated the evidence board in his house."

Ellery rocked the swing with her foot as she contemplated what that must have been like for her siblings. "Where did your grandma go?"

"South Carolina."

The hair on the back of Ellery's neck rose. She swallowed hard. "W-where in South Carolina?"

"Hilton Head. That's where she grew up. She still has family there."

Shock wrapped its long arms around her. Her insides spun like a washer, and perspiration prickled her scalp. The air pressed down on her. She knew she had to escape before Liam glimpsed her losing control. There were still some secrets she could not afford to reveal.

"D-do you have a bathroom?" The words rushed out louder than she anticipated.

"Across the hall from the kitchen."

"I might be a bit." Ellery dashed through the door and toward the small room off the entry.

Once inside, Ellery leaned against the cool wall and slid to the floor. All those years, her grandmother had been less than an hour from her. She closed her eyes and saw herself as Summer St. John, standing in her apartment window, praying someone would notice her and save her. It could have been her grandmother. It *should* have been. She had been so close, yet she never came.

SEVEN

The front door opened and slammed shut, resonating like a clap of thunder. Squeezing her hands into fists, Ellery braced herself for what was to come. Her cheeks warmed, and she ran her clammy palms down the sides of her sweatshirt as three strangers who felt familiar, yet foreign, entered the kitchen. From the photos she had spent two years studying, she recognized them all: Jacqui, Preston, and Baily.

Their voices rose and fell in a heated argument. Their words were a blur, not strong enough to crash through her inner turmoil. But when they saw Ellery, silence fell like a heavy curtain. Her breath hitched in her throat. A storm crashed over her. She was drowning under the pressure of their stare.

"So, you must be the flavor of the day," Jacqui, the eldest, said, a smile spreading across her face. "Edda called me on her way home."

"Of course she did." Liam scowled, pressing a reassuring hand against Ellery's back.

Preston grinned. "Don't think you're so special, Jacq. She called all of us. She couldn't wait to dish gossip on Liam's new woman." He turned his attention to Ellery, curiosity dancing in his eyes. "So, do you have a name?"

Panic exploded like fireworks in Ellery's stomach. She looked at Liam, but when he opened his mouth, she cut him off.

"Elle." Her voice was edged with uncertainty.

Preston's head bobbed, his eyes sparkling with mischief. "Oh, yeah. Edda mentioned Liam was dating a woman named after a letter in the alphabet." He grinned at Baily.

Baily puckered her lips in a fake pout. "All I got was that

she was worried about Liam bringing some floozie—her word, not mine—into the house while Dad was away."

Ellery cleared her throat. "Actually, my name's Ellery. Elle's what everyone calls me."

Jacqui lightly brushed her fingers across Ellery's shoulder as she glided past her. "Well, welcome to the nuthouse." With a grin, she made her way toward the kitchen, pausing at the doorway. She gave Liam the look. "Do we have cherries, or did you forget them again?"

Liam shot a cheeky grin at Ellery. Her eyes gleamed with understanding. "What'd I tell you?" He followed Jacqui into the prep kitchen, announcing loud enough for all to hear, "Elephants never forget!"

Suddenly, the sharp sound of a towel snapping repeatedly filled the air, followed by Liam's yelps. "Ow! What the heck? I give!"

A couple of minutes later, Jacqui emerged with a devilish grin, balancing a wooden tray laden with toppings, five ice cream scoops, bowls, spoons, and a thick stack of napkins. Liam followed; a bucket of vanilla hung in his left hand. The container of mint chocolate chip was pressed to the side of his head.

"Liam!" Preston snapped. "Have you learned nothing in thirty-eight years? If you're going to insult Jacqui, you've gotta keep your distance."

Liam lowered the bucket to expose his bright red ear. "And why is it we're not allowed to hit girls?" He grimaced at Jacqui.

"Because you'd get your butt kicked." Baily laughed. "Like you just did."

Ellery climbed onto the stool next to Jacqui. Suddenly, it was like someone had shot the starter pistol and sent the siblings on a wild race for survival. Their piranha-like behavior was amusing. They dove into the buckets of ice cream and toppings, fighting over them like small children. The whipped cream shot across the counter on more than one occasion, with Preston always the first to rescue the blobs before they melted. When the four of them finished, Ellery plopped a small scoop of ice cream into her bowl and helped herself to a spoon and napkin.

"If you're going to be part of this family, you need to eat way more than that." Preston dumped a massive scoop of ice cream into her bowl. Jacqui pulled the tray across the island toward Ellery.

Part of this family. The words ricocheted in her mind. The statement gnawed at her thoughts. She knew he meant—*as Liam's girlfriend*—but to her, it held a much deeper meaning.

To make peace, she drizzled some Magic Shell over the mound of ice cream, the rich chocolate cascading down the sides until it hardened. She drizzled a large spoonful of strawberry topping over it all.

"Now, that's more like it." Jacqui folded her hands and dropped them on the counter. "You could be one of us with that masterpiece."

Liam's expression shifted, his lips twitching into a subtle grin, a secret between them.

For several minutes, the room was filled with a symphony of clinking spoons tapping against the sides of the pottery bowls. A second round, almost as frenzied as the first, began, but this time, laughter mingled with groans of discomfort. Faces flushed with both joy and regret.

An enormous St. Bernard ambled into the room, his coat a blend of golden browns and whites. His droopy jowls flapped with each step. Liam nudged the tub of the vanilla ice cream closer to Jacqui. She scooped two generous servings into a bowl and set it on the floor.

"This is Huck," Jacqui introduced the dog. "He's the size of a refrigerator, but he won't hurt you. For some reason, he always knows when we're about done. He thinks his job is to bat cleanup."

Huck plunged his muzzle into the bowl, and the ice cream disappeared in just a few licks. Suddenly, a foul odor wafted through the air. Ellery fought to keep her expression neutral, but finally, her nose wrinkled, and she pressed her hand to her face.

"Ahhh, Huck!" Jacqui exclaimed, leaning away from the dog. "This is not uncommon."

Everyone clapped their hands over their mouth and nose. Despite the smell, a giggle escaped Ellery as she glanced around the table.

Seconds later, Preston dropped his hand and sniffed the air. A single nod gave the *all-clear*. He scraped the edges of his bowl, pushed it to the middle of the island, and shoved the last bite into his mouth, laying a hand on his stomach. "So, Elle, do you have a last name, or is that just a letter too?" He chuckled. "Maybe Elle Jay or Elle Kay?"

Ellery swallowed the bite of ice cream she had just put in her mouth. Trying to swallow before it had melted triggered a jolt of pain that surged through her head like a bolt of lightning. She pressed her tongue against the roof of her mouth and a hand against her forehead in a futile attempt to curb the discomfort.

"Gray." She heard the awkwardness in her voice, a strained blend of embarrassment and agony. She squeezed one eye shut and pressed a hand to her forehead.

"Ice cream headache? That's a Chambers family thing. We all get them," Preston replied with a casual nonchalance. He scanned the table. "I'm surprised you're the first of the night."

Jacqui leaned forward slightly. "What did you say your last name was?"

"Gray."

"So, not another letter, but a color?" Preston continued to laugh.

"Gray? Ellery Gray?" Jacqui's voice carried a subtle lilt. "Like the author? That reclusive woman the world knows almost nothing about?"

Baily's spoon clattered as it accidentally dropped onto the stone countertop. "That woman's an enigma," she mused, almost to herself. "I've always loved her books, but anybody who won't let the world know who she is has to be hiding something." Baily took another bite of ice cream, shifting it around her mouth as it melted. Suddenly, she pushed it into her cheek. "I wonder if there's any truth in her books." Her gaze passed from Ellery to Jacqui.

Ellery's eyes met Liam's, a flicker of unease crossing her face. "You're right. She does have a lot to hide." Her voice was filled with the gravity of her reality.

"Wait. You know her?" Preston pulled his head back.

"Oh my gosh, Preston. You're dumber than a box of rocks!" Jacqui turned toward Ellery. "You're her? Ellery Gray? The author?"

Ellery bobbed her head once. "I am." Her heart tried to escape through her chest as the revelation was unleashed.

Liam's shoulders slumped, his open mouth sending her a clear message. "You never told me that."

Ellery nervously played with her fingers beneath the counter. "I haven't told anyone. Until now, only a handful of people knew."

Preston playfully punched his brother in the shoulder. "Seriously? You had no clue your girlfriend's famous?"

Liam's jaw pulsed. The woman before him was still a stranger. "She's not my girlfriend." He paused briefly. "And she's not Ellery Gray."

Ellery gritted her teeth and tipped her chin down. Her gaze was like a blade as she shot him a warning.

Baily pulled back in bewilderment. "She just told us she's Ellery Gray."

Liam's expression was a storm of emotions as he wrestled with the betrayal he felt. "That's the person she's pretended to be for the past eighteen years." His voice trembled with anger. "And before that, she was pretending to be someone else."

"Liam, please," Ellery begged. "Please don't. Let me."

He shot a stern look toward her. Even though he saw how much it hurt her, he ignored her plea. "But that's not who she is." He shifted his jaw and stared at her. "She's been hiding something, alright. She's been hiding the fact that she's our *sister*." The information hung in the confused silence as he sneered at Ellery, his eyes not softening until he saw the pain on her face. "She's Chloe."

Ellery felt like she was drowning in silence as four sets of eyes stared at her, waiting for an explanation. They hadn't been ready to hear the truth. She'd felt it before Liam set the freight train in motion. The need to flee surged inside her, but the air was so thick with questions that it was impossible to peel herself from the stool. Every second felt like an eternity.

"What are you saying?" Preston exclaimed loudly, grabbing Liam's arm and swiveling his chair to face him. He shot a piercing look in Ellery's direction. "This is Chloe? *Our* sister Chloe? The one that disappeared almost thirty-seven years ago?" Ellery could feel the shockwaves pulsing through the room as they stared at her.

Preston continued. "This is the sister Mom ignored the rest of us to go find?" Without looking at her, he waved an angry finger in her direction. "You're saying that's her?" Even the room seemed to hold its breath, waiting for a response. Liam deflated, unable or unwilling to defend her. Ellery wasn't sure which.

"You sat here for an hour, watching us, listening to us, trying to decide if you even wanted to be part of our family, didn't you?" Jacqui tipped her head back and huffed. "Have you done your research on us? Oh, who am I kidding? You're an author. That's what you do. You probably have an entire book on us. So, let's see how I do. Before you came to Hunters Cove, you already knew I worked for Dad, and Preston has a law firm. You knew Liam was a painter. You probably own one of his paintings." Ellery swallowed hard. "And you must have known that Baily, your twin sister, owns the bakery in town. You knew all of that, didn't you?" Jacqui's eyes were steel as she stared into Ellery's. "But until a few minutes ago, we didn't even know you were alive."

She grabbed Ellery's arm. "So, what'd you decide? Are we good enough to claim as your family?" Jacqui roughly released her arm and leaned away. "Don't answer that. I don't care."

"I didn't know. I didn't know I was Chloe."

Jacqui's hands shook in anger. The sharpness of her words sliced through Ellery. "Well, you've had to have known for a while. Your first book came out almost ten years ago, and you were hiding under this fake name then."

Baily stood abruptly, her legs colliding with her stool, sending it toppling. "Ten years," she spat, her voice trembling with anger. "For ten years, you've let our family suffer while you hid behind fame, standing just out of the spotlight." Her stare pierced Ellery. "How could you do that—to us? To our parents?"

"It wasn't like that." The urgency in Liam's voice drew everyone's gaze.

"So now you're going to defend her? A minute ago, you were as angry as the rest of us."

Liam ignored Preston's accusation. "That's not how it happened. She told me she only found out she was Chloe two years ago."

Jacqui clicked her tongue. "So, ten years was *too long* for us to suffer, but two years was okay?" Her voice was smothered with thick sarcasm. Her jaw pulsed. "Good to know. Two years of subjecting family to pain is the limit." She scanned the faces of her siblings. "Did you all hear that?"

Ellery firmly dropped the side of her hand on the counter. "Don't you think I suffered? The woman who took me was Satan. She starved me and beat me repeatedly after my dad…"

"Don't!" Baily waved an accusatory finger at Ellery. "Don't you dare! Whoever you're referring to as *Dad* is *not* your dad. Weston Chambers is your father—nobody else."

Suddenly, Baily's tone shifted, uncertainty rising. "If any of this is even true."

Baily rounded the corner of the island. She pressed her hands firmly against her hips and leaned dangerously close to Ellery. "How do we know? You're a storyteller. You could be lying to us just like you lied about being Ellery Gray all these years."

Even without the presence of rocks, Ellery felt the thud of

the stoning she was receiving. "I didn't lie about being Ellery Gray. I legally changed my name eighteen years ago before the fire…"

Jacqui leaned toward her, holding her hands up in question. "What fire?"

Ellery tucked her hands between her knees. "That's not important. My name is legally Ellery Gray."

"She has DNA results that prove she's our sister," Liam said. "Show them."

Ellery exhaled deeply, hoping the single sheet of paper filled with numbers and a few words would be enough to ward off their doubts. On wobbly legs, she made her way to the foyer and removed the folded paper from her bag.

Returning to the kitchen, she handed the page to Liam, who flattened it and laid it before his brother. Preston studied the details comparing shared DNA between Ellery and their mother.

He shrugged dismissively. "This is just some online test. Sure, it shows you share fifty percent DNA with Mom, but this would be really easy to fake. Anyone who's even a little tech savvy could have made this." He gave Ellery a dry stare. "I've seen people try to pass off crap like this before. It'd never stand up in court. Documents are easy to falsify. Five minutes on Google, and you've got everything you need."

"So, let's run another test." Liam put his hand on Preston's arm. "Quinn could oversee it."

Baily huffed bitterly. "How can you believe anything she says? She's playing you, and you're too stupid to see it. You're the perfect mark. None of the rest of us are that gullible."

"What reason would I have to lie?" Ellery squeezed her hands into balls beneath the counter.

"Money," Baily growled.

"I have money. I don't need money," Ellery shot back, her tone defiant.

Baily pulled her arms across her chest. "Maybe a story for your next novel, or maybe…"

"Stop it, Bai. Assuming Quinn agrees, we can have the test

run tomorrow and have it back within the week. In the meantime, not a word to anyone. I don't want this getting back to Mom and Dad until we know for sure." She side-eyed Ellery. "We've been here before. You're not the first person to claim you're our sister. You're just the first one to go after the softest heart."

Baily moved back to the end of the counter and righted the stool. "I already know what the results will say. Just look at you. You're the only one with dark hair. And anyone can change their eye color with a pair of contacts. We're supposed to be twins, but we look nothing alike." A malicious grin spread across Baily's face. "What're you gonna do when the test proves you're a liar? What rich family are you gonna target next?"

"Grandma Maggie had dark hair, Bai. Hair color doesn't necessarily prove Ellery's not a Chambers. I'm not a defense attorney like Preston, but I know the law. Hair and eye color are circumstantial evidence, not definitive proof."

"Two minutes ago, you didn't believe her either." Baily squeezed her fists until her knuckles turned white.

"I'm not saying I do now, but until we have proof, one way or the other, we just have to wait."

Baily nodded toward Ellery. "Regardless, I don't trust this *liar* farther than I can throw her."

"Do you have anything else to tell us?" Jacqui leaned back in her chair.

"I know you have no reason to believe me, but I'm telling you the truth. Why would I lie? If you'd rather I leave…"

Baily scoffed. "I vote hell yes."

Ellery's shoulders drooped forward. "I'll do whatever you want. I didn't mean to disrupt your family."

"Bullshit! You did too."

"Liam, we need to talk." Preston ignored Baily's outburst. Instead, he pointed at Ellery with a side jerk of his head. His meaning was unmistakable, yet he clarified it for his brother. "And by *we*, I mean just the family. What'da you wanna do with her?"

Liam summoned Ellery with a hooked finger. "Come with me."

Without a word to anyone, Ellery followed him to the door. He helped her into her jacket, picked up her bag, and handed it to her before pulling his car keys from his front pocket.

"I'm sorry. I didn't think they would react this badly." Regret edged his words as Ellery stared at him. "I'm honestly shocked. But then again, I thought you'd told me the truth—all of it." Liam dangled the keys before her. "Go back to the B&B. I'll have Preston drop me off in town."

Bits and pieces of the sibling's conversation cut into Ellery. Tears rimmed her eyes, and she started to shake.

"Drop my car at the gallery in the morning. We can talk then." A few moments of silence wedged between them. "I feel awful about what I did, but I…" He bit his lip. "Never mind."

He opened the door, but a sudden urgency propelled him to halt her at the threshold, and he threw an arm in front of her. "Whatever you do, don't leave. Promise?" Ellery's eyes were glassy; even the tiniest movements would send her tears cascading. "Listen to me. If you leave now, they'll think you're lying."

Ellery defiantly raised her chin. "And what do you think?"

"I don't know. I want to believe you, but you haven't been entirely honest with me." His expression softened momentarily, but his fear was undeniable. "But here's the thing. Now that they know you're Ellery Gray, the author, there's no telling what they would do with that information. They could ruin you. I don't think they would, but…" Liam glanced toward the breakfast nook for a brief second. "Baily has no filter. You saw that for yourself. I'll try to do damage control. But I still don't understand why you didn't tell me who you were." The statement was charged with betrayal.

Ellery stared into his familiar eyes, identical to the ones she had seen in the mirror every morning. "I hadn't planned to tell anyone, but they figured it out, and I couldn't add more lies to my life." She tucked her trembling hands into the pocket of her sweatshirt.

"We'll talk in the morning. Meet me at the gallery at eight. I have an appointment for a commission at eleven."

Ellery heard the door close behind her. The angry whispers from the kitchen played in her mind as she walked to Liam's car. She was right to think things would fall apart. They always did.

EIGHT

A warm golden glow from the streetlight hovered over Liam's car when Ellery parked it in front of the gallery. The engine gave a soft moan before falling silent. She had no intention of parking his vehicle at Harmony House. It would prompt too many questions from the owners.

The soft crunch of gravel underfoot accompanied her to the B&B as she walked along the path. The moonlight cast a silvery glow, the only beauty in Ellery's agonizing night.

She carefully tiptoed up the back porch, her entire body on high alert. The door creaked in protest as she pushed it shut behind her. Miraculously, the sounds had seemingly gone unnoticed.

Navigating the back hallway, she reached her room. The lock clicked behind her, locking out the people she had prayed would welcome her with open arms. She pressed her head against the door and tried to calm her nerves. Several breaths of lavender and faint traces of vanilla attacked her unease, sending it packing. But when she turned on the light, panic rose into her throat.

The room was pristine, as if she were entering it for the first time. Her bed had been neatly made, and the covers had been turned down. Two foil-wrapped chocolates lay on her pillow. A collection of clean towels hung neatly near the sink, and a pair of plush white bath sheets had been tucked into the wicker basket near the soaker tub.

As she exited the bathroom, her skin crawled upon realizing something was amiss. The suitcases, which she had carefully concealed beneath the low shelf in the closet, had been moved.

They rested side-by-side on luggage racks positioned against one wall. The lids had been left open in a blatant invasion of her privacy.

Panic pounded inside her as she rifled through her belongings, searching for the one thing that could give her away. The nausea that stirred in her stomach slowly dissipated when her hand touched it. Relief washed over her, unraveling the tension coiled within her. She released the breath she had been holding for much too long.

Clutched in her hand was the first book she had written. The cover was worn from numerous readings. Karma's tiny print mocked her in the margins of every chapter. Each disgusting comment was a scar, a reminder of when the world was darker. On the last page, three handwritten sentences haunted Ellery.

Summer, you're a disgusting piece of trash. I won't allow you to exist in this world with me. Believe me, when I find you, I'll make you pay.

The only thing that comforted her was knowing that Karma was dead, buried in a grave somewhere in Beaufort, South Carolina. Karma was prolific in her comments for Ellery. Her distinctive handwriting and disgusting comments appeared on nearly every page. The ink smudges were like dark marks on her soul.

Ellery felt the floor collapse beneath her, and she dropped to her knees. If whoever had cleaned the room found the book, they would have been able to connect the dots, piecing together the truth. Until the DNA results came back, and all the Chamberses had been told, no one could know who she was and why she was in Hunters Cove—and even then, she was not sure she wanted them to know.

A soft knock on the door nearly made her jump out of her skin. Ellery slid the book under the bed and straightened the bed skirt. She glanced at her reflection in the mirror as she approached the door. Her eyes were somewhat glazed, and her hair appeared as if it hadn't been combed in a week. She prayed that whoever stood on the other side would be kind enough not to acknowledge the turmoil they were sure to see.

"Elle?" a voice called from the other side of the door. "I wanted to check on you to see if you need anything before I turn in. Tea? A magazine? A book?"

Ellery pulled the door open a crack, allowing just enough space for a sliver of light to escape into the hallway. She slipped into the shadow of the door, concealing her face from Susan's view. Only her forehead was visible from the hallway. "I-I think I'm okay. I was just going to jump in the shower."

"Oh, I'm sorry. I'll let you go. Paula's off tonight, but I'll be here. If you need anything, don't hesitate to text."

"Thank you." Ellery started to push the door closed but stopped when she heard Susan's voice.

"Breakfast will be at nine. I have…"

"No need for breakfast. I have an appointment at eight."

"Okay. I'll drop off pastries and a pot of coffee around six thirty. I'll leave the tray out here in case you aren't up."

"Thank you." Ellery felt herself begin to crumble. "Have a good night."

"Sweet dreams." Ellery heard Susan retreat to the third-floor owner's suite before she dropped onto the bed.

Sweet dreams were not possible. Not tonight, and the way things were going, maybe not ever.

The night stretched endlessly, every minute heavy with deep torment as Ellery tossed and turned. Replays of the meeting with her siblings kept her from closing her eyes because when she did, she was haunted by nightmares of everyone trying to destroy her.

At 6:28 a.m., she stood at her door, straining to hear Susan delivering the coffee and pastries. After hearing her retreat downstairs, Ellery swung the door open. The smell wafted toward her. She snatched the tray and nudged the door closed with her hip. Within half an hour, she had drained the pot of coffee, and all that remained of the flaky strawberry cream cheese croissants were a few crumbs.

An envelope with her name had been propped on the tray. Due to a friend's emergency, Paula and Susan would be gone for a few days, but a woman named Claudette would be staying at the B&B. For that, she was grateful.

At 7:55, Ellery stepped into the crisp morning air. She pulled her hands into the sleeves of her sweatshirt and headed down the path. Eight minutes later, as she approached the gallery's entrance, she noticed Liam anxiously pacing in front of the windows. He pointed to his phone before twisting the deadbolt on the door and pulling it open. "You're late."

"Sorry," Ellery whispered.

"My car was here, but you weren't. I told you to leave it at the B&B. I thought you left town."

Ellery handed him his keys. "I wanted to, but I didn't."

A woman stepped out of the back room and moved toward them. Before closing the distance, she came to a dead stop. Her mouth dropped open. "Even without the DNA test, I can tell she's your sister. She has your eyes. How did the siblings not see that last night?"

"They were too angry to see anything."

The woman offered her hand to Ellery. "I'll apologize for the family's behavior last night. Eventually, they will, but for now... I'm Quinn, Preston's wife." Ellery nodded but said nothing. "Right. You already know that. You probably know everything about us, and we know virtually nothing about you."

"I was accused of that last night too. You're all the same. It's like a mean girls' clique you want to be a part of but can't." Ellery stared at Quinn.

"Yeah, it does feel that way sometimes. They're a tight-knit bunch. They didn't handle me or Harley..."

"Harley?"

"Jacqui's husband," Liam said.

"As I was saying, they don't handle outsiders well. Ask

Harley about that." Quinn chuckled. "Anyway, Preston told me bits and pieces about last night, but he was too angry to talk much. Liam filled me in this morning."

Ellery locked eyes with Liam; a storm of emotion whirled in her gaze. "I don't understand why they're so angry with me. It's not like I kidnapped myself. And I would never have chosen to stay with a woman who almost killed me a dozen times had I known I didn't really belong to her."

Quinn's gaze was gentle. "I can't imagine what life was like for you. That woman sounds like she was… As a doctor, I won't call her crazy, but..." For a fleeting moment, a wave of compassion created a bridge between them. Yet, almost as quickly, the tenderness in her expression toughened. "The problem everyone has is that you've known you were Chloe for two years, and you didn't come forward as soon as you found out. That's what the siblings are the most upset about."

"I get it, but I didn't…"

"Look, I'm not the bad guy here." Quinn's voice was gentler than it had been. "The Chambers siblings are a close bunch. When their mom left in search of you, all they had was each other. Weston was so busy building his empire that he hired Edda to raise them." Her expression was almost cartoonish. "And you met that woman. The thing is, that family would do anything for you—once you earn their respect. Just don't expect it to happen overnight."

"I know, but…"

"No buts. The only way you're going to earn their trust is to be honest about everything. We'll start by getting blood samples from you and Liam. That way, we'll know if you're full siblings, half-siblings, or not related at all." She moved toward the back room. "And if the latter is true, which isn't likely based on your eyes, you'll walk away and never speak of the family again." Quinn met her gaze. "Just as they'll never speak of you."

Ellery's head bobbed like a small boat tossed on a restless sea. "Okay."

Quinn led the way to the painting studio, where she had everything laid out on a low table. Five minutes later, she had two vials of blood, one with Liam's name on it and the other with Ellery's.

She began wiping down the counter. "I'll put a rush on this. I should have it back in a few days."

The promise felt leaden, like a burden on her soul. Ellery almost hoped it would come back as not being a match. Then, she could walk away and return to hiding amid millions of people in New York rather than in a town of a thousand.

Liam unrolled his sleeve. "Promise me you'll call me first. I want to be the one to break the news to the family. Whether it's a match or not, I want to know."

"You do know your brother's gonna drive me nuts while we wait for the results." She grinned as she packed everything into a plastic box and closed the lid. "But I agree. You deserve to know first."

Quinn pulled her purse over her shoulder. "It was nice to meet you, Elle. I enjoy your books. I went back and reread parts of your first one last night. Knowing they aren't fiction was like a dagger to my heart. I hope one day, we can sit down and talk about your life—as a family."

Ellery's eyes took on a glassy sheen. "Almost every word is true." Heat rose on her cheeks as she felt the need to defend herself.

Quinn shook her head in disbelief. "I'm sorry. I can't imagine how awful your life was." She lifted the plastic box between them. "I hope this comes back proving you're a Chambers. You've suffered enough." She peeked at her phone before tucking it into her purse. "I have to get going if I'm going to drop this at the lab and not be late for rounds."

Liam trailed Quinn to the door. A low murmur of whispers wrapped around them like a shroud, locking Ellery out of their world.

NINE

Waiting for the results felt like an endless march through a swamp, each step a struggle against the uncertainty of what lay ahead. Minutes felt like hours, and hours felt like days. Ellery aimlessly wandered around Hunters Cove and neighboring towns. During the daylight hours, keeping busy helped her ward off worrisome thoughts that had the potential to send her spinning out of control, but by nightfall, those insuppressible thoughts turned her world upside down.

To avoid rehashing her worries in the evenings, Ellery wandered through the B&B, looking at old photo albums and reading about the home's history. Afraid to return to her room, she settled into the cozy lobby, where Claudette poured two glasses of white wine.

Ellery shared fond memories of her years caring for Millie and Gus. She chose her words carefully, concerned about revealing her true identity. Claudette listened intently, her eyes filled with empathy. When Ellery finished speaking, she opened up about her own struggles, describing her mother's battle with dementia.

Every so often, Ellery glanced toward the stairs, but the thought of retreating to the solitude of her room was unbearable, so instead, she lingered, savoring the temporary escape from her predicament.

In the early morning of the fourth day, after Quinn drew blood for the DNA test, Ellery's phone pinged.

Results are in.

Gallery at 7:30.

Ellery felt like she would burst, yet her unease made no sense. She knew the DNA results she had given to the family had not been forged. Vanessa Chambers was her mother every bit as much as she was everyone else's.

After slipping on a pair of jeans, she pulled on a zip-front sweatshirt. A wave of gratitude washed over her. Claudette had taken care of her dirty clothes while Ellery battled her emotions.

She swiped a toothbrush over her teeth and ran a brush through her tousled hair. She pitched both items onto the bathroom counter and exited her room on a mission.

Running down the front steps, she paused momentarily in the kitchen doorway. "Sorry, Claudette. No breakfast for me. I have a meeting."

Leaning against the counter, Claudette snickered. "For someone who doesn't know a soul in this town, you sure have a lot of meetings." Her eyes twinkled with curiosity. As Ellery stepped away from the kitchen door, Claudette followed. "By the way, Paula and Susan are due back today, so I might not be here when you return."

A rush of gratitude filled Ellery. She turned around and threw her arms around the woman. "Thank you for being here. You'll never know how much I needed our time together." With a final squeeze, she released Claudette and turned toward the door. She bolted into the fresh morning air, facing the promise of a new beginning.

Arriving twenty minutes earlier than Liam instructed, Ellery found the gallery dark. She pounded on the door with a sense of urgency prickling under her skin. The sound echoed in the entryway for what felt like an eternity. Frustrated by his lack of response, she fished her phone out of her pocket and texted Liam.

Outside! Where are you?

Wrapping a hand over her eyes to shield them from the early morning sunlight, Ellery pressed her face against the glass. When Liam finally rounded the corner, excitement coursed through her. Unable to contain herself, she shook her fists like a child on Christmas morning.

As he drew near, she saw him swipe his hands through his damp, uncombed hair. The seams of his T-shirt were on the outside, indicating how quickly he had dressed. When the lock clicked open, she burst through the door, her excitement propelling her forward, nearly knocking him off balance.

"What does it say?" Ellery bent over, pressing her hands to her knees. She panted for several seconds while she pulled herself together. Her face flushed. She straightened her back, raising a hand between them. "No. Don't tell me. I know what it says. You're my full brother. I've known that for two years." She stood fully erect, pressing a hand to her stomach. "Quinn was right, I look…"

"How much coffee have you had this morning?"

Ellery exhaled deeply. "None."

Liam's eyes bulged in surprise. "You could have fooled me." He closed the door behind her and pressed his palms down in front of him. "Quinn'll be here in ten minutes. Just calm down. She'll share the results when she gets here."

Ellery began to pace. She tugged on the strings of her hood, knotting and unknotting them repeatedly. Suddenly, she stopped midstride to point at Liam's shirt. "You might want to fix that." Without waiting for a response, she resumed pacing, her movements almost frantic. "If the results show I am Chloe…" Her voice trailed off. She stopped and turned toward him, her face full of hope. "When will we tell the family? 'Cause I think they need to know soon. Don't you…"

"Take a breath, Elle." Liam pulled his shirt off, turned it right side out, and slid it back over his head. He placed his hands on her shoulders. "Seriously. You're going to have a heart attack if you don't calm down."

A soft tap on the door jolted Ellery from her thoughts. She

ran to the door, bumping into it with her shoulder. With trembling fingers, she twisted the lock. The click echoed loudly. She reached for Quinn with a firm grip, pulling her inside.

"I am, right? I'm Chloe, right?" Her body wavered between certainty and doubt.

Quinn grinned at Liam. "Has she been like this since she got here?"

"This is her at about level five." Liam held his hand level in front of his waist. "You should have seen her before." He laughed.

Quinn gestured toward the back room. "How about we move out of sight of the gossips?"

Liam arranged three bar stools around a small, high-top table where he met with clients.

Quinn hung her bag on the back of her stool. She inhaled deeply, holding Liam's gaze for a fleeting moment. Ellery's foot shook, and she repeatedly ran her palms down her thighs while waiting to hear what she already knew.

"You were right. You're a sibling."

Ellery's head dropped forward as if her relief was too heavy to bear. She cradled her forehead in her hands. A whisper escaped her, barely audible over her heavy breathing. "I knew it." She glanced at Liam; her eyes were mirrors of the frustration that swamped her. "I didn't forge the other results, but the rest of the family was so skeptical that I began to doubt myself."

Liam touched her arm. "You don't have to doubt yourself anymore. You are Chloe."

Quinn cleared her throat, the sound foreboding. "That's the thing," she said, shuffling through some papers. "The test didn't prove you were *Chloe*. It only proved you're a full sibling to Liam." The silence that followed the revelation was unnerving.

Liam's expression morphed into confusion. "What's that supposed to mean?"

"Well, we have to consider all possibilities. Your mom was gone for a long time. Preston told me there was a time you kids didn't see her for over a year. That means there was a possibility she had another child with someone else during that time.”

“That makes no sense. You just said Elle and I are full siblings. That means we had to have had the same…” He pulled his head back. “Are you saying Mom could have cheated on Dad—more than once?”

“I’m not saying it, but your siblings might. So, to ensure there wasn’t a doubt in the world, I tested everyone, including your parents.”

Ellery’s mouth dropped open. “So, they know about me?”

“No. I took hair samples from their homes when they were out. That’s why it took a little longer than normal.”

“So, then, she *is* Chloe,” Liam declared.

Quinn’s head wobbled between yes and no. “Most likely. She’s definitely a *sibling* to all of you. But there was one more thing I needed to know. There’s the possibility Elle could have been born before the rest of you. She could have been born before they were married and placed for adoption. Or maybe she was born *after* your mom left? She could have been pregnant when she moved away from Hunters Cove.”

“And?” Liam asked impatiently.

“The epigenetic marks in DNA allow us to reasonably tell how old a person is.”

“And?” Liam and Ellery asked in unison.

“Ellery’s and Baily’s were different but similar enough that we can conclude they were likely born around the same time.” She nodded at Ellery. “So, based on the testing, I can comfortably say you are Chloe.”

Tears trickled down Ellery’s face, peppering her sweatshirt with dark spots. “I knew it. I knew I wasn’t lying.”

“I think the siblings did too, but this isn’t the first time someone’s claimed to be their sister. But it will be the last.”

Ellery’s hands trembled as her eyes met Liam’s. “When do we…”

“As soon as I can round everyone up.”

Quinn threw her purse over her shoulder. “Just so you know, your dad’s home, so you’ll have to meet at our house. I’ll pick up ice cream on the way home.”

A small crease grew between Ellery’s eyes. “But it’s morning.”

“If you’re going to fit into this family, you need to learn a thing or two.” Liam raised his chin. “It’s never too early for ice cream.”

“Will you be there, Quinn?” The words came out more as a command rather than a question.

“If you want me to.” Quinn ran a hand down Ellery’s arm.

“Definitely. There might be questions we can’t answer.” She wagged a finger between her and Liam.

“Then I’ll be there. But I’d better get home with the ice cream before the family starts showing up. So, give me a head start before you send the text.”

Liam walked Quinn to the door, returning moments later. The brightness of his expression died almost instantly when he saw Ellery.

“Are you okay? You should be thrilled, but you don’t look happy at all.”

Ellery’s gaze remained glued to the floor. “After what happened the other night…” Her knee bounced nervously, and she folded and unfolded her hands. “Let’s just say I’m less than optimistic.”

TEN

Liam and Ellery pulled in behind Jacqui. Three car doors slammed, a percussive start to their tense encounter. They joined Jacqui on the sidewalk. She had already assumed the stance near the front steps—arms folded in a barrier against Ellery. She shifted her gaze between them. Unresolved emotions electrified the air. "I suppose you two already know the results. I'm sure Quinn told you," Jacqui glared at Ellery, "or you wouldn't still be here."

Liam averted his eyes. When Ellery opened her mouth, he grabbed her arm in warning.

Jacqui pushed her way past her and entered the house without a knock, slamming the door in Ellery's face. The mountains she would have to climb to prove herself worthy would be steep.

It was apparent from the abandoned cars in the long driveway that Liam and Ellery were the last to arrive. The feeling in the room grew heavy the minute she stepped into the kitchen. She noted that everyone sat in the same place as the main house. It was clear they were a family of traditions. So, again, Ellery moved to the back side of the island, opposite Liam and next to Jacqui.

Quinn entered with a heavy tray cradled in her arms. The handle of the ice cream bucket hung over her wrist and swung back and forth like a pendulum. Ellery was the only one to help her.

When Quinn finally sat down, all was quiet. Instead of

diving in like the family had done the last time, the ice cream went untouched.

"Thanks, Quinn, but I don't want any ice cream." Baily's posture was rigid, and her voice thick with anger as she squinted at Ellery. "This isn't exactly a celebration."

"Same," Jacqui agreed.

Preston helped himself to a bowl and handed one to Liam. Jacqui's fingers tapped the counter as she impatiently waited for them.

Quinn made eye contact with each person. "I know this doesn't feel right meeting here instead of at your dad's, but…"

"Just tell us. Don't make us sit here with this imposter one more second," Baily grumbled.

Quinn shifted on her stool before turning toward Ellery. "Without a doubt, this is your sister Chloe."

Baily's expression darkened, and anger lines deepened around her mouth. "What? How is that possible? She doesn't even look like us." The pitch of her voice raised. "I don't believe it. She must have paid somebody off."

"She didn't pay anyone off, and I resent that you don't trust me." Baily mouthed "sorry," but the word was not audible. "And I disagree about her not looking like you. Other than hair color, she's the spitting image of Jacqui."

Baily slammed a fist onto the unforgiving quartz surface. Her eyes bored into Ellery. "This makes me sick. DNA doesn't make you family." Each word stabbed at Ellery's heart. In a fierce gesture, she swiped her arm around the group, clearly leaving Ellery out of the circle. "*We* are family. You pranced in here thinking we would gush all over you." An evil scowl marked her face. "Well, we're not."

"Baily!" Preston bellowed. "That's enough."

Jacqui grabbed a chunk of hair and twisted it around her finger. Her shoulders drooped, and her previous resistance fell away as she surrendered to the results. "I guess it's good we know the truth—whether we like it or not. We need to get Chloe…"

"It's Elle." Her calm voice belied the emotion that stirred inside.

"What?" Lines deepened on Jacqui's forehead.

"My name," she clarified. "It's Elle."

A sharp laugh from the end of the counter sliced through the tension. The sound echoed with a biting edge as Baily locked eyes with Ellery. "Your *name* is Chloe," she declared, her words dripping with disdain.

The whooshing in Ellery's ears was so loud, she could barely focus. She scanned her siblings' faces, wondering if others could hear what she did. Her pulse jumped near her throat. She pressed a hand to it.

"If that's a problem, you should walk away." Baily's voice was gravelly; hostility oozed from her. Ellery felt the heat of Baily's glare. "It might be better if you did."

"Baily, stop!" Preston's voice boomed. "Chl…" He closed his eyes briefly. "Elle isn't the enemy. She's our sister."

Baily shot to her feet, rage oozing from her. "Are you kidding me right now? Have you forgotten that Mom left us because of *her*?" Her words were steeped in resentment from old wounds.

Liam leaned forward. "She was eight days old, Bai. She couldn't have stopped that woman from taking her."

"Maybe not, but she shouldn't have sat on the information for two years when she found out."

"What would it have mattered? It wouldn't change anything. Mom still would have left us." Liam paused, glancing at Ellery. "We should just be grateful we have Chloe back."

Baily's eyes intensified, and her voice dripped with sarcasm. "Didn't you hear? She's *not* Chloe." Baily clenched her fists at her sides. "You tell me why we should be grateful." A suffocating pause pulled the air from the room. "So Mom can leave us again?" She waved a finger at Ellery. "So she can spend all of her time with her, trying to make up for the years she missed out on?"

A lump swelled in Ellery's throat. Her voice trembled as she whispered, "I never came here to take your mom away."

Jacqui touched Ellery's arm. "I understand Baily's frustration. I think we all agree with it. We all feel it. But whether we like it or not, she's your mom too."

Baily's emotions swirled like a tempest of anger. "I call B.S. on that. She doesn't get to waltz in here for the good times when she didn't suffer like the rest of us."

The feeling of the room shifted dramatically as a deep voice filled the space. "Who's suffering?" The presence of the imposing figure in the doorway commanded attention.

Ellery held her breath. Her eyes darted toward Liam, hoping he would keep her secret from their father. It was her news to share, and the middle of Baily's temper tantrum was not the time or place.

"N-no one, Dad," Liam stammered.

Weston's eyes lingered on Ellery for several seconds too long before turning toward Preston. "Who's this?" He tilted his chin toward her, his fingers combing his salt-and-pepper hair.

Preston followed his father's gaze before looking at Liam. Ellery could see the pleading in Liam's eyes.

"Dad, this is Elle Gray." Preston flung a hand in her direction without making eye contact.

Deep lines cut between Weston's eyes as he fixed his stare on her. "What brings you to Preston and Quinn's?"

"I'm…" Ellery opened her mouth but could not find the words to explain her appearance in Hunters Cove.

Liam's jaw tensed. Finally, he swiveled around on his chair. "Dad, this is…*Chloe*."

Weston's mouth dropped open, his eyes wide with shock as he processed Liam's words. "Chloe?" he whispered. "Chloe Chambers?" He turned toward Jacqui as if seeking confirmation.

Jacqui nodded. "Yes, Dad. Quinn ran the DNA tests. She really is Chloe."

Baily snapped her fingers. "Oh, but don't call her Chloe. That name's not good enough for her."

"Chloe?" Weston muttered, his eyes reflecting his disbelief.

Preston nodded. "It's true. She found us earlier this week."

With a sharp inhale, Weston shook his head vehemently. Suddenly, he pivoted on his heels and bolted toward the front door, the slam reverberating in the stillness, a final punctuation.

Baily leaned back on her stool, an evil smirk pulling her mouth to one side. "Hmm," she sneered at Ellery. "Seems he's about as taken with you as we are. See, no one wants you here."

Jacqui shot her a warning look. "Baily! That's enough. Grow up."

Ellery slid off the stool, her breath coming in short gasps as she rushed out of the house. Despair squeezed her, and she fought to stifle the sob.

At the bottom of the steps, she caught a glimpse of Weston's pickup disappearing down the highway. A fresh wave of anguish washed over her, and she instinctively covered her mouth, desperate to keep her grief from spilling out.

Rejection cut into her so deeply that she could barely breathe. Without a second thought, she took off at a dead run, plunging into the thick forest to the side of Preston and Quinn's house. Each step was a desperate bid for freedom—to put as much distance between her and the Chamberses as she could. But was it even possible now that she had met her family?

ELEVEN

From the gallery to Preston and Quinn's house took less than five minutes. Ellery needed to return to the B&B, get packed, and be gone before anyone came looking for her.

Baily and Ellery should have shared a unique bond, having been womb mates for almost nine months. It was apparent they did not. As Ellery sprinted through the woods that ran along the lake, jumping over the tree roots and rotting logs, she felt the gravity of Baily's disdain. It seemed almost impossible to fathom a time when Baily might ever view her with anything but contempt.

She replayed the conversation, picturing the knowing looks that only siblings who had been together for years could interpret. Jacqui's admission that they tolerated her but were not happy about it was a lot to stomach. As far as they were concerned, she would always be the outsider.

Worst of all was her father's rejection. He walked away rather than running toward her. That stung the most. It was almost as if he blamed her—just like Baily did.

As she ran, her thoughts turned to her past. It was impossible to shake her profound relief upon learning the news of Karma's death. For years, freedom had been an elusive dream, saddled by the suffocating chains of her mother's manipulation and madness. Destiny, Karma's biological daughter, born ten months after Summer was gone, had burst into her life.

Before Karma disappeared to die alone after she had been diagnosed with an aggressive form of cancer, abandoning

Destiny, she had unraveled a truth so damaging that it would destroy Ellery if it came out. Ellery's life as Summer had not been snuffed out by the fire. Instead, she had gone into hiding, recreating herself as Ellery Gray, to escape her evil mother. Had Karma not passed away, the woman would have made her pay.

Ellery felt like her soul was being ripped from her as she climbed the back steps of the Harmony House, taking them two at a time. The scent of pine cleaning products surprised her when she entered her room. She stood still for a moment, trying to pull herself together. But knowing she didn't have a second to spare, she grabbed her few clothes from the hangers and shoved them into her suitcase. She pitched the few items that would not fit into her bag into the trash. Throwing her tote and a plastic bag over her shoulder, she staggered under the weight of her bags, the edges clinking against the surface of each step as she made her way downstairs.

As Ellery entered the lobby, Claudette paused her cleaning. Dust floated in the stream of sunlight that seeped through the picture window. "Are you leaving?"

"I am." She glanced at the clock. "But I'm in a bit of a hurry. You have my credit card number…"

"Yes. I hope you plan to visit again. Paula and Susan will be so disappointed they didn't get to say goodbye."

Ellery said nothing. Lies and deceit were already such a massive part of her life that she couldn't speak one more. Within seconds, she was out the door. She tossed her bags into the trunk. As she pulled out of the B&B, Liam's Jeep came into view, navigating the corner two blocks north and heading toward the Harmony House from the opposite direction.

Ellery's saving grace was that he had no idea what kind of car she drove.

When Ellery reached Minneapolis, the rhythmic thumping

of her heart began to settle, each passing mile soothing the chaos she felt. By the time she entered Madison, Wisconsin, she could breathe without gulping air. And when she passed the Schenectady city limit sign, it was like her lungs had rediscovered air.

The headlights of the oncoming traffic, mingling with her tears, felt like torture as Ellery continued toward home, stopping only for gas and food. Her call to Destiny was brief, only long enough to let her know she was on her way. She refused to discuss the details, saying she would share what happened after a bath and a long nap.

When Ellery stepped over the threshold of her house, a sigh of relief escaped. She unceremoniously dropped her suitcases on her bedroom floor, the thud echoing in the stillness. Shedding layers of her journey, clothing she had worn the previous day when she faced her family, she tossed them into a chair. Without speaking to Destiny, she slipped into a hot tub of bubbly water.

After indulging in solitude, washing away the week's rejection, she felt a renewed calm. She dressed in a fresh nightgown before pulling down the shades and drawing the curtains to shut out the afternoon sunlight that streamed through her southern windows. The outside world faded away as she drifted off to sleep.

By 3:00 a.m., bathed in the soft glow of the small light over the sink, Ellery sat at the table, the rich aroma of freshly brewed coffee wafting through the small space. She cradled the steaming mug, blowing across the top to cool it. Moments later, Destiny shuffled in, wrapped in one of Millie's well-loved quilts. As she approached the counter, a yawn stretched across her face, revealing the remnants of sleep clinging to her. With a slight nod, she reached for a mug hanging from the hooks beneath the upper cabinet, filling it generously with milk before adding coffee.

"Okay, I'm ready," she muttered, breaking the heavy ten-minute silence that had settled between them. "Tell me what happened."

Ellery hesitated. She took a slow sip of her steaming coffee. "Everything…" That word was like a dense fog cutting through her thoughts. "And nothing."

"It's too early for riddles." Destiny grabbed a frosted cinnamon croissant from a takeout container, cut it in two, placed half on each side, and pushed one in front of Ellery.

Ellery's thoughts were distant as she broke off a small piece and slipped it into her mouth. "Well, things went well with Liam." She paused briefly. "For the most part."

"But..." She dragged the word out as she watched Ellery.

Disappointment dampened her tone as she licked icing from her fingers. Finally, she added, "But not so well with the rest."

"Did you meet your parents?"

"My dad, yes. But that went about as well as trying to eat a soup sandwich. When he discovered who I was, he turned around and walked away." Ellery's shoulders slumped forward.

"Wow," Destiny said under her breath. "That's cold."

"I suppose it was like the first time I met you. Remember?"

"Yeah. You slammed the door in my face. It would have hit me had my nose been a millimeter longer." She grinned, dropping a hand over Ellery's.

"When you told me you were Karma's daughter, I thought maybe she'd come with you to find me." Ellery got up and made a second pot of coffee. "It wasn't until you yelled through the door that she'd died that I let you in."

Destiny stiffened, her posture radiating anger. "We're probably the only two people in the world who know what an evil person she was. I only listened to her when she told me about you—and how perfect you were."

Ellery stared at her coffee cup, the steam rising like secrets. "Perfect? We couldn't stand one another. Karma wanted nothing to do with me after my fa…" She faltered, swallowing the truth-coated lie Karma had fed her for years. "*Brant* died." She took a sip of coffee. "Have you found anything that explains...?"

With a shake of her head, Destiny redirected the conversation. "Oh, by the way, your garage is full of boxes I had moved from the apartment."

"I noticed. It was a little hard to ignore when I couldn't get my car in the garage." She swallowed the last of her coffee and placed the mug down with a soft clunk. "I assumed you wouldn't toss them without going through them."

"I should have done it there, but I couldn't stay in that apartment for one more minute. I had to get out of that place, or I would go insane."

Ellery rested an elbow on the table and leaned on the palm of her hand. "I get that."

Destiny held out a hand, palm up. "So, I thought maybe," she pleaded with the expression of a young child, "since you're home, you'd like to go through the boxes with me. There might be things in there that would explain more about your life with her."

"And yours." Ellery finished the last bite of her croissant.

"It appears neither of us is moving forward, so we might as well deal with our ugly pasts. So, how about starting today?"

"I can tell you're a lot younger than me. I just drove twenty hours, and I have the energy of a snail. But why not? I vote for tossing most of it."

"Not until we've gone through every box. There might be something in there that tells us about her family."

Ellery sensed Destiny needed to hold on to the unknown. "Okay. I'm game."

By noon, the living room was filled with a dozen or more empty boxes. Ellery's emotions ping-ponged as she rummaged through the remnants of a broken past now left in fragments. At the top of a box lay the framed photograph of her and Brant, the one her mother kept on her nightstand. It was the only one she had ever seen of them. But at some point, after Brant had *died*, Karma had destroyed the photo. Ellery's face was marred with angry scratches, most likely scribbled out by the scissors Karma had held to Ellery's neck more times than she could count.

The photo had been taken on her third birthday. It was the last birthday she had ever celebrated because four days later, an accident had stolen Brant's life and her mother's love.

Ellery grew warm, too warm. She ripped off her sweater, dropped it on the couch, and cradled the picture. When Brant died, she had been so young that she had very few memories, but the ones she had were precious. Ellery studied the photo for a long time. She traced Brant's beaming smile with the tip of her finger. With everything that had transpired in Hunters Cove, he might be the only father she would ever know.

The afternoon sun cast a warm golden hue across the living room as Ellery and Destiny hauled the last boxes in from the garage. After stacking them in a corner, Ellery dropped onto the couch. The memories were too much—physically and emotionally. Each item stirred a squall of nightmares that she lived again and again.

Suddenly, the doorbell chimed, sounding more like a low-pitched church bell rather than a simple *ding-dong*. Destiny glanced at Ellery. "Are you expecting someone?"

"No, but I talked to Amelia on the way back. She told me she'd drop by this week. She wants to talk about the new book." She stepped over a pile of junk on the floor. "You know, the book I haven't started yet." Ellery made a funny face.

When she swung open the door, a chill ran down her spine.

TWELVE

"I thought…" Ellery's face fell as a rush of air escaped. "I thought…" Her words tumbled out. "W-what are you doing here? How did you find me?"

The woman moved closer. "That doesn't really matter." Her gaze was locked on Ellery's face with a fierce intensity. "I've been looking for you since you disappeared."

Destiny pulled the door wider, its hinges protesting with a low, ominous creak. Her mouth fell agape in disbelief. Stealing a glance at Ellery, she saw the same shock mirrored in her expression. "Oh, no way!" she whispered. Ellery elbowed her gently in a subtle warning.

The woman tipped her chin down and glared at Destiny. Of the two, it was clear which one she had come for. Destiny instinctively took a step back.

The woman clutched a faded blanket, its fabric a patchwork of muted colors, worn down by time and heavy with memories. The edges were frayed and soft, unraveling like the stories they held. With a swift flick of her wrist, she released the blanket, allowing it to cascade to the ground in front of Ellery like a ghost emerging from the shadows.

"Remember this?" she asked.

Ellery's throat went dry as a flood of recollections surged. She tried to speak, but the words were impossible to find.

The intensity of the woman's stare sent shivers down her spine. It was as if she were peering into Ellery's soul. How could she ever have forgotten that blanket? It had been her steadfast companion, her only comfort until the fire stole it.

How did the woman get it?

"I thought you might. This one is your sister's. It's Baily's." The woman's voice had softened. A smile graced her face. "I'd hoped the person who took you had kept it. It was the only thing that kept me connected to you."

Suddenly, Vanessa stepped across the threshold and wrapped her arms around her daughter. She whispered against Ellery's hair. "I've prayed for this moment so many times—the day I would find you and hold you in my arms again."

Behind her, Jacqui and Liam stepped into view. They approached the house and stood as a supportive presence behind their mother.

"Why are you here?" Ellery stepped around Vanessa.

"To bring you *home*." That word was like a balm for her soul. It instantly began healing something deep inside. Liam stepped forward, closing the distance. But Ellery remained guarded as she studied him, searching for the truth in his words. "We lost you once. That can't happen again. None of us handled your return the way we should have."

Pressure stung Ellery's eyes. She fought the surge of emotions welling inside her. "Forgive me. Come in. I'm sorry about the mess. We've been sorting through…" She shook her head dismissively. "It's just a lot of stuff from the garage." Ellery grabbed a few things from the couch and tossed them into a pile.

"This is Destiny." Ellery was unsure exactly how much to say. She never told anyone that Destiny was Karma's daughter or why she was in New York. She'd only told Liam a woman had found her and revealed she was a Chambers.

"I'm Elle's roommate." Ellery's body stiffened, hoping Destiny wouldn't reveal anything else. "I go to school at SUNY. Elle offered me her extra room."

Vanessa tipped her head curtly but remained silent. Jacqui followed her mother's lead.

"Nice to meet you." Liam offered a hand, but his attention was drawn to the overcrowded space rather than his sister's roommate. "This is like stepping a hundred years into the past." His voice held a sense of awe as he zeroed in on a painting hanging near the window above the couch. "Wow! That's a Muirhead Bone. That thing's worth a small fortune."

Ellery glanced at the painting. "I know nothing about art." Destiny cleared her throat and caught Ellery's eyes, a reminder that she owned one of Liam's paintings. Ellery stared at her and slyly ran a finger across her throat in a warning to keep her mouth shut.

"Gus and Millie left me the house." A moment of nostalgia pressed down on her. She glanced around, taking in the room as if seeing it for the first time. "I haven't changed a thing since Millie passed. That was a handful of years ago."

Vanessa pulled her shoulders back. "I'm sorry, but who are Gus and Millie?"

"They were this sweet couple I cared for when I moved to New York." A soft memory played on Ellery's face.

Jacqui clicked her tongue, drawing herself into the conversation. "Where did you live before coming to Schenectady?"

Ellery felt a knot grow in her stomach. It was clear Jacqui was digging for information she was unprepared to give. "Down south." She swallowed hard, the bitterness of her half-truth deflating her. "It was just a blip on the map." She gestured to the couch. "Please, have a seat. Can I get you something to drink? We have… Honestly, I'm not sure what we have since I was gone. Des?"

"Pretty much anything you want," she said, already standing in the entryway of the kitchen.

"Something diet?" Jacqui propped herself on the front edge of the ancient couch as if it were disease-ridden. "Otherwise, water's fine."

"Liam?"

"Anything not diet, if you have it." Liam's casual demeanor was the opposite of his sister's as he dropped into a chair.

"M-Mrs. Chambers?" A small wave of uncertainty lifted the

pitch of Ellery's voice.

Vanessa's smile felt unnerving. "I would love for you to call me Mom. But I know that might be uncomfortable for you. So, Vanessa's fine until you're ready to make that commitment."

Ellery felt relief flood through her. She had passed the first of many hurdles with her mother. *Would she ever want to call her Mom?*

"Water's fine for me." Vanessa's words were clipped, yet they carried an undercurrent of excitement.

Destiny disappeared, returning minutes later with a tray of three soda cans and five Cape Cod goblets, two filled with water.

"We want you to come home. We talked after you left, and we all agree you belong in Hunters Cove." Jacqui scooted an inch away from the arm of the couch as her elbow made contact.

Her tone struck a hollow note. Jacqui, the attorney, spoke with the practiced precision of someone accustomed to navigating the complexities of contracts.

Ellery's mouth twisted. "And what about Baily?"

Liam grunted derisively, a smirk creeping onto his face. "Baily…well, Baily's Baily." It felt as though that phrase explained everything. He raised his fingers one by one, ticking off her character flaws with mocking precision. "She's always going to be pessimistic, stubborn, self-centered, impulsive, close-minded, and… It's just who she is." The look in Liam's eyes spoke volumes. "For obvious reasons."

Vanessa shifted uneasily in her chair. "I know where I stand with you kids. You've all made that abundantly clear. But I think, after you, Baily's suffered the most." Vanessa ran a finger around the rim of the vintage pink goblet. Ellery could almost feel her deep regret. "And I'm afraid I only made things worse for her." She looked from Liam to Jacqui. "For all of you."

Ellery almost felt sorry for her, but she was the reason the others had lost their mother when they were young. If Karma hadn't kidnapped her, her family wouldn't have been torn apart.

She cleared her throat, the sound breaking the angst she felt over Vanessa's admission. "What about your dad?"

Liam raised his glass. "He's your dad too. You're a Chambers as much as anyone else."

Jacqui paused, her fingers drumming an anxious rhythm on her thigh. "He wants you to come back too. Well, he didn't say it in those exact words, but he returned shortly after you left. He was as shocked to see you as we were."

Ellery rose from her seat, a whirlwind of thoughts swirling in her mind. She began to pace, the old wooden floor creaking beneath her. Suddenly, she came to a halt.

"I don't know." The sentence was mouthed rather than spoken aloud. She folded and unfolded her hands. "I'm not sure I can take any more rejection." Her emotion was a clear reflection of her past struggles.

Liam leaned back in his chair. "You won't have to." His lips curled downward into a half-scowl. "Well, there's Baily, but she treats us all that way."

Across from him, Destiny sat with her elbows resting heavily on her thighs, her fingers entwined as they supported her chin. "Elle, as much as I don't want to see you go..." She paused, looking up as she searched for the right words. "You owe it to yourself to finally have the family you deserve. One of us deserves to be happy." A knowing look crossed between them.

Moments passed as Ellery stared at Destiny. Both raised as Karma's daughters, the women's shared experiences with her were electrified in their eyes. Her head bobbed between a nod and a shake. Finally, her resolve pressed down on her shoulders. She made eye contact with each person. "Fine. But I need you to promise you won't tell anyone that I'm Ellery Gray, the author."

"We've already talked about that. No one's going to say a word." When Vanessa's eyes went soft, Ellery felt an exhaustive feeling of relief run through her.

Ellery stepped closer to Vanessa. "Who will people know me as? Chloe? Because that's not going to happen." The shadows of her past loomed large, threatening to engulf her. She slipped her trembling hands into her back pockets to still them. "And what exactly will they be told?"

Vanessa balanced her water glass on her thigh, her fingers delicately curling around it as if it were part of the family secret. "We want you to be part of that discussion."

An awkward silence fell across the room. Finally, Ellery turned toward Jacqui. "I hope you mean that, because I'm out if things don't go well. I have too much to protect." A spark of fear ignited in her stomach. They had no idea about the fire.

Jacqui's eyes latched onto her mother's. "Yes," Vanessa agreed.

Several moments passed before Ellery felt the word form. "Okay." It came out more like acceptance of a loss rather than a win. She glanced at her watch. "I'll call the B&B and see if I can move back in."

Her mother leaned forward a couple of inches. "Weston would like you to stay at the main house. I'd offer to let you stay with me, but my house is just a cottage. It only has one bedroom."

Ellery dropped her chin before giving Jacqui a sly look. "With Edda? You want me to stay in a house with the woman who calls me Alphabet?"

Liam raised a booted foot and rested it on his other knee, his laughter bubbling as he drained the last of the soda into his glass. "Hey, we all had to put up with her. You need to do your time." A grin played on his face. "Just think of it as your initiation into the family."

"Lovely," Ellery said, sarcasm oozing from her.

THIRTEEN

Liam carried Ellery's ancient suitcases down the uneven sidewalk. He stopped dead when he saw her unlock the trunk of an old Camry using a key. "You've got to be kidding me. This is your car?" He took a step back and studied it. "Shouldn't you be driving something a little more fitting of a bestselling author?"

Vanessa and Jacqui settled into the backseat. "Stop being a snob, Liam. Get in." Jacqui swung the door closed.

A guffaw cut sharply through the air. "Snob? Me?" Liam pointed to her with the one finger he had loosened from the suitcase handle as he moved toward the back of the car. "You're the snob. I saw how you sat on that couch."

"I want to get home sometime this month."

Liam gingerly closed the trunk, holding his palms outward as if he needed to be ready to catch it in case it fell apart. With a mischievous spark in her eye, Ellery punched him in the shoulder before thrusting the keys into his hand.

"I've made this trip twice in the last ten days. I cannot drive it again." Ellery climbed into the passenger's seat and slammed the door with what felt like the last energy she had.

Liam slid behind the wheel and folded his long legs into the cramped space. He searched for the ignition. "I haven't used a key to start a car in… Well, I don't know how long." When he turned the key, the engine roared to life, purring like a new car. "Is your odometer broken? Thirty-two thousand miles, and what year is it? Ninety-eight?"

"Ninety-six. The Walkers were old when they bought it." Memories surrounded her, and she stared into the past. "Until last week, it never traveled farther than ten miles on any trip."

Fifteen minutes later, they entered the airport terminal to drop off Vanessa and Jacqui. Liam opened his mom's door and offered his hand to help her out of the car. Ellery hesitantly got out also, ignoring the cacophony of honking horns from impatient drivers.

Liam hugged his mom before handing her a small overnight bag, but Ellery hid in his shadow.

"See you soon." He touched Jacqui's shoulder. "Love you both."

Ellery flinched from the pain that stabbed her in the heart. She could not recall ever being told those words. Even Millie and Gus, who showered her with kindness, never spoke them aloud—not to one another or to her. She knew they loved her, but hearing the words would have been nice.

Vanessa looked at Ellery, her eyes soft. "See you soon, honey." She smiled but did not attempt to approach.

Feeling the pressure of the moment, Ellery managed only a brief nod, her throat thick with emotion. She climbed back into the car. The door clicked shut, sealing her from this new life she was being forced to accept.

She kicked herself. This was all her fault. Why had she not left well enough alone?

After two days of traveling and a night spent in a hotel when he could no longer drive, Liam parked in front of the gallery. The glow of the neon *open* sign surprised Ellery as she climbed out of the car and followed her brother inside.

Behind the counter, Claudette sat engrossed in a thick book. Ellery let out a chuckle. "Do you work everywhere?"

Claudette glanced up, her expression sharp. "Don't wanna

work a full-time job because of my mom." She stared at Ellery. "I'm surprised you're back."

"It's a long story. Someday, I'll tell you about it."

"Can you finish out the day?" Liam handed her several large bills.

"I kind of planned on it." The tone of Claudette's voice waffled, depending on whom she spoke to. "I wasn't sure when you'd be back. Your mom assumed today, but she didn't know for sure."

"I'm gonna change clothes. Then, we'll head out to Dad's." He bounded up the stairs, leaving the women alone.

Ellery smiled at Claudette brightly. "I appreciate that you kept me company at the B&B."

"Mm-hmm." Claudette kept her eyes fixed on her book.

Claudette's reaction felt off. "It's nice that business owners have someone they can call when they need help."

"Mm-hmm." The woman's response was barely audible.

Frustrated, Ellery stepped toward the counter and glanced at the book that seemed to hold Claudette's entire world captive. "That must be one heck of a good book."

"Mm-hmm."

Ellery tucked her hands into the pockets of her jeans, wondering where the kind woman from the B&B had gone. "What's going on? Are you angry with me for the way I left the B&B the other day?"

Claudette finally looked up. "None of my business what people do." Her eyes quickly returned to her book.

Ellery was grateful to hear Liam descending the stairs. He was dressed in clean jeans and a Marlboro College sweatshirt.

"Is that where you went to school?" Ellery nodded to the logo on his shirt.

"I did. It was a tiny liberal arts college in Vermont."

"Was?" Ellery tilted her head in question.

"It closed a handful of years ago." He pointed to a small painting of several buildings that appeared more as large houses than a college campus. A vibrant tapestry of autumn leaves hung in the trees and were scattered across the ground. "But it was a perfect place to learn to paint."

"It's gorgeous. If it's half as pretty as your painting…" She stepped closer to the picture.

Liam's expression shifted. "Pretty, yes. But my father wasn't happy about me going there. He said you were wasting his money if you didn't go to school to become an attorney, doctor, accountant, or earn an MBA. That made me the black sheep of the family."

Ellery scanned the galley. "You aren't a black sheep. Your paintings are beautiful."

"I'd like to think so, but you won't find one hanging in Dad's house."

"Seriously?" Her jaw fell open. "What about your mom's?"

Liam smirked. "Her place is so tiny, there's not a lot of room for pictures. Still, she has several displayed."

"Well, if your dad considers you a black sheep for being an artist, then I'd be right there with you. He wouldn't think too highly of me either," Ellery said softly.

"I suppose that could be true, but I doubt it. You're a female. He's partial to the woman." Liam turned toward Claudette. "Thanks for helping out." With that, he led Ellery toward the backdoor.

"Wait! What about my car?" She gestured toward the front of the gallery.

"Good point. You can follow me out to Dad's."

"Bye, Claudette," Ellery called as she passed through the gallery.

"Whatever."

A hollow feeling settled in Ellery. It was clear Claudette was not her biggest fan after she left the B&B the way she had. Or maybe there was more. Perhaps Baily had gotten to her. If her sister had her way, Ellery would become the pariah of the Midwest.

FOURTEEN

A silver Land Rover caught their attention as they pulled into the driveway. A massive red bow sat majestically on the roof. Liam glanced at Ellery. "It looks like Mom wasn't happy with her ride to the airport in your old car." He turned to watch her reaction. "This is one of the things our parents are good at *grandstanding*. Everything is about how things look to everyone else. It's gotta be the biggest and the best."

Ellery froze in place. A wave of confusion rippled through her. "What?"

"No child of theirs is going to be seen driving a thirty-year-old car." Liam swung his thumb behind him, aimed at her Camry. "It would make *them* look bad. You'll get used to it. I promise."

The screen door let out a sharp bang. Weston and Vanessa headed toward her, walking shoulder to shoulder, hand in hand, as if they were a couple.

Vanessa's eyes sparkled with excitement. "Do you like it? Jacqui thought silver would be a better color than red. Maybe not quite as showy. But if you'd rather have a different…"

"I don't need a car." Annoyance flashed across Ellery's face. "Mine works just fine."

"But wouldn't having a car built for Minnesota winters be nice? You haven't experienced one yet. You'll see; you'll be grateful for a bigger car then."

"Look, I appreciate this, but I *have* a car." A hint of annoyance crept into her tone. "And I have enough money to buy any car I want—*when* I want." She paused briefly. "And now isn't the time."

The whirr of a lawnmower sounded in the distance. It was the only noise Ellery could hear above the screaming in her head. Weston pivoted on his heels and returned to the house without a word, his footsteps heavy with anger.

"Please don't think I'm being disrespectful. I may be a Chambers, but I don't need or want your money. I don't want any of you to think that's why I'm here. I came because I wanted to get to know my family. I wanted to come home."

Vanessa softened her expression. "Oh, Chloe, why would you think we would feel you only came for money?"

The sound of the name lifted Ellery's hair to attention. Goosebumps rose on her arms, and she clenched her jaw. "My name is not *Chloe*. I already told you that." Her words were firm. She pulled her shoulders back and stood tall. Ellery felt anger soar through every inch of her body. "I don't want to be called Chloe. Not now. Not ever." The air around her crackled. Her eyes were fierce as she glared at the woman whose eyes she shared. "My name is Elle, and that's what you will call me."

Vanessa fingered the hem of her sweater as she watched her daughter. "Alright. It sounds like we have a lot to discuss."

"Clearly," Ellery shot back.

Liam removed Ellery's keys from her hand. He returned with her suitcases and a few bags.

She held up a hand to stop him before he headed into the house. "I think it would be better if I stayed in town."

"Please don't. Weston wants you here, and so does the rest of the family." Vanessa's eyes pleaded with her.

Ellery's gaze was fixed on the front door. "That's funny. It doesn't seem like it. I've met Mr. Chambers twice now, and he walked away with barely a word both times. I think you both want me to stay here until you can convince me to be your long-lost Chloe." She took a step back, seeking distance. "You want to hide me here until I learn how a Chambers acts. Am I right?" She pointed to the SUV. "New cars, suitcases, clothes." Ellery shook her head. "I'm never going to be that person, so you can quit hoping."

Vanessa folded her hands in front of her. "I know that. I just think your father's still in shock." She leaned closer to Ellery as if trying to close the emotional gap. "He never believed we would find you, just as I never gave up hope. I always knew you would come back to us."

Ellery closed her eyes and rubbed her forehead. "So, I'm here now," her voice was as fragile as a butterfly wing, "and he acts like he's disappointed he has me back."

"That's not true. He loves you. He just doesn't know you yet. Can you please give him a chance?"

Ellery inhaled deeply, filling her lungs with the fresh, pine-scented air. "Fine." She rocked her head faintly. "Okay." Her voice was steadier, as if she were trying to convince herself as much as Vanessa. "But this goes both ways. He has to bend my way too."

Her mother cautiously draped an arm around Ellery's shoulder. "Let's get you settled. You must be exhausted from that drive. We can worry about everything else tomorrow."

Baily emerged suddenly, almost materializing out of thin air, a ghostly figure clad in running gear that clung to her thin body. She wiped the sweat from her face with the bottom of her pink T-shirt.

"Oh, look! The prodigal daughter has returned." Animosity was plastered on her face. With a sidelong glance at the Range Rover parked in the driveway, she added, "And just in time to stake claim to a share of the family's money."

Vanessa's eyes were hard. "Stop it, Baily. You know she didn't disappear on her own."

"For your information, Elle doesn't even want the car," Liam said.

"Of course not." Baily frowned as she stepped closer to Ellery. "You can't come on too strong in the beginning. That wouldn't be a good look. Isn't that right, *Chloe*?"

Ellery fixed a fiery glare on Baily. She could feel her heartbeat throbbing in her temple.

"Did you not hear me? I said, 'Right, *Chloe*?'" Ellery couldn't remember ever seeing her sister smile. A smirk was as close as she came.

"My name's Elle. What's your problem anyway? What did I ever do to you to make you hate me so much?"

Baily's sharp laughter sliced through the air. "What did you ever do to me? Let's start with *ruining my life*." Rage simmered on her face as she turned toward Vanessa. "I'm sure our mother can explain it to you." She ran the palm of one hand across her glistening forehead. "You'll do that, right, Mother? You can explain how you left us once, and now that your favorite twin is back, you won't have time for the rest of us again." With that, Baily jogged toward her cottage, leaving a trail of unresolved anger.

Liam followed her with his eyes. "Ignore her. She's been like this since the beginning of time."

"But it's gotten worse since I showed up, hasn't it?"

Vanessa sighed deeply. "It has. But she's not mad at you. It's me she hates."

"That's not the way it feels."

They silently watched as Baily stopped to chat with her teenage daughter, Piper, before heading into her house.

"I get it. She's somewhat self-centered, and I take most of the responsibility for that." Vanessa continued to watch Baily and Piper. "She's lashing out at everyone right now. You just happen to be in her crosshairs at the moment. I've got a lot to atone for, I'm afraid. I thought we were in a better place…"

"Until I showed up. Maybe I should…" Ellery's shoulders hunched forward.

"That's not an option." Vanessa led her into the house.

There were too many loose pieces tumbling through Ellery's thoughts. She felt like she was trying to piece together a puzzle without a picture to reference. Searching for the edge pieces, she knew only a handful of things. Vanessa's incessant chatter made Weston's silence all the louder. Jacqui and Preston had shifted from the fiery heat of conflict to a placid neutrality; they were Switzerland. Baily's contempt for her was overwhelming. And Edda, Weston's housekeeper, tolerated no one but Huck, the oversized St. Bernard. Her only saving grace was Liam. He was the first corner piece of the Chambers puzzle. He was not only her brother but, in the short time since she met him, he had become her best friend, beating out even Destiny.

The time on her phone read *10:34*. Then *11:47*. Each minute felt like an eternity as she tossed and turned. Her last thought faded at *2:29* as she drifted into a restless sleep. A dark tapestry of nightmares plagued her. Before her eyes, Vanessa morphed into Karma. Her gentle smile became a wicked smirk as flames engulfed the cabin before it exploded into nothingness.

Ellery woke with a start. An uneasiness swelled in her, the murkiness of the night momentarily swallowing her sense of place. Beads of sweat clung to her forehead, and her breath came in quick, shallow gasps. Fragments of elusive images flickered in her mind, leaving her with an unsettling sense of dread. She knew there was more in the light of that fire, but the abrupt wakening had robbed her of the answer. Still, the remnant lingered, a warning that something was not quite as it seemed.

Ellery knew nightmares and dreams were fragmented memories, pieces of the past intertwining with the present. She lay motionless, trapped in the torment, her heart racing as she wondered if these dreams would ever stop. Would the relentless grip of her past loosen, allowing her present to weave a brighter future? The truth settled over her like a suffocating fog. Thanks to Karma, she would *always* be lost in the shadows of her past.

FIFTEEN

"I still don't understand who you are, Alphabet." Edda set a plate laden with scrambled eggs and thick slices of bacon before Ellery. "Weston doesn't like strangers in his house. And if you're just a friend of Liam's, there's no reason for you to be here—especially without him."

"Her name's Elle, and she's a *family* friend." Vanessa moved deeper into the breakfast nook.

Edda rested her arms over her thick stomach and stared at Vanessa. "And it makes no sense why you get to come and go whenever you want. This isn't your house anymore." She scowled sharply before heading into the prep kitchen.

"Where's Weston?" Vanessa asked, ignoring the housekeeper. She poured herself a cup of coffee.

Ellery shrugged. Her mouth was full as she eagerly devoured her hot breakfast. "I haven't seen him." She wiped toast crumbs from her mouth with a white cloth napkin.

Vanessa's gaze drifted toward the kitchen. She leaned closer, lowering her voice to a whisper. "I want you to come with me today. We have lots to talk about." She tipped her head toward the kitchen. "The walls have ears…and a big mouth." She cast a knowing look at Ellery.

"I've figured that out." Ellery slowly chewed a large bite of bacon. "Edda might not be the nicest person, but this breakfast is delicious." Her fork clinked against the plate as she set it down.

Vanessa took a sip of coffee; a sly grin hiked up one corner of her mouth as her eyes flitted toward the kitchen. "That's the only reason Weston keeps her. The woman can cook. I'll give her that."

Just then, Edda stepped into the room. She shot a pointed look at Vanessa. "That's a hell of a lot more than you ever did around here." Edda swiped Ellery's empty juice glass from her placemat. "If you want anything else, you can get it yourself. I ain't running no restaurant." She stormed from the room.

For the first time, Ellery smiled at her mother. It was a moment that felt normal.

Vanessa lived just down the road from her estranged husband. It was a charming white cottage that looked more like homes in South Carolina than Minnesota. Clusters of tulips painted the flower beds in fiery reds and soft pinks. They intermingled with the sunny yellow daffodils. A winding stone walkway meandered through the lush greenery.

Ellery was in awe, her eyes sweeping over the tapestry of colors. "It's beautiful. Did you do all this?"

Vanessa tucked a strand of hair behind her ear. "Just wait a few weeks. When the summer flowers open, it'll take your breath away."

Her expression grew pensive as her mother retrieved her purse from the console. "Whenever I'm in the garden, I think of you." Her mouth turned downward. "Of course, I'd never tell your brothers and sisters that."

Ellery struggled to rein in her emotions. "And there it is. Don't you get it? Constantly thinking about me is the reason Baily hates me—and you. Instead of focusing on the children you still had, you searched for me. You took precious moments away from them, looking for someone you barely knew." Vanessa's Lexus still had that new car smell. It reminded Ellery of what Liam had said. *Everything had to appear perfect.* But their life was far from it. Looks were deceiving.

Claustrophobia stirred in Ellery. Her lungs tightened, and tiny gasps were all she could draw. Finally, she climbed out of the car and slammed the door, echoing her turbulent feelings more than she intended.

She stepped into the garden and followed a path to the backside of the house. After settling onto a stone bench at the end of the path, her gaze drifted over the water's shimmering surface.

Vanessa settled beside her, maintaining a respectable distance. The gentle rustle of new spring leaves provided the soundtrack for their thoughts.

Ellery knew the truth shackled Vanessa to her past choices. "I know my kids think I was a horrible mother." There was a ghost of regret in her eyes. "They still see me as Vanessa, a friend or a relative, rather than their mother. The same way you do." Regret hung in Vanessa's eyes as she tented her trembling fingers before her.

She took Ellery's hands in her own. "I know I hurt them. I've tried to make it right, but I take a dozen backward for every step I take forward." Her honesty was raw. She swiped at a lone tear that escaped. "Except for one year, when my dad had cancer, I never missed a birthday or a holiday."

Vanessa's voice trembled. "I thought I was doing enough. But clearly, I wasn't. When Baily was pregnant with Piper, I moved back to Hunters Cove." Her eyes drifted to the lake. "That was fifteen years ago, and I still feel like I'm walking on eggshells most of the time."

A robin landed near them, lingering only long enough to snatch one of the straw pieces Vanessa had scattered for the birds to build their nests. Like a banner, it fluttered in the wind as the momma bird flew toward a birch tree near the lake's edge. That small act of kindness proved her love for all creatures: animals and humans.

"My showing up here isn't helping your case." Ellery pulled her hands from her mother and folded them in her lap.

The gentle sound of water lapping along the shore broke the

stillness. "No. It's not. But Jacqui, Preston, and Liam have all come around. I'm sure Baily will too—eventually." There was a hint of hope in her voice. She glanced toward the house. "Let's go inside. I have something I want to show you."

As Ellery stepped onto the wraparound porch, the deck moaned. Vanessa led her into the two-story living room, where she immediately noticed two of Liam's paintings. A feeling of home washed over her as the morning sunlight poured into the room through enormous glass dormer windows.

"This is beautiful." Ellery marveled at the small house, her fingers gliding over the sleek surface of the quartz countertop separating the kitchen from the living room.

"Weston had it built for me." Her voice carried a heaviness that Ellery had heard before, a guilt that settled in like an unwelcome guest. "When I told him I was coming home, he offered to let me move into the main house, but I refused. It was too soon. There was too much baggage we needed to sort out." A pause hung heavily, wrapping the room in a past Ellery would only know pieces of. "Besides, I wasn't returning to him. I was coming back to the kids."

A glimmer of uncertainty clouded Ellery's face. "But Liam said you never divorced."

"We didn't." Her face looked statuesque, as if she were frozen in the past. "We still love each other. I think we always will. But as hard as I've tried, I can't seem to forgive myself for losing you." The painful truth manifested itself on her trembling lips. "For destroying our family. And honestly, I'm not sure Weston's forgiven me either."

Ellery studied a photo of her father. She had not seen his warm smile since arriving in Hunters Cove. A rush of emotion washed over her: regret, sorrow, and guilt. "Even though I know I did nothing wrong, I still carry this horrible guilt for disappearing, for tearing the family apart."

Vanessa hugged her warmly. As she pulled back, her hands found Ellery's shoulders, steadying her like a lighthouse in a storm. "This is not your fault. Of course, your sudden appearance has sent us back a few steps. But I guarantee you, there isn't one of us, Baily included, who wants to live the rest of our lives looking into the faces of strangers and wondering if they might be Chloe. Do you understand?"

Emotions swirled inside of Ellery. The lump in her throat made it difficult to breathe, let alone speak. So she offered a nod.

Vanessa embraced Ellery again in a cocoon of reassurance. "Good. We won't ever speak about you not belonging here again because you do. You're part of our family. It's the rest of us who need to get our act together."

Vanessa walked across the room and reached for a box on a high shelf near the fireplace. Motioning for Ellery to join her, she patted the spot beside her on the couch.

As she opened the box, a faint scent of nostalgia wafted out. Vanessa's fingers delicately ran along the top edge of the photo before handing it to Ellery. "That's you on the left."

"I had dark hair even back then. I never knew that. Of course, I've never seen a baby picture. Even when Brant was alive, Karma wasn't exactly the mothering type. And after he died, she destroyed every picture of me."

"Your hair was dark, a lot like Weston's mom. You and Baily looked absolutely nothing alike. Weston honestly asked if you were ours." She tapped the photo in Ellery's hands. "You and Baily both had blue eyes, but a baby's eye color often changes, so I wasn't sure if your eyes would have stayed blue or if they would have been darker, more like Weston's side. Even so, had I seen you on the street, I would have known you were *Chloe...*" She shrank back against the couch, almost burying herself in the cushions. "I'm sorry. I don't know how to identify you when I talk about you as a baby."

"I get it." Ellery's eyes reflected the complexities of the past.

"The moment I saw you in New York, I knew you were Chloe, even without the DNA test. You have the Abernathy eyes. All five of you were blessed with them." She straightened her back and folded her hands in front of one knee. "They are my mother's eyes—the narrow almond shape with the striking silver-blue hue I've seen nowhere else."

Ellery leaned forward and studied the photo again—those *eyes*. Beaufort and Hilton Head were less than an hour apart. Her grandmother must have visited Beaufort, but they would never have come in contact because Ellery hid in the shadows. If they had, would her grandmother have recognized her eyes— known she was Chloe?

Vanessa handed her a second picture, the glossy surface reflecting a moment lost in time. In the image, she and Baily were nestled together in the stroller, their small cherubic faces pressed intimately against one another as if caught in a timeless embrace. It appeared as if their mother had posed them.

"This was taken the morning you disappeared." The heft of the memory was evident in her mother's eyes as several moments of silence passed between them.

"After you were gone, Baily wouldn't stop crying." Her voice was stiff with pain. "She wanted only you. I held her for the next several days, too afraid that if I put her down, she'd disappear too.

"The day after you vanished, you and Baily were supposed to have your first baby photos taken. I forgot to cancel. The photographer arrived to a dozen police officers wandering in and out of the house. My father was the chief of police in Minnetonka. You were taken from Groveland Park, less than six blocks from our house."

Vanessa stared at the photo in Ellery's hands. "My father sent the poor photographer packing. No one was permitted to cross the police tape wrapped around the park or our house. He was sure he would find something that would lead him to the kidnapper, but he didn't."

She stared out the window as if she were looking into the past. "I never did have Baily's baby pictures taken. Honestly, I stopped having pictures taken at all. Other than school photos or a few Weston snapped here and there, there are almost no pictures of Baily." Her words sounded like a surrender to a failed past.

"Add that to the reasons Baily despises me." Ellery sagged into the plush sofa.

"I told you before. Baily's mad at me, not you. Her anger with you is misplaced. She doesn't know what to do with it." She picked up the picture of the girls. "She and I were just starting to bond again when you… Well, that doesn't matter." Vanessa patted her daughter's leg.

"When I showed up," Ellery finished her mother's sentence. "Had I not come to Hunters Cove, you could have rebuilt your relationship with her, right?"

"Perhaps, but there was no greater gift than finding you again."

"Karma told me…"

"Was Karma her real name?"

"No. That was the name she adopted after my father—I mean, Brant—died in the car accident."

"So, she resented you for living after he died?" Vanessa's eyes fell like a heavy curtain over a stage. "I get that. I'm afraid I did the same thing to your siblings."

Ellery's eyes were unblinking as she stared at Vanessa, wondering how anyone could compare her to the devil.

"Liam told me bits and pieces about your life, but not everything. The whole time you were gone, I prayed the person who had you would love you as much as we did. But now that I know that wasn't the case, it kills me." She tapped her chest. "All those years, the way that woman treated you. I'm so sorry."

Ellery's shoulders sagged, and she pressed her hands to her thighs, seeking grounding. "Karma always told me bad things happened wherever I went. She made sure I knew it was my fault my father died."

"What a horrible thing to tell a child," Vanessa blinked back tears.

"She wasn't wrong. Horrible stuff *does* follow me—Brant dying, Karma's hatred for me, the fire, coming here to face…"

The list of tragedies spilling from her felt like an unending stream of sorrow.

"Tell me about the fire." Vanessa's eyes held a curiosity that scared Ellery.

Fear squeezed Ellery's lungs. She had warned herself time and again, not to mention the fire. Now, Vanessa would pick at it like a fresh scab, opening a wound Ellery would not be able to close.

The thought of admitting anything left her feeling uneasy. "There's nothing to tell." Ellery tried to steady her voice despite the lies brewing inside her. "It was still dark out. I smelled smoke and ran into the woods to escape." The knot in her throat tightened as her mind drifted back to that fateful day. She saw the vivid image of the flames engulfing the cabin and the explosion that took everything, including her life as Summer St. John.

Ellery cleared her throat and buried the lie within the truth. "The cabin burned to the ground."

Vanessa hugged a pillow to her stomach. "You lost everything?"

"I had nothing to lose." Ellery stared out the window, afraid to look at Vanessa.

A thick silence filled the room uncomfortably. "And you didn't go back to your… Karma's?"

"No. I got on a bus and headed north." The words spilled out like a confession, a partial release of her burden. She paused, lost in thought. "That's how I ended up in Schenectady with Millie and Gus."

"And Karma never suspected anything?"

"She thought I died in the fire. That accident saved me. It was the only way I could ever escape her clutches." The word *accident* tightened across her chest.

"I don't know how you survived all those years. I'd have set that fire to escape her."

Ellery stifled a gasp. She could almost feel the heat from those flames. She squeezed and stretched her fingers repeatedly, taking a moment to steady herself. Vanessa was peeling back layers to get to the truth. If she kept probing, how long would Ellery be able to keep up the charade? Her hands trembled as the walls of the room began to move toward her.

Ellery's mouth went dry. "Can I use your bathroom?" Too afraid for her mother to see the rise of her panic, she focused her eyes on the floor.

"Of course, honey. It's down the hall and to your right."

When Ellery stepped into the bathroom, her heart thudded against her ribcage. Her trembling hands fumbled with the lock, the metal feeling slick in her clammy palms. Beads of sweat trickled down her forehead, peppering her T-shirt in a pattern of worry.

She leaned against the door, feeling its solidness as she fought the instability of her thoughts. "I'm okay. This is just my anxiety. I'm stronger." She whispered those words repeatedly, her voice barely audible above the pounding in her ears. Little by little, the mantra built a fragile barrier against the chaos inside her.

Even as the tightness loosened around her neck, she knew the decision to come to Hunters Cove had been a mistake. It had been so easy to slip away before. Why couldn't she do it again? This time, she just couldn't be so predictable.

SIXTEEN

Shoving open the heavy front door of the main house, Ellery felt an inexplicable chill drift through her. Her fingernails were tinged with dirt from helping Vanessa work in the gardens. The silence had not felt as heavy outdoors as it did inside. And her panic had room to run free.

The kitchen pulsed with tension. Ellery felt her muscles stiffen as she came face to face with Baily.

"Where's Edda?" Ellery's blood ran cold.

"She took the day off. I'm cooking tonight." Baily slid a large roast layered with thick chunks of carrots and potatoes into the oven.

After Baily slammed the warm door shut with a thud, she pivoted, her eyes narrowing in a fierce glare directed at Ellery. "Don't think I'm happy spending time with you either." The bitterness was strong as she responded to unspoken words.

Ellery stepped deeper into the kitchen. Her fingers were splayed in question as she threw them out to her sides. "I still don't understand why you hate me so much. I haven't done anything to you."

A sharp snort bounced off the kitchen walls. Baily's thin frame trembled with emotion. "You have no idea what you've done to us. How can you even ask that? You destroyed our family. You could never understand how much we suffered because of you."

"I didn't hurt you. Karma did." Ellery's head flinched backward. With Vanessa, she could admit her emotions. With her sister, she wasn't about to show her fear. "It's not like I ran away."

"Maybe not, but it would have been a hell of a lot better had you not shown up." The bitterness in Baily's voice resonated like a haunting melody.

"Better for whom?" Ellery locked eyes with her sister and waited for some big epiphany.

"All of us. We were finally beginning to feel like a family again." Baily poked a trembling finger at her. "And then you showed up."

"So, you're saying it'd be better if I left." Her tone was brimming with deep-seated hurt and anger. Ellery thrust a hand toward the backyard. "You'd honestly be okay knowing I'm out there living my life without you?"

"In a heartbeat. I guarantee you could walk away, and not one of us would come after you."

Ellery laughed. "That's funny, since your mom and Jacqui and Liam showed up on my doorstep in Schenectady."

"That was a mistake. Jacqui admitted it to me."

Ellery felt the knife twist. She couldn't imagine Jacqui saying that, but maybe she'd been wrong about her all this time. She sneered at Baily. "Tell me how you really feel."

"Well, *Chloe*." Baily pronounced the name deliberately, the syllables like a slow-motion slap to the face. "You aren't wanted here. You're like that kid from high school who always tries to sit at the cool kids' table, but…"

"Oh, so you were a mean girl growing up. I can see that." Ellery stepped closer, narrowing the gap between them. "You haven't changed much, have you?"

Baily's eyes blazed. "You don't know me. You know nothing about me."

"I know you better than you think I do. You're the exact opposite of me." Ellery spun on her heels and headed toward the foyer.

Baily grabbed her arm and jerked her around. Her fingers tightened around Ellery's arm. "Just because you're this *famous* author, you think you're so much better than the rest of us."

The heat prickled Ellery's skin. Her face contorted in anger as she fought to avoid decking her sister. "I don't think I'm better than anyone."

"You sure don't act like it. Why'd you come back here anyway?"

Ellery's gaze dropped, and her eyes glistened. It didn't matter how many times she tried to explain it to Baily, she would never accept her. But she tried again. "To find you and the rest of my family." She pressed her fingertips together. "I never had a real family." Her voice ached with honesty.

"So you thought you'd take mine?" Baily released a taunting laugh. She mockingly rubbed her eyes and created a cry-baby expression. "Am I supposed to feel sorry for you? My family doesn't switch sides so easily. They will never choose you over me."

Ellery stepped away from Baily. "They don't have to choose one of us over the other. I still don't understand why you're so bitter toward me. I didn't kidnap myself. I was eight days old."

"You've said that before. It's just words. So just shut up about it. And as for hating you, I have dozens of reasons." Baily's face was overcast with anger, and her eyes were cold as steel. She raised her hand and extended her index finger. "You're the reason I didn't have a mother for eighteen years. Oh, sure, she was in the house for the first three, but she wasn't *here*." She pointed to the floor. "Not when I got my period, had my first kiss, learned to drive, or needed a prom dress. And she wasn't here when I got pregnant while I was still in high school or when Dad forced Ben and me to get married at the courthouse. You don't think I needed a mother then? Someone to stand up for me?"

Baily didn't wait for an answer. She threw up a second finger. "Even after you left…"

"I didn't *leave*. I was taken." Frustration flushed up Ellery's face.

Eyes full of hatred, Baily glared at her sister. "You left. You maybe didn't walk away, but you left." She pointed a finger at Ellery. "*You* did this to our family."

Ellery took another step back, trying to anticipate Baily's actions, but her sister was too unpredictable. Taking her eyes off her was dangerous.

Resentment flashed on Baily's face. "Two. There were photos of you everywhere in this house. Even if we wanted to forget you, we couldn't. Every year, Mom had an age progression picture made for the media, and she framed them all. It was like you were never gone." Baily's hostility was like a brick wall, unforgiving.

She took a long draw of soda before slamming the can down on the counter. "Every time Mom left again, Dad put them all away." A snide grin flashed briefly across Baily's face before her hostility returned. "And every time she'd come home, she'd dig them out and line the house with them."

"How many pictures do you think there were of me in the house?" Silence engulfed the room. Finally, Baily held her thumb and finger together to form a circle. "Zero. That's right. Not one. There wasn't a picture until I got married—in jeans and a Pearl Jam T-shirt, thanks to Dad."

Baily moved to the far side of the island. "Three." She held up an equal number of fingers. "Whenever I wanted to spend time with Mom, she was too busy making phone calls and meeting with private investigators, or..." She paused, her shoulder sagging forward, "staring at pictures of you. She didn't have time for me or anyone else."

Ellery felt an ache of empathy for her sister. Karma had fractured so many people in her selfishness. She'd destroyed her family, ruined Ellery's childhood by treating her like trash, and demolished Brant's life, snaring him in her trap. The whole thing made Ellery sick.

Baily raised another finger, her expression marred by pain. "Whenever Mom was here, all she and Dad did was fight. Do you have any idea how devastating it is for a child to hear their parents scream at each other?" Her words were charged with such extreme emotion that Ellery felt Baily's pain in her chest. "They couldn't be in the same room together. And when they were, I hid in my bedroom closet, wrapped in an old quilt. Because lord knows none of our siblings thought to take me out of the house when the shit hit the fan."

Ellery opened her mouth to speak, but the fire in her sister's eyes stopped her. As she rounded the corner of the island, her ponytail snapped like a whip.

Five fingers hovered inches from Ellery's face. "Mom thought she could make up for her absence by buying our love. Most of the time, presents showed up without her." Her voice was coated in rage. "They were wrapped all pretty-like, with a big bow, delivered by a courier service. I know she never touched those gifts. And I'd bet you anything she had no idea what they were. Because she had a personal shopper on speed dial." She stabbed a finger at Ellery. "That's the kind of childhood I had because of you."

Ellery stepped back. "I'm sorry. I really am. But mine…"

"What was that?" Baily shouted. "You're sorry? If you were sorry, you'd have stayed away and let us continue healing without dragging us through the mud again." She shook her head wildly. "But no. You showed up and ripped the wound wide open."

Heat rushed up Ellery's face, darkening it. Her anger sliced through the air, a heat-seeking missile aimed at Baily. "You act like my childhood was full of sunshine and singing birds who tied ribbons in my hair." Her palm came down hard on the countertop. "That couldn't have been farther from the truth."

Baily's eyes blazed with fire. "I don't care what your life was like. This was your doing."

Ellery opened her mouth to speak, but Baily silenced her with a raised finger before she could utter a word.

"Six," she stated firmly. "Let's talk birthdays. Every year, my cake read *Happy Birthday, Baily and Chloe*." Resentment coated each word.

"What?" Ellery's face twisted in confusion.

Baily's expression deepened. "That's right. I shared my birthday with a ghost. They always sang happy birthday to

Baily *and Chloe.*" Her voice was thick with emotion. "And there were two stacks of gifts—one for each of us. It was like Mom expected you to miraculously appear to celebrate your birthday."

"But I…"

"When I was young, I never got to invite friends to my party because *you* didn't get to." Baily's voice cracked.

"That's awful. Why would they do that?"

Baily scrunched her face in response, but she didn't answer. "When I got older, I didn't want my friends at my birthday because I didn't want them to see how out of touch Mom was."

Gritting her teeth, she stared at Ellery. "I wish you'd never come back."

Ellery's face mirrored Baily's anger. "What they did to you was horrible, but at least you had a celebration, a family who loved you. The only party I had was when I was three, just before my dad died. And I only remember that because of one photo Karma scratched my face out of."

Baily kicked the island. The sound sliced through the air. "That man was not your father!"

Ellery exhaled sharply. "You can't have it both ways, Baily." Ellery's voice simmered with anger. "Brant's not my dad. Your dad's not my dad. Make up your mind?"

Baily's glare could have cut glass. An uncomfortable silence stretched like elastic between them.

"Brant was the only dad I knew. He's the only person who ever loved me. God knows Karma didn't."

Baily arched her neck. "Maybe you're just unlovable."

Memories knotted in Ellery's throat. "Don't think that's the first time I've heard that. Karma reminded me every chance she got after my…" Her words trailed off, stopping short of uttering the word *father* to keep from setting Baily off again.

"What were you going to say? Killed himself to get away from you?" Her words had barbs that dug in.

Pain crumpled her face—pressure built behind her eyes. "Brant was a good person. He loved me. It was Karma who hated me."

A smirk lit up Baily's face. "Well, she couldn't have been all bad, then."

Ellery closed her eyes briefly. "You're an awful lot like her."

"Am I, *Chloe*?" Baily flashed a devilish grin. She leaned in slightly as she emphasized the name Ellery dreaded. "Am I really, *Chloe*?"

Defiance flashed on Ellery's face. "My name is not Chloe. It's Elle."

Baily pressed her palms on the counter. "You're Chloe. You've always been Chloe. You always will be." She laughed mockingly.

"My name is Elle Gray."

"You think you're too good for the name you were given, don't you? But then again, who would want you to stake claim to our family? Other than Mom, everyone else wishes you'd never found us." She pushed herself upright. "I've been telling you, so you might as well admit it to yourself; no one wants you here, *Chloe*."

The finality of that statement echoed in Ellery's mind. A shiver ran down her spine. The hope of the family she had always dreamt of faded. The chilling reality of solitude replaced all hope. Her body melted inward as Baily's words sliced through her. Even if they were lies, they still stung.

"Did I hurt your feelings, *Chloe*?" Baily laughed sadistically. The sound was a dagger twisting deeper as she circled Ellery. "Poor *Chloe*. Poor baby *Chloe*."

The last of Ellery's patience snapped. She grabbed the front of Baily's shirt, yanking her forward until their faces were just inches apart. Anger flared in her eyes. "My name is not Chloe. I am so tired of your…"

A door slammed shut, bringing a sudden end to the fight. Weston stood framed in the sunlight pouring through the foyer sidelights.

"Enough!" He stomped into the kitchen. "I could hear you two outside. I won't listen to this crap in my house." The refrigerator door swung open, and he grabbed a bottle of beer. Tilting it to his lips, he downed half before slamming it on the quartz countertop.

Hatred was etched on his face when he looked at Ellery. "I sure as hell am glad you didn't show up sooner." His voice was low and venomous. "Listening to this bullshit would have done me in years ago." He started to walk away but abruptly spun around. "That woman did us a huge favor when she took you. By some miracle, she picked the right kid." Then, as quickly as he entered, he vanished into the depths of the house.

The viciousness of his words nearly dropped Ellery to her knees. Her stomach twisted as the message replayed in her mind, amplifying her despair.

"I told you. Maybe you should disappear again. It seems to be the one thing you're good at."

Ellery felt the sting of those words deep inside, but she clamped down on the swell of emotion threatening to spill over. Drawing a shuddering breath, she headed down the hall toward her bedroom.

Fifteen minutes blurred into what felt like an eternity. Hesitation and doubt swelled inside Ellery until she decided to leave. With a glance back at the life she was walking away from, she loaded the last of her belongings into the old car. Ellery slammed the trunk with every ounce of energy she had. The sound reverberated inside her bones. It was more than just a physical sensation. It was the severing of ties with her family and Hunters Cove.

SEVENTEEN

By the time Ellery reached St. Cloud, her vision was blurred, clouded with tears and exhaustion. Her eyes stung from the remnants of the fight at her father's house, and she felt like an elephant was standing atop her. The pain of rejection was deep.

The barbs of the words Baily had hurled at her drew blood. But it was her father's chilling remark about being relieved she had not found them earlier, and his comment about Karma choosing the right child to kidnap that shattered her. How could anyone be so heartless? The question twisted inside her like a knife.

A chill ran up Ellery's spine; an audible feeling of dread escaped. Fragmented thoughts cast long shadows. Could her father have had something to do with her disappearance? Her blood ran cold. Something wasn't right. A feeling of betrayal gnawed at her insides, and she could not shake the sense that a dark secret lurked beneath the surface of her family's facade.

Suddenly, an overwhelming burden settled over Ellery; her arms and legs felt leaden. She was like wax in a relentless flame, her dreams of a family melting before they could take shape. Her thoughts were fragmented. Pieces of Chloe Chambers, Summer St. John, and her current identity as Ellery Journey Gray spiraled around her, dissolving into a chaotic swirl of confusion. Each life drifted away, leaving Ellery in a haze, grappling to hold on to who she was and who she had become.

A sudden honk shattered her thoughts, jolting her back to the present. How long had she been sitting at the green light? She pressed the gas pedal too hard and felt the car lurch forward as she maneuvered it to the side of the road.

As she glanced to her right, the man sped past her, his irritation evident as his middle finger popped up. She watched him until he passed through the next light.

That incident, the man's face, and his middle finger would resurface at some point. Things always did. They stacked on top of one another, stirring her worries until they exploded. Ellery could let go of nothing—big or small—they haunted her dreams and thoughts. It was easier to be perfect when she lived in the shadows.

The haze of exhaustion rattled her. She had to get off the road for her safety and everyone else's. Ellery turned her attention to finding a hotel. Scanning her surroundings, she squinted against the sun that hung low in the sky, finally settling on an obscure but nice, off-brand hotel.

She kept her puffy eyes shielded behind her dark sunglasses, even in the lobby. Her tote bulged with the essentials she needed for the night. Each step to her room on the third floor felt heavier than the last. As she turned the corner, the heat inside her became overwhelming. A single tear slipped beneath the frame of her glasses, defying her efforts to hold it back. She wiped it away, but an uncontrollable stream followed.

After locking the door, Ellery sank onto the bed, her body crumbling like a wilted flower. She buried her face in a pillow as waves of grief washed over her.

Her mind swirled with memories of the day. Enough was enough. With three hundred and forty million people in the United States, she could hide and never come face-to-face with her family again. She could reinvent herself, change her name, and even her looks. Money wasn't an issue. She had enough to walk away from Amelia and the book industry.

The tears that had flowed so freely moments before had dried up, leaving her hollow. She was drained; her exhaustion was bone deep. There was not enough moisture in her for another tear to form. Yet even in the aching stillness, the room felt strangely comforting, a cocoon of solitude—similar to how she had existed for nearly two decades. It was time to return to the safety of that life.

Her reflection in the bathroom mirror was haunting even with her decision to leave. It was as if she were staring at a stranger, someone she no longer recognized.

Ellery could not recall ever caring about anything or anyone this deeply. Anger, fear, and sadness had all been part of her life, but this profound sense of loss frightened her.

For two years, her longing to be loved by the Chamberses had felt suffocating. Until she decided to seek them out, she had not had a moment's peace. But her family had turned away from her in big and small ways. Baily and her father's disgust for her bound them together, creating a fortress she could not penetrate. Jacqui had flown to New York with Liam and Vanessa, but she had not come for Ellery; she was there for her mother.

Trusting Vanessa was not as easy as it should have been. It was possible Ellery's return had eased her mother's guilt over losing her—rather than being thrilled to have her back. And Liam? He was the one person she trusted. But then again, they were two peas in a pod. He painted with a paintbrush, and she painted with words.

Ellery stepped out of the bathroom, droplets of water falling from the ends of her hair as she ran a wide-tooth comb through it. The steam followed her.

As she neared the nightstand, her phone buzzed. The screen was illuminated with a dozen notifications—missed calls from Liam and Vanessa and a string of texts from Quinn and Preston. One message stood out: Jacqui's plea to call Liam.

After settling into the overstuffed chair, Ellery listened to one voicemail after another. She would have had to have been a rock not to feel the emotion behind their words. Still, she could not be convinced to change her mind. The words were not much different than the last time she left.

Just as she was about to put the phone down, a new notification popped in. She hesitated momentarily, her finger undecidedly hovering over the button before finally opening it. The words jumped at her, grabbing her around the throat. Her resolve to leave wavered as she read the new message.

Preston here.
Elle, sometimes we don't
know what we have
until it's gone—again.
We blew your return big time.
Please let us know you're
okay. Call someone.

Preston's previous neutrality about her return disappeared, revealing his thoughts in those two dozen words. It felt like the scales had marginally tipped in her favor, igniting a flicker of hope.

Thoughts ricocheted through Ellery's mind. A storm of conflicting emotions pulled her in opposing directions—to return or not. Overwhelmed, Ellery flung her phone onto the bed.

Rejection was a constant in her life. She could hear the silence from the neighboring apartments when Karma's violence filled the halls. They had listened to her screams, yet they turned away, leaving her to navigate the darkness alone. The locals had branded her as something less than human.

But amid all the whispers of disdain, one name stabbed deeper than the rest—*Karma*. The woman delighted in her suffering by twisting the knife of rejection. Still, just when she thought no one could hurt her more, she met her sister and father.

Baily and Weston's presence introduced a new kind of torture, amplifying her sense of worthlessness with an ache she had never known. Walking back into that was a flat-out no.

Shortly after 10:00 p.m., she texted Liam.

Heading back to New York.
Let me go. Please.

After tossing her phone into her bag, she snapped off the light next to the bed. She had made her decision. She would never return to Hunters Cove again.

Ellery was utterly exhausted, yet sleep would not come. She watched the city lights sprawling across the velvety sky. Her mind swirled with thoughts, each crashing into the next: fragments of her past, the longing for a family, and what would always remain out of reach.

Time slipped away, hours blending into one another as she wrestled with her thoughts. The clock ticked closer to 2:00 a.m. before she surrendered to sleep.

Just before 8:00 a.m., Ellery emerged from her room. She wore the same rumpled clothes from the day before. Her eyes, puffy and red, were shielded by her dark sunglasses as she searched for an ice machine.

A few doors down, a sign directed her toward a small indent near the elevator. She filled the ice bucket and quickly returned to her room, hoping to avoid guests heading to breakfast.

Ellery made a makeshift compress of a clean washcloth and a handful of ice. She pressed it to her eyes and felt the coolness seep through, providing momentary relief.

Half an hour later, she placed a breakfast order with room service, a double meal that would need to carry her through the next twenty hours.

By the time room service arrived, the swelling had subsided enough to make her not look like she'd lost a fight with an onion; the puffiness could pass as allergies. Still, she slipped her sunglasses on before opening the door. Questions swirled as

Preston stepped into view, holding a cloche-covered plate and a tray loaded with extras: fruit, juice, and coffee.

"Room service." A half-smirk played on his face.

Ellery froze, her mouth opening and closing multiple times. "W-why are you..." Words momentarily eluded her as she swallowed hard.

He strolled into the room, balancing the heavy tray on one palm. "I was hungry." A grin played on his face as he lowered the tray onto the small table and lifted the cloche.

Preston's eyes shifted from her to the plate and back again. "For a skinny thing, you sure eat a lot."

"How did you find me?"

He turned toward her, waving a finger in the air. "Let's just say being an attorney has its perks. I called in a few favors." A noisy yawn escaped, and he shook his head. "I knew you were in St. Cloud, but I didn't know where until four thirty this morning."

Ellery's anger simmered just below the surface. "Did you get those favors because you were a lawyer or a Chambers?"

"Does it matter?"

Ellery turned toward the window and stared at the flurry of morning activity. "Your family seems to think they can do anything they want. People jump through hoops to earn their approval."

"You're a Chambers too." The words hung in the air, a pointed reminder of the very legacy she belonged to and resented.

"No. I'm not. Baily and your father made that very clear." She pushed the sheer fabric of the curtain aside, letting the light illuminate her frustration. "I'm an outsider—sort of like that odd cousin no one wants to admit is related."

Preston grinned. "Well, we don't have any crazy cousins, but we do have an aunt who's more than a little off her rocker."

Ellery crossed her arms defensively. "I'm serious, Preston."

He moved to the window and stood next to her. "Come on, Elle. You have to admit, you took us by surprise. A call or something before you just showed up..." His voice trailed off, and he turned toward her. "But you just appeared. We didn't have time to get used to the idea." He rocked his head. "Think of it this way. You've lived your whole life without a finger when suddenly, one just appears. It's gonna be awkward. Things aren't going to go smoothly right away."

Ellery cringed, a knot forming in her stomach. "Maybe so. I would have been a lot more excited if I were you. Why weren't you?"

Preston shrugged. "I heard what Baily and Dad said to you. I probably would have left too. I know Liam told you this before, but Baily's Baily. Because of how Mom handled everything, she suffered the most." Lines deepened across his forehead. "And believe me, she's made us all aware of how much. I don't know how Ben and Piper put up with her, but somehow, they make it work. Ben's a saint."

He plopped into one of the chairs at the table. A wave of delicious aromas wafted to greet him as he lifted the lid. "Holy crap! That really is a lot of food."

He raised two sets of silverware. "Look! Even the kitchen thought this was for more than just you."

Preston dove into the plate with a flourish, scooping up a forkful of fluffy scrambled eggs and eagerly shoving them into his mouth.

Ellery grinned, pulling out the other chair. A soft knock startled her as she settled into her seat. Her eyes flicked nervously between Preston and the door.

Preston shrugged nonchalantly. He casually broke off a piece of crispy bacon and stuffed it into his mouth. "Regardless of whoever's out there, they can order their own breakfast. We're not sharing." His words were muffled behind a mouthful of food.

Ellery apprehensively approached the door. Instead of peering through the peephole, she pressed her foot against the door's edge and nudged it open just a sliver.

"Aren't you going to invite us in?" Liam asked with a grin.

Ellery turned toward Preston. "Did you?"

Preston pointed to his mouth and mumbled something unintelligible as he chewed. A smile spread across his face as he crammed the other half of a bacon strip into his mouth.

Ellery stepped back, allowing Liam, Jacqui, and Vanessa to enter the room. Vanessa approached Ellery. With a gentle touch, she removed her daughter's sunglasses, the ones she wore to hide her puffy eyes.

"Oh, sweetie." Vanessa cupped Ellery's cheek. "I'm so sorry about what happened at the house. Your sister and your dad do not speak for the rest of us. We love you and want you to come home."

Unable to monitor her emotions, Ellery began to pace restlessly. She tugged at her hair, her fingers trembling.

"No. I can't. It's been one rejection after another. I told you in Schenectady that I couldn't do that anymore." She felt the crushing pain of being denied the world she belonged in. "Last night, I decided to go back into hiding and live a simple life without being surrounded by any of you."

"I understand. But there are more of us than there are of them. We all want you to come home. I promise you don't have to spend time with your dad and Baily."

Preston bit off a hunk of toast. "We'll protect you." He curled a bicep.

Liam pointed to himself. "Well, I will. I'll protect you." He flexed his bicep and looked at Preston. "I've got the pipes in the family.

"That's only because you push a paintbrush around all day. *I* do the important work." Preston tapped a finger against his temple.

Vanessa threw out a hand, palm up. "They never change."

Ellery bit her lip. "If I return, I won't move back into that house."

"You can stay with me," Liam said. "I have an extra bedroom above the gallery. It's not much, but it's yours."

Ellery felt the sincerity of his offer. As she studied the faces of those who came searching for her, she saw the progress of being accepted into the family.

Jacqui held her. "Welcome home." Her warm breath brushed against Ellery's cheek. As she pulled back, a smile lit her face. "I've always wanted a sister who wasn't a self-centered bit—brat!" she corrected, looking at her mom.

The room erupted in laughter.

"Your first choice of words was a lot more accurate." Liam grinned.

"Baily'll come around. It's just going to take time."

Preston burst out laughing. "You know the Vikings have a better chance of winning the Super Bowl than Baily does of becoming a nicer person, right?" His words hung in the air, a comical jab that momentarily eased the tension.

Vanessa draped an arm over Ellery's shoulders. "If she eggs you on, you have to walk away."

A hint of a grin spread across Liam's face. "We learned that a long time ago. Otherwise, just punch her."

"My bet's on Baily." Preston twisted his mouth. "You're too nice."

"All right, you two. No one's punching anyone. But as for your father, if you and Baily aren't at each other's throats, Weston will be fine."

Ellery's eyes darted nervously around the room. "I know this is going to sound awful, but I have to ask something." She played with her words in her head. "Is there any chance Weston may have been involved in my disappearance?"

Liam's head instantly twisted toward Preston, the question on his face.

Vanessa plucked at her hair, a nervous habit that revealed her discomfort. "Oh, honey, of course not. That was all on me. I was the one who fell asleep and let Karma into your life."

Ellery paused, her thoughts swirling as she wrestled with the question. "But that doesn't mean he…" She left the question unfinished. The moment stretched like taffy before she finally exhaled. "I just had to ask."

EIGHTEEN

The dawn had yet to break when Ellery opened her eyes. A soft glow filtering through the window illuminated the sitting area in Liam's extra bedroom. The town was still wrapped in dreams. She wished she was one of the people who found peace in Hunters Cove, but she wasn't sure that would ever happen.

Thoughts boomeranged through her mind, amplifying the contrast between her past and present selves—Summer and Ellery. In the shadows, Chloe lingered, finally set free from a past that had been taken from her. But now that her existence had been unearthed, Ellery yearned to lock her back in a closet.

The desire for a family tugged at her. Ellery had wanted to be part of the Chamberses, but the more she thought about the baggage that came with that and the reminders of all she had missed out on, she wasn't so sure.

Unable to sleep, she threw off the covers and sank into the swivel chair in the small alcove. Shadows danced across the park in the flickering streetlights. Bee's Bakery, across the street, was the only building that showed any sign of life.

Folding her arms along the edge of the windowsill, Ellery watched Ben and Baily inside the front windows. Baily pressed her hand to her husband's cheek before leaning in and kissing him tenderly. Ellery had never witnessed this softer side of her sister.

Suddenly, Baily stood alone in the front window, staring at the gallery apartment. Ellery wanted to hide, but she knew Baily couldn't see her with no backlight in the room. They made eye contact without her sister knowing it. It was the first time since

Ellery's arrival that Baily's eyes were not dark with hatred.

She stepped into the living room. A spotlight hung directly over Liam's head and illuminated his canvas.

Liam glanced up briefly before touching a small brush to the surface. "Why are you awake?"

"I just wanted a glass of water." Ellery stepped behind him, her eyes drifting to the painting. "Do you ever get tired of painting sunrises?"

He wiped his paintbrush on a piece of an old T-shirt. "No." After taking a long draw from his paint-marred glass, he wagged his head. "The colors of every sunrise are different. The cloud formations too. Do you ever get tired of putting words on paper?"

Ellery settled onto the couch. "No, but writing's different. My stories change a lot."

Standing, Liam tilted his neck from side to side, pressed his hands to the small of his back, and leaned backward. "I don't think I agree. Your books are a series—same people, same town. It's a continuation of the same tale." He cast a hand toward the window. "Sunrises are like that, a continuation of life—the next day of our story."

"I suppose." Ellery stared at the painting, contemplating the moments that led her to this point. Suddenly, she stepped away from Liam. "I think I'll go shower. I have an idea for the new book. I wanna get started."

Ellery waited for Liam to respond, but he was already lost in his own world. Perhaps they were more alike than she realized.

Before settling in to write, Ellery texted a list of things she wanted Destiny to ship to Liam's. She also wanted her to know she had transferred money into her checking account so she could pay for her summer classes at SUNY.

At almost nineteen, with Ellery's financial help, Destiny had earned her associate's degree in Beaufort. Her determination and dedication were not inherited from Karma; they were self-taught. It was called survival. A transfer student to the State University of New York, she embarked on her junior year, setting her sights on a degree in Criminal Justice. She had no intention of working for the legal system. After everything Karma had hidden from her, she had more interest in working in the private sector as a private investigator.

Had it not been for Destiny, Ellery would never have known her true identity—the missing Chloe Chambers. They were not bound by blood but by experience. Karma, a force of chaos, had crafted their lives with a single purpose: to destroy her daughters and dismantle them piece by piece while inflicting the most emotional pain possible. In that twisted bond of shared trauma, they found solace in each other.

It was nearly seven when Ellery planted herself at the desk in her room. She opened the document she had titled *Book 6*. Her fingers hovered above the keyboard before decisively typing the first line: *The truth was a lie.*

That simple sentence was charged with potential. In Ellery's previous books, her readers met Carma Graves—a name carefully modified to shield her personal life from prying eyes. Through the stories, they encountered Carma's destructive patterns and ups and downs. There was no mention of a fire; instead, they were told of an accident, a tragic drowning where the main character's body was never recovered.

As Ellery told the new story, she thought of Autumn St. Marie, a character who had risen from the ashes to become Sage Ashcroft. It would not be until this book that her readers would discover Autumn's and Sage's ties to Cally Bradford, a baby whose existence was marked by her disappearance within her first week of life.

The story pressed on her. It was close to home, maybe too close. But with careful planning and wording, she could hide the truth and deception within the pages.

She drew a deep breath. There was still so much to tell. But there was a fine line between staying safe and being stupid. Had she crossed it?

Ellery's fingers tapped out the story hiding inside her—Sage's journey as she unearthed the truth about Cally, the kidnapped daughter of a wealthy Ohio family.

She could feel a weight pressing down on her as she channeled her story, the lines between truth and fiction blurring. As she immersed herself in the unfolding tale, Sage became her friend, searching for the truth. The words flowed as if they had been waiting to break free. For Ellery, it was cathartic.

A soft creak announced Liam's arrival. He poked his head through the doorway and lifted a bag from the bakery. Ellery smiled. His interruption momentarily pulled her from her imaginative world. Looking back at her screen, she marveled at the thirty pages she had written. This story was alive, begging to be brought to life.

With a hint of curiosity, Ellery stared at the pink bag with its twisted handles as Liam removed the sandwiches. The white label, adorned with the elegant "Bee's Bakery" script, caught her attention.

"Did Baily know which sandwich was mine?" She unwrapped her turkey, cream cheese, and cranberry sandwich.

"Worried she'll poison you or something?" A teasing grin spread across his face.

"No. Too obvious. But maybe spit in it or wipe the bread under her armpits."

Liam grinned. "I can tell you're a writer. You have an imagination that doesn't quit. You'll be happy to know she wasn't even there. Ben made the sandwiches."

"Maybe she's convinced him…"

Liam shook his head confidently. "Wouldn't happen. I went to school with Ben. You won't find a nicer guy."

Doubt was imprinted on Ellery's face. "Then, how'd he end up with Baily?"

"Well, Bai got pregnant at the end of her senior year."

"She mentioned something about that during our fight, but… Well, I was too angry to care."

"Understandable. Anyway, Dad insisted they get married rather than tarnish the family name." A humorous expression crossed his face as he punched a fist across his body. "Like people can't count months." Liam tapped each finger to his thumb, mimicking a count. He opened the fridge and grabbed two cans of soda. "Dad hauled them to the justice of the peace five minutes after he found out."

"Shotgun wedding, huh?" Ellery paused to chew a bite of her sandwich. "But that baby couldn't be Piper. She's not old enough."

Liam leaned back on his stool. "No. The little girl died shortly after she was born."

Empathy shone in Ellery's eyes. "That's awful. But they stayed married?"

"They did, but only because, like I told you, Ben's a great guy. He's put up with a lot from Baily. It's weird, though. When she's with him, it's like she's a different person."

Ellery took a generous bite of her sandwich. After swallowing, she chuckled lightly. "Maybe you should handcuff them together, then."

Liam sighed. "How's the book coming?"

"It's falling into place." Ellery felt a wave of confidence course through her. "It's weird. Weeks ago, I felt like my words were locked in a prison. Now, I can barely type fast enough."

"Something inspired you. Any idea what?"

"Yeah, Amelia. She's been riding my butt to see something for months." Ellery pulled her shoulders back. "She thinks the book's a lot further along than it is." She shot him a smirk. "And I might have led her to believe that."

"Mmm. So, you're a liar." Liam winked before shoving the last bite of his ham and cheese sandwich into his mouth and glanced at his watch. "I've got to get back downstairs." His words were muffled behind the last of his sandwich. Balling the paper wrapper, he shot it into the garbage can. "Three-pointer.

And the crowd goes wild." Liam danced around the island, making a sound that was supposed to sound like cheering.

"I thought Claudette was helping you out today."

"She was supposed to, but she has a meeting at her mom's care facility. What's on your agenda for the afternoon?"

"More writing." Ellery rewrapped half of her lunch and placed it in the fridge.

Liam stopped at the top of the stairs. "Will you be done writing by six or so? There's somewhere I'd like to take you."

"I should be. Do I need to change?" Ellery wiped her hand down on her T-shirt and jeans and cast it out to the side.

Liam gave her a comedic look. "This is Hunters Cove. If you wear jeans without holes, people'll ask why you're dressed up."

"Got it. But what about dinner?"

"It's covered," Liam called out as he descended the stairs.

NINETEEN

Liam leaned against the doorframe of Ellery's bathroom. She stood at the mirror, her mouth open as she ran the mascara wand over her lashes.

"Do all women hold their mouths open when they put on that crap?" He opened his mouth and mimicked her.

Ellery glanced up, her eyes meeting his in the mirror's reflection. "Yeah. I believe it's a required middle school class—sex ed and mascara application."

"Interesting. All I ever learned in middle school was that you can light your farts on fire."

Ellery spun around. "What?"

"Yeah. It's called pyro flatulence."

"Makes me glad I didn't know you back then." Ellery laughed.

"Are you almost ready?"

"Done." She dropped her mascara tube into her make-up bag.

Liam steered her down the stairs and out the gallery's front door. He locked it behind him and turned left.

Ellery adjusted the collar of her jacket. "Had I known we were walking, I'd have worn different shoes."

Liam chuckled. "It's only two blocks." He pointed to her black boots. "Soldiers travel miles in those things."

Ellery looked at her boots. She snorted, tapping his arm with the back of her fingers. "These aren't army boots. They're fashionable. Well, they were ten years ago."

Liam cleared his throat as they turned left at the end of the block. "Do you ever spend money on clothes?"

"Clothes have never really been important." Her voice was reflective as memories unfurled. "Karma never spent a dime on me once I turned eight. So, I stole them from garage sales. Then, when I was with Millie and Gus, I rarely went anywhere. Most of my clothes are hand-me-downs from Amelia, my agent."

Liam's expression softened. "Based on those boots, maybe you should rethink shopping."

"Do I embarrass you? Is this one of those family 'it makes us look bad' things?"

"It doesn't bother me." Liam stopped in front of a brick building. "But when the town finds out you're a Chambers, the gossip mill's gonna be so hot, it'll burn down the town. You might not want to give them so much to talk about." He smirked, waiting for Ellery to say something, but she remained silent. "This is it." Liam nodded toward the building.

"Eddie's Bar? Your big plan for tonight was to go to a bar?" Ellery bit down on the side of her finger as she took in the building with peeling paint and a mismatched collection of empty chairs scattered around the tables on the patio. "And it's not even a nice bar."

"Oh, come on. This isn't just any bar. It's *Eddie's*." Liam gestured to the poster on the door. "And it's karaoke night."

Ellery pulled her neck back. "Wait! The poster says 'Piano by Liam Chambers.' Seriously?"

"I play every Thursday night from seven to ten."

"Wow! I'm impressed." She playfully punched him in the shoulder.

"There're a lot of things you don't know about me." Liam pushed the door open and ushered Ellery inside.

"Ed-die!" Liam called as if cheering on a baseball player. "This is Elle. Give her whatever she wants and put it on my tab. And make sure she eats at some point." He headed toward the piano.

Ellery moved closer to the bar. "I'll have a beer," she said, her voice steady despite the flutter in her stomach.

"So, you're a friend of Liam's?" Eddie filled her glass. Ellery hesitated, unsure how much to reveal, before giving a simple nod.

"You might want to rethink that decision." He chuckled, the corners of his eyes crinkling. The amber liquid swayed as he set the glass on the counter. "Honestly, Liam's a great guy. His family's decent, but he's more small-town than the rest." Ellery bobbed her head in agreement.

Eddie wiped his hands on a damp towel and tossed it back on the counter. "So, you've met his family, then?"

Beads of sweat rose at her hairline. She swallowed hard, the lie forming almost instinctively. "Just once."

"Based on your expression, it sounds like that was enough."

A dark-haired waitress stopped at the bar and placed an order with Eddie. She gave Ellery the once over. "I saw you come in with Liam. Are you dating?"

Ellery fought a wave of panic. "Oh, no. He's my…" Her throat went dry, and she grabbed her beer and sipped. "Friend," she blurted, the word rushing out like a burst of air. "We're just friends."

"Okay, then." The waitress's tone suddenly softened as she began arranging the drinks Eddie handed her. "I'm Rachel."

"I'm Elle."

The woman didn't appear interested in getting to know her. She pivoted as the first notes of a 70's song drifted through the air. "He's a pretty amazing guy. Liam deserves to have a special person in his life."

With that, she effortlessly lifted the heavy tray off the bar, balancing it on her arm, before gliding toward a table near the front.

Eddie leaned against the bar and watched her go. "She thinks that special person should be her, in case you didn't notice." He tapped his fingers on the bar. "Don't worry. Rachel's sweet, but I don't think Liam's interested in her."

Ellery almost sprayed a mouthful of beer at him. "I'm not

interested in Liam as a boyfriend. We really are just friends." Her cheeks flushed pink.

He winked at her. "Got it—just friends." Eddie stepped to the other end of the bar to attend to another customer.

The door to the bar swung open, and Preston and Quinn strode in first, followed closely by Jacqui and a man Ellery assumed was her husband.

"Elle!" Preston bellowed as he wrapped an arm over her shoulder. "We were hoping Liam could talk you into coming tonight."

Quinn grinned. "Yeah, between the people and the singing, we didn't know…"

"Elle, this is Harley." Jacqui motioned to a man with gorgeous brown eyes and hair, dressed in designer jeans and an expensive-looking polo shirt. "He's a realtor." She glanced around before whispering. "So, when the time's right, he can help you find your own place."

Ellery nodded in greeting. "Nice to meet you, Harley."

He swept her into a bear hug. "That's not how family greets each other."

Jacqui's eyes flared. "Harley," she hissed, her voice barely above a whisper. "Shut up."

The man pressed his lips together, turned a fake key, and mimed tossing it over his shoulder. "It's gonna come out sooner or later anyway."

"Well, that's not for you to decide. That's up to Mom and Dad," Jacqui snapped.

He closed his eyes and faintly shook his head before he sauntered to the bar where Preston and Quinn were already ordering drinks.

"I'm sorry." Jacqui looped her arm through Ellery's and guided her toward the table Liam had reserved for them. "Sometimes, he can be such a…" She plucked out a piece of hair that hung in her vision and said, "dick." Annoyance was etched on her face. "More than a dick."

Quinn laughed as she came up behind them. "She's right.

But then again, they all can be." She slid her chair closer to Ellery. "Do you sing?"

"Yeah, but I'm not super confident. I'm more of a shower singer, and even then, I whisper."

Quinn gulped her beer. "That's okay. Preston and Liam drown out the rest of us anyway."

Ellery smiled. "Then, yeah, I can sing, but I don't know many songs."

"You'll recognize the traditional family song. And if not, just dance."

Solos and groups butchered numerous songs. Occasionally, someone was so good that the bar went silent. The breaks between songs were only long enough to allow a guy named Baker to pull the words up on the screen at the back of the bar.

After a third beer, laughter bubbled uncontrollably. Ellery's initial hesitations melted away as she climbed the stairs onto the makeshift stage alongside her siblings. To the townspeople, she was an outsider, a guest invited into their tight-knit circle for a single night. But in her heart, Ellery had a different reality—*she belonged.*

As Liam played the first notes, apprehension swelled inside her. Ellery had listened to that song so many times during the last two years that she could have sung it in her sleep. But as a virtual stranger in the town, that particular song might not be the best choice. Yet, a rush of exhilaration flooded her. The rhythm took hold, and together they sang and danced to the song "We Are Family."

Quinn and Preston bumped into one another as they danced, arms flailing above their heads like flags in the wind. Nearby, Jacqui and Harley swayed, their bodies pressed together, moving in rhythm with the beat. Caught up in the moment, Ellery danced with abandon near the piano where Liam stood, his fingers flying across the keys.

Suddenly, the music stopped, plunging the lively scene into an unexpected silence. No one moved, not family or patron, as all eyes turned toward Baily.

TWENTY

An air of chaos descended on Eddie's Bar as a sharp-edged silence fell. The siblings stood frozen, their bodies rigid, lifeless mannequins: arms hanging limply at their sides and feet positioned apart to keep them from tumbling over. Their eyes were fixed on Baily.

Ellery felt her hair rise to attention. Beads of sweat formed on her forehead. This would be a scene that would rock the small town. And Baily was the wild card in the unfolding drama. How many secrets would she unleash?

Baily stiffened her back and crossed her arms defiantly. She held her chin high, a silent challenge to her siblings. The tension thickened as Ben quietly approached. He wrapped a hand around her arm and whispered something meant only for her before trying to pull her away, but Baily did not move. She glared at him and peeled his fingers loose.

"Baily," Jacqui finally hissed just loud enough for her to hear, her eyes darting across the crowd. "Not here. Not now."

Baily cackled, the sound blasting toward the crowd. "Why the hell not?" With a bold stride, she stepped onto the stage. Threateningly, she moved closer to Ellery. Liam stepped between them. "Everybody's gonna find out about this lying bitch sooner or later. It may as well be now."

Ellery's instincts screamed at her to run, but her feet felt as though they were encased in concrete.

"Not here, Baily. Let's go somewhere and talk about this." Liam's eyes silently begged the sound tech for assistance.

"Break," Baker called into the microphone. With a swift motion, he cut the stage mics, plunging the room into a brief intermission as recorded music filled the air, but the audience did not move.

Undeterred, Baily approached the sound module, grabbed the cord, and jerked the plug from the wall, plunging the room into silence. Once again, she stepped toward Ellery. Liam spread his arms, creating a barrier between his sisters.

"*I* am family. Me. You're just a…a wannabe. You will never be a Chambers." A sneer played on her face. "You're nothing." Liam wrapped his arms around Baily. "Did you hear me?" Baily yelled. She waved her arms as if trying to reach Ellery. "You. Are. Nothing. You will always be nothing."

Liam's grip on Baily loosened as Ben wrapped his arms around her waist from behind. Struggling to free herself, she planted the thick heel of her boot squarely on her husband's instep with a decisive force. The sudden impact made him cry out, releasing his grasp on Baily.

Ben bent forward, his body racked with pain. His face twisted into a tight ball of agony. The heels of his hands pressed against his knees so hard, his body quaked.

Quinn approached Ben, her voice low and soothing as she bent near him. Baily swung a fist at Ellery, but she leaned back, and Liam took the brunt of the strike.

Finally, Ben stood, his eyes glistening as he turned and limped out of the bar.

Liam pressed a hand against his cheek, the sting still fresh. "Bai, you're only going to make things worse." He instinctively opened and closed his mouth, trying to alleviate the throbbing.

Baily seemed impervious to the pain and chaos she had caused, shaking her hand only once, dismissing the ache she must have felt. "How will I make anything worse? Will she disappear again?" Wicked laughter rang out. "We can only hope."

Preston caught his brother's gaze and subtly lifted his chin toward Baily, then glanced at the back door. In silent agreement, the brothers each grabbed one of her arms and pulled her toward the exit. But Baily violently kicked at them, forcing them to release her.

She surveyed the crowd, their eyes glued to the unfolding drama like drivers in a gawker slowdown. With a steady hand, she pointed to Ellery. "You might as well know, this…" She gestured emphatically. "This woman is not who she claims to be."

That statement almost broke Ellery. Baily's lie swelled and twisted in her gut, nearly taking her to her knees.

"She's pretending to be Chloe Chambers." Baily's voice pierced the din. Gasps erupted, eyes darting around as patrons digested the bombshell revelation.

"That's right. She came to town claiming to be my twin sister who, thanks to my mother's ineptness, was kidnapped when we were babies." The glare she directed at Ellery burned with intensity. "Well, she's not." She poked a finger toward Quinn. "And somehow, she convinced my sister-in-law, the great Dr. Quinn Chambers, to create a fake DNA test."

Quinn stepped toward Baily, their eyes locked in an intense stare. "You know I would never do that. I took an oath to uphold…"

"Oh, shut up, Quinn." Baily dismissed her with a wave of her hand. "You can be bought, just like everybody else."

Preston's eyes flashed with rage as he pulled his wife to his side, out of Baily's reach. "You know Quinn would never do that. You all know her," he told the crowd, trying to protect his wife's reputation.

He clutched a microphone stand in one hand. "Please, everyone, since we can't convince Baily to walk away, I'm asking you to do so. I'll pay your tabs if you go home. Please just let us deal with this as a family."

Preston glared at Baily before turning back toward people he'd known most of his life. "I'm sure rumors are going to fly." A dark red rushed onto his cheeks, his vulnerability peeking through his normally tough facade. "Please put them to rest. We will answer questions soon." He moved toward Ellery and placed a protective arm around her neck. "For now, all you need to know is that this is our sister, Chloe."

"Bullshit!" Baily yelled over the noise of chair legs sliding against the tile floor. Her outburst caused a few patrons to turn their heads before joining the line of people heading toward the door. "This isn't over. Mark my words. This isn't the last you're gonna hear about this fake bitch." Baily raised a fist in the air as if in victory. "Don't you think I'd know if she were my twin?"

Preston stepped off the stage to speak with Eddie. Soon, the employees all disappeared as well. Eddie locked the front door from the outside, leaving the family alone in the bar.

Ellery sank onto the piano stool. She hung her head, anxiously weaving her fingers through her hair. Her thoughts were heavy with emotional fatigue. Despite the exhaustion that seeped into her bones, she remained vigilant, her gaze fixed on Baily. A protective instinct coursed through her, honed over years of navigating life with Karma, now intensified by the turbulent dynamic she shared with her sister.

The siblings formed a closed circle just feet away, their faces etched with anger. Baily stood in the center, a storm of unstable air. Her fingers splayed at her sides as if preparing for a gun battle.

Preston curled his arms over his head. A primal howl bled into the room. "What the hell did you just do?" He leaned closer but kept far enough away to keep his hands from tightening around her neck. "You know damn well that DNA test wasn't faked. Not only did you throw Elle under the bus, but you tried to ruin Quinn. What the hell's wrong with you?"

"Baily, what you did was downright hateful. I'm not sure any of us, including Elle, will ever forgive you." Jacqui flung her head and flipped her hair behind her shoulders. "And that includes Ben. What you did to him was despicable."

Baily laughed bitterly. "What *I* did? What about what *you* all did? I walk in here and see you all standing up there singing *our* song—the one we do every Thursday night." She aimed a fisted hand at Jacqui. "I've been your sister for almost thirty-seven years, but tonight," her voice shook with emotion as she pointed a finger at Ellery, "*she* took my place. You picked her over me."

"Elle didn't take your place," Liam snarled. "I told you we'd be here tonight, and you chose not to come. There's no reason all of us couldn't have been up here."

"Like hell." Baily's words were laced with venom. "There's no way I'd do anything with that...that imposter."

Jacqui's eyes were blazing when she faced Baily. "Elle's not an imposter. She's our sister—just like you."

"She may be *your* sister, but she'll never be mine," Baily hissed.

Liam fixed his eyes on Ellery but addressed Baily. "Elle's a hundred percent Chambers, just like the rest of us, and there's nothing you can do about it."

Quinn's brow wrinkled. "It's not Elle's fault she didn't grow up with the rest of you. I know she'd rather have been here than with that horrible woman who took her."

Baily looked desperately at Harley, but her brother-in-law's silence told her she was on her own.

"Why do you all call her Elle and not her real name?" Fury clutched Baily's words.

"Because *that* is her name," Jacqui said. "She legally changed it. I saw the records."

Baily's face flushed a deep shade of crimson, and her eyes burned with indignation. "Nothing's good enough for you—not the house, our father, or even your given name."

Ellery wobbled as she rose from the piano bench, her legs unsteady beneath her. She moved cautiously toward the narrow opening between Liam and Harley, using them as shields against Baily.

Fear pulled her backward, and she grabbed Liam's arm and steadied herself. "When I changed my name, I didn't know I'd been kidnapped. I didn't know I was Chloe Chambers."

"So change it back. I'm sure Jacqui or Preston would help. Seems to me, if you want to be a Chambers, you'd be anxious to have our name."

Ellery shouldered her way deeper into the circle. "That's not happening." Her voice strengthened as she moved toward Baily. "I've been Ellery Gray for over half my life. It's who I am. It's who I'll always be." Her conviction was deep.

"No. You won't change it because you think you're better than the rest of us." Baily's eyebrow arched incredulously. "You think you're hot shit just because you slap some words on a page that form a sentence. Well, congratulations! You're on the same level as a first grader."

Baily planted a hand against Ellery's chest and shoved her. She stumbled backward, failing to catch herself from falling. The sudden impact of Harley's knee against the back of her head sent a sharp throb radiating through her skull. Attempting to soothe the pain, she wrapped her arms around her head and cradled it, rubbing the spot with her thumbs.

Frantic pounding echoed through the room, drawing everyone's attention. Weston's face pressed against the door as he jerked on the handle repeatedly. Vanessa stood near him, keeping a safe distance.

Preston wove through the tables and scattered chairs, and unlocked the deadbolt. Quinn trailed closely behind, darting into the kitchen to grab a plastic bag of ice for Ellery's head.

Weston charged toward the back of the bar. He widened his path, shoving tables and chairs farther than Preston had, the legs scraping against the floor with a grating sound. "What the hell's going on? I got a call from Eddie telling me I'd better get down here because all hell was breaking loose."

Vanessa knelt next to Ellery. "Are you okay, honey?"

"For cryin' out loud. She's not a baby, Vanessa. Stop treating her like one." Weston huffed. "Maybe Baily finally knocked some sense into that one. Lord knows she could use it."

"What the hell's wrong with you, Dad? Baily's done nothing but harass Elle since she got here, and you just keep pretending she's perfect," Preston shook his head. "Baily's about as far from perfect as they come."

"Elle's your daughter too," Quinn said. "Why are you so awful to her?"

"She's a grown-up. She can fend for herself."

"Family's supposed to take care of family." Liam ran a hand around the group.

Weston took an intimidating step toward him. "Says who? The baby boy who still plays with paints and runs to his mommy anytime I look at him wrong?"

"Stop it, Weston! Stop being a bully!" Vanessa stepped in front of her ex, years of unresolved conflict lodged in the space between them. "You've always claimed you're the head of this family—so how about you try bringing us together rather than tearing us apart?" She placed a hand on his arm and lowered her voice. "Because what you're showing your children is not how to lead—it's how to destroy. You're destroying this family. And if you don't change, they'll all walk away from you one day."

"Oh, that's rich coming from you." Anger was chiseled deeply on Weston's face.

"You're right. I walked away." Sorrow flickered in her eyes. "There isn't a moment that I don't regret all the years I lost with our kids. But I didn't leave because I *hated* them. If *they* leave you, it's out of hatred. And that's on you."

Vanessa's eyes swept across her family. "It's taken me a long time to earn their love, even a little." Her tone was tender. "I won't take them for granted ever again."

Emotion hung heavily. "You haven't earned me back, Mother." Baily took a step toward her father, her voice barely a whisper. "I would never leave you, Dad."

"Of course you wouldn't." Liam's face was ripe with anger. "All you have to do is call his name, and he's buying you whatever you want. You'd never give that up."

Vanessa held up her hand, a warning for Liam to stop. "So, how do we pick up the pieces? How do we move forward as a family?"

Ellery pushed herself up from the floor, her body trembling as she stood. Her head throbbed. The room spun briefly, and she put one hand out to steady herself.

"Elle?" Quinn anxiously moved toward her.

"I'm okay." She closed her eyes as she raised a hand between them. "I can fix this." She met her father's eyes. Swallowing hard, she felt the bitter taste of defeat rise in her throat. "Baily's already told everyone I lied about being Chloe. So I'll leave Hunters Cove. Then, once I'm gone, you can tell everyone I was a fake—just like Baily said."

"That's not happening. You *are* Chloe. You belong in this family every bit as much as Baily. Maybe more." Jacqui glared at Baily.

"What's that supposed to mean?" Baily's eyes clouded as she met Jacqui's.

"It means I'm so sick of you making everything about you." The fire smoldered in Jacqui's words. "I love you, Bai, but I have to be honest. If someone made me choose..." Her voice trailed off briefly. "I'd pick Elle in a heartbeat."

A soft gasp fell from Baily.

"No one's asking anyone to choose," Vanessa said, trying to stop the spark Jacqui lit. "But, Baily, you have to let some of the past go, or you're going to spend your entire life being very unhappy."

Baily twisted her hands. "Well, at least I know where I stand with Jacqui and Mom." She looked at her brothers and tipped her chin upward. It was a move that challenged the others. "What about you two?"

The muscles of Preston's face flexed under the strain of the question. "I can't stand the fighting anymore. And you're the one who's fanning the flame. It's not Elle."

"Liam?"

He raised a shoulder toward his ear in hesitation. "I agree with Preston." Liam stepped toward Baily. "Bai, I love you, but you've been so unfair to Elle. Put yourself in her shoes. What if you'd been the one who was taken?"

The room grew deafeningly quiet.

Baily pressed her hands together, tears threatening to fall.

"That's the thing," Her words were barely a whisper as her gaze drifted toward each of her siblings before landing on Ellery. "I wouldn't have wanted to be kidnapped, but what was wrong with *me* that that whack job picked you instead?"

"What?" Preston's voice was sharp and incredulous. "Are you kidding me? That's why you're so pissed off all the time—because some freak stole Chloe instead of you?"

"No. That's not it. It's just something I've always wondered. Why her?"

Weston wrapped an arm around Baily's shoulders. Without a word, he led her out of the bar, leaving his family grappling with his decision to choose one over the rest of them.

TWENTY-ONE

Dawn was beginning to filter through the windows of the apartment when Ellery and Liam called it a night. They had gotten home from the ER around midnight. Wary of Baily's mood, instead of dropping Ben at the cottage, they brought him back to the apartment, tucking him into bed with his walking boot propped up and a heavy dose of painkillers.

With several dozen people at Eddie's when the secret unfolded and the rest of the town on speed dial, by the time Liam got home, he had received texts from Rose and Stephanie, volunteering to take the baking shift for Ben if someone would cover their daytime hours. Claudette and Abby had also heard about the fireworks and offered to run the bakery from 6:00 a.m. to the 2:00 p.m. close. Hans, who barely lifted his head to acknowledge anyone, would hear about the events during his regular lunch shift. Claudette would make sure of that. Whether Baily would show up at all was yet to be seen, and after what she pulled, no one in the family honestly cared. They were only concerned about Ben. So, Liam took on the job of ensuring the bakery doors remained open.

By the time Ellery woke, the sun was high in the sky. The blankets Liam had used were stacked neatly on the couch. She ran a brush through her hair and went to check on Ben. He leaned against the upholstered headboard with his foot propped up on a stack of folded blankets. The screen of his phone lit up as he scrolled through it.

"How's the foot?" Ellery sat gingerly on the edge of the bed.

Ben's head shake was barely visible. His eyes told her how

sorry he was for his wife's fireworks.

"Any word from Baily?" Ben's eyes said it all. "You know you did nothing wrong." Ellery tapped her thighs with her hands, wondering if she should ask the next question. "Has Baily always been this volatile?"

He briefly pressed his palms to his forehead. "There've been a few outbursts over the years, but I've never seen her like she was last night. I don't know why you set her off for some reason. She doesn't talk to me much anymore."

"After you left, she mentioned something odd."

Ben gripped his beard. "Lately, that's been her norm."

"She told us she wondered why Karma didn't take her instead of me. It was almost like she was—I don't know—maybe jealous or hurt. I couldn't tell."

Ben's eyes bulged. "What?" His mouth dropped open, and he locked his fingers behind his neck and pressed his forearms to the sides of his head in frustration. "That's so typical of her. Of course, she'd wonder about that. It's always about Baily. It always has been."

"She's never told you that before?"

"No. But she needs help. And this time, if she refuses, I'll take Piper and leave. We can't live like this anymore."

Ellery closed her eyes briefly. "I feel responsible for everything that happened last night."

He laid his hand on Ellery's knee. "Don't you dare. Most people would be ecstatic if they reconnected with someone missing for decades. I'm sorry Baily's not one of those people."

"I was hoping that was how this was going to go. You know, open arms and all." She met his gaze. "But it even took Preston and Jacqui a while to accept me."

"They're attorneys." Ben winced as he adjusted himself. "They're analytical, organized planners. They don't have a lot of emotion. They're very much like Weston. You and Liam are like your mom."

Ellery plumped the blankets and carefully adjusted his leg. "So, where does Baily fit in?"

"She doesn't. That's the problem. She's an outsider looking in." He stuck his bottom lip out. "I'm sure you feel the same way right now."

"Completely." Ellery handed Ben the water glass he was trying to reach.

"She's angry at your mom, so she wants to be nothing like her. She wants to be like Weston, but she's not. So, the way she deals with things is by creating drama." He handed Ellery his glass. "Honestly, she's a toxic person and maybe even a bit narcissistic."

"Why do you stay, then? Why don't you walk away?"

"Piper." His answer was instant. "Those two don't get along. When we're together, I spend every minute playing referee. But the thing is, if I take Piper and leave, Baily won't survive. I'm afraid she'd do something to herself."

"Really? She's suicidal?"

Ben nodded. "Vanessa did a number on her. Baily's always been needy, which is why I think Weston babies her."

Ellery crossed her arms and cupped her elbows in her hands. "I understand that. But if last night is any indication of how off she is, she should be hospitalized."

"Yeah, I know. But if I tell her that, it'll send her into a tailspin like we've never seen."

Liam burst into the room. "Baily's on her way up. I saw her coming across the street." He slipped out as fast as he entered.

Seconds later, Baily stood in the doorway, her hands pressed to her hips. "So, she got to you too, huh, Ben?" She grabbed Ellery by the arm, jerked her out of the room, and slammed the door.

Ellery stood outside the room with an ear pressed against the wall. After what happened at the bar, she was afraid for Ben, but the voice she heard coming from inside was sweet and loving. Where was that twin sister when she came to Hunters Cove?

After being convinced Baily would not hurt Ben, she went down to the gallery.

"Oh, thank God. I figured you might be bald and toothless after last night." Liam grinned.

"You couldn't have been too concerned. You left me up there with her. The only protection I had was one of Ben's crutches."

"I was on a phone call with a big client."

"So, money over sisters, then?" Ellery laughed.

Liam's head bobbled. "Well, of course. The great Weston Chambers raised me, and you know his slogan, right?" Mischief lit his eyes as Ellery shook her head. "It doesn't matter *who* you know. It's how much money you have that counts." She finished the last few words with him.

"Are you serious? He puts money above everything else?"

"Everything except Baily."

Suddenly, there was a rhythmic thudding coming from the stairway. Ellery and Liam watched as Ben and Baily rounded the corner, her arm protective around him.

"I'm taking Ben home." Her message was to Liam only. Baily's face was heavy with hatred as she turned toward Ellery. "This is on you." She pointed to Ben's foot. "Had you not come here, he wouldn't have had this accident."

Liam side-eyed Ellery. "It wasn't an accident, Bai."

Baily puffed out her chest and glared at Ellery. "Of course not. She did this, and she's gonna pay."

Ben hobbled to the door. "Baily, we talked about this upstairs. Let it go." Struggling with his crutches, Ben fought to open and hold the door for his wife. It struck Ellery as odd that even in his pain and frustration, he took such good care of Baily. In Ellery's mind, she didn't deserve someone like Ben.

"This isn't over," Baily hissed as she walked past Ellery.

The door slammed shut. Ellery kept her eyes on the ground when she ran past Liam and up the stairs.

TWENTY-TWO

Ellery lay on the bed, her body tucked inwards to shield herself from the world. She pressed her fists beneath her chin. The remnants of anger and disappointment pressed heavily on her, making her consider returning to Schenectady again. At least there, she could escape the cold words of Baily and her father.

The gentle knock startled her, yet she expected it. "I'm fine. I just want to be left alone," she called through the locked door. Liam dropped his head against the door. The *thunk* told her he was not happy with her response.

"Promise me you won't leave."

Ellery flopped onto her back and stared at the ceiling. The silence stretched between them until she finally gave in. "Fine. I won't leave."

"Thank you." Liam's words sounded more like a breath.

Memories churned inside Ellery. Karma's venomous tone was impossible to forget. The hatred of her words played on a loop inside her head daily. Blame, anger, and disgust kept her trapped in the past.

On the day of her father's accident, three-year-old Summer had just woken from a nap in the back seat after a morning spent at the park and a stop for ice cream.

They were nearly home when an SUV barreled toward them, traveling the wrong way down the freeway. Her father, unaware of what was about to happen, smiled at her in the rearview mirror, returning his eyes to the road just in time to swerve to the right, taking the brunt of the impact and sparing her life. The car spun in a circle, a kaleidoscope of sounds and colors as Summer hugged her doll. Then, there was a suffocating silence.

"Daddy," Summer said. It had felt more like a question. His head lolled to one side at an awkward angle. "Daddy?" she tried again, trying to reach him with her chubby fingers.

Suddenly, someone jerked the front door open, the hinges creaking loudly. He glanced at the person behind him and shook his head.

"Daddy?" she called a third time.

Desperation set in, and she repeatedly kicked the back of the seat and let out a bloodcurdling scream. Suddenly, a hand with long red fingernails unlocked the back door. It belonged to the woman who settled onto the seat beside her. Hope mingled with confusion as the lady softly asked her name. Summer rubbed her face on her doll's hair as she listened to the soothing voice telling her stories. Looking away was impossible. As long as she lived, she would never forget her. She had been a lifeline when she needed one the most.

During her two days in the hospital, muted voices became Summer's constant companion, while her mother's absence deepened her loneliness. Each time she cried, it was the hospital staff or a volunteer who offered comfort.

When her mother finally appeared, a surge of emotion bubbled through Summer. All she wanted was to be held, to know everything would be okay, but the woman was unreachable. When she spoke, it sounded like she had someone else's voice. Her jagged tone and harsh words made Summer recoil rather than cozy up to her.

The woman she had adored for three years had disappeared the minute her father was gone. She went from loving to vile in sixty seconds.

With an angry hand, her mother dragged her to the parking lot. Summer's shoes hadn't been tied, and her shirt was unbuttoned. Her feet barely touched the floor. She wanted to tell her she was hurting her, but the minute she made a sound, her mother tightened her grip, digging her fingernails deeper into her skin. Summer felt like a stranger was kidnapping her.

"Listen, girl." Her tone was unyielding. "I'm done playing your mother. So don't even think about calling me *Mom* or *Mommy* or any of those other stupid names." Her eyes seethed hatred. "From now on, my name's Karma. That's the only thing you'll call me. Understand?" Without waiting for a response, she started the car and sped out of the parking lot.

Summer had not been buckled into her booster seat. Each time Karma hit the brakes or passed another car, the vehicle lurched one way or another, making it impossible for Summer to remain on the seat. She repeatedly slammed her face and head against the floor, door, and the back of the seat. After several bumps, time seemed to slow, and she blinked several times to clear her vision. The longing to cry out for her mother was instinctual, but after Karma's stern warning, she covered her mouth with both hands and swallowed the sound instead.

Summer attempted to scramble into her seat multiple times, but with Karma weaving in and out of traffic, it was impossible to find her footing. She finally lay on the floor, braced between the front and back seats.

Speeding into their driveway, her mother slammed the brakes, stopping inches from the garage door. She spun around, balancing on her knees in the driver's seat, a monster in what had once been her mother's skin. "Get up! Get up, I said!" Summer scrambled to her feet, fear rising inside her. Karma pulled her hair so hard that Summer rose onto her tiptoes.

"Mommy, you're hurting…" She tried to slap her mother's hands away.

"What did I tell you? I'm not your mother. My name is Karma." She gave her hair a final jerk before letting go. "You're the reason your father's dead. You killed him." She slapped Summer's face, knocking her to the floor again. "You should have died, not him." The door banged shut as her mother stormed off, leaving her alone in the vehicle.

Summer lay on the back seat, sobbing. "I hate you," she whispered, too afraid to say it out loud. "I hate you! I hate you! I hate you!"

After several minutes, Summer went limp. Her mother's words finally sank in. Her father was dead. It was the first time anyone had spoken the devastating truth to her. At three, she understood death, having experienced it weeks before when Mr. Britches, her two-tone black and white cat, had slipped out of the house one afternoon and crossed paths with the neighbor's German Shepherd.

That evening, the family donned their finest clothes and held a funeral in their backyard. They laid Mr. Britches in a cardboard box and buried him beneath the red maple tree near the swing set.

Weeks passed, and Summer thought they would put her father in a hole near the cat, but that didn't happen. They never said goodbye. Every night, after Karma locked herself in her bedroom, Summer talked to him like he was still there.

Then, one day, a heavy wooden box with several knicks and scars appeared on the mantel. Even though it looked like it came from the clearance section of a discount store, its presence loomed large. Over the years, she often gazed curiously at it but dared not touch it. By the time the veil of innocence lifted, she knew the truth: the box held her father's ashes.

When she was four, they moved to an apartment with two bedrooms. Less than a year later, after listening to her mother screaming at the man who owned it every Friday afternoon, they hauled their stuff to a one-bedroom down the hall. That was where they remained until Summer moved out when she turned eighteen.

The living room was her bedroom, and the couch was her bed. On the nights her mother invited men into their apartment, the floor behind the sofa served as her refuge. She learned to stifle her presence, listening to muffled voices and occasional laughter behind her mother's door.

Once they moved to the small apartment, Karma seemed to have an endless supply of money for new clothes and food for herself. When Summer turned eight, her mother told her she was old enough to care for herself. Desperation set in once she learned what that meant. She resorted to pilfering food from grocery stores and gas stations, but it was not without guilt and a silent promise to pay them back *one day*. When that wasn't enough, she began scavenging through garbage cans behind local restaurants, searching for anything to fill her aching stomach.

Despite her best efforts, Summer's body remained painfully slender. Her frame elongated with age. Her pants hung like capris, and her tops like midriffs. In her mother's presence, Summer pulled the bottom of her shirt as far down as she dared to keep from getting the belt. In an act of desperation, she began swiping clothing from garage sales and off people's clotheslines. She even resorted to taking them from the laundry room in the apartment building. Each piece she acquired felt like a small victory, but they came with deep regret.

Summer had been a survivor, molded out of need. The rules of life had not been explained to her; they had been learned by trial and error. In a world where noise and actions could bring unwanted attention, she learned to hide. She was a loner who never attended school and knew enough to keep her mouth shut. When a woman from social services knocked on their door, Karma peered through the peephole, snapped her fingers, and hooked a thumb toward the bedroom. Her instincts kicked in. It was not the fun game of Hide-n-Seek that the other children enjoyed. This was an entirely different game—one saturated in caution. From the time she was young, Karma had brainwashed her to believe being sent to a foster home would be far worse than living with her.

Concealed beneath her mother's bed, she strained to hear their conversation. Karma spun a tale, convincing the woman that her daughter had moved to Minnesota. Having never been to school, Minnesota was a place that existed only as a name.

The lies kept coming. If Karma's mouth was open, a lie was flying out like dandelions in the wind. Even her birth date had been a lie. Summer believed she was eighteen years, fourteen weeks, and two days old when the cabin exploded. Now she knew the truth. Her birth certificate was as fake as everything else.

Two weeks before Summer St. John's tragic end, she had become a different person. Gone was the familiar name and image. In those two weeks, her dark hair had been dyed a dirty blonde, and her striking blue eyes hid behind green contacts. Summer had been replaced by Ellery Journey Gray. With nervous excitement, she had retrieved the official document from her post office box: a new social security card that bore her new identity and numbers.

Behind closed doors, she had crafted a new existence. The world around her remained unaware of this metamorphosis, and for as long as she could maintain it, she was determined to keep it that way.

Summer had worked since she was fourteen—bussing dishes for cash. She had juggled multiple jobs while weaving a narrative of being homeschooled to explain her unconventional schedule. Money was her way out. She had cleverly stashed it in numerous locations, each carefully selected to keep Karma from taking ownership. After finally breaking free of her mother, she took a pivotal step toward independence. Opening a savings account at the Worthington Credit Union felt like planting a flag in new territory.

Summer began planning her escape after she was out from beneath her mother's thumb. Just days before she was ready to pull the pin, Karma held a butcher knife to her throat, threatening that if she did not make a thousand dollars appear within the next two days, the money would be hers one way or another. As the next of kin, she would inherit every penny Summer had to her name. To prove she was not afraid to take a life, Karma poked the end of the butcher knife into the fleshy part of her daughter's arm. It opened like a split in the earth, blood oozing out onto the floor.

It had taken her thirty-two hours to arrange the final details of her escape. The bus ticket to New York—a state large enough to disappear in—a few clothes, proof of her new identity, and cash were packed in a sizable thread-worn backpack she had swiped from the chair at the coffee shop where she picked up random shifts.

With a chuckle that felt foreign to her, she had taken a thousand dollars from her savings account, leaving seventy-eight dollars for Karma to *inherit*. That was her final act of revenge.

On the day of the fire, the early morning had been still; the world outside was draped in shadows. She tucked her pillows under the comforter, shaping them like a body. With only the moonlight as her guide, Summer placed an oversized paraffin candle on the kitchen counter, setting it close to the long curtains that swayed in the open window.

In the still of the library, in a corner tucked away from the lobby, Summer had done her research, discovering which items would accelerate the fire. She tore open a bag of flour, dumping some of the contents onto the countertop near the candle and leaving the bag open. Several towels, soaked in hand sanitizer, lay on the other side. It appeared they had been used to wipe up an *accidental* spill from the gallon jug. The combination created the promise of a fire, and it was less evident than gasoline. The cabin had to burn to the ground, or the police would not believe she had been inside. But even then, there was the possibility cadaver dogs could call her out.

As she stood in the dim light of her kitchen, ready to strike a match and ignite the wick of the candle, the sudden rattling of the front door handle interrupted her plan. It was 4 a.m. Expecting it to be her creepy landlord, who periodically appeared at her window, she felt a chill crawl up her spine. Quietly grabbing her backpack, she moved swiftly out the back door and across the porch, carefully avoiding the loose boards that could give her away. With a surge of adrenaline, she dashed into the dark woods.

An ominous feeling ran through her as she pivoted back toward the house. Suddenly, a deafening, ground-trembling explosion knocked her to her knees. When she finally rose, blinking away the stars that danced in her vision, the cabin no longer resembled a shelter. It lay in ruins, flames lapping at the old logs. It hadn't burned; it was gone. That was better than she could have wished for.

The shock of the explosion crushed her. Her gaze swept across the debris, landing on a motionless form sprawled on the ground. Suddenly, the person rose and slunk into the woods, not more than twenty feet from Summer. It hadn't been her landlord who had been rattling the door handle.

Ellery sprang up in her bed, the image still replaying. She wasn't responsible for the fire that destroyed the cabin; she hadn't even struck the match. It was Karma. The woman she had believed was her mother had tried to kill her.

With a frantic shake of her head, Ellery fought to dispel the fog of confusion that clouded her thoughts. She needed clarity.

She slid off the bed and opened her computer. Goosebumps rose on her arms as the screen came to life.

It had been years since the house explosion—a moment frozen in her mind, a memory she had tried to bury, but one that wouldn't remain dead. The thought of searching for details made her stomach twist. The prospect of someone tracing her IP address back to Liam's and connecting her to Summer St. John filled her with dread.

Her fingers hovered over the keyboard. A range of emotions swept through her before she typed the words she had avoided for so long. Articles populated the screen, each headline echoing the same narrative: "Suspected Gas Leak Takes Life of Beaufort Woman." The words gripped her as she grappled with the haunting reality.

Ellery leaned back and stared at the ceiling, her mind racing with the new information. A gas leak? The thought buzzed like a swarm of angry bees. In her mind, she pictured the narrow gas stove in the corner of the cabin. It must have been at least fifty years old. From time to time, the pilot light would go out, she'd get a whiff of gas, and she would relight it. But that wasn't what happened when she snuck out the back door that morning.

There had been no gas smell. The pilot light had not been out.

Every part of her body pulsed as reality set in. Her fingertips and throat throbbed, making it nearly impossible to focus. She got up and walked around the room to clear her head before returning to the desk.

She closed her eyes and tried to clear her mind before rereading the article. Was it possible the fire wasn't an accident and that Ellery hadn't started it? Karma could have lit the candle and moved it close to the stove before blowing out the pilot light, leaving the deadly gas to build up in the cabin, causing it to explode.

If that were the case, then the woman hated her so much that she had chanced dying to snuff out Summer's life. Karma had barely escaped when the tiny building exploded, sending logs and debris across the yard. It had knocked her down. Her survival was a fluke that defied all odds.

Ellery's body had gone limp with exhaustion as the memories replayed. This time, the projector had not broken down in the middle; she saw the ending. Karma had tried to kill her, and she believed she had succeeded. Anger surged through Ellery, but somehow, she also felt profound relief. Fate had intervened at the last possible moment, snatching her back from the brink of death and saving her from something she could never have forgiven herself for. It had been nineteen years since that fateful night, almost two decades of believing she had started that fire. For the first time, she found the tiniest sense of peace.

She closed her laptop and slid her chair away from her desk. Memories flooded her as she thought about the hatred Karma spewed. But lately, with the pain of rejection so close, those turbulent years seemed like nothing compared to the agony she had faced since arriving in Hunters Cove. Ellery was an ant, fried through a magnifying glass held by her dad and sister as they tried to burn her sense of self-worth and belonging. Each sunrise brought intense angst, her stomach twisting in knots, palpitations racing through her like a runaway train.

Between her old life and this one, only her years with Millie and Gus held glimmers of tranquility. She longed for those days when she was a nobody, hiding in plain sight. But returning to Schenectady meant diving back into a world colored by the complexities of her relationship with Destiny. Their connection, though not defined by blood, was a tapestry of hardships suffered under the wicked hands of Karma. She would always fill the space between them, a constant reminder of all they had endured.

Ellery slipped her purse from the hook and pulled on a sweatshirt. She crept down the stairs, one at a time, pausing intermittently to listen for Liam. When she reached the landing, she peeked around the corner. He was engaged in a conversation with a client near the front door. Ellery slipped across the narrow hallway and through the back room, grateful for small favors. Cautiously, she opened the back door. After a glance to ensure she was not being watched, she closed the door with barely a sound.

Adrenaline coursed through her veins as she sprinted to her car. Guilt slapped her upside the head. She had promised she wouldn't leave, yet here she was, driving away again.

TWENTY-THREE

By now, the town's rumor mill would be out in full force. Speculation and judgment would fill the air. Ellery could almost hear the whispers. *That's the baby that was kidnapped. Are they even sure she's the one? She doesn't look much like the rest of the family. Look at that dark hair. I wonder where she's been all this time. Why do you suppose she showed up now? She looks poor. Just look at her clothes. I'm sure she needs money. Why else would she come?*

Why? Family. Love. Acceptance. It was as simple as that.

The urge to scream surged through her. "Leave me alone!" she wanted to shout, but she knew it was futile. It wouldn't stop tongues from wagging or end the stares. Until the scuttlebutt died down and the town found a new target, it wouldn't end.

As Ellery headed north, a rush of freedom surged through her. The town that had felt suffocating moments before was disappearing in her rearview mirror. The oppressive weight of her surroundings lifted, and the open road stretched before her like an invitation.

She glanced at the time on her phone. More than anything, she needed to get away for a few hours. Liam would be unaware of her escape for at least an hour or two, giving her time to experience things outside Hunters Cove.

As she drove through Brainerd and Nisswa, the scenery unfolded like one of Liam's paintings. It was possible he had painted the beautiful small town. Starving, she decided to stop for an early lunch at Grayson's, a delightful two-story restaurant on the southwest corner of Little Cullen Lake.

The building featured an entire wall of windows, upstairs

and down, that offered a view of the water. Inside, live-edge tables cut from local trees showcased the area's natural resources.

Once seated, Lori Weidemann, one of the owners, welcomed her with a plate of fresh bread and three butter flavors. Ellery inhaled the aroma and smiled before ordering a soda.

"I'd wager a bet you're not from Minnesota, are you?" Lori grinned. "Most people here, not all, call it pop."

"You're right. I'm from New York." Ellery felt a tiny lump in her throat.

Lori tilted her head. "Really? I would have guessed the South. I thought I heard a hint of an accent."

"No." The lie circled as she tried to cover her southern accent. "New York is home." Her pulse quickened. Every word felt like a cautious step on unfamiliar ground.

"Well, welcome to Minnesota. I, for one, am happy you're here—no matter where you're from." Lori winked before returning to the kitchen.

Ellery sat at a small two-person table, the lunch menu spread like a map before her. She was wavering between a salad and a sandwich when a familiar voice cut through the restaurant. Instinctively, her head snapped up. Her heart sank when she recognized Weston, flanked by three other men, confidently striding through the front door.

As they were ushered to their seats, Ellery raised the menu to veil her face. Shakily, she shifted to the opposite side of the table, positioning herself so her back was to them. The walls that held her fear at bay were beginning to crumble. Finally, she grabbed a twenty-dollar bill from her purse and dropped it onto the table. Before she could second-guess her decision, she slipped out of the restaurant.

Of all the eateries scattered along the highway, fate undeniably led her and her father to the same restaurant on the same day at the same time. But then again, Grayson's rustic charm and lake views offered the perfect place for Weston to meet clients, even if it was nearly twenty miles from his office in Brainerd.

Ellery headed back toward Nisswa, where she grabbed a Club House sandwich at Ganley's before wandering under Highway 371 toward the lake. It was the place she would least likely be recognized by the patrons who had seen the fireworks the night before.

The sun hung high in the sky, casting dappled light through the dense canopy of trees, prompting her to reach for the sunglasses she had purchased when she moved to Schenectady. After years of small frames, her large ones were trendy again.

Barely a bite into her sandwich, Ellery's phone began pinging. *Liam. Liam. Jacqui. Liam. Liam. Liam. Vanessa. Ben. Liam. Preston. Liam.* At least, based on the messages, she assumed the unknown number belonged to Ben. Each name flashed in rapid succession. It was evident Liam had rallied the troops when he discovered she was missing.

It was obvious no one wanted her to enjoy a peaceful lunch. She stared at her sandwich, missing only two small pieces. She could feel their concern seeping through the screen, almost as if they were hovering beside her.

Knowing she couldn't ignore them forever, she rewrapped the sandwich and set it on the bench while she added names and the extra number to a group text.

I'm fine.
Driving around.
Back tonight.

She clicked send and set her phone down. Instantly, she picked it up again and added—

Don't worry.

Messages erupted on her phone--ranging from a *thumbs up* to a *Thank God*. Amidst the responses, her mother's message stood out, a gentle reminder wrapped in concern, reminding her to *be careful*. And then came Liam's private text.

You promised you wouldn't leave.
Where are you? Really?

Her response was curt, likely leaving Liam with little comfort. She repeated what she'd told the group—nothing more. She took a bite of her sandwich and turned off her phone. The screen faded to black as a sense of relief washed over her. The invisible barrier between herself and her family had been locked, allowing her to enjoy the peaceful afternoon.

Ellery tossed her garbage into a can a few feet away and wandered back to the bench she had claimed before the park got busy. The lake held her eyes, but the glistening water and the people did not register. Instead, her thoughts swirled with the morning's revelation. *Karma had tried to kill her.* The woman harbored a deep-seated hatred for Summer, a loathing so intense that her need for money outweighed their eighteen-year bond. But then again, Karma had never intended to love her. It had all been a facade to trap Brant St. John. When his life came to an end, the relationship between mother and daughter snapped, revealing a void where something resembling affection had once lived. Without Brant, Summer was only a reminder of Karma's failed manipulation.

The storm that brewed around Ellery was hard to ignore. Anxiety twisted in her stomach. She could not shake the feeling she had somehow earned all the hatred heaved on her since birth: Karma's judgment, Baily's disapproval, and her father's disappointment. A gnawing doubt taunted her. Perhaps she was a wretched person, unworthy of love, for all three to wield their words like weapons against her.

Ellery's shoulders scooped forward, her sadness too heavy to carry as she turned inward, watching the haunting replay of her childhood. Suddenly, a fragile bud pushed through the crack in the concrete of her life, a reminder that even in desperation, there was hope. Karma could no longer hold sway over her, especially from the depths of hell, where Ellery was sure she lived. But realizing Karma's responsibility for the fire pulled her from the depth of despair after years of endless suffocation, Ellery could finally begin to reclaim her narrative.

Until hours ago, Ellery hadn't known Karma believed she'd been responsible for Summer's demise. The moment her mother staggered to her feet, her face contorted into a mask of malevolence. A wicked grin spread, and her eyes were bright in twisted delight. Karma was pure evil.

Ellery could imagine the look on Karma's face when she walked into the bank, waving her death certificate, ready to claim what she believed to be a windfall. The woman would lose it when she realized Ellery had bested her, leaving her with a paltry seventy-eight dollars.

After years of her mother's manipulation, Ellery had finally outsmarted the woman. A wave of triumph coursed through her, and she reveled in victory. Yet a nagging sensation, closer to home, poked at her. The chasm that separated her from her sister and father was vast and filled with hostility, not so unlike the relationship she had had with Karma.

Ellery knew all too well that hatred was a stubborn force that rose from wounds festering below the surface. *Hurt people hurt people.* She could name those individuals in her life on one hand.

Winning Baily's and her father's approval was like standing at the base of a towering mountain. The only way to climb it was to take that first step. Still, she questioned her efforts. No matter how many steps she made toward them, they erected barriers to keep her away. Was it worth it?

As she inhaled deeply, she felt a flicker of hope that cast a faint light on the uncertain path ahead. She was not leaving until she had exhausted every possible avenue to change their minds about her. After all, a sliver of hope was better than none.

She strolled back along the winding path and began stepping in and out of stores that offered unique treasures. The rich chocolate and fruity aromas greeted her as she entered The Chocolate Ox. Rows of retro candy mingled with the modern favorites, making her feel like she had stumbled into a secret world.

Time ticked away as she lingered over the bright-colored wrappers. Facing one wall, she was transported back to her younger self, a wide-eyed girl with her nose pressed against the Beaufort Candy Shop glass window—*dreaming*. She had watched families slip in and out with bags of sweet treats. Her mouth watered, and she longed for someone to notice her. She'd even resorted to praying, something she learned from Brant, for someone to take pity on her and offer her even a tiny threat. But it never happened.

A painfully thin girl with a wild tangle of dark hair, and a shirt that appeared to have fought its way out of the washing machine before soap laid claim to it, leaned against the window of the Chocolate Ox. One hand was pressed above her brow, shielding her eyes as she scanned the treats through the thick glass. It was eerie how similar the girl looked like Ellery had nearly thirty years before.

She quickly selected a few of her favorite items before picking ones she thought the girl might enjoy. At the counter, she requested separate purple bags. Joy stirred inside her as she stepped into the sunshine. Squinting, she plucked her sunglasses from her purse and slipped them on.

With a casual smile, she leaned against the weathered brick wall for a few seconds before addressing the young girl beside her.

"Hi. I'm Elle, What's your name?"

The girl, who could be no older than nine, eyed the two bags with incredible longing. "Summer," she said without peeling her eyes from the bags.

A sudden rush of adrenaline and disbelief shot through Ellery. Her eyes darted up and down the street, searching for anything that indicated she was being watched and that this was some elaborate setup. "W-what did you say?" Ellery's voice trembled at the coincidence.

"Summer," she repeated, her voice ladened with uncertainty.

Her hands trembled as she summoned her composure, returning her attention to the child. She released a long breath and offered a purple bag to the girl. "Can I give you this?"

The young girl's shrug was barely visible, belying the look of want on her face.

"It's okay. You can have it." Ellery extended her arm, brushing hands with the child who badly needed a bath and a lot of love. "You'd be doing me a huge favor. I bought way too much."

A crooked smile lit Summer's face. She snatched the bag from Ellery's hand and ran.

At the end of the block, she spun around and returned to Ellery, throwing her arms around her waist. "Thanks, lady," she whispered, her voice filled with gratitude. "Thanks for seein' me." Then she was gone, weaving her way through the crowd of shoppers.

A rush of emotion ran through Ellery so deeply she could barely breathe. She sank onto the bench, her elbows pressed to her knees. As a child, all she had ever wanted was to be seen.

As Ellery drifted through the shops, the shadows from the afternoon sun lengthened. Exiting each store, she searched for the girl. Had she only imagined her? Was she a memory from her past? Or had she been real? By 4:30, she had all but lost hope. Instead of routing herself back to Hunters Cove, she drove the streets and alleyways, searching for the young girl, who seemed to have disappeared into thin air.

Ellery shifted in her seat as she pulled back onto the highway, her fingers tapping the steering wheel as the car traveled back to Hunters Cove. The hum of the tires seemed almost hypnotic, yet her mind was a sea of tumultuous thoughts.

The girl had an unsettling presence. Innocence surrounded her, yet something in her eyes haunted Ellery. The two feelings clashed. Darkness exploded in Ellery's stomach. She attempted to shake off the feeling, but her unease only increased.

By the time she reached Brainerd, the sun was low enough in the sky that even the visor on the passenger's side didn't help. The brilliant light crept into the corners of her vision, blurring the roads.

Ellery slipped her hand inside the candy bag, glancing down to see what treat she had randomly selected. Just as she looked up, a deer stepped into her lane, its eyes glimmering like a pair of onyx stones. Time seemed to slow as she instinctively jerked the wheel to the right. The car veered sharply, bouncing across the uneven terrain of the ditch.

Her body slammed against the seatbelt as the old Camry careened toward a tree. She desperately attempted to regain control, but the collision was inevitable.

The last thing Ellery saw was the smear of blood on the steering wheel before her world faded to black.

PART TWO
Vanessa Chambers

TWENTY-FOUR

The waiting room lights had been purposely dimmed. The soothing atmosphere had little effect on those waiting for word about which side of the fence their loved ones were leaning.

"What happened?" Vanessa's heart galloped. She tossed her purse onto a padded chair and joined her family, who were huddled together, bracing themselves against the unknown.

Preston pulled his mother into a protective hug. "All we know is that she hit a tree just outside town."

"Why was she even over here?" Vanessa glanced toward the information desk, hoping for a doctor to appear.

Outside, the last remnants of daylight faded as Vanessa watched her family's reflections in the darkening windows. Each face was laden with worry, including her own.

She pivoted toward Quinn, her voice replete with impatience. "Have you been able to find out anything—doctor to doctor, I mean?"

Quinn shook her head. "Nothing. And they won't let anyone in her room. I thought we might have heard something by now."

Vanessa's eyes landed on Ben. "No Baily?"

He tilted his head toward a corner of the room, where Baily paged through a magazine. The muscles in her jaw flexed repeatedly. Her lips pressed together, forming a thin line that revealed her annoyance.

"Where's your dad?"

Liam shrugged. "I don't know. After I got the call from Destiny…"

Lines deepened at the corners of Vanessa's eyes. "Why'd

they call her? She's not her family."

"I guess they found her number in Elle's purse."

"So, Destiny called you?"

"She called the gallery phone. I supposed she found it online. As soon as I heard from her, I sent the family text, but Dad didn't respond, so I assumed..."

"Of course, he didn't." Vanessa turned toward Ben. "How'd you get Baily here?"

Ben cast a sideways glance at his wife. "She wasn't going to come, but I insisted." His voice carried a hint of regret. "I'm a little worried Bai could be responsible for Elle's accident," he whispered, "especially after what happened this morning."

Vanessa cocked her head. "This morning? Now, what happened?"

"Mom, let it go. Baily's an a-hole, and we all know it." Liam rubbed his temple.

Jacqui glanced over her shoulder, the creases in her forehead deepening. "Wouldn't have mattered if she hadn't come. Liam's got her pegged." She plucked her phone from her back pocket.

She pressed a few buttons and held it for Ben to see. "Are you kidding me?" He glared at his wife, who remained oblivious to the discussion about her.

"What is it?" Liam grabbed the phone. Anger reddened his face as he read. "Listen to this. 'Chloe has to go. I know you think so too, but you're just playing nice for Mom.'" Liam handed the phone to his sister. "Is Baily right? You don't want Elle here either?"

"No! Nothing could be further from the truth. I'm glad she's back." She glanced down at the message again. "And for the record, it made me furious that she called her Chloe."

"Yeah, I caught that. We need to have it out with..."

Suddenly, the room went quiet. Everyone shifted their eyes toward the heavy door as it swung open, and a doctor in a white lab coat stepped through.

"Chambers?" His eyes leaped from one group to the next.

The family surged forward, pressing so close to the doctor that he stepped back.

"How is she?" Vanessa nervously clasped her hands in front of her.

"Are you all family?"

"I'm her mother—Vanessa Chambers."

"And the best mother in the whole damn world." Baily words dripped with sarcasm.

"This isn't about you, Baily." Jacqui stepped in front of her sister, blocking her from joining the group.

Unfazed, she moved to the other side. "Nothing ever is."

Annoyance grew on Preston's face. "You're such a bit..." He cut himself off before throwing gasoline on the fire Baily started.

Ben gripped his wife's upper arm and guided her back to her corner. He bent near her and whispered something meant for her ears only before straightening. His orthopedic boot clunked against the floor as he made his trek back to the family.

Vanessa's face hardened. "Family drama, I'm afraid." It was a simple explanation, yet heavy with implication. "They're twins," she added, as if that alone explained their complicated history.

The man nodded. "I'm Dr. Torres," he said, introducing himself to the anxious faces that stared at him. "Siblings?" he inquired, swinging a finger across the group.

"Family." Vanessa rested a hand on Ben's back.

Dr. Torres's expression shifted. "I'm afraid Ellery..."

"Her name's Chloe," Baily called from the corner.

Vanessa closed her eyes briefly before making eye contact with the doctor. "Please ignore her."

"Your daughter's a lucky woman. Had she been going any faster, this would have been a very different conversation." In that one statement, Vanessa felt the reminder of how thin the line between life and death could be.

"Dr. Torres, I'm Dr. Quinn Chambers from St. Gabriel's in Hunters Cove." Torres nodded once. "I can help explain medical information to the family."

"That'd be helpful." His gaze met Vanessa's. Every nerve in her body started screaming as the hair rose on her arms.

"She has significant injuries." He read from the list on his clipboard. "Concussion, distal radius fracture, facial lacerations, organ contusions, two bruised ribs, and a nasal fracture." He handed the clipboard to Quinn to review. "We have her in a neck brace out of caution. "Fortunately, she doesn't appear to have any back injuries, but until she wakes up, we won't know for sure."

"She's not awake?" Liam looked from Torres to Quinn.

"Not yet. And I'm not going to lie. It is a little concerning." He uncomfortably adjusted his stance. "It's not unusual, but worrisome, nonetheless. With her concussion, there's been some bleeding on the brain."

"Can we see her?" Preston's face was hopeful.

"Because she's not awake yet, she can only have one visitor at a time." Torres's tone was firm yet sympathetic. He pressed a few keys on his phone.

Preston's attention shifted to his mother, whose face was a canvas of worry lines. "Mom, you go." He gently touched her shoulder.

Dr. Torres's phone buzzed, and he glanced at the screen before looking up. "It looks like someone's already in there."

Lines deepened on Vanessa's forehead. "Who?" Vanessa's eyes darted across her family, quickly accounting for each member. An unsettled feeling crept over her. The hair on her arms rose, urging her to turn around. Her heart sank when she turned. Baily's chair was empty, and she was nowhere to be seen.

"I'm not sure." Torres was unaware of Vanessa's concern.

"Would it be alright if I went back to see who's with her?" Vanessa's voice held an edge of concern. "I promise. It'll only be a second or two."

A small crack appeared in the doctor's stern facade. "Fine, but only two minutes, then one of you has to leave."

He waved his badge in front of the card reader, and the door opened. Hesitantly, Vanessa followed him inside.

"She's in room 6." He pointed to the right of the nurses' station. He held up a pair of fingers. "Two minutes. That's it."

Vanessa stepped into the room, prepared to confront Baily, but other than Ellery, there was no one there. She walked to the window and peeked behind the long curtain. The bathroom was empty also.

Her heart grew heavy, and the pressure at the corner of her eyes intensified when she stopped at the end of Ellery's bed. Her vision clouded as she saw her daughter, knowing how much the accident had destroyed. They had only found their way back to one another a week ago, and now she lay broken. The reality of almost losing Ellery again felt unbearable.

If the doctor hadn't told her what room she was in, Vanessa wasn't sure she would have recognized her behind the bandages across her face and the massive bruising. A sob slipped from her, but she muffled it with the back of her hand before lowering herself into the chair next to the bed. The seat felt warm beneath her. The doctor was right; someone had been there.

She laid a hand on Ellery's unbroken arm. Her skin felt cool, so Vanessa adjusted the covers, tucking her daughter's arm beneath the thin white blanket.

"Hi, honey. It's Mom." Her heart ached that her daughter had not yet begun calling her that. "I'm sorry. It's Vanessa." She watched the lights of the machines for a moment, checking for changes in Ellery's heart rate. When she saw none, she laid her forehead on the edge of the bed. "Please come back to us. It would destroy us if you left us again."

Vanessa closed her eyes and prayed to calm her nerves and irrepressible thoughts. Time fell away, and she lost herself in begging God not to take one more minute from them. Finally, feeling more settled, she placed a tender kiss on her daughter's forehead. She had done all she could do. It was in God's hands now.

As she approached the waiting room, she steeled herself for

a confrontation with Baily, but by the time she returned, Baily and Ben were nowhere to be seen. Weston had not shown up either.

Liam pulled her into an embrace. "I'm going to go see her. Anything I should know?"

She cupped Liam's face with her hand, her thumb brushing repeatedly against his cheek. "Prepare yourself, honey. She doesn't look good."

He laid his head against her shoulder briefly before disappearing down the hallway. Vanessa said a prayer for Liam and Ellery. If she died, he'd take it the hardest. The silence of the nearly empty room throbbed inside Vanessa. "Your father never showed?"

Jacqui's shoulders sagged. "No." She aimed a finger toward the vacant corner of the room. "And Ben took Baily home because... Well, because she was being Baily."

A soft puff of air fell from Vanessa. "I can't believe we almost lost her again. I don't know what..." Her voice was trembling.

Suddenly, Baily stormed into the room, bringing a whirl of anger and chaos with her. "You don't know what you'd do if you lost her again?" she spat, finishing her mom's sentence with a tone sharp enough to draw blood. She snatched her forgotten purse from a chair and flung it over her shoulder. "Of course you don't. It doesn't matter that the rest of us never left." A trail of bitterness was almost visible around her.

"Shut up, Baily," Preston snapped. "Get the hell out of here before..." He drove his fist into his other hand.

"Gladly. Didn't wanna be here in the first place." With a pivot, she stormed away, leaving the same way she arrived—sucking the air from the room.

Quinn touched her mother-in-law's arm. "Don't pay any attention to her, Vanessa. She's an expert at throwing her little tantrums. They've always gotten Weston's attention. Baily's perfected her little *'Daddy, I want...'* routine."

"Who was in Elle's room?" Jacqui asked.

"I don't know. There was no one there when I walked in."

Preston wrapped a comforting arm around his mother. "Why don't you go home? Quinn has to get home to Harlow anyway. She can drive your car, and you can return in the morning. I'll spend the night."

Vanessa nervously ran a finger along the edge of her sweater. "I think I should stay."

Quinn handed her mother-in-law her purse, not giving her a chance to object. Lovingly, she hooked her arm through Vanessa's, providing an anchor in the storm of uncertainty. "I think it's better if you go home and get some rest. You won't do Elle any good if you get sick."

As they approached the hallway, Quinn paused. She glanced over her shoulder. "Preston'll let us know if anything happens. Right?"

"Of course. You'll be the first person I call."

Quinn squeezed Vanessa's arm and led her through the hallway and out the front door.

TWENTY-FIVE

As the clock ticked toward 7:30 a.m., morning light filtered through the windows of the ICU waiting room. The scent of fresh pastries wafted through the air as Vanessa and Jacqui carried two small boxes of assorted treats and a beverage carrier filled with four steaming cups of coffee.

Vanessa placed the boxes of rolls on the counter and set a stack of napkins beside them. She turned toward the weary faces of the few waiting individuals whose eyes mirrored her own exhaustion.

"Help yourselves," she offered with a kind smile.

Jacqui leaned close to her mom. "Looks like Liam spent the night too." She nodded to the corner where he lay slumped in a chair, his long legs draped across the seat he had pulled toward him. "At least one of them is getting some sleep."

"It's guilt." Vanessa listened to her son's soft snoring. "Since Elle was staying with him, he feels guilty about the accident."

"Why? She's the one who snuck out. That was her choice. She's an adult."

Vanessa turned toward Jacqui, her eyes glistening. "You're right. But you know your brother. He carries the weight of the world." She squeezed Jacqui's arm. "Elle chose to reveal herself to him first. So…" She let the thought speak for itself.

"Honey," she whispered, gently shaking Liam's arm.

He stirred, his eyelids fluttering like the wings of a sleepy butterfly. It took a few blinks before his eyes finally opened. He let out a long yawn, stretching his arms above his head.

Vanessa dropped into the chair beside him and rested a hand on his shoulder. "I thought you'd go home last night since Preston offered to stay."

Liam gave her a knowing look as he untangled his legs from the confines of the chair and indicated for Jacqui to sit. He gratefully accepted the cup of coffee Vanessa offered.

"Is she awake yet?" Jacqui dropped into the chair.

"Not yet." Vanessa could hear the worry in his voice. Liam glanced at his watch. "Well, not since I came out here around four." He took a sip of the steaming coffee.

"Jacqui and I will stay today. You and Preston go home and get some sleep."

Liam let out a snort. His tousled hair and heavy eyelids betrayed his exhaustion. "That's not gonna happen."

Jacqui blew across the top of her coffee cup. "Are you leaving the gallery closed today?"

"No. Claudette's there." He yawned again. "But even if she weren't, I'd be here."

Preston suddenly appeared. Vanessa brightened at the sight of her son. She rose, her arms instinctively opening for a warm embrace. However, she instantly dropped back into her chair, hinting at her exhaustion.

"Are you okay, Mom?" Jacqui touched her knee. "What's going on?"

"It's nothing. I'm fine." She waved off Jacqui's concern. "I'm just emotional, and that's taking a toll on me right now." Vanessa pulled Preston in for a hug. "Any news?"

"You're sure you're okay, Mom?" Preston asked. Vanessa held up a hand in response. "Because…"

"I really am fine. How's Elle?"

Preston added a chair to the circle. He adjusted his position several times before refolding the collar of his shirt. "They need to buy more comfortable chairs." He finally met his mother's gaze. "She's still not awake, but the doctor was just in."

"What'd he say?" Vanessa handed Preston a cup of coffee.

"*She*. Dr. Kathleen Nield. It sounds like Elle's starting to respond to some of the tests." Exhausted, Preston rolled his neck in a circle. "And when I talked to her, she squeezed my hand."

Vanessa slumped into her chair and released a breath she had not realized she had been holding for the past sixteen hours. "Oh, thank God." Her gaze flickered upward in thanksgiving. "Did she say how long she thought it would be before she'll wake?"

"She isn't sure. It could be minutes, hours, or days. They don't really know." His eyes caught sight of the box on the counter. "Did you bring those?"

"Of course she did." Jacqui smiled, giving him a knowing stare. "Who else?"

"Bring me one too." Liam held out a gimme hand, his fingers wiggling like a small child. "You know what I like."

"So, it sounds like it's a waiting game." Jacqui felt crumbs from Preston's roll drop into her hair. "Seriously?"

He handed Liam a Boston cream pastry and brushed the side of his hand across his sister's head before sinking his teeth into a Bismarck. The raspberry oozed out. He caught the stream of jelly in his other hand just before it dropped onto the slacks he'd been wearing when he raced out of the office the day before.

"Did your father ever show?"

Disappointment weighed on Preston's face. "No. I left several messages for him but never got a response." He licked the jelly from his palm.

"Do you think he's okay?" Liam poked the last bite of his pastry into his mouth.

Vanessa gave a decisive nod. "I'm sure he's fine. He's just being Weston…" Her voice trailed off momentarily. "At least where Elle's concerned."

Preston helped himself to a white chocolate raspberry scone. "I don't understand what his deal is."

"It doesn't make sense to me either." A puzzled look etched on Vanessa's face.

As the subtle buzz of the hospital receded into the background, a nurse appeared in the doorway. "Ellery's awake," she said as she approached the group.

A tear instantly hovered at the corner of Vanessa's eye as emotion swelled inside her. "Thank you, Lord," she whispered. "Can we see her?"

The nurse paused, her gaze sweeping over their faces. "Dr. Nield's running some tests. I'll come get you when she's finished, but it'll be a while." Her face softened. "We aren't sure exactly how much she remembers. So, when you go in, please be patient."

"Thank you. You have no idea how grateful we are." Vanessa lightly touched her hand.

The nurse smiled. "I think I do. I'll be back in a while. But in the meantime, why don't you go to the cafeteria and get a decent breakfast? You'll have plenty of time. It could be a couple of hours before you can see her." With that, she slipped out of the room.

Vanessa pressed her palms together. "I can't tell you how relieved I am."

"We all are." Jacqui glanced toward the door. "She's right, though. If we don't eat..." She shook her head as she watched Preston shove the last of the second pastry into his mouth. "*Real food*, we're gonna end up in here ourselves."
Vanessa's expression shifted, and her body relaxed. "Okay. Let's go," she said, waving her brood toward the cafeteria with a flick of her hand.

TWENTY-SIX

Vanessa was perched anxiously on the edge of the hospital bed. She gripped Ellery's hand. The smell of disinfectant wafted through the room. Liam sat in the folding chair across from his mother, his back stiff and his eyes on Ellery's face.

Jacqui and Preston leaned against the windowsill, the early morning sun spilling into the room through the partially open vertical blinds.

"I'm so sorry," Ellery whispered, her voice raspy and low. Her gaze shifted between their faces. "I didn't mean to cause this much trouble."

The seriousness in the room shifted as Preston released a soft chuckle. "So you were okay with a *little* trouble, just not *this* much."

Jacqui elbowed him in the side but could not conceal her smile. "He's teasing, Elle."

The newest dose of painkillers was beginning to take hold. Between the pain and the drugs, Ellery's smile looked more like a stoned clown. "I-I really am sorry."

"We know you are, honey. No one chooses to drive a car into a tree." Vanessa squeezed her daughter's hand.

Liam cast a sidelong glance at his mother. The thought pressed down on Vanessa. "You didn't try…"

"No!" Ellery exclaimed, her cheeks flushing. "Never!" She made eye contact with every person. "I wouldn't do that to you. I wouldn't do that to me."

Weston burst into the room like a tornado tearing through a quiet town. "Then, what in the hell happened?"

Vanessa's eyes flashed daggers. Protecting her daughter from her estranged husband's storm was a full-time job. "Weston, she just woke up. Be gentle."

But Weston ignored her warning as he turned toward his daughter, lying frail and broken in the narrow bed. The tape across her broken nose hid only part of her blackened eyes.

"How in the hell does anybody drive a car that far off the road? Unless…" He stepped to the end of the bed that sat low to the floor, making his towering six-foot-four presence even more bewildering.

"Unless you were on your damn phone." The accusation was direct, and his eyes were unyielding. "That old piece of crap you drive doesn't have Bluetooth. Is that what happened? Were you distracted by your damn phone?"

The stiff neck brace confined Ellery's ability to shake her head. "No," she finally mouthed. "I wasn't."

"Then what the hell happened?" Weston knotted his arms and waited for an answer.

Ellery grimaced as she struggled for air.

"Small breaths, honey." Vanessa laid her hand on Ellery's arm.

"You have a couple of bruised ribs, Elle." Liam's face mimicked her pain as she breathed. "Air's gonna be hard for a while. Besides, you look like you lost a fight with a prizefighter, so nothing's gonna be easy for a week or so."

"Ha-ha," she whispered.

With Vanessa's steady guidance, Ellery gradually relaxed. Her labored gasps slowed and grew shallow.

Liam turned toward his dad. "How about you lay off and let her rest?"

Weston's eyebrows shot up, forming deep lines on his forehead, the muscles in his jaw flexing as he stared at his son. "How about you shut the hell up? I'm talking to Chloe."

"Her name's Elle, Dad." Preston's gaze shifted from his father to Jacqui.

Jacqui stepped close to her father, her fingertips lightly

resting on his arm, a gesture that was both grounding and pleading. "She had it legally changed, and that's what she prefers. So we have to respect her decision."

Weston sighed deeply, the sound heavy with frustration. "What the hell happened last night?"

Ellery's face twisted in panic, and she began gasping again. "I-I swerved to miss a deer."

"Bloody hell! A deer?" A shake of his head, a huff, and a scowl hammered home Weston's anger. "How in the hell do you not know you don't swerve for deer?" He turned one hand on its side and drove it forward. "If you can't miss 'em without a serious swerve, you hit 'em head-on."

Vanessa shot a warning glance. "Weston, stop."

Weston dismissed Vanessa's concern. His eyes drifted toward the machine next to the bed, ignoring the increase in her heart rate. "Of course, with that car of yours, it wouldn't have mattered much. Up here, we drive big vehicles." He raised his hand, fingers curled under until he ticked off each reason. "Winter. Potholes. Collisions. Deer. Had you been driving that Land Rover I bought you, you wouldn't be lyin' in this bed." His expression shifted as he turned toward the door, the volume of his voice increasing. "Instead, you're paying these highway robbers to let you sleep off a couple of black eyes and some bruises."

Preston shot a fiery look at his father. "Leave it alone, Dad. Now is not the time to be riding Elle's ass over something that can't be changed."

Ellery glanced at Liam. He raised a shoulder almost to his ear, his scowl deepening as he glared at his father. "He's not wrong. Not about sleeping it off here, but about the deer *and* driving a big vehicle."

A nurse burst into the room. Her jaw was firmly set in a mask of authority. "Keep the noise down, or you'll all have to leave."

Weston took a step back, coming alongside her. "Believe me, I'd rather be anywhere else than looking at that." He poked his chin at Ellery. With that, he stormed from the room.

Weston's appearance had left a black cloud hanging over all of them. Vanessa pressed her eyes closed and counted to ten. When she opened them, she could feel disappointment stamped all over her face.

"He..." She brushed a tear from Ellery's cheek. "Honey, sometimes your father is..." She hesitated, her face twisting as she tamped down her tangled emotions. "Well, sometimes he's an ass when he gets scared."

Ellery stared at the ceiling, forcing her eyes open to contain the waterfall that threatened to explode. "Then he's been scared since I got here." Vanessa could feel the pain in her grief-coated words.

Preston cocked his head in agreement. "Believe me, it started long before you got here. He comes from a long line of...unhinged individuals, lunatics, nutjobs, wackos..."

"Enough. Your sister doesn't need to hear the entire family history all at once." A soft grin twisted the edges of Vanessa's mouth. "Some things she just needs to find out for herself."

"I think she already knows. His folks were off, but his sister's a piece of work." A smile broke across Preston's face as his eyes connected with Jacqui's. "There're stories about our family that would curl your toes. If you decided to write those stories, you'd never run out of material. Interestingly, Dad's probably one of the more rational ones."

Ellery attempted a smile but instantly moaned. She clenched her teeth and spoke through her lips. "Is it too late to change my mind about being a Chambers?"

Liam chuckled. "Afraid so. You maybe should have done more digging before you decided we'd be a good family."

"Most of you are fine. But there's Baily," Ellery said.

"Let's just say the apple doesn't fall far from the tree." Jacqui flashed her a knowing smile.

Vanessa shook her head in warning. "We don't need to go there. Your dad's not nearly as bad as they're making you believe. Yes, he's opinionated, never considers anyone else's opinions, believes he's always in the right…"

"And everyone else is wrong." Liam dipped his head slightly.

Vanessa fell silent. Suddenly, her shoulders slumped in resignation. "Well, maybe he is that bad."

Laughter rippled through the room. Liam laid his finger to his lips. "Unless we want Nurse Cratchit hauling us out of here by our ears, we need to keep it down."

Preston moved to the end of the bed and lightly ran his shoulder into Jacqui's. "The thing is, Elle, when he loves, he loves hard. He might give us a lot of crap…"

"But he'd do anything for us." It was clear that Jacqui's loyalty was to Team Chambers.

A grin spread across Liam's face as he looked at his mother. "Yeah, like that time Preston got picked up by the cops after prom, and Dad purposely wore his pajamas to the police station to pick him up."

Jacqui held a hand over her mouth to stifle her laughter.

"What?" A crooked smile crossed Vanessa's face. "What happened?"

Preston wiggled his eyebrows at his mother. "Statute of limitations on groundings has run out, right?"

"I don't think so." The lightness of her tone suddenly dissolved as remorse moved in. "I missed so much of your lives. I regret so many choices I made."

"I did this." Ellery touched her mother's knee.

"Oh, honey, no, you didn't. You keep saying that, but it's not true. None of this is your fault. Karma did this. She's the one who took you from us and set the wheels of dysfunction in motion." She brushed Ellery's hair off her forehead.

Ellery closed her eyes. "I'm so tired." The admission had barely escaped before sleep took her.

"You sleep, sweetheart." Vanessa kissed her daughter's forehead, wishing she could have shielded her from the ugly side of Weston and Baily.

The muted beeping of machines was the only break in the

silence that blanketed the small room. Vanessa finally broke the stillness. Rising, she pushed her hair off her shoulders and glanced at Jacqui.

"Can you stay today so the boys can go home and sleep?"

"Of course. But where are you going?"

A dark expression settled on Vanessa's face. "To have it out with your father." With that, she stepped into the bright lights of the nurses' station and walked out of the ICU.

TWENTY-SEVEN

Without knocking, Vanessa opened the door and stepped across the threshold of the main house. The musty scent of stale beer immediately assaulted her senses. She hesitated for a moment before calling out.

"Weston?"

The kitchen was a snapshot of neglect. The toaster, still plugged in, bore numerous fingerprints. A small plate with a half-eaten slice of toast lay neglected on the counter. The sink was a graveyard for several empty beer bottles, a solitary knife, and the remnants of the broken butter dish Vanessa had bought in Italy. It was abundantly clear that Edda had the weekend off.

Vanessa fought the urge to clean up after her estranged husband. Instead, she looked away. She rotated the coffee carousel, selecting a French Vanilla pod. The lingering remnants of Weston's chaos disappeared as the sweet aroma began to weave through the air.

"Weston?" she tried again.

"Out here." The muffled voice came from somewhere outside.

Vanessa carried her coffee to the back screen porch overlooking the pool and the lake.

"Do you want coffee? Oh. So, it's a beer morning." Surprise spread across her face as she settled into a rocking chair and watched him tip his bottle back, swallowing the last of it.

"Third one." Weston pointed to a pair of empties on the floor. He opened the new bottle. "And that's just the start."

"And the ones in the sink?"

Weston's expression darkened. "Don't start. It's been a rough couple of days."

Vanessa settled into the chair a few feet from him, pulling her sweater closed against the morning chill. Boats bobbed on the lake's surface. Since the opening of fishing season, weekends on the lake were like rush hour.

"I suppose you're here to tell me I suck." Resignation was woven into his words. The silence that followed amplified his statement like letters on a billboard. "Well, save it. I already know."

Vanessa's eyes were fixed on the lake. "Good to know." She paused, blowing across her steaming coffee cup before taking a sip.

"Then I don't have to…" Suddenly, she turned toward him, her expression becoming fiery. "Yes, I do. What's wrong with you? How can you treat your daughter with such hatred?" No matter how long she waited, Weston refused to make eye contact.

She leaned forward and snapped her fingers. "Weston? Could you answer me, please? How can you hate our daughter that much? She's done nothing wrong."

He remained silent for a moment longer, his eyes clouding with emotion as he sucked down his beer. Weston pressed his hands to the arms of his chair, abruptly stood, and disappeared into the house. Seconds later, he emerged with another beer.

Bitterness sliced through Vanessa's voice. "Is that for courage, or are you hoping you'll get so sloshed I'll leave? This is not okay."

Without a word, Weston twisted the cap off the bottle and tossed it into an empty flowerpot on the low slate table in the center of the porch.

He lifted the bottle and swiftly gulped down a quarter of its contents as if trying to drown out the question. "Maybe both." He wiped his mouth on his sleeve.

Vanessa glared at him. "We need to talk. So, you need to stop drinking." Each word was deliberate, a command rather than a request. "Because we both know where this is going."

The silence screamed. It was a haunting melody Vanessa had heard many times before. Weston had never been a talker, but alcohol pulled him deeper into himself. Finally, she left the porch and returned with a cup of coffee. She set it on the table in front of him, a silent invitation to reclaim his senses. Then, she wrestled the bottle from his hand.

"Hey!" Weston hollered, trying to snatch it from her hand.

"Don't," she warned. "I'm dead serious. I need to know what's going on with you. Right now, you're treating Elle no better than that awful Karma woman did. And that's the last thing our daughter needs."

Weston stared out at the rippling water for a long time. With a resigned huff, he picked up the coffee cup and honored his wife's demand.

Silence stretched between them. Vanessa felt the unspoken tension that filled the air. "I'm not going anywhere. I'll stay until you talk to me. However long that takes."

After what felt like an eternity, Weston turned to face her, his eyes reflecting a vulnerability she hadn't seen in a long time. They glistened as he explained his pain. "She just shows up out of the blue. I thought she was dead."

Vanessa pulled her neck back, eyes narrowing as she tried to gauge Weston's reaction. "What made you think she was dead?"

Weston's face drained of color. "W-well," he stammered, his hands trembling. "Well, why wouldn't I? Someone took her, and I went to the worst-case scenario. That's what I do."

"But why would you go there—to death? Most children who disappear are found at some point in their life. Elle just happened to return later than most."

"Of course, you'd throw out statistics. The likelihood... Chances are... Most children..." Weston inhaled deeply and stared at Vanessa. "That's just like you. You saw it all: beginning, middle, and end. Our daughter was taken, she had a life, and then she came back. End of story." A long pause filled the space between them. He ran a hand through his hair, eyes darting to the ground. "I didn't see it that way. In my head, I figured she was abused, and whoever had her had killed her."

"Well, I never gave up hope. I knew she was alive. As her mother, I would have known if she were dead." She scanned the lake, seeing nothing but the past. "You're right, though. Elle was abused horribly." Her eyes met Weston's, her daughter's pain reflected on her face. "And that kills me because I was the one who let that woman into her life. But by some miracle, she came back to us. For that, we have to be grateful."

He set his nearly empty cup on the table in front of him. "I guess. But how damaged is she? How do we know she won't snap at some time? Destroy us more than we already are?"

Vanessa pushed his coffee cup to the side and sat on the table, facing him, her heart filled with conviction. "We've all been damaged by what happened. Her kidnapping broke us. But we're her family. We'll help her no matter how long it takes or what we need to do to get her through this—the same way we're trying to help Baily deal with life." Weston's expression softened to a hesitant nod of agreement.

She locked eyes with him. "Now that she's back, I can barely take my eyes off her. So, why aren't you overjoyed to have our family back together again? Why are you holding back?"

Weston stared at the dark beams of the porch, his face crumbling in frustration. "Why?" he snapped, climbing out of the chair and moving to the far side of the porch. Vanessa remained still as she watched him wrestle with the turmoil of his emotions.

Without warning, Weston spun around. He locked his fingers behind his head. "Because who's to say she won't leave again?"

Vanessa got up and joined him. "The way you've been acting, if I were Elle, I'd leave."

"That's not fair. In the eight days we had Chloe, I fell head over heels in love with that little girl. But then she was gone."

The pain of her absence echoed across the porch.

He ran the tip of his tennis shoe along the edge of the rug before looking up at Vanessa. "Then, it was like she fell from the sky. She was just suddenly here." He choked back a sob. "Not as the baby I knew, but as a grown woman, older than we were when she was born."

"You're right. We lost out on almost thirty-seven years, but…" Vanessa's voice trembled, "she came back. Do you really want to miss out on another moment? Shouldn't we be thrilled to have all five of our children back together again? Shouldn't that be enough?"

"No!" Weston's voice was charged with intensity. He dropped heavily into a different chair and wound his fingers through the bottom fringes of the hair on the back of his neck as he pressed his elbows to his knees. "It's not. I've been waiting for the other shoe to drop."

"What?" Vanessa asked. "I don't know what you mean."

Anger flashed in Weston's eyes. "Don't you get it? We had her, and then that woman took her. She reappeared but then left when things didn't go her way. Do you honestly believe she's committed to our family? Or will she run away again when things go south?"

Anger nearly knocked Vanessa to the ground. Threads of frustration knotted in her throat as she fought the desire to strangle her ex. She crossed her arms and pulled them against her ribcage to keep from striking him. "That's on you and Baily. You haven't exactly been welcoming." The words were a challenge—to do better—to be better—but Vanessa wasn't sure Weston was capable. "Elle would have been thrilled to be a part of this family from the get-go had both of you not done everything in your power to make her feel like she didn't belong." She stretched her neck upward. "I've never been so angry or embarrassed by anything in my entire life."

Weston shifted uncomfortably. "Okay. I get it. I've been awful to her, but I'm scared. Her return has sent me reeling, and I can't see straight. Sometimes I can't breathe."

"What are you afraid of?"

"Elle came back, and not even a week later, she had an accident that could have... We could have lost her again. Did you ever consider that?"

Vanessa's stomach clenched as she saw the worry on Weston's face. "Of course, I thought about that. I'm sure every one of us did. But I hear you say that you're afraid to love her because she might disappear again. Am I right?" Weston's nod was frail, almost as if he couldn't admit it to himself. "You have to understand that our kids could fall off the face of the earth at any point—with no warning. No one's guaranteed to live to a hundred. Just like we can't be certain we'll die before they do. Life is what it is. The days go fast, and the years go faster. We have no control over how many days we have. We just have to trust." Vanessa squeezed his hand.

"Right, like you trusted when Chloe disappeared?" His eyes shifted away from her. "If you honestly believed she'd come back, you wouldn't have left us to search for her."

Vanessa shoved his hand away and bit her cheeks to avoid saying the wrong thing. "I left because you made it very clear how much you hated me. You couldn't forgive or forget that our daughter disappeared under my watch. Did I screw up? Hell, yes! I was exhausted from being up all night, every night, with two babies. You slept through those nights, remember? Not once did you offer to watch the girls so I could sleep for an hour or two." Sadness welled inside Vanessa as she let that message sink in. "Then, after Chloe was taken, you hired a full-time nanny because you no longer trusted me. And you hired Edda to cook, clean, and take care of the other kids."

"I..." Weston stared, but Vanessa stopped him with a glare.

"I felt like such a failure. I'd gone from taking care of two babies and three others under seven to none. I wasn't just grieving the loss of Chloe, I was devastated over losing Baily and the rest of the kids too. You actually told them not to talk to me anymore because I needed to be 'in time out.' You told them I was a bad mom. Do you remember that?" Weston's shoulders slumped forward. "So, because you couldn't stand by my side through our grief, I didn't feel like I had a home, or a marriage, or a family. You'd taken them all from me. The only way I could bring our family back together was to find Chloe. To fix what I screwed up." She focused on the lake. The water was like glass, a reflection of the past. "*You* pushed me away just like you're doing to Elle."

Weston leaned forward, pressing the palms of his hands together as if in prayer. "You're right. I wish I could take it all back." His eyes met hers. "But I can't. You have to know the way I treated you kills me."

"Since I came home, you've never apologized to me—not once. This is the first time I've heard anything remotely apologetic. So, thank you for that." Vanessa sighed. "If you want to fix this, you have to stop treating your daughter like an outsider too. Don't make the same mistake twice."

He nervously folded and unfolded his hands. "Nessa, it's taken me thirty-seven years to deal with losing her and to forgive you. I've finally gotten there. Before our daughter showed up, we were finally in a good place—you, me, and the kids. Even Baily'd come around." His head moved back and forth, almost in slow motion. "But since she's come home, things have fallen apart again."

"That's on you. It didn't have to be that way."

Resting his arms on his knees, Weston folded his hands and stared at the floor. "I suppose you're right. But the thing is, I can't go through any of that again. I can't lose her a second time. It would kill me, and it would destroy the family."

He cupped his hands in front of him. "I feel like I'm holding this fragile butterfly, and if I move just wrong, it'll fly away. So, I don't want to hold her, or get close to her, or startle her."

"Don't you think I feel the same way?" Seconds passed without an answer. "Elle's not as fragile as we think. She survived a woman who did everything she could to break her, and she came out the other side stronger than ever. Our daughter's a survivor." A gentle grin crossed her face. "She took on a tree and won.”

Weston’s brows slanted inward. “You know what I mean.”

“I do.” Vanessa’s smile disappeared. “But you haven’t exactly been gentle with her. Honestly, you’ve been a little ‘get off my lawn’ crabby old man around her.” Vanessa lifted his chin with her fingers. “Not so unlike your father.”

His pain was visible in how he rested his arms across his knees and locked his fingers together. “If you don’t get attached, it doesn’t hurt so much when the butterfly flies away.”

“That’s true, but, Weston, if you don’t enjoy the butterfly when it’s near you, you’re missing out on everything good.”

Vanessa’s gaze drifted toward the lake. “I understand how you feel. I really do.” She blinked several times before turning to face him. “You struggle with forgiving her for leaving, but there’s nothing to forgive. She didn’t do any of this. You and I are very different in that respect. I spent years searching for her.” Vanessa clasped her hands in front of her. “And now that she’s back, I’m holding on with everything in me. I refuse to miss out on one second with her.”

Suddenly, the nagging feeling that had haunted Vanessa the night before resurfaced. She locked eyes with Weston, her back stiffening as she moved toward him.

“It was you. Wasn’t it?” She turned a hand over in question, pointing a finger at him.

“What are you talking about?” Confusion clouded his eyes.

“You were at the hospital last night before I went in to see Elle.”

The accusation hung between them as she watched Weston slump in his chair. “Yeah.” The word escaped like a reluctant confession. “And I was with the doctor in her room this morning.”

“Why didn’t you just tell us you were there?” Vanessa tried to decipher the storm brewing in her husband.

“I didn’t want any of you to know I was getting attached.” His face betrayed the facade of strength he usually wore like armor.

"I didn't even want to admit it to myself. If Elle had died, I had to be the strong one." His confession revealed the pressure he had placed on himself all those years. "Dad pounded into me that I was the cornerstone of the family—the one who had to hold everyone else together when things fell apart." His long pause suffocated Vanessa. "Since our daughter came back, I had to do it again. But it wasn't as easy this time. I was scared, and that fear turned into anger. And I took it out on her and on Liam since she trusted him the most."

His admission shattered Vanessa as it screamed of the burdens he had not admitted to anyone until now. She finally understood the conflict he'd faced all these years. A rock wasn't supposed to crack.

"Your father was wrong, Weston. Marriage burdens aren't meant to be carried alone. That's why you have a partner. The problem was, once we lost Chloe, you wouldn't let me be responsible for my share of anything."

"I tried to protect you, but I only pushed you away." His leg bounced nervously. "My dad repeatedly told me I wasn't doing enough. I felt like such a loser."

Vanessa suddenly knelt and wrapped her arms around him. As time ticked away, each second brought them closer.

"I didn't need your protection, Weston. I needed your love—your support."

Finally, Vanessa released him and perched herself on the edge of the low table. "I'm so sorry I put you in that position. My heart breaks, not just because I live with the nightmare of losing Chloe, but because I missed out on all those years with you and the kids."

She gently cupped his cheek. "Do you ever wonder why we never got divorced? All these years, we've been separated, but we never took the final step to make it official. Why do you think that is?"

Weston leaned forward, removed her hand from his face, and cradled her hands in his. The warmth of his grip sent a rush of memories flooding back. "I didn't want a divorce. I've never stopped loving you."

Vanessa's heart skipped a beat. The same flutter she felt when they first met at Snuffy's Drive-In reignited the fire in her. Honestly, it never fully extinguished. She searched his eyes, seeking the truth behind his words. Slowly, she leaned in and pressed her lips to his.

"And I've never stopped loving you. But you've always known that. We finally have our family back together. So, let's make the most of it. There are no guarantees it'll stay this way. Any one of us could be gone tomorrow."

"And that's the problem. I oversee land development and the building of massive structures. Everything has to happen perfectly, or the building could collapse. I don't deal well with unknowns."

"Well, I hate to tell you, but life's one big, messy unknown. Look at everything that's happened to us."

"You know we need to make a statement about Chl..." Weston stared at the rug and balled his hands into fists. "Elle's return. When I got home, a reporter was outside peeking into the windows." Uncertainty was written on his face. "We have to get this over with so we can move on with our lives."

Vanessa slid backward. "I got a call on the way back from Brainerd. They're moving Elle out of the ICU today. Can we at least wait until she's home before we make any statements?"

"I don't think we should. Before the gossip goes off the rails, we need to say something. I'll have Lana set something up for tomorrow." He held a hand in front of him. "If you're okay with that."

At that moment, their eyes locked, and an unspoken connection ignited between them. "I am." Vanessa watched the years fade away. For the first time in almost four decades, she knew they could confront whatever lay ahead as long as they did it together.

TWENTY-EIGHT

The stately clock tower, built in 1891, loomed over the courthouse. Its hands pointed to noon, marking a historic moment for the Chambers family. They gathered on the steps, a united front, prepared to share the news that had already created a buzz around Hunters Cove and the state of Minnesota.

The crowd before them swelled. With their cameras poised and notepads in hand, journalists and newspaper crews were joined by townspeople who had heard rumblings but needed to know the details.

Officers stood nearby, vigilant of the chaos that could erupt.

Baily had distanced herself from the family. Vanessa knew she was skeptical of their acceptance of Ellery. Even for the day, she couldn't find it in her to stand with her siblings on the courthouse steps. Weston, who had always had her back, had done a sudden one-eighty after their previous discussion. Vanessa knew she would be blamed for that turn. Baily would accuse her of threatening, warning, or promising Weston something to create his sudden change of heart. When they told her about the press conference, Baily did not hold back. She let her mother have it with both barrels, claiming she was manipulative and disgusting. But nothing could be further from the truth.

Vanessa could only focus on one problem at a time. When this died down, she would deal with Baily, but for now, Ellery was her primary concern. The doctor had cautioned them that too many people could lead to overwhelming physical and emotional stress. He seemed equally concerned about reporters discovering her location, stating it would complicate her healing.

For the first time since the accident, Vanessa was relieved that Ellery was thirty minutes away from the media circus that was about to ensue. Camera flashes, microphones shoved in their faces, and a barrage of questions would be overwhelming for the family, who was used to dealing with the media; for Ellery, who had spent her entire life hiding in the shadows, it would be incredibly daunting.

Weston and Vanessa stood shoulder to shoulder in a display of solidarity. Behind them, Jacqui, Preston, and Liam formed a tight cluster of support. The crowd's murmurs created a low hum that faded as Chief Jansen approached the makeshift podium.

Jansen adjusted the microphone attached to the portable speakers. "Thank you for being here today." He glanced to his left and gestured toward the family. "I spent yesterday afternoon with the Chambers family. While this is a truly unbelievable story—a kidnapped daughter returns after thirty-seven years— we ask that you respect the family's privacy. Give them time to acclimate to their new normal." The chief pressed his hands on the edge of the makeshift podium and let his words soak in.

"After the family speaks, there will be time for questions, but they will be limited." He scanned the sea of faces. "At this time, I'll turn the mic over to the family."

Weston and Vanessa stepped forward. The crowd hung on every word as they told the heartrending tale of their daughter's kidnapping. Vanessa stood tall as she recounted her relentless search for Chloe, now known as Elle Gray.

They shared how Elle's past as their kidnapped daughter came to light—a revelation conveyed to her by a friend who stumbled upon folders revealing her identity, and how that information sent Elle in search of the family she had lost. Their message was brief and pointed but powerful.

Reporters jostled for a chance to ask their questions. A deep voice cut through the crowd. "Bruce Duller, WCCO. Who took your daughter? And have they been arrested?"

Weston glanced in the direction of the voice. "She was kidnapped by a woman who has since passed away." He pointed to a waving hand on the other side of the crowd.

"Where's your daughter been all these years? Was she raised in Minnesota or taken out of state?" Marlene Allery from the *Hunters Cove Record* tapped a small notepad with her pen.

Vanessa stepped closer to the mic. She squared her shoulders and smiled at the woman she had known since returning to Hunters Cove. "She wasn't raised here. To protect her privacy, that is all we will share about her location." Her gaze remained firm, a protective mother shielding her daughter from the probing eyes of the town.

Hands waved, and reporters yelled to be recognized as the crowd moved forward. Vanessa felt her resolve to be strong waver as she faced a stream of questions.

A reporter shouted, "Ray Parisian, KBJR. What do you know about your daughter's life growing up with this woman?"

Vanessa felt heat rush to her face. A familiar ache began behind her eyes, threatening to cascade into tears, but she held her ground.

"We know very little. We'll let our daughter tell her story when she's ready."

"Mr. Chambers, where is your daughter? Why isn't she here?" Parisian asked.

Vanessa felt her face flush. It was the question the team had rehearsed tirelessly. They had formulated every possible response and finally settled on one.

"To protect Elle's privacy, we've chosen to keep her out of the spotlight for now."

"Where's your other daughter? The twin, Baily?" someone yelled from the crowd.

The mention of Baily struck Vanessa like a physical blow. She had counted on her to show unwavering support today, to stand beside them. Yet, as the moments ticked by, her daughter's absence left a hole that could not be filled.

"She's, ah…" Vanessa stammered, her voice faltering as she scanned the crowd. Panic erupted when she caught sight of a figure obscured by a floppy, wide-brimmed hat and dark sunglasses. A long trench coat hung nearly to the ground as the woman stood at the edge of the assembly. Anger coursed through her. Of course, Baily would lurk in the shadows, drawn to the unfolding drama like a moth to a flame. "She's with her sister." Vanessa finally managed to blurt, staring at the woman she believed to be Baily, her eyes warning her to keep her mouth shut. Still, she prepared for the expected rebuttal, but to her surprise, there was none.

Another flurry of questions erupted from the crowd. Voices overlapped in an urgent need to gather information for their articles. The family answered the first onslaught of inquiries but soon looked to Chief Jansen to shut it down. His voice boomed through the crowd, calling an end to the conference. Once again, he warned them to stay off private property and respect the family's privacy. Jansen and his lead deputy guided the family toward their vehicles, leaving the rest of the officers to hold the press at bay until the family drove away.

Thirty minutes later, Vanessa and Weston arrived in Brainerd at St. Joseph's Medical Center in separate vehicles. The parking lot was filled with onlookers. Vanessa parked, and Weston abandoned his car close to hers on the grass. The closer they got to the entrance, the more the crowd closed in.

Police officers formed a protective barrier as photographers and journalists strained to capture something. Weston grabbed Vanessa's hand and shouldered his way through the crowd.

Once inside, Vanessa sighed in relief, grateful for the reprieve from the suffocating press of bodies and voices. She felt her cheeks burn when the doors closed behind them, sealing off the chaos.

"How in the hell did they find out she was here?" Weston waved his hand through the air.

Vanessa rummaged through her purse for a tissue. "Maybe someone from the hospital. I'm honestly surprised it didn't get out earlier."

Weston signed their names on the visitors' log and turned toward the elevator, frustration evident in his stiff spine. "Or maybe it came from our daughter."

"Elle would rather die than deal with this mess. She's too much of an introvert."

"No. The other one." Weston guided her into the elevator after a handful of people exited.

Vanessa shook her head. "Baily would never do that." But even as the words left her mouth, they felt hollow.

"I wouldn't be so sure." Weston's thoughts echoed hers.

The morning sun streamed through the open blinds of Ellery's room on the second floor. Joy filled the air, punctuated by the boisterous laughter of Vanessa's father, Will, who had spent years as the Minnetonka police chief. His instinct to stay alert to the slightest sound or movement around him showed when Vanessa and Weston entered the room, his eyes immediately drawn to them.

Elle pressed her hand against her bruised ribs. "Please, don't make me laugh. It hurts too much." But the giggling did not stop.

"Hey, you two." Vanessa leaned down to peck her father's cheek. "Thanks for being here, Dad." Her eyes shifted to her daughter. "How are you feeling, sweetheart?"

"I can finally smile without feeling like my eyeballs will pop out of the socket."

"Well, that's an improvement." Vanessa settled into the chair next to her father.

Ellery shot a grin at Will. "Pops doesn't seem to care that it still hurts to laugh."

"It doesn't hurt *me*." Will winked at her.

Vanessa glanced over her shoulder at Weston. He stared out the second-floor window before closing the blinds. "The crowd's growing."

"Come and join us." Vanessa nodded to the chair on the other side of the bed. "There's not much we can do about what's going on out there."

Ellery's gaze fixed on her mother, her eyes narrowing in confusion, nearly hiding the signature Chambers silver-blue hue. "It's alright, honey." Vanessa squeezed her daughter's hand. Her eyes flashed toward Weston. "There's been a lot of air-clearing in the last twenty-four hours. Your dad has some things he needs to share with you."

Will stood. "Well, that's my cue. Sit here, Weston. I'm going to go down to the lobby to meet your mother," he told Vanessa. His eyes sparked with mischief as he smiled at his granddaughter, "Your Nan hates to be kept waiting."

A smirk crossed Vanessa's face. "Tell her how you learned Mom waits for no one, Dad."

"I can't." Will chuckled. "It'll hurt Elle's ribs."

"Now I have to know. Please?"

Will's shoulders slumped. "Fine. But don't say I didn't warn you." He sank back into his chair and made a face at Vanessa. "It was our first date, and I wanted to do something special that Della Mae wouldn't forget. So, I thought—*flowers*." A humorous audible sigh escaped him. "But of course, the florist was closed by the time the romance thought hit me upside the head."

Vanessa bit the inside of her cheeks to keep from howling, but a laugh unexpectedly escaped as she glanced at Ellery.

"About a mile from her house, I passed what I would call a mansion." Will's eyes glazed over as if he were trapped in that moment. Finally, he swiped his arm through the air. "Their front yard was filled with flowers as far as you could see. In the front corner, near the street, was a rose bed with almost every color you could imagine. And near that were the biggest lilies I'd ever seen. Problem solved." Pops grinned.

"You were going to give her stolen flowers?" Ellery giggled. "And you called yourself a cop?"

The wrinkles around Will's eyes deepened. "Not then, I wasn't. I was just a stupid young man looking for love."

"So, that made it okay?"

Will threw his hands out to his sides. "Do you want to hear the story or not?" Ellery nodded, pressing her lips closed and laying the tip of her finger against them.

"Anyway, I parked in an alley about a block from the house and snuck into their yard. When I got to the corner of the house, I dropped to my stomach and belly-crawled to the garden. I pulled out my pocketknife." He brandished the same small knife he had used in the story. "And cut a dozen roses and three huge white lilies."

Ellery watched Weston, doubled over in laughter, snorts spilling out like bubbles from a child's wand. "I don't get it."

"Oh, you will, honey." Vanessa covered her mouth to suppress a laugh. "Go ahead, Dad. Bring it home."

Will's lips vibrated as he released a stream of air through them. "So, there I was, sliding backward out of the garden." His chin dropped, and he shook his head once as if he didn't believe it himself. "At that moment, the owners decided to let their mastiff out." His eyebrows humorously hitched up as he made a face at Ellery. "That dog must have weighed three hundred pounds."

Weston erupted into gasps of laughter. Ellery couldn't help but smile at his infectious energy.

Pops's eyes sparkled. "Instead of running, I froze. I lay there, my face pressed into what smelled like fresh manure, praying the dog wouldn't see me." A chuckle floated in the air. "But that damn dog wandered right up to me and plopped down on my back."

Shocked by that image, Ellery's mouth formed a silent O. "I tried to wrestle that dog off of me for nearly five minutes, but he was double my size, and I was battling the smell of cow shit." He glanced at Vanessa, who was laughing so hard, she had tears streaming down her face.

"Then..." His pause was dramatic. He opened his mouth several times as his face changed from one emotion to the next. "The owner came out, snatched the bouquet from my hand, and called the dog off me. They disappeared into the house without a word—just like it happened every day." He held his palm out and stared at it. "I spent the next five minutes plucking rose thorns from my hand."

Ellery's cheeks flushed as she finally managed to squeeze out a question between gasps of laughter. "H-how late w-were you?"

"Only half an hour," Will said with mock seriousness.

The remnants of Vanessa's laughter drifted away. She smiled at Ellery. "And…" Her eyes twinkled with mischief as she prompted her father to share the rest of the story.

A humorous expression played on Will's face that made Ellery giggle harder. "That heartless hussy slammed the door in my face."

Just then, a woman dressed in a floral blazer and navy slacks entered the hospital room with a confident stride, a striking figure reminiscent of Vanessa—but with a few more storylines on her face. She was followed closely by Preston, who looked like a puppy trailing its master.

"Dang tootin' I did! I'm a lady," she announced, her southern drawl wrapping around the words. "No man makes a lady wait. Besides, he smelled like he was wearing pasture-fresh cologne. I'd rather have licked a rusty nail than go anywhere with him."

Weston swiped a hand across his eyes and met his mother-in-law with a warm embrace. "Long time no see, Della Mae."

She wagged a finger at him. "The road goes both ways, sonny."

Della Mae put her arm around Preston. "Now, here's a boy who knows how to treat a lady."

"I made sure I got to the airport early." Preston held a thumb up. "I'd never be late to pick up Nan. I know the rules."

Della Mae brushed her fingers across her grandson's cheek before pointedly glancing from Will to Weston and back. "Stop kissin' my butt, boy. My will's already carved in stone," she declared, playfully slapping his cheek twice. "You ain't getting a penny more."

Preston made a comical, exaggerated face at Ellery over his Nan's shoulder.

The woman approached the bed with a warm smile. "And this must be my pretty as a peach granddaughter." She leaned closer to Ellery. "Well, once those black eyes and that swollen nose heal," she wagged her head back and forth, "I'm sure you'll look lovely."

Vanessa nearly floated around the bed and hugged her mother.

"Nice to meet you, Mrs. Cole." Ellery's voice was edged with nervousness.

"Call me Nan, honey. All my grandkids do."

Ellery's smile brightened. "Nice to meet you, Nan."

"Same here, darlin'." Nan's voice was thick with emotion as her eyes glistened with droplets of gratitude. "I've prayed for this day so many times over the years. God is good!" she declared, raising a hand in the air. "I knew someday we'd find you again." She fixed her eyes on her estranged husband. "Even without Barney Fife's help." She snickered. "I'm just sorry it took so long. But ya know, your grandpa couldn't find his shoes if they were the only things in the closet."

Will draped an arm around his estranged wife's shoulder and smiled. "Come on, Della Mae. The kids need some time with their girl."

"For cryin' out loud! I just got…" Her mouth widened in exasperation. Will pressed a hand over it to silence her.

"I'll go with you and Pops." Preston came up alongside her and hooked his arm through hers. "The cafeteria food's not half bad."

Della Mae blankly stared at her grandson. "You're so full of crap, your eyes are turnin' brown, boy." She shook off her escorts with a dramatic flair, her spirit as fiery as ever as she headed toward the door. "Jesus might have turned water into wine, but there's no way in hell any amount of praying's gonna turn a hunk of what passes for hospital ground beef into a steak." And with that, she swept out of the room, a whirlwind of energy followed by her entourage.

The quiet settled in, leaving Vanessa, Weston, and Ellery alone for the first time.

PART THREE

Ellery Gray

TWENTY-NINE

Two days later, Ellery sat in a wheelchair outside a door marked *"Deliveries Only."* The door was tucked into an alcove, sheltering it from prying eyes. Still, she nervously drummed her fingers against the armrest, expecting a rogue reporter to appear.

Vanessa stood beside her, a nearly empty overnight bag slung over her shoulder. Inside had been a stylish workout outfit to wear home. The tag showed a price that made Ellery's mouth drop open. She had not spent that much on her entire closet full of clothes.

Suddenly, Vanessa's Lexus glided into view. Weston eased the vehicle into the recess of the brick building. The nurse locked the wheels on Ellery's chair. With practiced ease, she transitioned her into the back seat. Behind the tinted windows, she finally felt like she could take her first real breath since the world discovered she was Chloe Chambers.

Weston deliberately passed in front of the hospital, a sly grin spreading. "Look at the commotion you caused," he teased, locking eyes with Ellery in the rearview mirror. "They're so busy watching the front door that we could have parachuted out your window, and they wouldn't have noticed."

Her mouth dropped open as she took in the scene outside. Hordes of reporters and camera crews pressed together as they waited for word of her release. "I knew they were out there, but I had no idea there were that many." An almost electric current coursed through her as she thought of facing that spotlight.

Weston cocked an eyebrow, turning his gaze briefly to Vanessa. "Somehow, they knew you were going home today. As Nan would say, small-town gossip travels faster than green grass through a goose." He flipped on his blinker. "If one person knows, everybody else knows within the hour."

"The only thing that matters is that our daughter is coming home."

Ellery suddenly felt the toll of the accident and the four days in the hospital had taken on her. She dropped her head against the headrest and closed her eyes. A wave of exhaustion crashed over her. It was not just fatigue but a weariness that seeped deep into her bones. Her whole body felt fragile, as if her muscles had shriveled, leaving her without the strength to lift even a finger. It was an exhaustion that went beyond the accident. It was from a lifetime steeped in fatigue.

"We have a surprise for you." Vanessa peeked into the back seat.

"That's nice," Ellery murmured, keeping her eyes closed. "I can't wait to get back to Liam's and fall into bed."

"That's part of the surprise. You aren't going back to Liam's."

Ellery's eyes shot open. "What?"

"You're moving back into the main house." Weston smiled at her in the rearview mirror.

The unexpected twist sent a ripple of emotions crashing through Ellery. "I already tried that. It didn't go well."

"Things are different now, honey." Vanessa rested her hand on Weston's shoulder. "You and your dad have worked things out. You understand why he was so... Well, you understand each other better now."

Ellery ran her fingers down her light blue cast. A frown crept onto her face. "Yes, but I don't think Edda wants me there."

"I'm sure you already figured this out, but Edda has the personality of a porcupine. And she's always been that way. It's not just you." Weston picked up speed.

Shifting lanes to pass a white van cruising the speed limit, he glanced at the side. A sigh of frustration escaped. He hooked a thumb toward the television production van heading south on

Highway 371, its colorful branding unmistakable. "I hope like hell they're heading back to the cities and not to our house."

Ellery sank deeper into her seat, feeling the headrest cradle her as Weston pressed the accelerator, the engine's pitch rising.

"The last thing we need is to have a bunch of reporters snooping around before you're ready to face the world."

Ellery sank deeper into her seat. "I know I have to talk to them at some point, but I'd prefer to wait until I don't look like I lost the fight with the tree." She stared out the window. The vegetation blurred together into a solid wall of green. Suddenly, she felt disoriented. Was it the speed of the car or her exhaustion playing tricks on her?

"You don't have to do anything until you're ready. But you should consider whether you're ready to admit to being author Ellery Gray. You know we'll keep your secret if that's what you want. But you need to know that people aren't going to stop digging until they know the truth. Your return is only the beginning, I'm afraid," Vanessa said.

The thought of admitting the truth to the world swirled around Ellery like a tornado. She felt the storm swell. "One thing at a time, if that's okay?"

"Of course. You rest now."

The sunlight flickered through Ellery's closed eyelids. Golds and soft shadows passed before her. Even with the calming warmth against her face, her mind was a cyclone of thoughts, each vying for attention in her ultra-introverted life.

The decision to reveal the truth about her identity as author Ellery Gray loomed over her. Readers would eventually realize that her past was a memoir, not a fictional story. It would throw her into the spotlight, pulling her into the light. She felt nauseous at the thought. If just thinking about it caused that reaction, how could she ever let anyone else into her world?

She had lived in the shadows from the minute Karma took her. Never attending school and digging through dumpsters under the cover of night had been her life for her first eighteen years. And caring for Millie and Gus had kept her out of the public's eye for another eighteen. Being a Chambers, especially the child who had been kidnapped and suddenly reappeared, was a beacon to the world that screamed *Look at me!* If she added that she was author Ellery Gray, she might as well be standing naked in the middle of the town square. Every piece of her life would be exposed—including the fire she may or may not have set.

As she wrestled with the burden of her public persona and the secrets she had kept buried, Ellery knew the courage it would take to navigate her new reality. A delicate balance between vulnerability and fierce self-preservation had kept her safe all this time. She was unsure she was ready to let that slip through her fingers.

The driveway at the main house was nearly deserted when her father eased into the garage and cut the engine. The silence was replaced by the low whirr of the garage door motor as it shut out the outside world. Ellery felt a wave of relief. All she wanted was a long nap and a few hours of uninterrupted solitude.

She gingerly stepped down on her right foot, feeling lingering discomfort rather than sharp pain. Although the swelling had receded, the discoloration reminded her that her ankle was not one hundred percent yet. Weston grabbed her bag and followed her closely, not quite holding on to her arm but ready to catch her if she needed him.

Edda swung open the door between the house and the garage. "I took care of the room like you asked," she told Vanessa, her words gentler than Ellery remembered. Then she turned her focus to Ellery. "I...I, ah..." She folded her hands and cast her eyes to the floor. "I, ah, I..." she stammered again. Finally, in a burst of exasperation, she blurted, "I have a big mouth."

Ellery tried not to grin as she followed her mother into the house. "It's okay, Edda. You didn't know."

Edda shot a scowl in Weston's direction. Her voice rose in indignation as she planted her fists on her hips. "That's right. I didn't know. I've worked here for over forty years. You'd think I could be trusted with family secrets. But noooo." Her voice was filled with mild outrage. Seconds after she disappeared, the slamming of drawers and cupboards echoed from the kitchen.

Vanessa smiled. "Noooo," she mimicked. She leaned closer to Ellery and Weston. "At least she admitted she has a big mouth."

Ellery stifled a laugh, grateful to share such a loving moment with her parents.

Weston led the way down the hallway, past walls of family photos, moments frozen in time. She and her mother followed. Ellery stopped at the short hallway leading to the room she had used prior. "Wait? Where are you going?"

Weston halted, turning toward her with an apologetic look. "When you were here before, we…" His voice trailed off as he cast a sideways glance at Vanessa. "*I* insisted we put you in the guest room." He glanced up the stairs. "But you have your own room up there, just like everyone else."

Ellery's mind whirled with a tumult of unfamiliar emotions. The feeling was overwhelming. Growing up, she had never had anything to call her own. Yet, fifteen hundred miles away, her family had kept a room just for her.

Pressure built in Ellery's eyes as she limped up the stairs in front of her parents. When she reached the landing, she found herself in a long, dimly lit hallway. The walls were lined with doors, each adorned with name placards.

Vanessa gestured to the far end of the corridor. "There's another guest room and a private bath on that end." She turned and pointed toward the door behind the stairs. "That's the game room. It was the *playroom* until Jacqui decided she was too old for such nonsense. Now, it's more of a media room with a wide-screen TV and a dozen recliners. It's the perfect spot for family movie nights."

"There are some old gaming consoles in there too. Preston and Liam, well, and the grandkids, play them occasionally. But just so you know, you take your life in your hands if you step between them and the TV." Weston raised an eyebrow.

Vanessa turned right and stopped before a door with a placard stating *Elle*. Confusion crossed Ellery's face. "We changed the name yesterday." She ran her finger across the sign. "There's something else you should know. All the rooms have been updated except this one."

"Vanessa couldn't stand to change anything about it." Weston touched the nameplate. "We kept the old one, just in case... Never mind. Anyway, your room looks exactly like your room in Minnetonka before you were..." He dropped the words like a hot potato. "I can't seem to keep my foot out of my mouth today."

Ellery wrapped her good arm around him. "It's okay. We'll figure it out."

"When you're ready, we'll remodel. There's a queen-sized bed in there, so you'll have a place to sleep." A soft memory passed between Weston and Vanessa. "Your mom never wanted you kids to disturb me, so she always slept in one of the bedrooms rather than risking waking me up. I don't think that bed's ever been slept in."

Ellery felt her heart swell. If she waited a second longer, it would burst. "Can we open the door already?" Her hands trembled with excitement.

"Of course," Vanessa replied, pressing down on the lever and pushing the door open with a soft creak.

Cautiously, Ellery stepped inside, fearful of disturbing the past. Weston and Vanessa lingered in the doorway.

Her gaze immediately landed on the white crib draped in a lacy pink canopy. She brushed her fingers across the surface before picking up a soft, plush teddy bear.

"That was a gift from Nan and Pops." Vanessa stepped into the room. Ellery hugged it before returning it to the crib.

"I never had a stuffed animal," she said to herself.

"I'm sorry, honey."

A pink, white, and mint green gingham-check quilt hung on the side of the crib. Ellery bent down and pressed her cheek against it.

"That's one of the two quilts your Grandma Chambers made for you."

"Did I use..."

"All eight days." Ellery could see the memory in her mother's eyes. "I'm sure it smells dusty."

With a silent nod, Ellery continued around the room. The changing table, a bookshelf loaded with baby books, and a mint green upholstered rocker lined one side of the room.

"I can't believe you decorated a room for me even though I wasn't here." Ellery felt the love of every carefully chosen element.

"Your mom always knew you'd come home. I should have trusted her." Weston leaned against the doorframe and watched.

"This is just so different than how I grew up. Our entire apartment could have fit in this room."

Vanessa moved near Ellery and soothingly rubbed a hand on her back. "It breaks my heart that you missed out on so much."

Fueled by everything Ellery had lost, anger suddenly surged within her. Her muscles tensed. Yet, amid the turmoil, a surprising warmth spread through her. Changing the past was impossible, and being angry about it would only cause more heartache. Ellery stared out the window into the past. Would she have become the compassionate person she was now had Karma not altered the course of her life? Would she still possess the kind heart and appreciation for the simplest joys life offered? Or would she have mirrored her sister's bitterness, living in a world painted with a shade of anger? The answer haunted her like a forgotten melody. But she understood that experiencing both worlds made her appreciate life more than the rest of her siblings.

"Thank you for this," she murmured into her mother's shoulder. "It's the best surprise I've ever gotten."

"This isn't your surprise, Elle." Weston grinned. "That's arriving later." He glanced at his watch. "But if I were you, I'd sneak in a nap. I think you're gonna need it."

His words left Ellery both curious and excited.

"Edda will bring lunch in an hour or so. The bathroom's between here and the game room." Vanessa cupped her daughter's cheek. Her eyes glimmered with love as she pulled her close. "Welcome home, honey."

When she let go, Weston, still somewhat apprehensive about getting too close to his daughter, wrapped an arm over her shoulder in a companionable hug. "Vanessa never gave up hope." His Adam's apple bobbed, and he swallowed hard. "I thought she was nuts to think she could find a needle in a haystack." His eyes grew glossy. "But here you are, and I couldn't be more grateful."

Ellery was left in the past as the door clicked behind her parents. She stood in the center of the room, picturing what might have been. The walls echoed the lively chaos of five children under seven. She could almost hear the squeals of delight and the teasing, a whirlwind of love.

It must have been heavenly.

THIRTY

It was nearly five thirty when Ellery awoke to a commotion outside her bedroom door. She swung her legs over the edge of the bed and made her way to the mirror, half awake and still unaccustomed to her surroundings.

The face that stared back had sleep lines pressed into her cheeks and wild hair that stood on end. A soft smile lit up her face as she recalled Brant St. John's morning greeting. "Good morning, Sunshine. Did you comb your hair with an eggbeater?" he would ask, a twinkle in his eye that always made her bury her face against him and say, "Daddy!"

Ellery ran a finger down her part, separating the strands that had somehow switched sides. Then, she finger-combed the rest of her hair before stepping into the hallway.

The once-closed doors stood ajar, allowing the late afternoon sunlight to spill into the corridor. The ruckus from minutes before had faded into an eerie silence, leaving Ellery to question if the sound had been part of a dream. With no one around, Ellery turned toward the stairs. A single floorboard squeaked as she reached the top.

"Oh, no, you don't!" Jacqui popped out of the room at the far end of the hallway. She was clad in knit shorts and a T-shirt, her feet tucked into cozy slippers.

"What's going on?" Ellery was still trying to shake off the thick fog of sleep.

Suddenly, Liam emerged from his room, closely followed by Preston. They were similarly dressed.

Confusion was stamped on Ellery's face. "Seriously, what's

happening?"

Preston flashed a cheeky smile, put his reassuring hands on her shoulders, and turned her toward her room. "It's a sleepover, Elle!"

"A what?" Ellery could not wrap her head around her siblings' sudden appearance, let alone a slumber party.

"A sleepover. It's like family meeting night, but longer." An unmistakable spark of mischief lit his eyes as Liam stretched out that last word. "Just go with it."

Ellery crossed her arms. "I know what a sleepover is, but aren't you a little..."

"Old? Are you kidding?" The smirk on Preston's face spread. "You're never too old for a sleepover."

"Why are you doing this?" Her eyes narrowed in suspicion as she tried to read her siblings.

With an impish gleam, Jacqui smiled. "Because you missed out on all those years of Liam and Preston duking it out and Baily whining that everyone was picking on her, and..."

"And..." Liam interrupted, his chin jutting defiantly in Jacqui's direction, "the years of little Miss Perfect telling us all what to do."

Jacqui stuck her tongue out at him. "Come on. You might need some help getting dressed with that cast."

Baily emerged from her room, zipping an oversized sweatshirt that covered her pajamas. The fabric hung loosely, accentuating her guarded demeanor. The hoodie wasn't meant for warmth. It was a pointed barrier meant to set her apart, to protest her attendance at the required family gathering.

Ellery pulled back in surprise. "You're here."

Baily folded her arms in a message of defiance. "Not..." she started, but the word barely left her mouth before Liam stepped in.

"Baily!" he scolded, his sharp look attempting to dissolve her rebellion.

With a dramatic eye roll, Baily deflated. Her body crumbled inward. "Yes." Without another word, she retreated into her room. The door slammed, punctuating her rebellion.

Ellery threw her shoulders back. "It's Tuesday. Don't you have to work tomorrow?"

"Don't worry about us." Jacqui ran an arm through Ellery's elbow and steered her toward her room. She held up the bag. "You're the only one not wearing pajamas." Her knowing smile hinted at their late-night shenanigans.

Five minutes later, Ellery stepped into the hallway, dressed in pale blue camouflage shorts cinched at the waist and a matching solid blue T-shirt. Jacqui had tied Ellery's long brown hair into a high ponytail that brushed her shoulders. Her feet were snug in suede slippers lined with sheepskin fleece. She felt like she belonged for the first time since arriving in Hunters Cove.

Baily trudged down the hallway, her footsteps heavy with reluctance. "Where are the guys?" Ellery asked.

"Ice cream," she muttered as she descended the stairs, her entire body flopping like a ragdoll.

"How's the ankle?" Jacqui asked. "Do you need help on the steps?"

"It's fine." Ellery brushed off her sister's worry. "It was just a minor sprain. It's just a little stiff." She followed Jacqui downstairs, wondering if there was more to the sleepover than they had let on.

When the girls walked in, Liam and Preston were already engaged in a fierce tug-o-war over a bucket of chocolate ice cream.

"Do they do this often?" Ellery watched her brothers fight like children.

"Eat ice cream or fight?" Jacqui smiled. "Both. They never grew up."

The bucket slipped from Preston's grasp, and Liam triumphantly pumped a fist. "Winner! Winner! Chicken dinner!" He danced around the island, proving his sister's point.

"Oh, come on, I was distracted!" Preston pouted, shooting a wink at Ellery. "Sometimes you just have to let the baby win."

Liam's eyes went humorously dark, and his face twisted in challenge. "Two outta three," he challenged.

"I didn't even want chocolate," Preston admitted, looking at each of his siblings. "I just didn't want Liam to have it." His crooked smile and a single eyebrow dance made Ellery laugh.

Liam leaned against the counter and helped himself to a spoonful of ice cream from the bucket. "When we were kids, it was a tradition." He grimaced as he swallowed the cold clump in his mouth. "We promised we'd meet once a month when we moved out. Baily even made us pinky-swear. But then… Well, life happened, and people got busy, so it fell by the wayside. But I have a feeling now that we're all back together, we might revive it."

"Of course," Baily grouched from her end of the island, "for her, we'll do it more often."

"Enough!" Preston warned as he lowered his chin, his eyes dark in an impressive display of authority that commanded everyone's attention. Suddenly, he dove for the whipped cream can and held it in the air, butt dancing on his stool. "And that's how it's done—distract and dive." His antics sparked laughter as the chaos of grabbing and loading bowls with topping unfolded before her.

Liam slid a bowl of already scooped ice cream toward Ellery. "It's hard to scoop with one hand."

"Thanks." She patiently waited for the strawberry topping and the hard-shell chocolate to be available.

"You sure can tell you didn't have to fight for anything growing up." Baily's stare was hard, meant to hurt Ellery. The air thickened as anger radiated from the siblings, their eyes aimed at Baily.

Ellery drew a deep breath and held it. The room felt as if the walls were leaning in. Finally, she held up a hand and faced her sister. "It's okay. You're right, Baily. I didn't experience anything like this. But I fought every day just to survive. This…" Her eyes narrowed as she waved her hand over the food. "This is like a miracle to me. I rarely had ice cream until

I moved in with Millie and Gus."

Baily was the first to look away, her contempt momentarily stifled. Ellery's shoulders relaxed as she turned her attention to her other siblings. "I'm thankful to be here." She shifted her gaze back to Baily. "I'm even grateful you're here."

Ellery took a bite of ice cream and mumbled, "Sort of." That admission drew snorts of laughter from the others. But Baily feigned indifference, keeping her eyes focused on her bowl. Ellery knew she had to keep the flame low to walk through the fire with Baily. But it also meant not taking her crap either.

An hour of nonstop chatter and clinking of spoons against porcelain wrapped around Ellery's heart, making her feel complete. The sound sparked a feeling of deep belonging, which she had never experienced.

She watched the faces glow with laughter over shared stories from the past. Baily kept her resentment to a minimum, sitting quietly but not unengaged. Ellery's heart grew as she watched each of her siblings, knowing she finally belonged.

Suddenly, Liam tugged the neck of his T-shirt over his nose, scrunching his face as the smell filled the air. "Aw, Huck! What the heck?"

A collective protest against the St. Bernard's odor erupted. Faces twisted in disgust. Jacqui clamped a hand over her nose in a futile attempt to filter the assault. Ellery waved her good arm through the air as if trying to shoo away a swarm of flies. The scene was chaotic yet strangely comical.

"What's going on?" Vanessa stepped into the kitchen. Suddenly, her eyes bulged in horror, and a reflexive gag escaped.

"Huck! That's what's going on." Jacqui said behind her hand.

Despite the stench, the corners of her mouth lifted. "I hate to tell you, but Huck's in the pool house with Dad, Pops, and Nan."

All eyes turned toward Preston. "You're disgusting!"

"Hey! He who smelt it dealt it." Preston smirked.

Liam shot to his feet. "You're not blaming this one on me."

Others joined in, complaining about Preston's deadly gas that seemed to be on round two. Jacqui flung open the French doors of the screened porch and pressed her face against the mesh. The others followed—everyone except the offender. With a smirk, he finished his ice cream before helping himself to Liam's.

Ellery watched from the doorway as Edda stepped into the breakfast nook, brandishing a can of air freshener like a weapon. She was on a mission to destroy the unseen enemy. She headed over to Preston, whose smirk would not leave his face.

Aiming the can at his backside, she pressed her thumb against the button like she was squashing a bug.

When the lemony air overpowered Preston's stench, Edda spun the can and tucked it back in her apron pocket. "My work here is done," she said, tittering.

"You can come back now," Preston announced moments later. "Air's clear."

"For how long?" Jacqui pinched her nose closed again.

Preston pressed his hand to his stomach. "I think the tank's empty."

In no hurry to experience another round of what happened earlier, the siblings lingered on the porch, sharing stories about Preston's disgusting habit he should have outgrown. When they finally returned, the aroma of freshly made popcorn wafted through the air, pushing aside the citrusy scent.

"Popcorn?" Ellery asked. "I'm so full…"

"Nope. Nope. Nope. Don't even say it." Liam waved his hand to dismiss her concerns. "It doesn't matter if you are. It's a sleepover tradition. Edda always makes popcorn. Trust me, you'll be hungry again by the time we start watching movies."

Ellery twisted her mouth, hesitation showing on her face. "I, ah, I have a confession." All eyes turned toward her. "I've never seen a movie. When you mentioned George Clooney the other day, I had to look him up."

"You've got to be kidding!" Baily exclaimed. "You're

lying."

"I'm not. Karma said if I had time to sit around watching a stupid show, I had time to clean." She gave a gentle shrug. "And when I was taking care of Millie and Gus, I was on duty twenty-four hours a day." Ellery looked at Baily. "They didn't even own a TV."

The group went silent as they absorbed the reality of her words. That admission was another in a long list of ways their experiences were a hundred miles apart.

"Wow! Well, then, you've come to the right place," Jacqui said.

"I think we have every movie ever released between nineteen eighty-two and two thousand six, when Baily graduated."

"You're kidding, right?" Ellery's face twisted in surprise. The thought of that many movies did not compute in her sheltered mind.

"Pretty close." Preston lowered his voice and glanced toward the kitchen. "I mean, there were some movies Mom threw out when she would visit, but thanks to Dad, we rescued them." He pressed a finger to his lips. "He built a secret compartment in the back of one of the closets to hide our contraband."

Liam tapped his brother's arm with the back of his fingers. His face was all kinds of humorous. "I'm pretty sure Preston hid more than movies back there. We should probably check what's in there."

"Preston Dallas! Are you kidding me?" Vanessa suddenly appeared with the first bowl of popcorn.

Liam held his palms up. "Crap! She's using middle names. You know you're in trouble when she uses both your names."

"So, Mom, Quinn wanted…"

"Are you trying to change the subject?" A grin slipped across Vanessa's face.

"You know it." Preston locked his hands around one knee and leaned back. "Anyway, Quinn wanted me to ask you something. I know I was named after your great uncle, but…"

"Who was I named after?" Ellery's gaze fixed on her mother.

Vanessa folded her hands on the quartz countertop, leaning in with a spark of nostalgia on her face. "Well, when I graduated high school, my parents took me to Greece. We rented two rooms from a woman named Chloe." Vanessa smiled, the memory sweeping her back in time. "I instantly fell in love with the name." Her eyes momentarily drifted to Jacqui. "I completely forgot about it until I learned we were having twins. I spent months looking for two names that would go well together, but it wasn't until Nan mentioned that trip that the name came back to me."

That small piece of information was a gift, her reward for returning. It was more than she had ever known about herself.

Preston raised a finger and stuck his tongue out at Ellery. "So, if you're done interrupting, it's my turn. Quinn wants to know how we each got our middle name."

Vanessa's face turned a brilliant shade of red. "Umm, well, umm," she stammered. "That was your father's doing."

"So, you picked our first names, and he picked the middle ones?" Jacqui asked.

Vanessa's head bobbed. "Sort of." She pressed her shoulders down and caught Jacqui's eyes. "In September of nineteen eighty, we took a trip with friends to Australia."

"And you fell in love with the city of Sydney." Jacqui smiled. "That makes total sense—a reminder of where you visited."

"Something like that." Vanessa made eye contact with Preston. "In August of nineteen eighty-three, your dad had a business trip in Dallas, so I went with him."

"You must have loved…" Preston's eyes widened as they trailed from Vanessa to Liam. He scoffed loudly. "Nine months before Liam was born, you were in Phoenix, right?" He faked a gag. "Does anyone see the pattern? Our middle names aren't places they liked. It's where we were conceived."

Liam's face went white. "You named us after places you and Dad had sex? Gross!" He pretended to erase away the thought with his palm.

The room burst into chaos, the siblings' voices rising as they shared their disgust for how they were named. But amid the discussion, a heated debate emerged over who had their beginning in the best city. Finally, laughter rang out as they grappled with the reality of their unique middle names.

When the noise died down, Ellery timidly asked, "Baily's middle name is Savannah, right?" Vanessa nodded. "But mine's Jade. Why?"

Vanessa opened her mouth to respond but clearly could not find the right words amidst a cascade of emotions. "I guess we didn't feel it was right to give you both the same middle name. We wanted you to have your own identities." Her voice faltered. "And since Baily was born first…"

Baily slapped her hand against the counter, making everyone jump. Her eyes narrowed into slits as she fixed an intense glare at her twin sister. "See! You were *never* meant to be part of this family. You were an accident."

"Baily!" Vanessa exclaimed, her voice heavy with anger. "That's not true! Elle was always meant to be part of this family."

Preston seized Baily's arm firmly, pulling her away from the room to prevent her from unleashing another round of rude comments.

Vanessa hugged Ellery, drawing her close as muffled words came from the other room. "You're a Chambers, and you always will be. Never let Baily or anyone else tell you you're not." There was a layer of fierce protectiveness in her voice.

Ellery glanced from Jacqui to Liam. "I'm sorry," Liam mouthed. "She's Baily," he said aloud. The more she heard that statement, the more she understood it.

THIRTY-ONE

A week and a half later, Ellery's black eyes had faded to a pale yellow, light enough to be masked with heavy foundation. Jacqui ran a brush through thick makeup, dabbing the sallow skin beneath her sister's eyes. With a delicate stroke, she applied a highlighter to Ellery's cheeks, making Ellery's eyes sparkle.

"There. That should do it." Jacqui dropped her brushes back into her cosmetic bag.

Ellery stared into the mirror. Never had she considered herself beautiful, but with Jacqui's magic, she saw someone else staring back. Her blue Chambers eyes were even more striking if that was possible. Ellery felt her confidence ignite as her reflection revealed a person she barely recognized.

Her gaze was fixed on the mirror. "Thank you." Ellery held up her cast. "Now, if you could just cover this up."

"If they ask about it, just tell them you had an accident." Jacqui weaved her fingers through Ellery's curls. "Then move on to the next question. Don't let them dwell on any one question. Keep it moving."

"Says the attorney." Ellery grinned.

"I'm giving you good advice—*for free*." Jacqui feigned a serious tone. "And that doesn't happen often in my line of work."

Ellery leveled her chin and admired her reflection again.

"That's it. Be confident and sweet. Look who I'm telling to be sweet. You're probably the nicest person I know." Her smile was a mirror to the affection that was growing between them. "I'm lucky I get to call you my sister."

There was a soft knock. "Girls, are you ready?" The thick wood door muffled Vanessa's voice.

"We'll be down in one minute." Jacqui grabbed Ellery's hand. "Before we go, I have something for you." She reached into her pocket, retrieved a small object, pressed it into Ellery's palm, and closed her fingers around it.

"What's this?" Ellery opened her hand and examined it.

"It's a 1936 Liberty half-dollar." Jacqui tapped the coin.

Ellery pulled her neck back; her face was marked with confusion. "And?"

The sunshine cast a warm glow on Jacqui as she recounted the story. "It belonged to Pops. It's from the year he was born." Her eyes remained on the coin. "On the day Pops was born, his dad traded a handful of change for it."

Jacqui's face grew somber. "Pops was born during the Great Depression, and his parents didn't have a penny to spare, but somehow, his dad saved enough for this coin." Its significance deepened in Ellery.

"Pops tells the story better, but during the Depression, there were numerous times they almost starved to death because they didn't have enough money. Yet his father refused to spend that coin."

Ellery felt the family's pain. She had experienced it living with Karma. There were days when she ate less than a bite of a stranger's *secondhand food*. She wondered if their shared experience would bring them closer.

"When Pops was eight, his mom got sick. The doctor told the family to start planning her funeral. Pops was devastated. He wanted to do something special for his mom, so he took the coin to buy her a gift."

There was a moment of silence as she paused, drawing a long breath. "By the time he got to the checkout counter, his grief spilled out like rain. He held his coin in one hand and, in the other, a bracelet he wanted his mom to wear when they buried her. He wiped his face on his sleeve and waited his turn."

Ellery felt heavy, laden down by the image of her

grandfather as a young boy facing his mother's death. It made her heart hurt.

"Suddenly, the man in front of him reached toward Pop's face and..." Jacqui held a hand toward the side of Ellery's head, reenacting the moment, "pulled a half-dollar coin out of his ear and handed it to him." Her eyes sparkled. "He said, 'Son, your momma'd want you to wash those ears better. There's no telling what else might be in there.' Pops reached up and poked a finger in his ear as he watched the man disappear."

"And that's when he decided the coin was lucky." Jacqui smiled.

"What about his mom?" Ellery asked.

A grin tugged up Jacqui's lips. "A week later, she was out in the barn milking cows. She lived to a hundred and two. And Pops buried her with the bracelet."

"Wow!" Ellery flipped the coin over in her hand. "It must be lucky. But if it's Pops's, why do you have it?"

"We share it. Whoever needs a little luck has it." A gentle sigh escaped. "Liam wanted you to have it today." Jacqui glanced down at the coin lying in Ellery's hand. "Do you know he had it in his pocket when we came to Schenectady...and again when you were in the hospital?"

Ellery's fingers curled around the warm metal. Butterflies fluttered in her stomach. If she ever needed luck, it was today. She searched for reassurance in Jacqui's eyes. "Are you sure you want me to have it? I mean, I could jinx it."

"Believe me. That won't happen."

The stakes were high today. The thought of Pop's story swam through Ellery as another soft knock echoed against the door.

"Girls, we need to leave." Urgency filled Vanessa's voice.

Jacqui pulled the door open. "We're ready."

Vanessa grabbed the doorframe to steady herself as she looked at Ellery. "Oh my gosh. You're so beautiful." Her voice was almost reverent as she took in her daughter. "Other than hair color, you two look almost identical." Finally, Vanessa clasped her hands together. "But your dad's going to lay on the horn if we don't get out there."

Ellery tucked the coin into her front pocket and hugged Jacqui. The press had been camping out across the road for nearly a week. Since the news broke, their cameras had been aimed at the house like predatory eyes. No matter how often the police escorted them off the property, they found their way back.

Today was the day she would face them, tell her story—or at least a version of it—with a bit of security. She traced the coin's outline with her finger, hoping it wouldn't let her down, and followed the others to the car.

Ellery settled into the backseat of the Lexus with Jacqui. Just as they began to back up, the back door opened.

"Move over." Baily poked Jacqui in the shoulder.

Vanessa turned her head sharply. "I didn't think you were coming."

"Yeah, well, I wasn't going to, but… Well, here I am," she snarled, slamming the door.

Ellery slipped her hand into her pocket and fingered the coin. She stared out the window and smiled, a secret little joy hidden from view.

As they pulled into Hunters Cove Park, the sun hung high in the sky, spotlighting the crowd. Like ants heading for food, the masses continued to arrive, traveling toward the lake, not away from it. Reporters, journalists, and townsfolk lined up in front of the gazebo. Ellery felt her pulse in her whole body as the buzz of excitement increased.

Weston pulled into a parking space reserved by Chief Jansen's team. When the hum of the engine faded, he turned toward Ellery. "Are you okay?"

Ellery nodded, even though a wave of uncertainty deep

inside weakened her legs. "I think so." She leaned forward. "I'm grateful you're both here with me." Jacqui gave her a reassuring smile, but Baily turned away.

"Preston texted. He and Liam are already down there." Vanessa turned her phone off and tucked it into her purse.

Ellery stole a deep breath, her heart picking up speed as they approached the lake. The officers' presence felt both reassuring and intimidating. The gazebo loomed ahead. She blinked several times to clear her vision. Focusing on her mother's back, she counted her steps and breathed deep and slow.

The Chamberses gathered on the stairs, a united front—with one blonde exception. Ellery felt her pulse quicken beneath her skin. She could even feel it in her fingertips. Public speaking was unfamiliar. Other than the past few weeks with her new family, she had never spoken to more than two people at a time. She touched her throat as a lump began to grow. Vanessa offered a bottle of water and rubbed her back. Both grounded her momentarily.

As Chief Jansen stepped forward, the crowd's murmurs quieted. He leaned on the makeshift podium and scanned the sea of faces, each eager to learn Ellery's story.

Jansen waited for the crowd to quiet. "Thank you for being here. Today, you will hear from the woman who was kidnapped thirty-seven years ago. The name given to her at birth was Chloe Jade Chambers." He turned his gaze toward her. "Today, she is known as Elle Gray. Please refer to her as such both when you address her and in the news."

"I'm only going to say this once," he declared, his intense gaze piercing the crowd. "Be respectful of Miss Gray and her family." His tone was both a warning and a plea.

His eyes flicked down to his notes. "Thank you to the Brainerd and St. Cloud police departments for their assistance today. If you show respect, we shouldn't need them." The microphone crackled, and Jansen pulled back, a pregnant pause punctuating his message. "Understand?" Heads bobbed. He gestured with a final nod toward the family and stepped to the side.

Ellery felt her parents slip their hands into the crook of her elbows and guide her down the stairs. The crowd blurred into a swirl of colors and sounds, making her feel like she was floating rather than walking as they approached the podium.

Weston adjusted the microphone for her. The breakfast Edda had insisted she eat was curling into a fist and seemed to want to fight its way out. Ellery felt her father nudge her closer to the mic. She briefly closed her eyes. The coin popped into her mind. Ellery reached for it, her fingers wrapping around the warm metal as she pulled it from her pocket. That simple act settled her.

"Hello," she finally said as a surprising surge of peace flowed through her. Squeezing the sides of the podium, she plunged into the depths of her story. "My name is Elle Gray." She stole a glance at Vanessa. "I was born to Weston and Vanessa Chambers. They gave me the name Chloe Jade. On June tenth of nineteen eighty-eight, I was taken from a park in Minnetonka, Minnesota. I was eight days old." She subtly gestured toward her parents. "I had three older siblings and a twin sister."

Ellery swallowed hard. That first part was simple, straightforward facts. It was the next part that would feel like walking on broken glass. She had to choose her path carefully. Honesty tugged at her, but a fierce instinct to protect Destiny held her back. Destiny's only crime was circumstantial—being born to Karma.

"The woman who took me went by one name: *Karma*." That name caused a buzz through the assembly. When Ellery began speaking again, the crowd went silent. "She used me as bait to trap a man into marrying her, claiming I was his daughter." Ellery's eyes swept over the crowd. "The man I believed to be my dad was killed in a car accident when I was three. And Karma died three years ago."

"I was raised in the South until I was eighteen. Shortly after my birthday..." She looked at Vanessa. "Or what I believed to be my birthday, I legally changed my name and moved north."

"Miss Gray," someone yelled from the crowd, "how did you discover you were a Chambers?"

Ellery shoved her hand in her pocket and closed it around the coin. She waited for the right words to reveal themselves. "A friend found information in Karma's belongings after she passed."

"Dawn Roussin, *Brainerd Dispatch*," the woman said, introducing herself. "Did Karma ever try to find you after you moved?" Roussin held her phone in the air, recording every word.

"I don't know. I never spoke with her after I left." Ellery gestured to a man in a navy polo shirt with a logo that Ellery could not identify.

"Tim Braxmeier, Lakeland TV." He nodded in greeting. "I assume this Karma woman changed your name after taking you. Are you willing to share that name?"

Ellery squared her shoulders. "I am not. It's a name I would rather forget." She dismissed him by signaling a woman with a small notepad.

"Paula Palmer, KBJR News. Are you aware there's a famous author who conceals her identity by the name of Ellery Gray?" Her pen was poised, ready for a response.

"I am." The answer was purposely curt. She had no intention of going there.

"Are you her?" the woman asked. A profound silence fell over the group.

Ellery felt a wild adrenaline rush as her heart leaped into her throat. "I'm sure many people share my name, just as I'm sure many share yours." Her voice was steady despite the pandemonium churning the breakfast she should have skipped. She gestured to a woman in the front row.

"Shari Horton, *Aitkin Independent Age*." The woman smiled warmly. For the first time, Ellery felt someone saw her, not just a headline or the drama from her past. "When did you learn you were Chloe Chambers, Miss Gray?"

Ellery hesitated, recalling the day her world tilted sideways. "When the friend came to me with the information." Her voice sounded steadier than she felt.

"But when was that?"

"Two years ago." Ellery pointed to another journalist. But before the woman could open her mouth, an inquiry crashed through the air, silencing the crowd and waiting for an answer.

"Sharon LaRocque. *Star Tribune*. Why didn't you come forward then? What made you wait?"

Ellery had rehearsed her response to that question countless times, but it was a lie. The truth was, she hadn't come forward out of fear of rejection, but that was too personal. So, she stood behind a shield she hoped would end that question for good.

"I wasn't sure I wanted to leave the life I had caring for the elderly couple." She should have added *who had been dead for five years,* but she did not.

"What were their names?" a voice called from the back.

"What does that have to do with my disappearance?" Ellery shot back, her eyes darkening. She searched the crowd of faces, finally gesturing to a reporter standing in the front row.

"Verna Jeanotte, *Voyageur Press*. Miss Gray, how has your transition to the family and Hunters Cove been?" The question resonated deeply. She was grateful someone truly cared about her journey.

Ellery glanced over her shoulder, smiling at her siblings whose support she could not do without. "I'm..." she paused briefly. "I'm home," she finally said, fighting back tears.

A voice cut through the tender moment. "What happened to your arm?"

She raised her cast for everyone to see. "Let's just say my name's not Grace for a reason." Laughter cut through the air.

Weston stepped forward. "Vanessa and I are extremely grateful to have our daughter back. Her siblings couldn't be happier." As he scanned the crowd, the sincerity in his eyes reflected the seriousness of their ordeal. He wrapped an arm across Ellery's back. "For now, we'd like time to be a family. I ask you to please give us the time to heal."

Cameras flashed as the officers escorted the family back to Vanessa's car. Ellery felt her pulse slow. Preston and Liam slipped across the street while Chief Jansen offered his final warning, once again instructing the crowd to respect the family's privacy.

Ellery climbed into the car next to Jacqui. She held the coin in front of her sister. Once again, Jacqui folded Ellery's fingers closed over the good luck charm. "You keep it for now. You might need it again."

"Of course, you gave her the coin." Baily sneered at Jacqui. "I've never even touched it."

Ellery paid no attention to Baily's complaint. She was lost in Jacqui's statement. Did she know something, or was she just being kind?

THIRTY-TWO

Ellery stood in the kitchen with Edda. The afternoon sunlight filtered through the window. Three glass shelves lined with plants brightened the room, bringing the outside into the vast space. Edda was sharing a story about Liam when Vanessa walked through the door.

"What are you two up to?" She headed toward the coffee maker.

"Keeping track of the number of times you walk into this house uninvited," Edda snapped. "You do remember you don't live here, right?" The housekeeper knotted her arms in front of her.

Unfazed by Edda's attitude, Vanessa winked at Ellery before turning her attention to the woman. "Edda, you've been a godsend to this family. I can't thank you enough for all you've done for us over the years." Then she unexpectedly threw her arms around the woman and hugged her close, grinning at her daughter over Edda's shoulder.

The housekeeper stiffened and tried to pull away, but Vanessa locked her fingers behind her, giving Ellery a mischievous grin.

Edda grimaced. She wiggled her arms into the space between them, trying to free herself from the unwanted closeness. Finally, she shoved Vanessa away. "Geez! That was disgusting. Don't touch me again."

Vanessa pressed a hand to her chest with a melodramatic reaction. "What? You don't appreciate my hugs? Well, I'm not a fan of your snarky comments." She tightened her lips. "So, no more hugs if you agree to stop with the spiteful comments.

Deal?"

Edda opened her mouth and closed it again. She tried once more, but the same silence engulfed her. Her shoulders slumped in defeat. "Fine," she hissed, storming from the room.

Celebrating the win, Vanessa brushed her hands together. "To quote Edda, 'My work here's done'." A hint of triumph gleamed in her eyes as she savored the small victory.

Ellery's expression shifted. Her grin was replaced by a pensive stare. "You've changed. You used to be so formal, almost stiff around me." She folded her arms, cupping her elbows in her palms. "Now, you're lighter…" Ellery tilted her head back and forth. "Kind of fun even."

"Oh, honey." Vanessa reached out, her fingers brushing against Ellery's cheek. "This is who I was before you disappeared from my life. Do you think I could be raised by two people like Pops and Nan and not pick up a line or two along the way?" She lifted her mug and took a slow sip. "When you disappeared, I did too. It's only recently I found the person I used to be."

Ellery tilted her head slightly, her eyes studying her mom. "You weren't like this when you came to see me in Schenectady. Not at all."

"I know. I was afraid one of us would say the wrong thing, and you'd disappear forever. I felt like I was walking on eggshells." A look of relief fell across her face. "But now, I know you're staying. You are staying, right?"

Ellery leaned in and wrapped her arms around Vanessa. "I'm not going anywhere," she whispered into her mother's neck. Vanessa set her cup on the counter and surrendered fully to her daughter's embrace. Suddenly, Ellery blurted, "I'm not leaving, *Mom*."

She felt her mother's arms tighten around her. When they finally separated, she saw the gratitude in Vanessa's eyes, a mirror into her soul.

"Does this mean…"

With a nod, Ellery responded without letting her mother

finish. "It does. You and Dad have shown me what being part of a family means." Vanessa pulled her into another embrace. Ellery did not want her to let go.

"I don't remember Karma ever hugging me, even when I was little. My da… Brant did," she corrected, "but I was so young, I barely remember how that felt."

Edda strode back into the kitchen. "How about you two get outta here," she grumbled.

Vanessa released her daughter, got up, and threw her arms around the older woman. "It's so hard to break bad habits. They say it takes twenty-one days." She let go of Edda. "Prepare to be hugged *a lot*." A glint sparkled in her eyes.

Edda's gaze hardened. "Touch me again…" Her voice trailed off.

"What?" Vanessa leaned in, her ear cocked toward Edda. "What was that? Did you say you wanted another hug?"

"Never mind." Edda's shoulders stiffened as she glanced between the two women. Her fists were clenched at her sides, and her knuckles had turned white. "I have work to do. Would you mind leaving? Please?" Edda asked.

"Not at all." Vanessa gave her a goofy smile. "I need to talk to Elle about her birthday party." Vanessa hooked an arm through her daughter's. "Would you bring us some cookies and iced tea, Edda?"

"Get it…" Edda clamped her mouth shut and inhaled deeply. "I mean, *got it*." The hardness in her eyes spoke volumes. "I'll bring them out to the porch right away." Her words were as stiff as her posture.

"Thank you," Vanessa called over her shoulder. "You can dump my coffee."

"What? But you just made…" Vanessa spun around, her smile broadening as she locked eyes with the housekeeper. Edda raised her palms in surrender. "W-what, ah, what…" she stammered. "What I meant to ask was what you want me to do with the mug?"

"Maybe try washing it. I hear they have these new

inventions called dishwashers."

"Aren't you afraid she'll spit in our drinks?" Ellery whispered as they walked toward the screen porch.

"No. Cameras." The word came out as a whisper. Vanessa glanced behind her to ensure Edda wasn't listening. "I might have told her there're cameras in every room. Except for the bathrooms."

Ellery laughed, settling into a cushioned chair. "And she believed you?"

"Of course." Vanessa's eyes twinkled with delight over the success of her ruse. She sank into a nearby chair. "Years ago, I sat at the island paging through a catalog of spy cameras, pretending to talk to a friend on the phone. I bragged about how amazing they were, and that they're so small, no one knows they're there." She smiled at Ellery. "It's possible I mentioned I ordered a slew of them for the house."

"You're bad." Ellery shook her head. "Like really bad."

"We all have a dark side," she whispered as Edda walked in with a tray.

"Anything else?" Edda asked, her hands tucked into her front apron pockets.

"This is fine for now." Vanessa's smile was both sweet and somewhat disarming. "I'll let you know if we need anything else. But thank you. This was very nice of you."

Edda frowned. "If you need me, you might need to text me. I'll be upstairs cleaning."

"Oh, no need." Vanessa glanced at Ellery. "I can see where you are on my phone."

Edda swallowed hard, turned, and headed upstairs.

"You're unbelievable." Ellery shook her head disapprovingly. Yet, the grin on her face said otherwise.

"Sometimes you have to do what you have to do."

Vanessa leaned forward and took both glasses from the tray. The ice clinked against the sides as she handed one to Ellery. "Let's talk about the birthday party. We don't have much time with your and Baily's birthdays next week. I should have started planning earlier, but there's been so much happening with your accident and all."

She took a long sip, savoring the taste before resting the glass on her thigh and wrapping her hand around it. "Since it's the first time you get to celebrate your birthdays togeth…"

"I don't want a party," Ellery said firmly.

"Honey, of course you do. You told me you haven't celebrated your birthday since Brant died. It's important…"

"I don't want a party." Her tone left no room for discussion, and her gaze was unyielding. "Listen to me."

With a gentle nod, Vanessa gave in. "Alright, I'm listening."

Ellery glanced up, following the massive wooden beams with her eyes from one end of the porch to the other. "Baily already hates me."

"She doesn't hate you, Elle. She's just jealous of your relationship with the rest of the family."

Ellery set her iced tea on the table and turned toward her mother, her striking blue eyes a pool of emotion. "Please, let me talk." Vanessa resignedly sank into her chair. "Baily told me she shared every birthday with my ghost." She paused, raising her hand to silence any impending interruption, knowing how intensely her mother would react. "And now that I'm back, she should get to have one birthday without any reminders of me."

A frown creased Vanessa's forehead as she considered her daughter's words. "My gosh. You are the kindest person. How that evil woman raised you, and you still turned out so caring, is beyond me."

To Ellery, the answer was simple. "Being like her wasn't an option. She hated everyone, and I didn't want to be like that."

A wistful look crossed Vanessa's face as she considered her daughter's words. "Over the last few weeks, I've wondered how you might have turned out had you been raised here with us. Don't get me wrong, I would never have chosen for you to be raised by that awful woman. But you were. And I am so grateful that something good came from it. *You.*" A gentle smile broke across Vanessa's face. "You're the person you are today because of all you went through."

Vanessa laced her fingers with Ellery's. "I have no idea if Baily would still be this angry if you'd grown up together. Would you have been best friends? Would you have giggled together long into the night? Would you have gone on double dates? Or would you have hated one another anyway? I don't know if anyone can answer that. I think we'll only know moving forward."

Ellery's response came in a slow, deliberate nod. "And that's why I want Baily to have a birthday party that's all her own."

A tiny smile surfaced on Vanessa's face. "I understand, but…"

"No," Ellery interrupted, her voice carrying the strength of her conviction. "This is the way it has to be." She shifted her gaze toward Baily's cottage. "Maybe next year, things will be different. But this is the way I want it this year. I want her to feel like she's the most important person in the world. Because right now, I think she feels like she's been forgotten at home while everyone else is off having an amazing vacation."

Vanessa let out a soft snort. "If that's what you want, we'll do it your way. I don't like it, but I understand." Her eyes glimmered with disappointment.

Ellery clasped her hands together. "Good." She felt a spark of hope.

"You know it'll take some convincing to get your dad to agree."

"Then do your best to convince him because this is what I want. It's what I need." Ellery folded and steepled her fingers. "This is the only way I can think of to get into Baily's good graces."

"Alright," Vanessa said, with a shake of her head. She checked the calendar on her phone. "I have a lot to do to prepare for this party to make it special for your sister."

"I'll help. I'll do whatever you need me to do." Ellery paused briefly. "But I won't be there."

Her mother opened her mouth to protest. She pressed her hands to her thighs and looked at Ellery. "And you're sure this is what you want?" Her eyes bored so deeply into her daughter's soul that Ellery had to look away.

"More than anything." Ellery's gaze drifted to the end of the dock where Baily sat. A heavy sadness stole her smile. "I want to heal our relationship. I want us to be more than sisters. I want us to be friends."

THIRTY-THREE

Ellery spent the morning nestled beneath her covers, hiding in the quiet of her bedroom. As she stared at the ceiling, memories drifted like clouds, each filled with anguish from the past.

Today marked her thirty-seventh birthday, but the day held an unshakeable sense of emptiness instead of joy. It brought back memories of her life with Karma, years of living as Summer, a child who was invisible to the person who should have loved her the most.

Karma always celebrated her own birthday with a cake and a stack of gifts she purchased and wrapped. Summer was never allowed to have a piece of her mother's cake. But afterward, when she was forced to clean up the mess of her mother's solo party, she licked the crumbs from the plate and off the tabletop.

After one of those celebrations, she asked about the date of her birthday. Karma's eyes flared, and Summer melted into the wall to escape the belt she knew would come if she uttered one more word. Finally, Karma screamed *June ten, eighty-eight*. She marked it on a calendar she stole from the drugstore. Every night, she crossed off the date with a black X. When June 10th arrived, her mother was nowhere to be found. The day disappeared without so much as a whisper.

The following year, just before her eighth birthday, Summer stole a candle and a card from a gift store. Every year after, she lit the multi-colored candle and sang "Happy Birthday" to herself, carefully hiding her celebration from Karma. She would open the card and smile at the words she had painstakingly printed in her inventive spelling. The message was part of her wish every year—that the life she had been born into was a mistake. The card was signed, *Your real family*.

Ellery closed her eyes and listened to the quiet. Millie had always insisted that God was listening, even when hope felt like a dream. He had heard her, had given her the *real family* she wished for.

Finally, she tossed the covers back, pulled a sweatshirt over her pajamas, and went downstairs. The house was steeped in profound silence, surrounding her like a thick fog, amplifying the feeling of isolation.

Everyone, including Edda, had gone to Baily's surprise party. She imagined the party: her siblings, parents, Nan, and Pops gathered without her. But instead of feeling sorry for herself, she focused on the fact that Baily would celebrate one birthday without the shadow of *Chloe* hanging over her.

She opened the fridge, the cool air washing over her as she peered inside. Edda had left an egg bake. A folded note with her name sat atop. *Happy Birthday, Elle! I thought you might enjoy this.* The initial warmth she felt was overcome by butterflies dancing in her stomach. She knew she had done the right thing by letting Baily celebrate without her. Still, after being part of a family for several weeks, memories of her previous life with Karma crept in, complicating her emotions.

As she wandered around the house, Ellery wondered about each item Vanessa had sitting out. Had they been purchased on a trip? Were they a gift? Did they hold special meaning? Her fingers brushed against the edges of framed photos lining the walls, each one an event she had not been a part of.

Climbing the staircase, she ventured into her siblings' rooms. Each held the ghosts of their past, revealing them through photos, posters, and decorations. Her room had been frozen in time. She had not asked for it to be redecorated yet, not because she wasn't ready, but because she did not want to be a burden.

Curiosity pulled her to the guestroom, tucked away at the

end of the hall. The room appeared untouched, as if it had never played host to anyone. Yet, it sparked with cleanliness that spoke to Edda's meticulous nature. Suddenly, Ellery burst out laughing. Edda had the mouth of a trucker, but she could care for a room with such a gentle hand.

Ellery's imagination took flight as she envisioned the party unfolding. She could hear the laughter of her siblings as they egged one another on, and she could see her nieces and nephews flitting about, duplicates of their parents. Pops would be regaling the family with off-color stories that would have anyone who would listen clutching their sides, begging him to stop. And Nan, well, all Nan had to do was open her mouth, and everyone would die laughing. Between her southern accent and her witticisms, she was hysterical.

Ellery knew the celebration would wind down by 7:00. Vanessa had hired a clean-up crew, allowing the *family* to linger in each other's company before heading home.

The word *family* snagged in Ellery's throat. She was part of the Chamberses, bound by blood but missing the history. But at that moment, alone in the sprawling mansion, she felt the chasm between them. Her choice to stay behind echoed loudly. Her siblings, parents, and grandparents begged her to come, but she refused. Today was about Baily.

Ellery returned to her room and crawled beneath the covers, but sleep eluded her no matter how hard she tried. Thoughts poked at her like an impatient child.

Suddenly, she scrambled out of bed and sat at the changing table Weston had converted into a makeshift desk, its surface cluttered with notes Ellery had handwritten. Her computer screen flickered to life, and she pulled up her novel. Despite the challenge of typing with a cast, she quickly found her rhythm.

The words began to fall from her as if they had been waiting to be unleashed. With each keystroke, the characters came alive.

Time slipped away unnoticed as she lost herself in the unfolding narrative. When the lateness of the day registered, she reluctantly tore herself away to change out of her pajamas, use the bathroom, and grab something to keep her going. She placed a handful of crackers and a soda on a plate, hoping they would help her power through another chapter.

As she sank deeper into the story, the outside world faded again.

For the briefest of moments, Ellery sat with her fingers hovering over the keyboard, lost in thought. Suddenly, a sharp knock on her bedroom door startled her. She quickly glanced at her phone—*7:47 p.m.* She had spent nearly the entire day lost in her newest book.

"Come in," she said, stretching her back after hours of sitting at her computer.

The door creaked open, and Liam stepped in. "Whatcha doing?"

Ellery tucked a few strands of hair behind her ear. "Writing. It's been a while. It feels good to be back at it."

"I bet it does." He tried to peek over her shoulder, but she closed the lid. "I feel the same way when I paint. But I can't just close the lid when you walk in."

"It's not ready for anyone to see—not even you." She hooked her arm over the back of the chair. "How was the party? Was Baily surprised?"

"It was good." A broad smile lit Liam's face. "But *surprised* wasn't the word for it."

"Why? What happened?"

Liam chuckled. "She walked into the Country Club and almost peed her pants when everyone yelled surprise." Liam's expression quickly changed. "I'm not sure why. She has a party every year." He picked up her bear and absently tossed it into the air a few times before returning it. "She went from thrilled to *Baily* in record time. But then Mom explained what you did for her, and she pulled her act together. So, I'd say it was a good day."

Ellery pulled her arm into her lap, feeling a wave of relief. "Good. I'm glad it went well."

Liam glanced at the crumpled waxy cracker sleeve and the

empty can of soda lying on its side. "If I know you, that's all you ate today, right?"

She cast him a lopsided smile. "Yes. But the book was…"

"Elle, you have to eat. You can't live on crap." He rocked the empty can between his thumb and fingers for emphasis. With a gentle tug, he pulled her to her feet. "Mom brought leftovers home from the party. Come downstairs and at least have something to fill your stomach."

"Fine." Ellery followed him out of that room. As they descended the stairs, the quiet felt unnerving. "Where're Mom and Dad?"

"They were out by the pool when I came to find you."

"Surprise!" The chorus of voices erupted like a shotgun blast, reverberating through the room, momentarily catching Ellery off guard. Liam reached out to catch her as she stumbled backward in shock.

"Surprise." The message was soft, more personal than the jarring surprise. "Happy birthday, Elle."

Harlow, leaning against her father, could not contain her excitement. "It's your birthday party!"

Preston extricated himself from his daughter, a proud smile on his face. "Yes, it is. Happy birthday, Elle." He opened his arms for a hug, but Ellery was fuming.

"No. No, it's not." Ellery emphatically pushed him away. "This isn't my day. It's Baily's." Her mouth locked in an angry line as she scanned the room for her sister. "This is supposed to be her day."

Suddenly, Baily and Ben came through the front door. "I had my party. This one's for you."

Ben casually held a pink and white birthday cake before her, tipping it so Ellery could see her name written in pale green frosting. "Baily just decorated it. That's why we're late."

Ellery's gaze swept the room. "Why are you all being so nice to me? This is supposed to be Baily's birthday." Her voice quivered.

"Elle, it's your day too," Ben reassured her, looking at his wife. "This was all Baily's idea—for everyone to gather here for your birthday."

Ellery locked eyes with Baily. "Why?"

Baily stared at her for several seconds. "I don't know," she finally admitted, her shoulders lifting. "It just didn't feel right to celebrate my birthday without a cake that said Baily and Chloe or having *Happy Birthday* sung just to me." Her eyes fixed intently on Ellery, revealing a hint of vulnerability. "I'm still not happy about any of this, but for tonight…" Her gaze shifted to her husband. "…I promised to be nice."

Ellery felt nothing but joy when she threw her arms around Baily. "Thank you." Though Baily's arms remained by her sides, a subtle shift in her demeanor transcended the moment.

Suddenly, a chorus of eager voices erupted from the breakfast area. "We want cake! We want cake! We want cake!" Noah and Graham's chant bounced off the walls, drawing everyone toward the island where Ben had placed the cake.

Quinn wagged her head. "It's not like they haven't already had three pieces," she said with a mom look.

"Four!" Graham yelled.

"And a half," Noah added, unable to contain a fit of giggles that gurgled inside him.

As the joyful singing filled the room with warmth, Ellery started to cry. For the first time that she could genuinely remember—beyond the lone photograph of her and Brant and the cupcake Millie had her neighbor make every year—Ellery felt whole. The room was thick with laughter, love, and an unmistakable sense of belonging. And she stood dead center.

THIRTY-FOUR

Ellery leaned against a post on the screen porch and watched Baily stroll down the long dock. The mid-morning sun glinted off her coffee mug. Fresh off her shift at the bakery, where she spent the early mornings decorating cakes, Baily appeared exhausted. Her shoulders sagged as she trudged down the narrow walkway.

A knot wound tighter in Ellery's stomach as she picked up a plate of Edda's warm chocolate chip cookies and crossed the yard. With every stride, the need to bridge the distance between her and her sister grew stronger. She wondered if Baily would even hear her out. The sole advantage of meeting her at the water end of the dock meant it would be unlikely she'd be gone by the time Ellery's feet hit the first board.

Her sandals softly slapped the bottoms of her feet as she wandered down the narrow walkway. Baily glanced up, her eyes instantly returning to the lake when she realized it was her. "What are you doing here?"

The Baily of the night before was gone, and in her place was the sullen, angry sister she had become accustomed to. She dropped into one of the chairs and held up the plate. "I brought cookies." She set the plate and her phone on the dock.

Her sister cast a skeptical eye at her. "You do know I own a bakery, right?"

Ellery closed her eyes briefly and summoned a smile that wouldn't send her sister running. "I thought maybe we could talk."

"Right," Baily scoffed.

"What you did for me last night…" Her voice trailed off as she searched for the right words. With Baily, there was a fine line between striking a match and experiencing the explosion. "I just wanted to thank you." A warm blush crept onto her cheeks. "No one's ever cared about me that much."

Baily huffed, her eyes returning to the lake as if uninterested. "Yeah, you already said that."

Ellery's heart sank. "Sorry. It just meant a lot to me. I wanted you to know." Studying her sister's face, she hoped her gratitude would be the one thing that would break through her apathetic exterior.

Baily's eyebrows arched high above the frames of her sunglasses. "You told me that too." Her words were dismissive. But shooing her away with a backhanded wave was too much. Still, Ellery did not move.

"I just don't understand why you hate me so much?" Ellery's voice trembled.

Baily inhaled deeply, her shoulders rising and falling as she stared at Ellery. "Hate you? I barely know you."

"Then let's change that."

"Not interested." She threw her legs over the side of the deck chair and faced Ellery. "You showed up and expected us to welcome you with open arms like you're royalty or something. And then, when I didn't, you got upset." She sneered. "I'm not like the rest."

Ellery shook her head. "I never thought that. I never expected any of you to fall in love with me when I told you who I was."

"Well, that's the way it seemed." Baily pressed her elbows against her thighs and stared at the water. A good minute ticked away before she opened her mouth again. "I know this doesn't matter to you, but I finally had my mother back. I had her attention, something I missed out on growing up."

Ellery threw her shoulders back. "It *does* matter to me. I don't understand how any of this is my fault."

Baily ripped off her sunglasses, sending them to the dock

near her phone and coffee mug. With fiery eyes, she bore down on her sister with such contempt that Ellery had to look away.

"How *isn't* it your fault?" Baily shot back. "Once Mom accepted you weren't coming back, our lives were back on track." She clasped her fingers closed to ward off the chaos of emotions inside. Her eyes softened for a split second before they turned hard again. "Mom and Dad were starting to reconnect. We could finally talk about the past without Mom blubbering about you." She glared at Ellery, her eyes as cold as ice. "And then you show up and toss our lives into bedlam again."

Baily's words stung, yet, at the same time, they angered Ellery. "I'm not going to apologize for coming home to my family. It's not like they chose to give me away."

"I wouldn't be so sure."

There was that feeling again—that perhaps her father or someone else had been involved in her disappearance. The words stabbed at her, but the implication hurt more. "Do you know something I don't?"

Baily held up two fingers. "Two babies is a lot. One too many." She folded one under. Her sister's vicious grin took her back to her days with Karma.

Hurt glistened in her eyes. "That was mean. Why would you say that?"

"In case you didn't notice, Dad wasn't exactly thrilled with your sudden appearance."

Palpitations kicked Ellery's chest. "Are you saying that he…"

Baily rose, closing the space between them. "I'm not saying anything. I might have to deal with you being back here, but it'll take me a long time to accept you as my sister—if that ever happens." She poked a challenging finger into Ellery's shoulder. "For now, you're nobody to me."

Ellery held her ground. "You're right about one thing. You do have to deal with me being here because I'm not going anywhere." Her eyes flared as she slid closer to her sister.

"Wanna bet?" Baily drove her shoulder into Ellery's stomach, sending her off the end of the dock.

Instinctively, Ellery grabbed for Baily, her fingers grasping her sister's T-shirt, sending them both into the water.

Panic surged through Ellery as she broke the surface. "I can't swim! I can't swim!" she yelled, thrashing wildly with one arm, trying to keep her already-soaked cast above her head.

Baily watched her briefly before clutching her by her good arm and pulling her to her feet.

"The water's not above your head, idiot," she hissed, climbing up the stairs near the end of the dock.

Adrenaline coursed through her, sending her body into fight or flight mode. Flight won out. Ellery was done trying to make friends. Her legs trembled, and her face flushed with embarrassment as she followed Baily up the stairs.

"Here." Baily tossed her a towel, which she pulled from the deck box. Ellery shivered as she ran the towel down her legs and arms, trying to dry the top edge of her cast. Baily handed her a second one. "Wrap this around you. You'll be fine. A blow dryer'll take care of that," she said, nodding at the cast.

Wrapping the dry towel around herself, Ellery stared at her sister. "Why'd you do that?"

Baily burst out laughing. "I can't swim! I can't swim!" she sputtered, thrashing about as she mimicked Ellery's panic. "You're pretty damn pathetic."

Anger ignited inside Ellery, and she hissed her words through her clenched jaw. "If being raised by an evil woman who never fed me, never bought me clothes, and never let me go to school makes me pathetic…" she shot back, her piercing gaze driving into her sister, "then I guess I am." Hot tears suddenly rolled down her cheeks. "But at least I don't hurt people just because I'm afraid they might get more attention than me."

She grabbed her phone and retreated down the dock, trying to put as much space as possible between her and her sister. As she neared the shore, Baily's haunting voice cut through the quiet, the weight of the emotion making Ellery freeze in place.

"Do you want to know why I live here?" Baily's tone was hollow, almost haunting. "In this house, on Dad's property?"

Ellery turned; an undercurrent of unease gripped her. She wasn't sure if it was another trick or if Baily finally decided to open up about her deplorable behavior.

"Because I'm scared," she admitted, her voice trembling. "Scared as hell."

The rawness of her words pulled Ellery closer. "Of what?"

Moments of silence stretched before them; discomfort tapped at Ellery's stomach. "Remember that night at Eddie's when I wondered why that woman took you instead of me?" Ellery nodded, making her way toward her sister. "That question ran through me every single day when I walked by your room. But I spent more time worrying about *being* taken," she admitted, her arms betraying her terror as she shook them as if trying to throw off her fears.

"Mom and Dad didn't trust me to go anywhere alone. They constantly reminded me that *you* disappeared, so I needed to be extra careful because maybe that weirdo might come for me too."

The revelation slapped Ellery across the face. Suddenly, she felt like she was splashing in the freezing water again—only this time, she had to save Baily. She moved closer and dropped onto a chair. "They honestly said that?"

Baily shook her head, her eyes glistening in the sunlight. "Not in so many words. But I've spent my entire life looking over my shoulder, feeling like someone's watching me." Ellery finally saw the invisible chains Baily lived with.

"For years, I slept curled in a ball or in my closet beneath a thick quilt at night, thinking no one would look for me there." Ellery recognized that feeling. As she listened to Baily, memories pressed down so hard, she could barely breathe. "Jacqui would never let me sleep in her room. And the boys? Well…"

"And Mom was gone, so I had no one." Ellery could see

what that aching admission was doing to her. Her sister folded herself in half and pressed her face to her knees.

"Baily. I'm so sorry for everything you went through. You shouldn't have had to suffer like that."

Her sister sat up, her eyes an ocean of pain. "I work the middle of the night shift at the bakery so I don't have to interact with anyone I don't know." She twisted the end of her towel. "And I have PTSD because of what happened to *you*."

Baily's eyes drifted to the main house. "Living close to Dad is the only place I feel safe. I can breathe when I'm here." She rolled her neck in a circle. "Ben puts up with me, and Piper hates me. She says I'm too controlling." Baily grew silent. Ellery saw her weighing another thought. "Do you know why Ben and I only have one kid?"

Ellery's hand turned upward in question.

"Because I'm scared shitless. I couldn't keep two kids safe. How can anyone watch two at once?" She turned toward Ellery. "Mom couldn't."

Ellery gasped. Baily's pain was spilling over onto her. She was absorbing it rather than being her sounding board.

Baily stared into the waves. "Then you show up, and suddenly, I feel like that scared little girl again, wondering if you led that insane woman back here. I worry she wants me this time." The desperation on her face was thick. "I jump at every sound, and I'm constantly aware of my surroundings. It's exhausting being on high alert twenty-four-seven. When I fall asleep—if I *can* sleep—I have the same nightmare. I'm being kidnapped, and you're laughing. 'It's your turn now!' you yell as that deranged woman drags me away."

A shiver ran up Ellery's spine. She wrapped her hands inside the ends of her towel and pulled it tighter around her. "I wouldn't wish what happened to me on my worst enemy." Ellery shook her head. "And I would never want it for you."

Baily lifted her legs onto the deck chair. "Logically, I know that. But I can't stop the nightmares. And every time I'm around you, I get this churning in my stomach that I can't shake."

Ellery's face softened. "Karma's gone, Bai. She can't hurt you. But I'm here, and I want to help." She took her sister's hand. "Would it help if I went to therapy with you?"

Baily's shoulders fell, and her face crumbled. "You'd do that for me?"

"I'd do anything to have you back in my life," Ellery said, the emotion in her eyes reflecting her sister's.

Baily stared at her for the longest time. "Wow," she finally whispered, wiping her eyes with the thick towel. Suddenly, the corners of her mouth twitched upward. "I guess if you do that for me, the least I can do is teach you to swim."

"Wonderful," Ellery said sarcastically. "We don't have to tell anybody about this little incident." She wagged a finger at the lake.

Baily chuckled, her expression brightening. "Oh, come on. It's too good not to share."

"Of course it is. But maybe we could…"

"Nope. This is one of those sibling things. So, it's coming out."

THIRTY-FIVE

Ellery sat on the edge of her bed. Her thumbs tapped out the message three times, each refining her thoughts. Finally satisfied, she tapped *send* and fell backward onto the mattress, wondering if it had been a mistake. Almost instantly, her phone buzzed to life, notifications chiming like a chorus.

This better be important.
I have a life, you know.

Doing what?

Checking the expiration date
on the mayo.

You're a dork, Preston!

Strawberry cheesecake ice cream!

I heard they have garlic
ice cream. Maybe…

Ellery's phone vibrated again, the screen lighting up with three notifications, each an emphatic "NO!" The moment she read them, she laughed until she cried. She dried her face on the bottom of her T-shirt and reveled in her newfound family. Seconds later, a text from Liam pinged. A smile spread across her face.

Don't forget the cherries.
Good Lord, whatever you do,
don't forget the cherries.

After slipping on her tennis shoes, she grabbed her purse, hooking it over her shoulder before heading to her dad's office.

She knocked on the doorframe, wanting to catch his attention before entering. "Could I borrow your car for an hour or so before you take off? I have to go to the grocery store."

Weston glanced up from his computer, the afternoon light catching the creases of his forehead. "Secret sibling meeting?" His smile told her he knew more than she thought—much more.

Ellery straightened her shoulders in surprise. "I didn't think you knew about those."

Weston leaned back in his chair, a grin spreading across his face. "Do you know why I keep Edda—even though it's just the two of us here?" Ellery raised a shoulder.

"It's not because she's good at what she does." Weston closed his laptop before pivoting his chair and fully engaging her. His smile grew as he crossed his hands in his lap. "It's because she has a big mouth."

Ellery's eyes were fixed on him, unsure what to make of his claim. He smiled. "I know everything that happens here."

"Remind me to make that woman my best friend." Ellery's mind raced with thoughts of potential gossip and family secrets she had yet to uncover. She might be onto something.

Weston stood in the doorway. "Come with me." Ellery followed him to the garage. "Your car." He pointed to the Range Rover he had offered her weeks before. "Now that your cast's off, I figure it's safe for you to drive again." He held out a set of keys he had grabbed from a hook near the door but quickly withdrew them, a teasing glint in his eyes. "As long as you can tell me what to do if a deer steps in your lane."

Ellery's shoulders fell. "Don't swerve. Hit it head-on if you can't stop or miss it safely." She scowled at her dad. "It seems so mean to kill a deer like that."

"Better him than you." Her father gave her the *look* Ellery had read about. It brought a smile to her face. "Promise?" He dangled the keys over her hand.

"Promise. Anything else I should know?"

After a moment of contemplation, his expression shifted. "Yes, there is." His face was serious enough to make her lean in. "If you hit a skunk, park your car a long way down the road." He winked at her. "I'm only sort of kidding about that one."

Ellery wrapped her hand around the keys. "Thank you. I can afford to buy a car, though. You didn't have to do this."

"All the kids got a car when they graduated high school." He held his hands out to his sides. "You just got yours a little late."

Ellery's stomach plummeted. "You know I never actually graduated, right?"

"I do. But I'd say you've done pretty dang well for yourself, all things considered." He touched her shoulder. "If you ever decided you want your GED, there's a program at the school we could get you in."

Ellery stepped forward and threw her arms around Weston. She pressed her cheek against his chest. "Thank you, Dad." At that moment, she felt complete, like she was finally back where she belonged.

"I'll be gone by the time you get back. So, be careful." His words felt like love. "And maybe try to leave the house in one piece tonight, okay? I get so tired of Edda complaining about everything you kids do," Weston said with a chuckle as he headed inside.

"We're not exactly kids, Dad."

"You are to me." He pulled her into a warm hug.

A peacefulness Ellery had not felt before washed over her as she drove into town. She turned on KOOL 108 and listened to songs she had no idea existed. Her dad was right about one thing—this vehicle would fare far better in a battle with a tree than her old one.

Just before the clock struck six, her siblings began to arrive. Ellery had meticulously arranged every topping she could find on the large wooden tray Edda kept on the counter. The ice cream remained in the freezer until everyone was there.

When Preston walked in, he shed his tie and jacket, tossing them over a living room chair.

"Long day?" Jacqui hooked an arm through his and walked him into the breakfast nook.

"No. It wasn't bad. But I had a client toward the end of the day who couldn't take a hint that her issue wasn't legal. I literally pushed her out the door. What I really need is a beer." His face twisted as he addressed Liam. "What do you think a beer float would taste like?" His face was hopeful. "Could you eat one without throwing up?"

Liam's face twisted in disgust. "No. Just the thought of it makes me want to gag."

Unfazed, Preston shrugged. "Okay, then. I guess I'll go with extra."

The lines between Baily's eyes deepened. "Extra what?"

"Extra everything." A hint of a smile played on his face.

Ellery removed the lids and set the buckets of ice cream on the island, taking a cautious step back as the piranhas attacked. She sat and watched momentarily, still unable to accept how four usually well-mannered individuals could act like wild animals.

Liam pushed the strawberry topping and the chocolate shell in her direction, his eyes watching her as he shoved a huge spoonful of what could only be called slop into his mouth.

"Not today, brother. Today, I'm eating like a Chambers." A grin widened across her face.

Preston shoved the tray toward her. "About damn time."

Beaming excitedly, Ellery lifted her spoon high, a cascade of chocolate syrup and caramel dripping onto the countertop. "I'd like to make a toast."

"Ooh. Look at you, all fancy," Baily teased.

"Alright. Get your spoons up here," Ellery demanded, reaching across the island. Immediately, the others followed suit. Five overflowing spoons of ice cream and toppings dripped onto the quartz countertop. "To ice cream—that's so much better with toppings." She raised her hand to signal she was not finished. "And to people—who are so much better with siblings."

"Ah, that was so sweet." Liam's voice was dripping with sarcasm. He leaned forward, his eyes full of mischief. "I'd like to add something." He held his spoon higher. "To Jacqui, Preston, Bai, and Elle." A crooked grin hiked up the corner of his mouth. "I need some money. Send it with Zelle."

Preston pushed Liam's arm down, ready to interject his own toast. "Liam's a dork. Liam smells—pew. Mom should have stopped at perfection, but then she gave birth to you."

Liam's voice grew louder. "Preston's a..."

"Children!" Jacqui interjected sharply. "Are you quite done?"

Preston tilted his chin, feigning an overly serious demeanor, and looked at his sister. "Yes, Mother," he replied.

"Liam?" Jacqui asked. He nodded, resignation written on his face. "Go ahead and finish your toast, Elle," she prompted.

Gratitude danced inside Ellery as she glanced around the island. "I just want to thank you for accepting me into the family. That's what tonight's about. I love you guys."

"My arm hurts," Baily complained with an exaggerated pout. "Are we done yet?"

"Yes. Sorry." Ellery chuckled. "Go ahead."

"We're not accepting you into the family, Elle. You *are* family. We're just glad to have you back." Liam smiled at her across the counter.

Suddenly, the doorbell rang, slicing through the air like a

flat note in an opera. Ellery flinched at the off-key sound. "Dad told me somebody's coming to fix that."

The others watched one another as if playing the game of Clue, curious about who was at the door but, more importantly, waiting to determine who dared leave the ice cream long enough to answer it. Finally, Preston pushed back his stool and made his way to the door. Unconcerned about protecting his family, Huck plopped near Jacqui's feet, waiting for leftover ice cream.

Liam made a face. "Pfft. Some watchdog you are."

Silence filled the room when the front door slammed shut, and Preston returned, his face marked with trepidation.

"Who was it?" Baily's face was laden with concern.

"It was a reporter from New York." He made eye contact with Ellery. "She said she knew you were Ellery Gray." The muscles in Preston's jaw flexed. "*The* Ellery Gray." He spoke her name like a four-letter word.

"What?" Liam grabbed Preston's arm. "How?"

"No clue." Preston's eyes met Ellery's, seemingly searching for answers she did not have. "She said she was promised an exclusive interview with you."

Shivers ran down Ellery's spine. She felt the walls move toward her. Her body collapsed inward as the world imploded around her, and an anxiety attack grabbed hold. Hunters Cove and the rest of the world had finally shifted the spotlight on some other human-interest story. Now, it would start all over again. All she wanted was to fade into obscurity—rather than be thrust back into the unyielding glare of public attention.

THIRTY-SIX

The breakfast nook was thick with an uneasy silence after the news of the reporter at the door. It was possible it would be the only quiet the family would know until everything blew over again—if that was even possible. Once Ellery's identity was known, the small, quiet moments amidst the Chamberses' fame would fade quickly.

Her name would be the talk of the country. Gossip would spread like wildfire. Heads would turn as she walked by. Once the world knew what Ellery looked like, where she lived, that she was a Chambers—famous in their own right—and that her stories were more fact than fiction, she would always be under public scrutiny.

Ellery swallowed hard. The taste of dread knotted in her throat as she met the eyes of her siblings. They were looking to her for answers she didn't have. And it was not only family; she could almost hear the murmurs of the outside world creeping closer, hungry for the next chapter in her life, for their next big story.

She hunched over the counter, her hands trembling uncontrollably. Tucking them beneath her legs, she hoped to find a sense of calm, but it evaded her. "H-How did that reporter find me?" she whispered to no one.

"And who offered them an exclusive interview? Other than family, who even knows about Elle?" Liam lowered his chin and stared at Ellery. "What about Destiny?"

She immediately shook her head. "No way. She'd never tell anyone."

Baily erupted like a shaken soda bottle. Her frustration violently bubbled over. "Oh great. The media frenzy's starting all over again because of you." She stood quickly, ramming her stool against the wall. In a fit of anger, she shoved her bowl across the island. "None of us is ever going to be out of your shadow. We're never going to have a minute's peace. You just keep walking into that big damn spotlight." She waved her hand through the air like she was reading a marquee. "Come see the bearded lady," she announced like a carnie might. "Only yours reads, 'Come see the woman who put her family through hell—not once, not twice, but three times.' It's getting old, *Chloe*."

Ellery opened her mouth to protest the name Baily called her but instantly closed it. Her sister's words swirled around her like a relentless tornado threatening to sweep her into the lake of despair where she could not save herself. Each word twisted like a knife, deepening her hurt and fanning her unease. It had taken weeks for Baily not to cringe every time they were together. Ellery squeezed her eyes shut, desperate to shield herself from the world. But the pain of losing ground with Baily hurt worse. A single tear escaped, signaling the beginning of the end.

"Baily's not wrong, you know." Jacqui leaned closer to Ellery.

"Jacqui!" Liam warned, his eyes pointing toward their sister.

She placed a reassuring hand on Ellery's shoulder. "I just mean, the part about the family being thrown into the spotlight again." Her demeanor shifted as she turned toward Baily. There was a protective fire in her eyes. "But it's not Elle's fault, Bai. She didn't do this. It could have happened to any one of us. It could have just as easily been you who was kidnapped and set all of this in motion."

Baily stood rigid, anger seething from her. Bending forward, she pressed her hands against the top of the counter so hard that her fingers turned red. "But. It. Wasn't!" she shot back loudly. She pointed her chin toward Ellery. "It was her," Baily barked as she stormed out the back door.

"Ignore her." Empathy oozed from Preston. "She's just being her jerky self, Elle. Jacqui's right. This isn't on you."

Suddenly, a voice boomed from outside. "Get the hell off my property!"

"Stay here. Out of sight," Liam hissed. "No matter what, do not come outside."

He and Preston burst through the door of the screen porch and ran toward Baily. Jacqui followed close behind. Ellery remained concealed near the entrance to the porch, pressing herself against the edge of the French doors, making herself as small as possible. That was the one thing she was good at. She watched the confrontation unfold through the fronds of a massive potted fern.

Baily snatched the woman's phone, threw it to the ground, and drove her heel into it.

"What the hell are you doing?" the woman yelled. "How dare you?"

"How dare *I*?" Baily shouted, her face a mask of rage. "Maybe you shouldn't be recording things that are none of your damn business."

"I told you not to bother us again," Preston roared, each word dripping with anger. "As an attorney, I'm going to remind you that you're trespassing on private property. Now, get the hell out of here, and don't come back."

"But this *is* my business." The reporter bent down to retrieve her useless phone. "I was told I would get an exclusive interview if I..."

"And who told you that?" Jacqui barked as she folded her arms. "And before you answer, you should know I'm also an attorney."

"I can't reveal my source."

Baily's eyes flashed with annoyance as she glanced toward the house. "For crying out loud. Don't you see? Elle probably called her," she exclaimed, her voice rising as she dramatically waved her arms above her head. "Ooo, look at me. I haven't had attention for at least five minutes."

The reporter followed Baily's eyes toward the house. "So, you're admitting your sister is Ellery Gray, the author?" The woman pointed toward the screen porch. "And she's inside?"

Liam glared at Baily. "We're not admitting anything," he snapped, "least of all to you."

"You're barking up the wrong tree," Preston growled. "Now, get the hell out of here."

"If I'm not mistaken, this house belongs to Weston and Vanessa Chambers." Her finger sliced through the air as she pointed it across the siblings. "Are any of you Weston or Vanessa?" she asked with a sly smirk. "Yeah, I didn't think so."

"We have a right to be here. You don't," Preston countered.

The reporter's lips screwed into a wicked smile. "But the property doesn't belong to you. So, you're trying to toss me off property you have no legal right to either." The woman closed her tablet. "I think I'll wait to speak with one of them."

Just then, the wail of sirens sliced through the quiet, a chilling sound that drew the reporter's attention.

Ellery had hung up the phone only minutes before the sirens sounded. The call wasn't easy to make. She was too used to hiding and handling problems on her own. Her fingers almost defied her as she dialed 911.

"I called them," Jacqui claimed, glancing toward the porch. "They've been on the phone listening to your lies the entire time. And since we live in Hunters Cove, they'll protect us over some two-bit reporter. So, if I were you, I'd get the hell out of here before the police show up and haul your ass to jail."

Frustration flashed across the woman's face as she turned toward the garage. "This isn't over. I'll get the story."

"Not here, you won't," Liam yelled.

Ellery collapsed against the edge of the doorframe. Her body trembled. Her emotions were an open wound that oozed. The ice cream in her stomach slithered its way into her throat as she gently banged her head against her knees as she listened to her siblings discuss her.

"I told you." Baily's words were ripe with arrogance. One hand clenched into a fist, and she slammed it into the palm of her other. "Since she's been here, there's been nothing but chaos. This is a damn circus." She glanced toward the house. "She's the ringmaster, and we're her entertainment." Her shoulders dipped forward. "I don't want to be part of her game anymore. I can't."

"And what are you going to do about it?" Liam tucked a hand into his back pocket. "She's our sister."

"I don't know yet. But I'll figure it out. And when I do, that bitch won't see what hit her."

Jacqui's eyes flickered toward the screen porch. "What would happen if it came out that Elle really is Ellery Gray? Could anything beyond that send the family into the spotlight?"

Suddenly, Ben burst out of the cottage with Piper on his heels. "What's going on? The sirens are getting clo…"

"Piper, get in the house!" Baily screamed. Despite the urgency in her mother's voice, her daughter stood rooted in place.

"Why? What's…" Piper's eyes held confusion.

"I told you to get in the damn house." Baily clapped twice as if she were training a dog. "Now, go!"

Piper finally turned and ran.

"Ben, can you meet the cops and bring them back here?" Liam's message came out more as an instruction than an ask. "I don't want them talking to Elle."

"Sure, but…" Ben's expression was marked with curiosity as he turned away, disappearing around the corner of the garage.

Baily spread her feet and knotted her arms, anger radiating from her stance. "Why do you always protect her? She's obviously not some frail princess who needs saving. Look how she's manipulated all of us."

"Bai, stop!" Preston shouted. "I can't take any more of your condescending commentaries on Elle. She hasn't manipulated anybody. We'd do the same if this were happening to you."

"Really?" Baily shot back, her foot slamming down as she

leaned into the circle, challenging them all with her fierce gaze. "You all destroyed me. Your version of protection made me afraid of my own shadow. From the time I was old enough to understand what happened to *Chloe*, I've been scared shitless, thanks to all of you." She held up a hand to silence any objections. "The only time I can put myself out there is at Eddie's when we sing our song. And even then, have you ever noticed that I stand *behind* the piano?" Baily looked from one to the other, but no one responded. "Yeah, I didn't think so."

Emotional pain surged through Ellery. Baily's sharp tongue cut through her, reminding her how deep the chasm of hatred ran. The others felt their job was to shield Ellery, not love her unconditionally as siblings should.

Jacqui asked the question again. "What else could happen if the truth about Elle comes out?"

Ellery's mind spiraled. *What else?* If the truth about the fire, which she desperately wanted to believe was ignited by Karma, came out, then everything would shatter like glass. Panic surged in her. Prison was a terrifying possibility that would not reflect well on the perfect family.

THIRTY-SEVEN

Ellery followed Liam through the dimly lit backdoor of the gallery. The old stairs creaked beneath them.

"I could have stayed at the house tonight. I didn't have to come here." Her eyes darted around the familiar space, taking in a new painting Liam had begun. "I love the colors."

Liam shrugged off his sweatshirt and tossed it into a chair. "I wasn't leaving you there with that reporter snooping around." He massaged the back of his neck with both hands.

"I'm not sure they'll stop until they get what they want." Ellery wandered into the kitchen for a drink of water. She studied the photo attached to Liam's fridge with a magnetic paint can. "Who's the picture of the woman?" Ellery studied it while she grabbed a glass from the cupboard and ran the water over her finger until it was cold enough to drink.

Liam stood in the doorway, his expression shifting from surprise to mild discomfort. "Crap! I forgot that was there." He ran a hand through his hair. "Well…" His lips twisted into a grimace. "That's my, ah, wife."

Ellery's mouth dropped open as she studied the photograph. "Your wife?" Bewilderment painted her face. She leaned closer, staring at the woman with the jet-black hair and olive skin. "Care to elaborate?"

Liam opened his mouth repeatedly, obviously struggling with his thoughts. "Her name's Jessie," he finally said. "We were married twelve years ago. And we're not together anymore. That's about it."

"No. It's not." Ellery plucked the photo from the fridge

door, grabbed Liam's arm, and pulled him into the living room. "I want the whole story, not just the Cliff Notes."

He sighed. The sound carried both his resignation and unspoken memories. "I'd rather talk about that reporter and how we're going to handle her."

A knot swelled in Ellery's stomach, twisting uncomfortably. "Well, I don't. At least not tonight. I know we have to deal with it, but it's been one heck of a night, and I would prefer to think about anything else." She paused, a smile breaking free. "Like the wife I never knew you had."

"Fine." Liam shrugged away his resignation. "I met her in Mexico when I was down there chasing inspiration. We connected instantly." He held his hands out as if he were questioning the story himself. "And we got married a month later."

"What?" She tightened her fingers around her water glass as it started to slip from her hand. "A month? I'm sure that went over well with Mom and Dad."

Liam scoffed, the sound bittersweet. "That's part of why Dad thinks I'm a loser." He shifted uncomfortably.

"He doesn't think you're a loser. He just doesn't understand us creative types." Ellery dropped onto the couch. She pulled her knees up and wrapped her arms around them. "Don't leave me hanging. What happened?"

Liam sat on the other end and stared at the ceiling. "Jessie's a bit of a free spirit." He rocked a hand in front of him. "Maybe more than a bit. She gets bored easily. So, she's always off searching for her next adventure. I got tired of that lifestyle. So, I moved back to Minnesota a year later, and she went… Honestly, I don't know where she went when I left."

"You never got divorced?"

"No," he whispered, his eyes latched onto hers. "It kind of runs in our family. No divorces, but long separations are not uncommon." He tucked a leg beneath him and sat sideways on the couch. "Periodically, I get these letters from her telling me where she is and begging me to join her. Before I opened the gallery, from time to time, I'd go find her, always hoping she'd changed." He stared out the window. "But Jessie's a dreamer. She paints pictures in her imagination like I paint them on canvas." He shifted. "Only my pictures don't hurt her like hers haunt me."

"How long's it been since you've seen her?"

"Six years." He glanced at his watch. "Four months and seven days."

"But who's keeping track, right?" Ellery teased. "You must still love her if you're counting days."

"No, that's when I moved back to Minnesota for good. I set my watch to track it for some reason." His expression darkened as he rested his arm across the back of the couch. "I think I'll always love her." Ellery could hear the agony in his voice. "The problem is that Jessie chases shiny objects, and I was never shiny enough to hold her interest for long."

Ellery held the photo between them. "Did this just come, or did you dig it out?"

"It came a few days ago."

"Does she send them to torture you?"

"Who knows anything with Jessie? Her last message claims she's coming to Hunters Cove."

"Seriously? How do you feel about that?" Ellery pulled a throw from the back of the couch and covered her legs.

"I don't know. She's never been to Minnesota. I'm not even sure why she's coming." He plucked the photo from Ellery's hand and stared at it.

Ellery set her glass on the coffee table. "If you believed she was ready to settle down, would you let her back into your life?"

"Not in a million years. I can't do that again." He turned the photo face down on the couch. "No matter how many times she promises it'll work this time, it doesn't, and she always disappears. I can't put my heart out there again." Liam's voice cracked, revealing his raw pain.

"Then why are you letting her come? Why not just tell her no?"

Liam snorted. "You don't tell Jessie anything. Like I said, she's a free spirit."

"Why haven't you gotten divorced, then? Maybe that would help you move on."

"That's the plan," Liam stated firmly. "When I found out she was coming, I had Preston draw up divorce papers." A deep sadness hung on his face. "It hurts even to say that. But it's time we go our separate ways—for good."

"When's she supposed to get here?"

"Who knows? She may never even show up. I'm probably just another one of her adventures or a pit stop before she disappears again. Believe me, the sooner those papers are signed, the sooner I get her out of my life."

Ellery could hear both a deep-seated sadness and relief. She knew suffering. Their experiences might not have been the same—but hurt was hurt. "I'm always here if you need to talk."

Liam dropped his feet back to the floor. "Actually, I do. I need to know what we're planning to do about this reporter," he said, changing the subject.

"I don't know." Ellery's body folded inward. "I honestly don't. I don't even want to think about it."

"You could always ditch Ellery Gray and change your name back to Chloe Chambers."

"That's not an option." Ellery's tone left little room for discussion. "I spent the first eighteen years of my life as Summer, and I've been Ellery since then. I'm finally just finding out who I am." She hugged her knees to her chest and rested her chin against them. "Would I do it differently if I'd known I was Chloe Chambers? Probably, but it's too late now. Baily wasn't wrong about the family and the spotlight. If it comes out who I am, it'll happen again."

"No one's blaming you for the press coverage when you were taken or when you came back. And this, well, did you honestly believe you could always hide behind your computer screen without someone finding out you were the great Ellery Gray?" His expression slid from teasing to serious. "How did

Destiny find you anyway?"

"Through my agent, Amelia." She rocked back and forth, trying to recall everything she'd told Liam about Destiny. Being Karma's daughter was something she had purposely left out. "Destiny remained in the apartment." Ellery almost choked on the bitter lie she was weaving together.

"When Destiny went through Karma's stuff, she discovered who I was. So, she contacted Amelia through social media backchannels and told her about Karma. Amelia knew the stories were true." She paused, biting down on her lower lip, a habit she'd picked up when talking about the past. "Amelia gave me Destiny's number because she thought I should know Karma was dead." Ellery clutched a pillow. "I'm sure Amelia hoped I'd step out of the shadows once the dust settled. I'm sure she thinks it'd be good for sales."

"What about Amelia? Could she have let it slip?"

Ellery examined her painted toenails. The cheap pink polish was chipped and badly in need of a redo.

"N..." The thought trailed off, and she glanced away momentarily. "I-I don't think so. She knows how important it is for me to fly under the radar after living with Karma." Ellery stared out the window. "I'm pretty sure she'd have let that be my call."

"I know I asked you this earlier, but isn't it possible Destiny..."

"Never." Her ponytail wildly swung from side to side. "If she got involved, reporters would find her. They'd be hounding her night and day. She's going to school to be a PI. If she stepped into the limelight, she'd never make it as a PI."

"Is there anyone else?"

"Unless one of the family..." Suddenly, she stopped dead. "Or Edda?" She stared out the window, seeing nothing, as she considered the possibility. "Dad told me she has a big mouth."

"Well, that's true, but Edda's as faithful as she is...obnoxious." His grin told Ellery exactly how he felt. "If Dad asked her not to share something, she'd lock it up tight."

"Then I'm at a loss." Ellery tucked a chunk of hair behind her ear. "And you don't think Baily would have…"

"No. If it brought *you* attention, she'd be completely against it. She's very jealous of you—and anyone who's not her."

Liam's phone suddenly buzzed. He read the text. "Preston wants to meet in his office tomorrow morning to figure this out."

"Do you need me to cover the gallery?"

"Not on your life. You need to be part of this discussion. For now, you're attached to one of us at the hip." Liam scrunched his face. "Well, maybe not Baily. You could end up in the lake again."

Ellery's cheeks burned. "She told you about that?"

"Oh, she tells everybody—every chance she gets." Liam's grin morphed into a yawn. "I'll make a few calls tonight and see who I can get to cover." As he stood, stretching his arms over his head, the photograph of Jessie caught the light. He grabbed the picture. "After that, I'm putting this in the box with all the other stuff she's sent me over the past twelve years, and when she knocks on my door, I'll hand it all to her and send her packing."

"Do you think that's possible? Are you going to be able to let go after that long?"

Liam snorted. "I guess we'll see. But after it's all packed, I'm going to bed." His eyes met hers. "And I think you should do the same. It's been one hell of a night."

He was almost to the bedroom when Ellery stopped him. "Thank you."

"For what?"

"You could have turned your back on me so many times during the past several weeks, but you didn't."

An impish grin grew across Liam's face. "It doesn't mean I won't." He smiled as he closed his bedroom door.

That last statement haunted Ellery. If she feared anything, it was Liam turning against her. He was the one person she had been able to count on.

THIRTY-EIGHT

Ellery sat perched on a stool in the gallery, her fingers tapping out a rhythm on the countertop while she watched Liam pace back and forth near her. A deep line ran between his eyes, and from time to time, he would swipe a shaky hand through his hair.

"Any ideas?" she asked as he passed for what felt like the hundredth time.

Liam halted abruptly, a questioning look flashing across his face. "About what?"

"The reporter? I'm assuming that's why you're so upset." Ellery instinctively pulled her neck back. "Or is something else bothering you?"

Liam rolled his shoulders backward, trying to release the tension that had stiffened his muscles. "Jessie texted again last night. She claims she's on her way."

"Really? Do you believe her? When she says she's on her way, what does that mean?"

"I don't know. It could mean days, weeks, months. She has no concept of time." His eyes dropped to his watch. "She could show up today for all I know. I doubt it, but she could."

"Do you think she'd tell you she's coming and then just show up instantly?" Ellery tucked a fist under her chin.

"I don't trust her. She does this to me all the time." He pressed his hand against his stomach. "There's not enough antacid in the world to stop the churning going on inside here this morning. Why do I let her do this?"

"She gets under your skin, doesn't she?"

Liam's initial shake of his head transitioned to a reluctant nod. "I wish she didn't."

"Okay. Then, let's talk about something else. Jessie and the reporter are both off-limits for now. Deal?"

"Good luck with that. We both know it'll sneak back in like a turd that's not quite ready to take the plunge."

Ellery's nose scrunched. "That's disgusting." But she was not about to give up. She took Liam's doubt as a challenge. She tapped her steepled fingers together until a thought came to her. "Why's Stephanie coming to watch the shop this morning? What happened to Claudette?"

"When I called her, she told me she's not filling in for anybody anymore."

"That's odd. When I was staying at the Harmony House, she told me she needed the money to take care of her mom."

"Well, you know me, I was only half listening. As soon as Claudette said she couldn't, my mind was already calling someone else. But I swear she said she moved her mom to Safe Haven in Brainerd. That place is the Cadillac of memory care." Liam started to pace again.

"How's she paying for…" Ellery's jaw dropped, and she slowly sat upright as a realization sunk in. "Oh, no. No," she muttered. Fragments of memories clawed into her.

She slid off the stool and strode to the door, her steps much longer than usual. Fear propelled her forward. "I'll meet you in Preston's office. I have to check on something," she called over her shoulder.

Liam stopped pacing. "What? Where are you going?" But Ellery was already out the door.

Thoughts violently thrashed as she barreled across the street and down the steps toward the lake. The world around her blurred into a haze. By the time she reached the walking path, she was running.

Ellery flew up the back stairs of the B&B, every muscle in her legs straining as she took them two at a time.

She threw the back door open with such force that it hit the logs with a resounding thud. Sharp gulps cut through the air as Ellery dashed through the narrow hallway.

Paula and Susan were behind the counter with Mary Lou, arranging her rescued flowers into bouquets for the rooms. Ellery grabbed the edge of the counter and bent forward, gasping for breath.

"Are you okay?" Paula set the flowers down and rounded the counter.

Ellery lifted a finger, indicating she needed a moment.

Paula shrugged. "This is Mary Lou Allard. Mary Lou, this is Elle."

"Nice to meet you. You're famous around Hunters Cove," Mary Lou said, extending her hand. Still bent over, Ellery gave her a thumbs-up. "I've been friends with your mother since your folks first moved to town."

When she finally straightened, she pressed a hand to her side, massaging a cramp. She nodded to the woman.

"Is Clau-Claudette here t-today?" Ellery's voice came in spurts.

"No," Susan said. "Unfortunately, she's not working anymore. Not just for us but for anyone. She told Paula she was retiring."

Ellery felt like she could almost breathe normally. "Did she say why?"

Susan looked at Paula, who had again picked up a large bouquet of roses and carnations.

"Not really. It sounded like she'd come into some money, so she was moving her mom to a care facility in Brainerd." Paula glanced at Susan. "But if she won the lottery, we're gonna start playing it twice a week."

"She told me the same thing," Mary Lou said. "If you're playing the lottery, I want in."

Ellery's shoulders sagged momentarily. The lottery Claudette won had nothing to do with matching numbers and everything to do with finding her book. Suddenly, a thought buzzed through her. She straightened, urgency radiating through her. "Is anybody staying in the room I used?"

"The couple checked out this morning," Susan said. "I was just heading up to clean before the new guests arrive."

A rush of adrenaline shot through her. "I need to look for something I may have left there." She dashed up the stairs, each step matching her racing heartbeat.

Adrenaline pumped through her when she flung the door open. Desperation sent her to her knees at the end of the bed. The coolness of the hardwood floor was a sharp contrast to the heat rising within her.

"Please be there. Please be there." Ellery's pulse beat at breakneck speed as she threw the bed skirt up and searched beneath the bed, but there wasn't even a dust bunny. Her body went weak, and she felt as if she could crumble into a million pieces.

Pushing herself to her feet, she dashed to the closet and flung the door open, nearly removing it from its hinges. Light washed over the small space when she yanked the chain above her head. She ran her hand over the high shelf but found nothing. Panic swelled.

She peered behind the curtains and checked the windowsill. She jerked the roller blind down and let it go, wildly spinning until it reached the top. Each empty drawer revealed the same.

Desperation clawed at her as she crouched to search behind the dresser. Her world spun into a vortex of fear. Finally, she lifted the mattress as she prayed to find the book. But there was just more emptiness.

Just then, Susan appeared in the doorway. Ellery slid down the wall, her back scraping against the rough boards. She pressed her forehead to her knees.

"What are you looking for? Maybe I picked it up when I was cleaning."

Ellery's eyes fluttered shut, fighting the urge to cry. When she finally opened them, the truth hit her even harder. "It's a book." Ellery did not dare divulge anything else.

"There're no books in the Lost and Found. I went through

the box a couple of days ago," Susan said.

"Could Paula have found it?" Ellery's voice was smothered in heavy frustration.

"Found what?" Paula entered the room, balancing a large vase of flowers in each arm.

"Elle thinks she left a book in here."

Paula shook her head, her hair lightly brushing her shoulders. "Haven't seen one." She set a vase on the small table. "But did you check the bookshelf downstairs?"

Ellery's hopes skyrocketed. The possibility lifted her from the floor, and she pushed past the women and thundered down the stairs. Racing across the room, she almost skidded into the large bookshelf. Her fingers rapidly grazed the titles as she checked every black spine.

With no luck, panic clawed at her. Ellery pulled sections of books from the shelf and ran her hand behind them in case it had somehow gotten lodged there. She even checked behind the shelf but found nothing.

Her shoulders slumped in defeat as Susan stepped into the lobby and moved behind the counter.

"I wonder if Claudette found it. You could ask her."

Ellery's chest heaved as she moved toward Susan, a deep feeling of unease growing inside her. "Do you have her address or phone number?"

Susan stepped behind the counter and scribbled something on a scrap of paper. "I'm not sure if she'll be there, though. She told Paula she was leaving Hunters Cove."

"As in moving? To Brainerd?" Ellery clamped her teeth together, already knowing the answer. The pieces were suddenly falling into place.

Susan's shoulders lifted in a casual shrug. "I assume so, but…"

Ellery snatched the paper from Susan's hand, her face locked in determination. "Thank you," she called, racing toward the back door. She narrowly dodged a couple exiting one of the rooms; their expressions of surprise were a blur as Ellery darted past.

By the time she reached Preston's office, her chest heaved, each breath a struggle. "W-wait. I-I think I..." she panted, bending forward as she fought to regain the ability to speak normally for the second time in fifteen minutes. "Know wh-who." She held her thumb and little finger to the side of her face like a phone. "L-later," she sputtered, dashing out the back door and toward her car, parked behind the gallery several businesses away.

THIRTY-NINE

As Ellery sped down Highway 371 toward Brainerd, the tall pines lining the road cast flickering shadows across her windshield, matching the disturbance fluttering inside. Panic drummed inside her. The realization that Claudette had orchestrated such a betrayal was disgusting. If it was true, the woman was on about the same level as Karma.

The scene unfolded like a crime drama, pieces falling into place with eerie clarity. She had access to Ellery's room at the B&B while Susan and Paula were away. Claudette had spent most of her time cleaning while Ellery was there, placing her on the *most likely culprit* list.

And then there was the motive: her mother needed twenty-four-hour care, an impossibility since Claudette had to work to pay to keep the lights on. Ellery knew all too well that desperation made people do awful things.

As the highway stretched before her, Ellery's thoughts spun—from disbelief to understanding to anger and back. There were moments she wanted to rip Claudette apart. Other times, she felt the woman's hopelessness. As the miles passed, narrowing the distance between them, she knew the connection between Claudette and the reporter showing up was not merely a coincidence. It had been a planned and calculated attempt to extort money.

Ellery trusted very few people. It took a lot to lower her defenses enough to let them in. Somehow, she had been in such a vulnerable place when trying to reconnect with her family that she let her guard down, and Claudette had nudged her way in.

That had been a massive mistake, one she would never make again.

On the outskirts of town, the magnitude of the confrontation about to go down grew heavier. Ellery set her navigation to the Safe Haven Memory Care facility. Instead of tamping it down, she allowed her anger to boil. The thirty-minute drive felt like an eternity. Her fists clenched the steering wheel as thoughts of betrayal ignited her rage. How could anyone be so cruel as to strip away her choice to live her life the way she wanted? What gave anyone that right? The fact Claudette did it for self-serving purposes was beyond evil.

Upon arrival, Ellery parked in the spot closest to the front door. Sitting in the warm sunshine, she played the *What if?* game. What if Claudette apologized? What if it had all been a misunderstanding? What if she hadn't been the one who had stabbed her in the back? Or what if it had been a guest who'd found the book and sold it to the press? Then, she would walk away and deal with the outcome if that were the case. *But what if it wasn't?*

Finally, she climbed out of her car and entered the outer door. A woman smiled and buzzed her in through the main door that was kept locked to protect the residents. She forced a smile onto her face, becoming a player in Claudette's cruel little game.

"Good morning. Who are you visiting today?" The receptionist tapped her finger on a sign-in book.

Ellery's throat went dry. "I, ah, I'm visiting Claudette Mayer's mother," she said, hoping the woman would not probe deeper into their non-existent relationship.

"Oh, Ida's such a sweetheart," the woman gushed. "We're so happy she's here. Does she know you're coming?" A laugh escaped her. "Silly me. What am I thinking? This is Memory Care. Of course, she doesn't know."

The woman waited for Ellery to finish signing in before grabbing the clipboard from the counter. She raised her glasses and studied the board, reading the visitor list out loud.

Ellery felt a wave of irritation. She wanted to confront Claudette, not waste time listening to the receptionist carry on. Biting the inside of her cheeks to stifle a retort, she feigned interest in an activities calendar posted on the countertop.

"It looks like her daughter's in with her, but there's plenty of room. If you need another chair, feel free to grab one from the hallway."

"Thank you," Ellery managed to say, carefully monitoring her tone. "I can't remember her room number."

"One-twenty-four," the woman chirped, hooking her thumb down the hallway as the phone rang.

Grateful to whoever was on the other end of the line, Ellery spun around and disappeared down the corridor. The faint hum of fluorescent lights tugged at the hairs on the back of her neck. As she approached Ida's room, she could hear Claudette's soft voice as she spoke with her mother. Had Ellery not known better, she would have sworn she was talking to a small child.

She leaned a shoulder against the rough paperboard wall and strained to catch snippets of their conversation.

A woman wearing navy blue scrubs pushed a large cart toward her. "Can I help you?"

"No, thank you. I just didn't want to interrupt." The woman offered an understanding nod before continuing on her way.

Once again, Ellery leaned close to the doorway. When the room fell silent, she quietly stepped inside. She remained in the doorway until Claudette noticed her. The woman jumped when she saw her. Her reaction told Ellery everything she needed to know.

"Elle?" Surprise flooded Claudette's face. "W-what are you doing here?"

Without uttering a word, Ellery closed the door behind her. Suddenly, the gravity of the situation hit her, and her legs almost gave out. She moved toward a chair, running her hand along the wall for support until she could drop into it. Her gaze was fixed on Ida, who lay motionless in her bed. Compassion suddenly overpowered her. She slapped it away, searching for the rage that propelled her only moments before. Ellery rocked the chair for several seconds, stoking her anger.

"This is a very nice place you found for your mom," she finally said, taking in the layout of the room. "I bet it cost a fortune." There was a sharpness to her voice. She hoped Claudette would feel it, to know even a tenth of the pain she felt.

Claudette stole a glance at her mother. Ellery saw her body shrink inward before she suddenly pulled her shoulders back. "She doesn't have long left. They just started her on hospice."

"I'm sorry to hear that." Suddenly, anger surged through her, smothering the compassion she felt. This wasn't the time to waffle. She scolded herself for taking her eye off the ball of the situation *Claudette* had created. Stiffening her back, Ellery slid to the front of the chair and locked her hands together. "It's nice you can spend so much time with her." Her head bobbed suspiciously. "Liam, Susan, and Paula told me you weren't filling in for them anymore. So, I assume you're spending all your time here now." Again, she scanned the room. "In this *really* nice place."

As Ellery stared at Ida, empathy battled with her anger. Instantly, she clamped down on her emotions, only allowing room for her rage to seep through. "I heard you also moved to Brainerd. That surprises me since your mom doesn't have... Well, you know. You said it yourself." She hesitated, looking at Ida again before locking eyes with Claudette. "I would have thought you'd have stayed in Hunters Cove, knowing there isn't much time left. It's so much cheaper there."

Suddenly, Claudette turned away from Ellery. The soft rustle of the bed covers filled the wordless silence as she smoothed them around her mother's frail body. Her trembling hands ignited a fire in Ellery. That fear said it all. Claudette knew she'd made a mistake. No, it wasn't a mistake. Mistakes could be forgiven. There was a fix for them. This had been done on purpose.

"Why are you here?" Claudette finally asked. "I'm guessing

you didn't come to see my mom. So, what do you want?"

Every nerve of Ellery's body tingled as if it were on fire. "What do I want? Hmm. How 'bout we talk about what I *didn't* want?" Her eyes flared. "I didn't want my family to be accosted by that reporter yesterday." The lines around Claudette's mouth deepened. "That's right. It seems someone promised her an exclusive interview. Any idea who might have done that?"

Claudette opened her mouth but closed it again, clearly unable to defend her actions.

"Why? Why did you do it?"

The woman sat on the edge of her mother's bed, the pressure air mattress sinking beneath her. The sun that had been shining through the window when Ellery arrived lay hidden behind a cloud, bathing the room in a deep gloom. Claudette drew a deep breath and released it slowly. "I don't know," she finally admitted, her voice fragile.

"Yes, you do. Tell me." Ellery gritted her teeth, keeping her emotions in check until she heard Claudette's lame excuse. "Tell me why you felt it was okay to throw my life under the bus rather than talk to me?"

For several seconds, Claudette watched her mother, who had fallen into a deep sleep. Finally, she cast a hand toward Ellery. "You're one of them. None of you have never had to work for anything in your entire lives."

"How dare you?" Ellery hissed. "You know full well I didn't grow up a Chambers." Her expression intensified; her jaw shifted to the right, and she glared at Claudette. "It seems you know everything about me." An accusatory finger poked toward the woman. "Especially since you stole my book."

Claudette's eyes drifted to the floor. Her body shrank as she resignedly abandoned the unspoken lie she could no longer defend.

Warmth flushed up Ellery's cheeks. "That's what I thought."

"All I wanted was for Mom to die someplace nice."

"I understand that. I even feel for you." The empathy Ellery felt was short-lived. "But I don't understand how you could deliberately hurt me for your own gain." Ellery's jaw pulsed. "So, how much did you get for my story?"

"What?"

"You heard me. How much did you get to betray me?"

"What does that matter? You have money. Your family has money. I just wanted to get ahead for once. Does that make me a bad person?"

"Stealing? Backstabbing? Lying?" Ellery's nod was deliberate. "Yeah, I'm pretty sure that makes you a bad person." Her glare was red hot. "Besides, this isn't about money. It's about peace." A deep ache resonated within. "*My* peace." Her eyes drifted toward Ida. "And you took that away from me." Ellery folded her hands in her lap. "How does that make you feel?"

Claudette sat like a small child, refusing to admit guilt.

Ellery swept a hand across the room. "You know, Claudette, your mother might have a beautiful place to pass into her forever home, but because of what you did, you'll never have a day's peace. You'll regret this decision your entire life. And I guarantee you, if your mother were coherent, she wouldn't have wanted you to do what you did."

Claudette kept her weight low as she moved to her mother's recliner beside the bed. She collapsed into it and folded her hands. "What do you want from me?"

"I want you to fix this."

"How?" Claudette leaned forward. "If I admit I lied about the interview with you, I'll have to repay the money." Her eyes flitted around the room. "And a lot of it's already been spent." A look of desperation crossed her face as her nose crinkled and tears glistened. "Why don't you want people to know who you are anyway? What difference does it make if the world knows?"

The fire! Ellery wanted to scream. Instead, she glared at Claudette while she gathered her thoughts. "I already told you. It's about spending the rest of my life in peace. You read how awful my childhood was. Now that I have a real family, I just want to live a normal life. I want to forget everything that happened to me in the past. But that's impossible now that you've plunged your fingers into my life and plucked out the parts that benefited you." She rubbed her thumb and fingers together, indicating Claudette's goal of money. "But because of you, my family will always be in the crosshairs."

Claudette shrugged. "I'm sure this will all blow over in a few weeks. Then you can…"

Ellery abruptly stood, the small rocker sliding backward, slamming against the wall. "What gives you the right to make decisions for me? Why do you get to play God? This little move of yours puts you on the same level as Karma. You both felt your wants were more important than mine."

Claudette's fingers moved restlessly, tapping the arms of the chair as she processed Ellery's fury. "I guess I didn't think about it like that," she finally admitted.

"Of course you didn't." Ellery cast a glance toward Ida. "I honestly believe you love your mom so much that you would do anything for her, but what you did to me is deplorable." With that, she started toward the door. "And I expect you to fix it."

"How?" Claudette's voice screamed desperation, yet Ellery was unmoved. "How am I supposed to do that? Please tell me."

"Return my book for starters," Ellery said, her arms crossed.

"I can't." She shook her head. "They already paid me for it, and there's no way to get it back."

"Hmm. Then I guess you'll need to figure out another way." Ellery spun around when she reached the door. "You know, Claudette, had you asked, had you genuinely apologized for what you did to me, I would have given you the money you needed to pay those people back. But all you've done is make excuses, throw shrugs at me like it was no big deal." Ellery stared at Claudette until she turned away." It doesn't feel like you think you did anything wrong. So, I guess you'll have to figure it out alone."

"A-And if I don't?" Claudette stammered.

Ellery shrugged, the gesture contrasting sharply with the gravity of the conversation. "It's not an option." The sentence was direct. She could not have misunderstood it. Ellery jerked the door open and left Claudette to drown in worry.

FORTY

As Ellery headed toward Hunters Cove, her apprehension swelled. The browns and greens of early summer swirled past her, barely registering. She was consumed with Claudette's decision to destroy her life and her refusal to take responsibility for her actions.

Guilt gnawed at her. Ellery had always prided herself on her compassion, yet, with Claudette, she wavered between empathy and betrayal. When she began leaning too far toward empathy, she reminded herself about the woman's scheme. That was all it took for the bitter taste of injustice to take over.

Whether Claudette deserved redemption or a second chance slashed at Ellery. She could save herself by giving her the money to repay the reporter, but Claudette's lack of remorse for what she'd done cut the deepest, sending them into a stalemate. And worse, now that the word was out that she might be reclusive author, Ellery Gray, even if the money were returned and they shut down the reporter, the story would eventually grow legs. Other journalists would catch wind and begin poking around, searching for an article that would put them on the map.

And the book with Karma's annotations? Whoever had that in their clutches had all the information they needed, even without the interview.

As the miles between her and Hunters Cove faded, she felt more lost than ever. The struggle to reconcile her empathy with the pain inflicted upon her felt insurmountable. The opposing emotions crashed into one another, leaving her more confused than before.

Every nerve was on high alert as she steered into the alleyway behind Preston's office. Her body felt jellylike. When she stepped out of her car, her legs wobbled beneath her, and she grabbed the door to steady herself.

Stepping into her brother's office through the back door, Ellery dropped to her knees. Preston dove toward her, hooking an arm through hers and lifting her to her feet. He guided her to a chair and stood in front of her in case she went down again.

"Lana, grab Elle a diet soda and a glass of ice, please," Preston called from his doorway.

Ellery closed her eyes and focused on slowly inhaling and exhaling as she tried to ground herself. Preston tapped a message on his phone before dropping it on his desk.

"What happened?" He poured the soda into a tall glass and handed it to her.

A surge of emotions nearly took her down as she re-lived her confrontation with Claudette.

Liam burst into the office and dropped into the chair beside her. "A fight with another tree?" he asked, trying to lighten the mood.

"It was Claudette." Anger blazed on Ellery's face. "She stole the book and sold my story to that reporter."

Liam's brows pressed inward as his head pivoted toward his brother. "What book?"

Ellery sank deeper into the chair. "The first book I wrote." She closed her eyes for a moment before gazing at Preston. Droplets of memories, reminders of her ugly past, trailed down her cheeks. "The one that proved I was Chloe." Her voice cracked, a reminder of how broken she was. "Karma recorded her thoughts in the margins, claiming it was *her* story and that she would sue me for the rights. She maintained I was her daughter, Summer."

"But that's all true, right?" Preston stepped back. "Quinn told me the books are not about kidnapping, only about how you were raised. Correct?" Ellery nodded. "So, since they have no idea Summer was kidnapped, no one can connect her to our family—or to you. So, if anyone tries to connect those dots, it would only be speculation based on the claims of an insane woman. Or am I missing something?"

Her face went white, and the room began to spin. She clutched the arms of the chair and waited it out. "There's more." Ellery released a long breath. "Karma wrote that I hadn't drowned like I wrote in the book. She said she was made to believe I died in the fire, but somehow, I…"

"Wait. What fire?" Liam asked, casting a sideways glance toward Preston. "I feel like I'm playing catch-up. You've mentioned a fire before, but you always wave it off as nothing. Clearly, it's not nothing."

Ellery's hands trembled as she grabbed a box of tissues from Preston's desk. She sobbed. The grief-filled sound was enough to break even her brothers. Unsure how to help, they offered her solace in soda, an endless supply of tissues, a trash can, a shoulder to cry on, and time.

After what felt like an eternity, Ellery finally exhaled a long, shuddering breath. She wiped her face and blew her nose.

Preston sat on his desk. "Okay, so legally, we can stop this from going further. We can file theft charges against Claudette, and we can nail the buyer for receiving stolen property. A big magazine would likely settle to protect their name, but…"

Liam held up a hand to stop Preston. He intertwined his fingers with his sister's, offering support. "Tell us about the fire. I can see it's eating you up."

Ellery's gaze shifted from one brother to the other as memories flooded back. A wave of pain washed over her, settling in her lungs. She gulped a mouthful of air, but it didn't ease the tightness that clutched her chest.

Ellery steadied herself in the fact she could trust Liam and Preston. "When I was eighteen, I moved out of Karma's apartment. I rented a tiny cabin that wasn't much bigger than a bedroom." Liam handed her a tissue to wipe away the tears that partnered with the memory. "I worked at a small café to support myself. The owner agreed to pay me in cash until I could find my social security number." Ellery let go of Liam's hand and absently twisted the tissue. "I finally had money." Embarrassment squeezed her eyes shut. "And I wasn't eating from garbage cans."

"I hate that woman for what she did to you." Rage flared in Liam's eyes.

Preston grabbed a legal pad and pen. The repeated clicking sound sent her tumbling backward into an incident with Karma that ended with a pen plunged into Summer's leg. With trembling hands, she absently touched her leg where the scar lay hidden beneath her jeans.

"What was the address of the cabin?" Ellery was grateful that Preston's words rescued her from the memory.

Still, she shifted uncomfortably in her chair, picturing the rundown cabin. The address was engrained in her memory, but she did not trust herself. "It's been a long time, but I think it was 209 Kerr Street in Beaufort, South Carolina." Preston scribbled the address on the pad.

Liam offered her the soda. "Go ahead when you're ready, Elle."

Ellery grasped the cold glass, needing both hands to bring it to her mouth. Two sips later, she returned it to Liam and ran her palms against the thighs of her jeans. "It took several months to put all the pieces together. I changed my name, got a new social security number, and began hiding all the money I made." Her eyes found Preston's. "The social security number I finally found digging through Karma's stuff belonged to someone who had passed away around the time I was born. Someone also named Summer."

"Stolen?" Liam looked to Preston for confirmation.

"It happens more often than you think." Preston scratched another note on the paper. "Do you remember that number?" She shook her head. "It's okay." But his eyes told Ellery otherwise.

"I knew the only way I could ever escape Karma was to make her believe I died." Nearly two decades later, relaying the story to her family, the decision rode the line between brilliant and absurd.

The fear in Liam's eyes was palpable. "Please tell me you weren't going to take your…" The words faded.

"No," she insisted, shaking her head. "I told you that before. No matter how much I hated my life, I would never do that." She grabbed another tissue. "But I was going to burn down the cabin and make it look like an accident. If Karma believed the fire took me, I'd be free of her control." Her eyes met Preston's, desperation carving deeply on her face. "It was the only way I could move on." Cotton had glued itself to the inside of her mouth. She grabbed the soda and guzzled it, trying to wash away the dryness.

Understanding flickered on Preston's face. "So, you set the cabin on fire and escaped, hoping they'd think you died because no one would be able to locate you—in or out of the cabin?"

"That was the plan, but that's not what happened." She pressed both hands against her face. "I never lit the match."

Liam sat upright. "Then how did the fire start?"

"I don't know." Her voice trembled as she closed her eyes, haunted by the image of Karma running from the cabin. "I decided to burn the cabin down before dawn so no one would see me disappear into the woods. Before I even picked up the matchbook, the front door handle wiggled—like someone was trying to get in. I knew I had to be quick. But as I was getting ready to light the candle, I got a strong whiff of smoke."

She mindlessly stared at the wall behind Preston's desk. "My mind was so jumbled that I convinced myself I had already lit it. So, I grabbed my backpack and ran out the back door. I crouched down and waited for the flames, but it took longer than it should have. For a moment, I debated returning to see if the candle had gone out."

"Did you see who was trying to get into the cabin?"

The memory played out in the emotions that crossed her face. "By that time, I'd convinced myself it was my imagination playing tricks on me." She swallowed hard. "Just before I stepped out of the woods to go back into the cabin, a huge explosion threw me onto the ground. Too stunned to move, I watched as pieces of the cabin rained down in the opening. Finally, I couldn't stand it anymore, and I covered my face with my backpack." Her chin quivered. "When I opened my eyes, there was nothing left. *Nothing*."

Preston leaned forward. "So, if you didn't set the fire, who did?" He tapped the end of his pen against the side of his face.

Ellery lifted her feet onto the edge of the chair, curling herself into a protective ball. She wrapped her arms tightly around her knees, locking her fingers together. "For years, I tried to figure it out." She closed her eyes briefly. Those few seconds allowed her to replay the explosion and what she believed to be true. "It was Karma. I'm sure of it."

"Karma as in fate or Karma as in Karma, the woman?" Liam asked.

"It was her. I know it was. For the last two decades, I've blamed myself for that fire, but recently, whenever I close my eyes, I see her outside the cabin after the explosion." Ellery grew quiet as she plucked the image from her thoughts. "For a long time, she lay on the ground, face down. Then, finally, she staggered into the woods not far from me." She locked eyes with Preston. "That's what happened. I know it now."

"Are you kidding? Karma tried to kill you?" Liam processed the thought out loud.

"Yes. I'm sure of it. All this time, I believed the fire was my fault, but now I'm sure it was hers. Initially, I didn't know if what I saw was real or if I just wanted someone else to blame." Ellery clutched a sob between her teeth. Rather than let it take her down, she slowly exhaled it. "I found an online article that claimed it may have been a gas leak, but that would have been impossible."

"Mmm. Maybe not." Preston rubbed his chin with his thumb and fingers, deep in thought, as his eyes drifted toward Liam. Finally, his hand dropped into his lap. "You read everything Karma wrote in the margins of your book, right?"

Ellery nodded. "Did she say anything in there that made you think she started the fire?"

Rolling the question around, Ellery let her feet drop to the floor. Her eyes followed the pattern of the wood grain floor as memories of Karma's wild scrawl played before her. "I don't know. It's a jumbled mess up here." She tapped a finger to her temple.

"It's alright. But somehow, we need to get our hands on that book." Preston slid off his desk. "I'll be right back." A plan played on his face as he left his office.

Ellery collapsed deeper into her chair, feeling the weight of the world suffocating her.

Liam watched her for several moments. "It'll be okay, Elle," he said, bending forward, resting his arms on his thighs. "I wish you'd have told me about the fire before."

"I-I couldn't." Adrenaline rushed through her as fear clutched her throat. Ellery felt her confession drive a wedge between them. She reached out and brushed her fingers against his hand. "I'm sorry. I'm sorry," she repeated with more commitment. "I'm so used to hiding, protecting myself that I sometimes forget I have family to lean on now."

"Lana's gonna check on the cabin. She's also looking for information on how the fire started," Preston said as he walked into the office.

Ellery felt her emotions spin into a squall. He held up a hand. "She'll be discreet. If I didn't trust her implicitly, she wouldn't be working here."

"So, if Karma started the fire, then Elle's off the hook?" Liam's face looked hopeful.

The question was loaded. Ellery knew there were too many moving pieces for it to end that easily.

"The problem is, I was the last one there." Ellery's voice was laden with guilt. "Unless there's a way to prove Karma was there that morning, who's gonna believe me?" She glanced at Preston. "There's something else. After I got the advance on my first book, I anonymously sent cash to the owners to cover the cost of the cabin. I wanted to make sure they got their money. That's not what I'm worried about. But if they got an insurance payout, and it looked like someone started the fire…"

Preston's expression shifted. "Yeah. It'd be a felony." He pressed the intercom button. "Lana, see if you can find out if the owners filed an insurance claim on that place."

"On it, boss."

"How?" Ellery met his eyes. "How will she be able to get that information without an agent questioning why someone's poking around decades later?"

"Attorneys have back doors," he explained matter-of-factly.

Liam twisted his mouth, processing their conversation. "So that's why you've never wanted to come out as Ellery Gray? Because the locals would know you didn't die in that fire?"

"That was a huge part of it. But I was more afraid that Karma would find me." Ellery shrank inward. "That's the last thing I ever wanted."

"But she's gone. That leaves the cabin as our only concern." Deep lines spread across his forehead. "Right? Or is there more? Is there anything else? Anything?"

"I worry about Destiny." A frown pulled down the corners of her mouth. Leaving out the information that Destiny was Karma's daughter left a sour taste in Ellery's mouth, but she didn't have a choice. "If this comes out, because she's staying in my house in Schenectady, people will connect her to me, and I won't be able to protect her."

"Let's take Destiny out of the picture for a minute. We'll come back to her," Preston said, looking at Liam, concerns about this new revelation reflected on both of their faces. "We have our work cut out for us." Determination set Preston's jaw. "First, we have to keep that reporter away from Elle. Second, we need to find out how that cabin burned. Lana's working on the second one."

"What do you want me to do?" Liam uncrossed his legs and dropped his booted foot to the floor.

"Play fullback." Preston's words were firm. "Protect Elle at all costs. Hide her anywhere except with family."

His eyes met Ellery's. "As for you, when we find you a place, you have to stay hidden. Don't go near windows or doors. Got it? And wherever you are, don't leave unless one of us comes for you." He wagged a finger between him and Liam.

"What about Mom and Dad?"

"We're not gonna tell them yet. The fewer people who know about this, the better." Preston cocked his head as the plan began to grow legs. "Let's tell them you needed to go back to Schenectady to deal with some issues with the house."

"That's believable." Liam directed his gaze toward his sister. "Now, we need to find a place where you'll be safe."

Ellery rocked as she considered options. "How about in plain sight? I could stay at the B&B. I trust Paula and Susan implicitly. And, while I'm there, I could get some writing done."

Preston nodded thoughtfully. "That would work. But under no circumstances can you come out of your room." He tilted his chin down, emphasizing the seriousness of the matter. "It's possible that reporter might spend a night or two on the other side of your wall."

"What if we buy out all the rooms for a couple of weeks and send Paula and Susan on vacation?" Liam asked.

Preston shook his head. "People'd know something was up. They're moving into their busy season. And with any luck, it might not take that long to figure this out." He turned back toward Ellery, his face stern and uncompromising. "If we find out you didn't cause that fire, and no insurance claim was filed, you have to come forward and admit you're Ellery Gray. I know that's not what you want to do, but it's the only way to save the family from being harassed by reporters twenty-four-seven."

Ellery swallowed hard. "Okay," she agreed, fear poking at her stomach.

FORTY-ONE

Within two hours, Ellery was hidden away in a downstairs room off the lobby of the Harmony House. The air was thick with secrecy within the confines of the room that felt both protective and isolating. It had been strategically chosen for its minimal traffic, closeness to the kitchen, and emergency access to what Liam humorously referred to as *her babysitters*: Paula and Susan. The placard on the door had been changed to read *Storage*. Only one guest room was in that short hallway, and, with a push to reopen a room that had been closed for remodeling, it would remain empty.

When she arrived, the roller shades had been lowered and the curtains drawn. Someone had taken extra care to hang a thick wool blanket over the curtain rod, stapling it to the log wall above the window. If not for the clock on the nightstand or the time on her phone, it would be impossible to differentiate day and night.

Knowing the lake was on the other side of that window drove her insane. Like a dream, it called her to sit near the shore. Until Ellery arrived in Hunters Cove, she had not realized how much she needed the water—not for swimming—Baily had made that abundantly clear the day she pushed her in. But its crystal-clear tranquility allowed her to breathe. It was what Ellery imagined freedom to feel like.

Paula and Susan had been summoned, one after the other, to the back door of the law office. Each was sworn to secrecy, a rarity in a small town where whispers traveled in the wind. Determined to ensure Ellery's comfort and safety, Preston pressed several hundred dollars into their palms for food and essentials. He covered the seven-day room rate in cash and handed each of them an envelope for their silence before sending them out the back, instructing them not to return to the B&B immediately.

Preston had repeatedly warned Ellery to remain behind that locked door. She had repeated the rules to him: if someone knocked, she was to remain silent. If they called out *Hope*, it signaled that the person on the other side of the door was a friend, someone in the know. They would let themselves in with a key while she stepped into the bathroom so she would not be exposed to a random passerby.

Her heart felt heavy as she closed the door and turned the deadbolt that afternoon. Her days of freedom had been temporarily jerked away. Memories took her back to the days spent at Millie and Gus's, hiding beneath a baseball cap and oversized sunglasses. Once they passed, she was alone—until Destiny showed up, imploding everything she had ever believed.

She had just settled down at the small table, her computer screen brightening, when she heard a soft knock on the door. "Hope? I have your lunch."

With light footsteps, Ellery slipped into the bathroom, her heart racing as the deadbolt clicked open. When the door shut, she peeked around the corner.

"I'm so glad to see you. I have a feeling I'm going to get really lonely."

"Whenever you want company, just ask." Paula set the tray down near Ellery's computer. "Susan and I feel awful about what Claudette did to you. We thought we could trust her. I guess she wasn't the person we thought she was."

"That was all on her. You had nothing to do with what she did." A smile broke across her face as she lifted the silver cloche. "Ooh! A turkey croissant and chips. You know me well."

"Susan's out shopping for groceries. Is there anything you

want? Fruit? Snacks? Sodas?"

Ellery cast a hand toward the closet. "Liam loaded me with enough junk food to fill a dozen vending machines. If you never brought me a meal, I could survive for weeks." She laughed. "Honestly, I'm okay. I'll happily eat whatever you bring."

"Okay, but let one of us know if you want anything at all."

Ellery nervously rubbed one thumb with the other. "Is the B&B full?"

"It is, except for the room next door. It will be until the middle of October when the leaves fall off the trees. Because of cancellations, we get a random person here and there, but most people have been in the reservation book since last year." She bent down and appeared to snatch something from the floor. "But you're safe here." Paula dropped the tiny item into the trashcan near the table. "I'll be back around six. If you need anything before then, or you want someone to talk to, text one of us."

"Thank you. You and Susan are godsends. I don't know how to repay you."

Paula winked. "How about a book dedication?" And with that, she was gone.

The deadbolt felt like a sentence. The only difference between her and a prisoner was that the miscreant trying to get to her was locked out rather than in.

Each day seamlessly blended into the next. Ellery would rise by 7:00 a.m. After a leisurely shower and a hot cup of coffee, she would put in her earbuds and watch the local news on her computer, searching for stories about herself. Then, she would exercise, careful not to make a sound. She cherished her fleeting interactions with Susan and Paula. When they were with her, she did not feel so alone.

Liam and Preston checked in frequently throughout the day,

but it wasn't the same as human contact. Preston promised things were progressing, yet the details were like loose threads. Liam's texts were much more entertaining and read like a gossip column.

Her mother's texts were mainly about the house complications she had been led to believe were the reason Ellery disappeared, and her dad begged her to return to share some of *Edda being Edda*. Jacqui checked in each day to see if she would be back for karaoke night. From Baily, there were crickets. She had not expected anything more.

With no social media to distract her, Ellery immersed herself in writing. The story flowed effortlessly; each sentence felt like it had been waiting for its time to be revealed. She texted Amelia one evening, sharing her progress, but she left the story details a secret.

On her third night at the B&B, a full moon slipped past the edge of the thick blanket and through the curtains, casting a narrow sliver of light into her room. The moment felt almost sacred. Unable to sleep, Ellery climbed out of bed and stood in the center of her room. She dropped the digital clock on its face and turned her phone upside-down before unplugging the nightlight that illuminated the bathroom.

Cautiously, she lifted the blanket and roller shade almost imperceptibly but instantly recoiled as if it had burned her fingers. She pressed her back against the wall, recalling the figure who stood outside her window clad in a hooded sweatshirt and jeans.

Fear sucked her under as she dove beneath the covers. Curled into a tight ball, she could not shake the unsettling sensation. It may have been nothing more than a coincidence, someone as curious about the moon as she had been—but the feeling would not go away. It took an agonizing hour before her breathing steadied. Even then, the image of the shadowy figure lingered.

Around 2:30 a.m., exhaustion finally pulled her into a fitful sleep filled with all too real nightmares.

Shower, eat, watch the news, exercise, write. Rinse and repeat. The days blurred together, and the calendar's significance was lost. Without the alert on Ellery's phone, she wouldn't have been able to tell a Tuesday from a Sunday.

Around 9:30 one morning, Ellery was toying with ideas for the next chapter when a soft knock drew her attention. "Hope?" the familiar voice called. Grateful for company, Ellery unlocked the door and pulled it open a crack, forgetting Preston's orders, but it wasn't Susan who stood on the other side.

She attempted to slam the door shut, but a concrete block-sized foot wedged itself into the opening between the door and the frame. Adrenaline surged as Ellery attempted to battle the ogre, but it was like holding back a tsunami with her bare hands.

The man burst into the room and grabbed her, slapping a hand over her mouth. He hoisted her off the ground, her bare feet dangling against his shins. A woman with eyes as cold as steel slipped into the room. As she turned to lock the door, recognition hit Ellery like a sledgehammer, and she went limp in the giant's arms, surrendering not to the enormous figure holding her but to the sinister reality that had come crashing into her life. This woman was the devil—the reporter Claudette had sold their souls to.

"Well, well, well. Ellery Gray, we finally meet—face to face. You're a hard person to find." The woman scowled at the man. "Set her down."

When Ellery's feet touched the floor, she quickly backed away. "What-what's going on?" Adrenaline shot through her as she faced her biggest nightmare.

An evil smile darkened the woman's face. "Like you don't know." She dropped into the chair closest to the door. "I suppose you're wondering who I am. Well, I won't keep you in suspense any longer. I'm Molly King from *Hidden Magazine*." She gestured casually toward the monster on her right. "Parker Doeren, my, ah, photographer."

Doeren lurched toward her. "Don't try anything stupid." He ground a fist into his palm.

Ellery pulled her hands into her sleeves. "Why are you here? What do you want?"

King scoffed. "We were promised an exclusive interview with you. But somehow, you've managed to slip away every time we've gotten close." Her laughter was as cold as ice. "Well, not this time. We had no idea you were staying here until we just happened to book a room—right next door."

"But…"

"Right. Looks like somebody screwed up." She tilted her head slightly. "Or maybe not."

Thoughts of betrayal batted at Ellery. Had Paula or Susan double-crossed her? That was impossible. They would never do that, but then again, she would never have believed Claudette would have either.

With a wink at Parker, King mocked, "Meet Mr. and Mrs. Doeren, from Oceanside, Oregon, visiting family in the Brainerd area. It's amazing how gullible small-town people are." Her laugh was pure evil.

Her voice rose an octave, and she feigned a panicked traveler. "I don't know what we're going to do. We made this reservation almost a year ago. How could you not have it? This won't look good on a Better Business Bureau or Yelp review. We'll take anything." King huffed.

"A glass pressed to the wall, and you can hear damn near every word said in this room." King flickered an eyebrow. "For future reference, the real tipoff was a shower running in a storage room."

Ellery straightened her back, determination surging as she faced her nightmare. "I don't know who you think I am, but I believe you're mistaking me for someone else."

"No." Molly shook her head dismissively. "I don't think so." She leaned deeper into the upholstered chair, her posture relaxed yet predatory.

Ellery inched toward the small table and hastily closed her laptop. She reached behind her and pressed her hand over her phone, but before she could call for help, the giant lunged toward her and wrestled it from her, shoving it into his front pants pocket.

The reporter smirked. "And now you know why he's here. So, if I were you, I wouldn't scream or make any sudden moves. He could snap your neck with his thumbs."

Ellery touched the side of her neck as she dropped onto the edge of the bed.

"Maybe you could explain something to me." King's eyes were as sinister as Karma's. "Since you're the daughter of..." she glanced down at her tablet, "Weston and Vanessa Chambers, one of the wealthiest families in Minnesota, why are you holed up in a dumpy B&B? Why not your own place? Or living with Mommy and Daddy in that mansion of theirs?"

The knot in Ellery's throat was almost unbearable. "I'm a Chambers, but I'm not the Ellery Gray you're looking for."

Fierce and relentless, Molly King leaned forward. "You're not, huh? Well, we'll see about that. You let me know how many of these statements are about you—*not the right Ellery Gray.*" King tapped her tablet. "Some sicko kidnapped you from a park in Minnetonka when you were eight days old and passed you off as her kid to trap some dumb male. She raised you in the South. At eighteen, you changed your name to Ellery Gray and moved to Schenectady, New York, where you lived and worked as a caretaker for August and Matilda Walker, AKA Gus and Millie. Gus died in 2018, and Millie in 2022." An evil smirk slid across King's face. "How am I doing?"

The goon snapped a picture of her with his phone before dropping into the matching chair.

King glanced up. "Looks like you're not convinced yet." She returned her eyes to her tablet. "When the Walkers died, they left you everything: lock, stock, and barrel. Currently, someone named Destiny lives in that house but is not listed on the deed. She attends SUNY."

A nasty smile crossed King's face. "Not bad, huh?" She lowered her eyes and searched for where she left off. "You've written five books about your life, marketing them as fiction rather than a memoir, but people are beginning to wonder." King glanced up briefly. "Your agent's name is Amelia Lopez, and you have a new book coming out within the year. I assume that's why you were so eager to close your computer."

The muscles in Ellery's face went rigid, and her eyes bored into the woman across from her. Her heart pounded against her ribs like a caged animal. She knew that a glance elsewhere could open her up for a physical attack. Her years with Karma taught her two things: don't let anyone see your fear and create a diversion. The third was one she kept in her back pocket. If she could generate enough commotion, maybe someone would hear her.

"How about you tell me something," Ellery spat, pointing toward the beast. "If he's a photographer, why is he taking pictures with his phone? Where's his fancy equipment?" Suddenly, she sprang to her feet, her hands clenched at her sides. "And if you're a decent reporter at all, why do you write for some second-rate tabloid? Yeah, I know all about *Hidden Magazine*. Why aren't you working for a real magazine?"

King slid to the front of her chair and planted both feet on the floor. "Shut your damn mouth, or Parker'll shut it for you," she warned. The growl of her voice sent shivers down Ellery's spine. She smoothed her slacks before looking up. "You don't know anything about me."

Ellery's indignation flared. "And you know nothing about me," she yelled.

King raised her tablet. "I wouldn't call this list *nothing*."

"Everything you said either came from my press conference, a news source, or could be found by any armchair detective online. That last bit about Ellery Gray, the author, is available too. Anyone can look up agents and when books are being released."

King's eyes flicked to her henchman. He strained to lift his massive bulk from the chair. "Sit your ass on that bed, or I'll do it for you," he growled, coming toward her. "And keep your mouth shut."

Ellery stared at the ogre. She sank onto the bed, her mind racing. King never mentioned having the book. Either Claudette lied about where the book was, or the reporter was saving that bombshell as her trump card.

The sharp lines of the reporter's face sliced into Ellery. "Here's something I don't know. Why does your sister Baily hate you so much? I mean, a little cash," she rubbed her thumb against her fingers as if the image would ignite a fire, "and she was willing to sing like a bird."

The shocking statement sent sparks through Ellery. Her skin felt like it was on fire. "I don't believe you. I may not be her favorite person, but Baily doesn't need money. She'd never betray her family like that."

"Oh, wouldn't she?" King leaned back in her chair, her attention turning to the glowing light of her tablet. "So, how much of what I said was true?"

Suddenly, there was a wild pounding on the door. "Police!"

FORTY-TWO

Adrenaline shot through Ellery as she eyed her captors. When King held a hand toward the goon, signaling to stay put, Ellery raced toward the door, twisted the lock, and flung it open. She pushed past the officers and fell into Preston's arms, her sobs escaping in ragged gasps.

"Shhh." Preston wrapped an arm around her and led her into the kitchen adjacent to her room.

Her voice trembled as she tried to speak. "H-how did you k-know?"

"Susan heard voices in your room. She called me, and I called Jansen." As they spoke, loud voices reverberated in the hallway. "Stay here." He held a hand behind him as he left the room.

Ellery stood utterly still, focused on the conversation next door. Finally, Susan guided her onto a wooden stool and took one of Ellery's hands.

"We're reporters," King yelled. "You can't arrest us for doing our job. We've done nothing wrong."

"The last I checked, your job doesn't allow you to break into another guest's room," the officer shouted back.

"We didn't break in," Doeren argued, the pitch of his voice rising.

"Really?" The word was dripping with sarcasm. "So, this woman just opened the door and said, 'Come on in,' to a couple of lowlifes from a magazine whose sole purpose is to destroy people's lives?" He shook his head. "I highly doubt it."

"Doesn't matter," the second cop chimed in. "The

cameras'll tell us if you forced your way in or not." He pointed toward the surveillance equipment ten feet from Ellery's door. "For now, you two can sit in jail while we take our time figuring this out." The click of the handcuffs echoed down the hallway.

When the police paraded the two through the lobby and out the front door, Preston returned to the kitchen. A heavy sigh of relief fell from him. "Why didn't you call?"

"He took... Wait! That guy has my phone," Ellery stammered, pointing to the door.

Preston disappeared, returning minutes later, holding the phone up like a trophy. "Now they can add *stealing* to their list of crimes."

"I'm going to let you two talk." Susan's eyes flickered between them. "Are you sure you're okay? Can I bring either of you anything?"

"No. We're good," Preston answered for both of them. He took Ellery's arm and guided her back to her room.

When the door closed, Ellery imagined herself back in the room with King and Doeren. She longed to open the blinds but knew it was impossible.

"So, tell me what happened." Preston settled into the same chair the reporter had sat in.

"I-I'm sorry," Ellery stammered as she fought back tears. She flung her hands out to her sides. "I don't know how I could have been so stupid. There was a knock, and someone called *Hope*. I thought it was Susan." The memory rushed at her. "When it wasn't her, I tried to shut the door, but you saw how big that guy was."

Preston rocked his head with a smile. "I would've paid big money to see you fight that guy."

Ellery blinked several times. "Why are you laughing?" She struggled to reconcile his amusement with her panic. "So, what happens now?"

"Nothing. You didn't start that fire. I was on my way over to tell you when Susan called."

Her mouth dropped open. "What? How do you know?"

"The article you found was correct. It was a gas explosion." Preston paused a moment for her to absorb the information. He wagged his head slightly. "Because you smelled smoke before you lit the match, it's possible Karma started a fire outside and shut off the pilot light on the stove, but it's just as likely it was a random gas explosion. The fire marshal's report listed it as a faulty stove." He exhaled deeply, the sound resonating with unspoken relief. "Either way, you were lucky to get out of there alive."

Ellery raced to the window. She threw the blanket over the rod, swept the curtains aside, and pulled up the shade. She pushed the window open and gulped in the fresh air. "So, I won't be arrested?"

"Not unless there's something else you want to tell me."

Ellery's shoulders sagged as the tension she had been holding slipped away. A smile spread across her face. "Nothing. Wait. What about the insurance?" Ellery braced herself for the answer she feared.

"They had a policy, but because it was deemed a gas leak…" He raised a palm. "Anyway, unless they can prove Karma started it, which they can't, then no one was at fault."

Ellery pressed the palms of her hands together. "I know I need to tell my story—the whole story, but…"

"You're not telling it to that soul-sucking tabloid." Preston leaned back in his chair.

"What about Claudette? She sold the story to…" Ellery pulled back, unable to state the obvious.

"That's Claudette's problem. She got herself into this mess."

"You know what's weird about that? That reporter never mentioned having my book. She had all this other information, but there was nothing about Karma's comments or the book. Why wouldn't she have told me that?"

Preston scoffed. "If I were a betting man, which I am, I'd say Claudette was hedging her bets."

"I don't even know what that means."

"It means she tried to sell the exclusive to one magazine and probably the book to another." Preston shrugged. "Or, she could still have the book—hoping for a higher bidder."

"But she said she didn't."

Preston's head bobbed. "And you're going to believe her after everything that's happened?"

The seriousness of Claudette's betrayal hit with a one-two punch. "I think I'll ask her again. Give her a chance to come clean." She scanned the room, hoping beyond hope the book would magically appear. "I guess there is something else you should know."

"Oh?"

"King claimed they paid Baily for information about me."

Preston raised an eyebrow. "Oh really? If that's true, there's gonna be hell to pay."

FORTY-THREE

Once again, Ellery stood at a makeshift podium in the gazebo by the lake. The warm breeze ruffled the edges of her notes as she stared into the crowd of reporters from across the country. Each one was eager to capture the story of the elusive author who was known to the public by name only. Her return to her family had been a regional news story. However, the unveiling of Ellery Gray, the author, was a national sensation. Amelia, her agent, stood at her side, ready to field questions about keeping Ellery's secret.

As Ellery began to share her story, her voice was unsteady as memories of her life flashed before her. She recounted the kidnapping as it had been told to her and ended with the arrest of Molly King and her goon, choosing her words carefully, conscious of the people she felt compelled to protect.

"Miss Gray, Shari Horton, *Aitkin Independent Age*," a woman in the front row introduced herself. "I understand why you felt you couldn't come forward when this Karma woman was alive, but when you found out she passed, what stopped you then?"

Ellery stole a fleeting glance at Amelia before answering. "I just wanted my privacy." She knew if she slipped up, any response could unravel her story and send them running toward Destiny.

"So, why now?" Horton asked.

The soft splash of the waves along the shore broke the silence while Ellery wrestled with the question. She shifted away from the mic and cleared her throat, attempting to quell the nervousness that sloshed in her stomach.

"When I realized *Hidden Magazine* was snooping around claiming to have information about me—which they did not," she reiterated firmly, "I knew it would only be a matter of time before someone else claimed the same. So, I..." She made direct eye contact with Preston. "So *we* decided to come forward before another tabloid echoed those claims."

A voice cut through the chatter. "Dawn Roussin, *Brainerd Dispatch*. Rumor has it a local sold your story to Molly King. If so, are you willing to share the person's name? Also, will charges be filed against them?"

"I'm afraid it is true." Ellery fidgeted with the edges of her notes. "But because we're dealing with that as a family, the person's name will not be revealed."

"Ron Sass, NBC," a reporter introduced himself. "You write fiction, yet anyone who knows your story now recognizes there's more fact than fiction in your words. What percentage of your books are based on actual events?"

Ellery felt Amelia squeeze her elbow in a show of support. Whatever she said, Amelia would back her. She opened her mouth but hesitated. Finally, she responded. "Ninety..." She paused, then added, "Five. I would say ninety-five percent of the stories are true. I changed names, shifted locations, and adjusted a few minor details." She glanced into the sea of faces, trying to read the crowd. "But the truth is the truth."

"Would you say your books are more memoir than fiction, then?" Sass pressed.

"Does it matter? It's a story. Like any book, people will read it and take what they need from it." She gestured to another reporter.

"Betty Davis, E! News. We know you weren't in contact with the woman who raised you, but do you have information about her life in the years following your escape?" She held her pen up, indicating she had a second question. "And do you plan to include more about her in your next book?"

Ellery clutched the sides of the podium to steady herself. "I know nothing about her except that she passed away almost three years ago." The lie stung like a deep papercut. Ellery knew everything about those years; Destiny had shared it all. She stood tall. "And as for the book…" she smiled, masking the unease of the question, "you'll have to wait for it to come out."

After several more questions, Chief Jansen thanked everyone for their patience and courtesy. With that, officers led Ellery and her family to a line of patrol cars, ready to take them to safety before releasing the press.

July's early evening sun cast a warm glow over the backyard. The aroma of steaks wafted through the air as Weston flipped them before dousing them with beer and seasoning. Vanessa and Edda worked in the kitchen, slicing fresh veggies and pulling side dishes.

Ellery, Jacqui, and Quinn set up the food table. Giggles filled the air as they struggled to move three long tables with benches only on one side into a circle. The arrangement allowed enough seating to accommodate the entire family, including Pops and Nan, who had decided to stay for a few days.

The guys entertained the cousins with a game of badminton that periodically devolved into piling on one uncle or another.

Everyone was accounted for except Baily. When she finally arrived, she claimed a lawn chair next to the cooler. Still sulking over being asked whether she had accepted money in exchange for information about Ellery, she opened a beer and stared at the lake. She had given no definitive answer. There had been a great deal of huffing on her part, indicating at least a hint of truth.

"Dinner!" Vanessa called out, setting the last item on the serving table. Like moths to a flame, the grandkids rushed the table, nearly toppling it as they jostled for position.

Ellery wrapped her arm around her mother's waist. She watched the chaos unfold, the unfiltered joy of the whole family gathered together. Four months ago, she would never have believed it possible.

Within fifteen minutes, the food table resembled a battlefield after a skirmish. Food was spilled from one end to the other. Once loaded with steak, salads, and desserts, the tin plates now lay scattered, nearly bare except for the remnants of the meal clinging to the surface. Vanessa's message that *No one stops eating until they're miserable!* had been achieved.

Amidst the wreckage, the kids were sprawled out on the soft grass, watching the clouds float across the sky. Moans from being overly full, and a few words drifted in and out of the adult conversations.

"Look," Harlow yelled, pointing above the shore.

A drone passed overhead, turned over the house, and hovered over them, clearly interrupting their celebratory dinner.

Fueled by fury, Weston leaped to his feet, shaking his fist at the intruder. "What the hell?" he shouted, pitching a rock at it as it hovered above them. "Whoever you are, get the hell out of here and leave us alone."

Noah mimicked his grandfather, but his aim faltered, and the rock veered far off course. Soon, the grandkids were scavenging rocks from Vanessa's garden and taking shots. The encouragement from their dads and grandfather turned the moment into a carnival of chaos, ending when one of the rocks landed in the middle of a bowl of coleslaw, sending it spraying.

"Okay, enough." Vanessa shook a finger in warning. "Unless you plan to pick those rocks up before the lawn service comes tomorrow, you need to stop."

The remotely operated craft exited abruptly, gliding toward the lake and disappearing down the shore.

Baily, who had not spoken one word since arriving, glared at Ellery. "It's never gonna end," she shouted. "We just keep getting dragged into your drama."

"Baily," Ben warned, looking at his wife over the top of his sunglasses. "That's enough."

"How can you take her side? We can't even have a family

dinner without…" Her words fell off, and she pointed to where the drone had been. "We have no privacy, and I'm so tired of it." Baily unwound her long legs from the picnic table bench and headed across the yard to her cottage.

Ben watched her go. "I'm sorry. I…"

"Don't apologize," Weston said, taking a swig of beer. "It's my fault. I should've paddled that girl more when she was little."

Liam shot a grin at his brother. "Yeah, like you did to me and Preston."

Preston's eyes brightened, and he pointed at Liam. "Mostly you." He chuckled. "Do you remember Dad's rule? If you laughed when you got spanked, you got it again." Preston poked a finger in the air. "As I recall, Liam almost always qualified for the finals."

Vanessa laughed as she covered her mouth to keep her wine from spraying everyone around her.

Jacqui folded her arms and rested her elbows on the table's edge. "Well, I don't ever remember getting spanked."

Preston let out a snort. "Of course not. You were Dad's informant."

"I was not," Jacqui muttered, her cheeks flushing in indignation.

Weston tipped his head, a smirk dancing on his lips. "Yeah. You kind of were."

"Dad!" Jacqui warned. Finally, her irritation melted into resignation. "Well, you were the one who hired me." Mischief twinkled in her eyes. "That's right. Dad paid me five dollars every time I caught either of you doing something wrong."

"What?" Liam's face contorted in disbelief as he turned to his dad. "Do you know how often we got in trouble for things we never did? She lied." He glanced at Jacqui. "Liar! Liar! Pants on fire! You did those things, and we got our butts kicked."

Preston eyed Jacqui with a hint of skepticism. "Are you kidding me? You turned us in for crap you did?"

"It's possible." The expression that spread across Jacqui's face made everyone laugh, except the boys. "There was one time I needed a new dress for a dance, so…"

"Unbelievable!" Preston dramatically threw his hands in the air. "You might want to reclaim some of your cash, Dad."

"Yeah. And Preston and I would like all those allowances you took from us back."

Edda set her fork beside her plate and wiped her face on her napkin. "Well, I got ten dollars every time I turned in one of you little hoodlums."

Preston looked between Jacqui and Edda. "So, who was it that turned me in for calling Liam a butt-crack?"

Edda laughed. "Your memory's going, boy. You didn't call Liam a buttcrack; you called *me* one."

Preston tucked a finger into the corner of his mouth. "Oh, yeah. I do remember that." Suddenly, he sat upright. "And you know what else I remember?" Edda shook her head. "The day you stopped using bar soap to wash out our mouths—and went to dish soap."

"It squirts farther and lasts longer," Edda said unapologetically.

Laughter erupted around the table.

Vanessa's mouth dropped open as she stared at Weston. "This was how you raised our children?"

Weston's laugh was rich. "It's a dog-eat-dog world, Nessa. They had to learn to survive. I was just giving those boys opportunities to practice."

FORTY-FOUR

It had been weeks since Ellery staked her claim to fame. Her life as a celebrity was finally beginning to fade. She reveled in the simplicity of walking down the streets, where people no longer asked for her autograph. Mundane conversations about the weather or the upcoming Dam Festival were a relief. So, when the city council approached her about posting a sign claiming "The Home of Ellery Gray, Author of the *Through the Fire* Series, she declined before Mayor Zajac finished the sentence. Home meant family—not being accosted by tourists. That was the last thing she wanted.

The Chambers family gathered for dinner and laughter every Saturday night, regardless of the weather. Without fail, Baily found a reason to storm off in a flurry of emotion, yet Ben and Piper remained, anchoring themselves to the family.

In late August, as the days were getting shorter and began to fade into gentle twilight before falling into darkness, the Chambers family had one particularly perfect evening. Ellery's heart was full as she took in her siblings. *She was home.*

As darkness settled in, everyone headed out at the same time. Conversations lingered, full of playful arguments, a continuation of those that had started at dinner. Ellery had gotten used to the long Minnesota goodbyes. It was one of her favorite parts of the evening.

Once the last taillights disappeared, Huck waddled inside and headed for his bed in Weston's office.

Ellery found solace on the screen porch with her folks, where the moon's magic shimmered across the lake, far outweighing any words they could have shared. She pulled her sweatshirt tighter and drank in the love surrounding her like a blanket.

Throughout the summer, her mom had begun spending the night at the main house several times a week. Ellery loved their mornings together. It was something she never had with Karma.

With her head resting against the back of the chair, Ellery allowed herself to drift for a moment. A smile spread across her face as she drank in the sheer good fortune of finding her family. Everything was right in her world.

Suddenly, a raucous clatter echoed from the kitchen, breaking the magic.

"Sounds like Huck found himself something to eat," Weston said, with a hint of amusement, rising from his chair to investigate.

Even before crossing the threshold, Weston spat, "Who the hell are you?" His voice was sharp as he flipped on another light.

Stepping deeper into the breakfast nook, Ellery and Vanessa nearly plowed into him from behind.

Shock lit Ellery's eyes. "Destiny? What are you doing here?"

She glanced at Vanessa before focusing on Ellery. "Remember those boxes we were going through when you left?" Ellery nodded. "Well, I finally finished looking through them."

Vanessa smiled. "You know you're always welcome here, but I wish we'd known you were coming. We could have…"

Without looking at her, Ellery held a hand up to stop her mother. "And what'd you find?"

Destiny's eyes shifted to Weston. "How about you tell them, *Dad*?"

Confusion hung like a thick fog. Vanessa's gaze shifted to her husband. His face drained of color. "What's she talking about?"

"I, I…" Weston stammered. "Who the hell are you?" His

face twisted in confusion.

Ellery stepped next to Destiny, desperation creeping onto her face. "What's going on? What was in there that makes you think…" Dinner began crawling out of her stomach at the sheer possibility that flashed before her.

Destiny handed her a folded sheet of paper. "This."

Ellery's hands shook as she opened it. Her eyes darted across the page. She felt the ground shift and her knees buckle as her body seemed to fold in on itself.

"Oh, my God," she mumbled. "This can't be right?"

"Why not?" Destiny challenged. "Every *truth* she ever told was a lie. But this," she said, slapping the paper with the back of her fingers, "this is the truth."

"What's going on?" Vanessa stepped around the end of the island. "What is that?"

Ellery once again ignored her mother. "But she lied so many times. How do we know…" She pulled back her words and stared at her father.

Vanessa snatched the paper from Ellery's hands and read it. Time moved in slow motion as she watched the realization cross her mother's face. Finally, Vanessa lifted her gaze to Weston. "How in the hell can you be Destiny's father?"

Weston dropped his head back before addressing the accusation. "When…" A deep sigh slipped out. "I dated some while we were apart, as I'm sure you did." He sighed heavily. "One night, years ago, I met a woman at a bar in Brainerd who kept buying me drinks." He shook his head as if to clear the cobwebs of the nightmare. "One thing led to another, and…"

"How long have you known?" Ferocity narrowed Vanessa's eyes.

He turned his palms up and stared at Destiny. "Since she… since *you* were born, but I never saw you. I didn't even know your name. I never even saw a picture. That woman wouldn't let me be involved in your life—except for money. A generous amount was transferred into Ann's account for your care every month."

Ellery angrily crossed her arms. "And with all your money, you never tried to get custody?"

"By then, your mom had just moved back, and things were finally becoming somewhat normal. I should have."

Destiny's laughter rang out bitterly. "It wouldn't have mattered. Don't you get it? My mother used you. She set you up. All she wanted was your money. You would have never gotten me."

Ellery froze in place; her throat had gone dry. She could not find the words to convey the tangled web of lies that had just unraveled. But there was more to come. Baily was right. She had trapped her family in a never-ending carousel of drama.

"So, you had a kid." Vanessa waved the birth certificate in Weston's face. "And you never once thought to mention it to any of us?"

Weston's expression carried heavy shame. "It was a one-night stand. I was so plastered, I don't even remember what the woman looked like."

"Did you even check to see if she was your daughter before you paid her off?" Vanessa's voice was sharp with pain.

"I did." His eyes were on his newest daughter. "I'm, I'm sorry. I'm not a monster."

Destiny and Ellery exchanged a knowing look. The shock that was about to be unleashed would take them down.

"Where's your mother now?" Vanessa demanded, her voice rising in intensity.

Destiny glanced at Ellery before meeting Vanessa's gaze. "She died almost three years ago."

The room fell into an uneasy silence. Vanessa's eyes widened as she began piecing together the fragments that sank like a stone in the lake, leaving ripples no one could stop.

"The same as…" The word fell into a black hole. Vanessa's arms dropped limply to her sides. "Oh, no. Hell, no!" she cried. "That woman's ruined our lives enough." She slammed her hand on the counter. "How could you? How could you sleep with a woman as evil as Karma?"

"I didn't know she was Karma. I hadn't even heard that name. The woman told me her name was Ann Smith."

Weston stepped toward Vanessa and tried to embrace her, but she recoiled. "Don't." She pushed his arms away. "Don't touch me."

Ellery's piercing scream shattered the already uneasy silence. From the shadows of the dimly lit kitchen, a woman appeared, her long, dark hair disheveled and her eyes wild. Her face contorted with a raw hatred. Clutched in her hand was a butcher knife, its blade catching the light, reflecting like a deadly beacon.

"Karma," Ellery whispered. The haunting word sent icy shivers down her spine as she raised a finger in warning. Her throat ached, and the room felt like all the air had been sucked from it.

Weston spun around, adrenaline surging through his veins. He positioned himself in front of Vanessa. "What in the hell?" he shouted, his voice sharp with confusion. "Karma? I thought you were…"

Karma's eyes narrowed to slits as she glared at Ellery. "You liar. I didn't raise my daughter…" She waved the knife between Ellery and Destiny. "Either of my daughters, to lie."

"Elle's *my* daughter," Vanessa hollered, trying to push her way past Weston to get to Karma. "You stole her…"

A chilling cackle sliced through the air as Karma pointed the knife at Vanessa. "You weren't a mom—or a wife. Where were you when your husband got so drunk, he couldn't keep his pants on?" She lightly held a hand over her stomach. "When he planted Destiny in me, where were you then?" She touched the tip of the knife blade with her finger, letting a drop of blood drip onto the white quartz, and stared at Vanessa. "I'm waiting."

Ellery could see the rage swelling inside her mother. Vanessa's jaw twitched as she tried to get to Karma again, but Weston held out a protective arm, refusing to let her pass. "I was searching for my daughter, you bitch," she hissed. "The one you stole from us."

Karma raised the knife above her head. "I'll deal with you later. But I have a score to settle with these two first." She shifted her weight forward. Rage claimed her face as she glared at Ellery. "Well, Ellery Gray, how dare you paint me as a shitty mother in your little books!"

"You *were* a shitty mother," Destiny exclaimed, jumping to Ellery's defense. "You didn't care about anybody but yourself."

Karma held the knife toward Destiny. "You shut the hell up. I'll get to you and your disloyalty when I finish with that one. You," Karma spat, eyes fixed on Ellery, "you were supposed to have died in that fire. Yet, here you are, living like the Queen of England with people who didn't want you in the first place."

"Shut up," Weston shouted, the muscles in his arms flexing as he punched his hand into his fist. "That's a lie."

"Oh? You tell me what kind of mother falls asleep when she's supposed to be watching her precious babies." Karma's expression shifted to one of amusement. "Oh, that's right. You told me that night you couldn't keep your hands off me in my hotel room." A smirk spread as she looked at Vanessa. "He didn't think much of you then. I doubt much has changed."

Destiny twisted her feet, inching sideways toward the end of the counter, the movement so subtle that no one except Ellery noticed. "You're a pathological liar," she spat. "All those *truths* you used to feed us were lies. Don't believe a word she says, Vanessa." She inched sideways again, her expression a fierce scowl. "What kind of a person kidnaps a baby just to trap some poor slob and then tries to kill her when she can't manipulate her anymore?" Once again, she shifted sideways. "And who gets somebody drunk enough to have sex with her just to replace the kid she *thought she* killed? And then blackmail the guy to keep him paying child support. That would be the horrible, disgusting Karma—my mother."

Ellery glanced at Destiny, finally catching on to her plan. She had to distract Karma. "And that would be the same mother who paraded a string of men through our apartment every night while I lay behind the couch, too afraid to make a sound?"

Karma's upper lip curled with rage, her eyes darkening into slits as she glared at Ellery. "I did what I had to do to feed you," she snapped.

Ellery let out a loud, mocking laugh as she stepped in the opposite direction. "Feed me? I ate from garbage cans. Do you remember all those days you made me watch you stuff your face with three-course meals? How does that make you a good mother?"

"How in the hell did you find us?" Destiny asked, sliding one foot to the right.

"I've been here for months, waiting for you to show up. It took you long enough." She shifted the tip of the knife between the two. "Having you both in the same place makes my plan to kill you all a hell of a lot easier."

"You're disgusting," Ellery spat. "I hated you when I was under your thumb, and I still do."

"Shut the hell up! Look at you. You're still under my thumb," Karma shouted, leaning in. "I didn't come here to listen to you shoot your mouth off. I'm your mother. Show some damn respect."

Ellery burst out laughing. "Respect. That's a good one."

Karma pointed her knife at Ellery again. "I'll be taking every penny of that money you made writing about *my* life. A bestselling author—there must be millions by now."

Ellery's fear swelled as she saw Destiny shift again. She met her father's eyes, begging him to stand down as he inched toward Karma from the other side. "*Your* life? That was *my* life."

"You wouldn't have had anything interesting to write about had I not given it to you." Karma shook the knife at Ellery.

Vanessa's voice dripped with disdain. "You'll rot in prison for how you treated these girls. Elle told us…"

Karma took a step back, rage bubbling over. "Her name is Summer." Each word was slowly squeezed out between her clenched teeth. "And you'll pay for turning her against me."

"You did that," Vanessa said. "She said you were Satan on

steroids."

While Karma was arguing with Vanessa, Destiny wrapped her hand around a heavy iron candlestick and tucked it behind her back before drawing Karma's attention again. "Vanessa's right, *Mother*," she spewed, her words tumbling like an avalanche. "You're going to spend the rest of your life behind bars with people who are just like you."

"Shut up!" Karma screamed, her face twisting in rage, a storm brewing in her eyes as she wildly waved the knife through the air.

"You're a loser. You lose at everything. You lost Ellery. You lost me. And you're going to lose your life rotting in some hellhole." Destiny's chin jutted outward in defiance.

"Shut the hell up!" Karma screamed again. "I. Am. Your. Mother. You will respect me."

"You're no mother of mine, and you sure as hell don't deserve respect." Destiny gripped the top of the candlestick as her mouth curved into a smirk. "As of this moment, I disown you," she said flippantly. "And Elle disowns you too."

Karma lunged at her daughter, plunging the knife downward. Destiny shifted to the right. The blade snapped off when it slammed against the quartz with deadly force. Before Karma righted herself, Destiny swung the candlestick with both hands, striking her in the back of the head. The woman's forehead slammed into the stone countertop. Her eyes drifted backward as she slid off the island and onto the floor.

Vanessa darted toward Ellery and pulled her into an embrace. The world around them faded as they stood in that moment. Had Destiny not had the wherewithal to grab the candlestick, someone could have died.

Ellery reached out and pulled her sister into their circle. Vanessa wrapped her arms around both women.

FORTY-FIVE

Shards of red and blue rhythmically flashed as officers moved in and out of the house with a defined mission. An ambulance had come and gone. The siren scream had faded into the distance, leaving the air quieter than Ellery remembered since moving to Hunters Cove. Even the pair of Barred owls, who almost always performed a duet, had gone silent.

When they wheeled her down the sidewalk, Karma had been handcuffed to the stretcher. Whether the restraints were necessary was debatable. The woman didn't appear to be going anywhere on her own, at least not for some time. But that moment, seeing her locked up and hauled away, felt like a gift.

Relief washed over Ellery as the EMTs loaded her into the cabin of the ambulance. She would finally pay her dues for the despicable things she'd done. Death would have let Karma off too easily—but a lifetime of being locked behind bars felt like justice. For the first time, Ellery was glad Karma had faked her death. *This.* This was truly karma.

Inside, Weston and Vanessa sat on opposite sides of the living room, giving their statements to Chief Jansen. With the half-sister bombshell, things were strained; their body language spoke volumes. Without knowing the whole story, Jansen did his best to calm the couple amid the overwhelmingness of what could have been.

Ellery dropped onto the wicker loveseat beside Destiny. She stared into the night, wondering why Baily and Ben had not shown up with all the commotion.

"D-do you think I'm gonna be arrested?" Destiny's voice

quivered. She pulled her trembling hands inside her sweatshirt and folded her arms across her stomach.

"No," Ellery said resolutely, "I don't. If it hadn't been for you, Karma would have killed me." She zipped her sweatshirt, sheltering herself against the cool evening air and that thought. "I'm sure she planned to kill us all. Had you not knocked her out… Well, we know what could have happened." A shiver ran through her. Ellery folded her hands tightly. Residual fear tensed every muscle in her body. "We both told them you didn't have a choice. I'm sure Mom and Dad are telling them the same thing."

Destiny leaned back. "I did what I had to do. I couldn't let her hurt any of you. If she killed me…" Her voice fell silent. "If she'd killed me, it wouldn't have mattered. I don't have family." Her face fell, and her body curled forward. "But you all have each other."

Ellery slid closer to her. "You've been my family since you showed up at my house. And now, it's official. Because whether you like it or not, you're a Chambers, just like me."

Doubt flashed across Destiny's face. "Half-Chambers. What's the likelihood they'll ever accept me as their sister?"

"It may take some time, but they'll come around. Plus, you have me in your corner. That's more than I had. And if my family's learned anything in the last few months, it's that they shouldn't underestimate me." She lightly nudged her shoulder with Destiny's. "Besides, we need to stick together in this war against Baily when this hits the news."

Suddenly, Ellery's head twisted toward the trees that bordered the yard. "Did you hear that?" she asked as she tried to see into the darkness.

Destiny shook her head but stopped midway, her gaze drifting toward the woods. "I thought I heard someone calling for help."

Ellery stood, ready to confront whatever haunted the shadows, but Destiny pulled her back down. "After everything that's happened tonight, we're not going in there alone."

As an officer stepped from the house, Ellery reached out, her fingers brushing against the man's arm. "I think there's someone in the woods," she whispered, pointing past the end of the house. The officer glanced toward the trees. "It sounded like they called for help."

"How do we know it's not another of Karma's tricks? I wouldn't put it past her to have set a trap ahead of time." Destiny clung to Ellery's arm.

"Hagen! I need you!" the officer yelled to his partner. "Sounds like there might be someone hiding in the woods."

Officer Hagen pointed toward the house with her flashlight. "Inside. Now."

Ellery quickly followed Destiny through the front door. She slid the foyer window open and leaned close.

The other officer stepped forward, aiming his gun into the murky depths of the forest, searching for movement. "Hello? Is anyone in here?"

"Come out with your hands up," Hagen commanded.

A weak voice called back. "Help me. Please help me."

The shadows swallowed the officers as they disappeared into the trees, their light fading into nothing. Moments later, dread gnawed at Ellery as the distant sound of an ambulance pierced the air. A third officer headed toward the woods while a fourth waited in the driveway.

"What if it's family?" she whispered, almost to herself. Panic rushed through her as she burst out the door and followed the bouncing light.

She trailed so closely that she almost plowed into the officer when he stopped. Ellery veered around him at the last second, stumbling into the illuminated area. Her heart sank. "No. It can't be," she mumbled when she saw the small girl lying on the ground. Handcuffs attached to her arms and legs had been used to chain her between two trees.

"Do you know her?" Hagen asked.

"Yeah, sort of. Her name's Summer." Ellery dropped beside the little girl, trying to process the horror before her.

"Summer? Like the name that woman gave to you?"

"Yeah." Ellery turned her attention to the girl. "Did Karma do this to you?" Ellery's heart ached at the sight of the girl's dirty, tear-streaked face.

The child nodded, sobbing as one of the officers snipped the chains with a bolt cutter.

"Is Karma your mother?" Ellery scooped her onto her lap, defying warnings not to touch the child to preserve evidence.

The little girl shook her head fervently. "She told me it was a game. She said it was pretend." Summer sobbed as she gazed directly into Ellery's eyes. Her deep sadness and the hopelessness on her face sent chills up her spine. "I wanted to go home. But Karma said my mother didn't want me anymore." Summer ran a sleeve across her eyes.

"That's not true. Your mother wants you, honey. She loves you. She'll be so excited to have your home." Ellery felt her heart implode with anger as she gently rocked the child. "Why did she call you Summer?"

"It was part of the game." The child rubbed an eye with her fist. "But that's not my real name. It's Hattie." Ellery felt the girl's tiny body collapse in relief. "She said she'd kill me if I ever told anybody." Hattie rested her head against Ellery's chest. "When you gave me that candy, I wanted to tell you, but I was scared."

Ellery tightened her arms around the fragile child. Until now, only she and Destiny knew the horrors she had endured. Hattie had become a member of their club, a group that should never have existed in the first place.

"You're a brave girl, *Hattie*." Ellery emphasized her name. "You're safe now. Karma's gone. She can't hurt you anymore." The knot growing in Ellery's throat trapped her words. Finally, she whispered, "These nice officers will make sure you get home."

Hattie grasped Ellery's arm, her eyes glimmering with hope. "Don't leave me. Please stay until my mom comes?" Her voice was filled with panic, and her eyes brimmed with tears.

"Absolutely." Ellery's smile was warm. It was the smile of a mother, one Vanessa had shown her. "I'll be right by your side."

As they emerged from the dense trees, with Hattie carefully strapped onto a backboard carried by two EMTs, Baily stepped in front of Ellery.

She poked a finger at her. "More drama!" she growled. "You dragged that insane woman back here. I knew you would. She could have killed us all. No one in this family wants you here. Why can't you take a hint?"

"Stay with me!" Hattie yelled. Ellery recognized the panic in her voice as the paramedics loaded her into the ambulance. "You promised."

"I'm coming, Hattie," Ellery called before returning her attention to Baily, her resolve hardening. "Karma destroyed that little girl's life. I need to be with her right now. But when we find her family, you and I will finish this. Until then, stay the hell out of my sight."

Ellery shoved Baily aside, her heart racing as she slid into the back of the ambulance. Hattie grasped her hand tightly, pulling it close to her face. The young girl did not smile, but Ellery saw hope in her eyes.

"Elle." The name echoed, muffled by the commotion around them. "Elle."

Her gaze drifted toward the back doors. Liam's eyes were wide as he clutched the hand of a small boy. "My son!" he shouted just before the doors swung shut, separating them.

The ambulance rocked down the long driveway before merging onto the highway. Ellery's thoughts, swirling like leaves caught in a gust of wind, began to settle.

With her eyes on Hattie, she reflected on her life. The truth was a fine golden strand, shimmering but fragile, dangling from the heavens. It was meant to be fiercely held on to, knowing there would always be those who thought they knew better. Those who would try to manipulate, cut, or even destroy it in a fire. But eventually, the truth would come out. It always did.

Karma's truth was a lie. Every. Single. Word. But for Liam and his newfound son, Destiny and their father, and Ellery and her family, the truth had finally made its way home.

Unless someone else was harboring secrets.

ACKNOWLEDGMENT

Every time I sat down to write, the words eagerly greeted me as if they desperately longed to be unleashed. I can hardly contain my excitement for the second book in the series to reveal itself to me.

No book comes to fruition without the support of a dedicated team of people who have my best interests at heart. I am eternally grateful to each of you. I truly could not take this journey alone.

Mitch Perrine – Not only are you the best husband, but you are the love of my life. Your tireless encouragement has pulled me through my moments of doubt. I am so lucky to have someone who knows exactly what I need, often before I do. Thank you for your love and support.

Bridget Christianson, Laura Chevalier, DeeAnn Eickhoff, Barb McMahon, Cheryl Meld, Linda O'Neil, and Ruth Novack – My incredible dream team of beta readers. You transform my rough drafts into shimmering narratives. I am beyond grateful for your time, dedication, and commitment to my second act.

Beth Lynne of BZHercules.com – While others hone the story's edges, you dive deep into the fabric of my words, uncovering even the smallest errors. I am so grateful for your attention to detail. I am truly fortunate to have you on my side.

Connie Huse Mckanna – The name you chose for the town, Hunters Cove, perfectly captures the charm of the quaint Minnesota town. I also appreciate the introduction of the character Clara Olson, the owner of Clara's. While not at the forefront of this book, readers can look forward to deeper connections with her through the series.

Friends – I want to offer a heartfelt thank you to each of you who discovered yourselves woven into the story. Your presence and friendship have left an indelible mark on my life in unimaginable ways. I wanted to honor you in some way. I am so grateful for all of you.

My readers – You are my lifeblood, the driving force that keeps me tapping away at the keyboard and awake all night, creating new stories. Your messages inspire me to continue writing tales you want to read. Your continued support—be it through purchasing books, sharing your thoughts, or leaving reviews—means the world to me. Nothing fuels my passion more than knowing my words find a home in your heart.

AUTHOR'S MESSAGE

I'm going to give it to you straight. My mom taught me to lie. We're not talking whoppers to escape punishment, just using my imagination to create stories. She used to say, "Watch people and make their story bigger—more interesting."

Because my older sister wanted to be a teacher, I had the privilege of learning to read at three. By four, under my mom's encouragement, I became a writer. Armed with a kaleidoscope of neon notebooks and psychedelic pencils, I wrote my tales. Each word was read and cherished by my mom.

With a sharp understanding of both writing and the chaos of large families, merging the two for this book felt almost effortless. The shared interactions between the siblings could easily reflect those of my family or my husband's. Huck, the loveable yet gassy St. Bernard, was a throwback to my childhood dog, Barney. As for gassy Preston? With five brothers and six more on my husband's side, any one of them could fit that role—and likely did more than once.

This story has taken up space in the corners of my mind for as long as I can remember. Yet it wasn't until this past winter that I finally felt the nudge to put it on paper. Sitting down to write, I was reminded of an Italian proverb: "Hope is the last thing ever lost." Whether the main character was living as Summer or Ellery, one undeniable thread wove through her journey—her unwavering hope.

So today and always, let hope guide you through every chapter of your life.